Ask for a Convertible

Ask for a Convertible

·STORIES·

Danit Brown

PANTHEON BOOKS NEW YORK

 Published in the United States by Pantheon Books, a division of Random House, Inc., New York, and in Canada by Random House of Canada Limited, Toronto.

Pantheon Books and colophon are registered trademarks of Random House, Inc.

These stories were originally published in the following: "Running" in *American Literary Review;* "Thanksgiving" in *Crab Orchard Review;* "Descent" in *Glimmer Train;* "Ask for a Convertible" in *The Massachusetts Review;* "The Dangers of Salmonella" and "Hands Across America" on www.nextbook.org; "Selling the Apartment" in *One Story;* and "How to Clean Up Any Stain" in *StoryQuarterly.*

Library of Congress Cataloging-in-Publication Data

Brown, Danit.
Ask for a convertible : stories / Danit Brown.
p. cm.
ISBN-13: 978-0-375-42454-0
I. Title.
PS3602.R6943A93 2008
813'.6—dc22
2007039745

www.pantheonbooks.com

Printed in the United States of America
First Edition

2 4 6 8 9 7 5 3 1

For Bill and for Ziv:
You are my home.

Contents

Ask for a Convertible

Descent

When Osnat's grandmother came to visit, she brought Osnat underwear and socks, bananas and eggs fresh from the *lool.* "Eat a banana," she said. "Come on. Eat a banana. Eat it. Eat a banana. Eat it. Eat a banana. Eat a banana. Eat it. Eat a banana." She was crazy. Osnat's parents knew she was crazy, but they yelled at her anyway: "Quit it with the bananas. She doesn't want a banana." Osnat's grandmother smiled. Her eyes were blue, but her skin was brown and shriveled. She grabbed Osnat's head and kissed the top of it over and over: "Muah muah muah muah muah. Come on. Eat a banana. Eat it. Eat a banana. Eat a banana."

The evening before their flight, there was a big family dinner with lots of yellow food: potatoes, *bourekas, shkedei marak.*

"Are you wearing your yellow socks?" Osnat's grandmother asked Osnat. Osnat's grandmother believed yellow was a good color for traveling, and had knitted the socks herself. They were thick and made Osnat's shoes feel too tight, but when she started to take them off, her mother said, "Don't. Don't get her started." For emphasis, she shook the can of baby corn she was draining. Osnat hated baby corn, but her mother said it kept the salad from being too green.

In the next room, Osnat's aunt was setting the table with plastic yellow plates. When she came in for the silverware, Osnat's mother told her, "I can feel it. I'm going to have to teach Hebrew at some damn school for the rest of my life."

"It's America," Osnat's aunt said. "You'll be rich and won't have to work at all."

"But I like working."

"Not me," Osnat said. "I wish it could always be vacation."

The two women turned and looked at her. "Where's your grandmother?" her aunt asked.

Out in the living room, Osnat's grandmother was watching the news in Arabic. She didn't know Arabic, but she liked the announcer's mustache. She wrapped her arms around Osnat and whispered, "When you come back, find yourself a boyfriend with a mustache like that." The tops of her hands were crisscrossed with blue veins. The palms were warm and papery.

"We're not coming back," Osnat told her.

Her grandmother sighed. "No," she said. "I guess you aren't. This is why you should never marry Americans." Later, when she saw the cheesecake meant for dessert, she said, "This is beige, not yellow." Osnat's mother inhaled sharply. Osnat's grandmother smiled. "Just kidding." She cut herself a big slice. "This isn't a big deal," she said. "I left my mother and my sisters when I was nineteen, you know. And look at me now. You worry that I'll forget to turn off the gas, but I always remember."

"Or else someone finds you lying on the floor," Osnat's aunt said.

"Enough," Osnat's mother said. "She has a pilot light now."

"Come on," Osnat's grandmother said, pushing the cheesecake toward Osnat. "Have a piece of cake. It's delicious. Have some. Have a piece. Have a piece of cake."

At the airport, the air smelled like toilet bowl cleaner and sweat, and the fluorescent lights made people's skin look gray. At the foot of the escalators that led to the departure gates, Osnat's aunt hugged Osnat's mother so tightly her fingertips turned white.

On the plane, Osnat watched Tel Aviv's lights flickering below them. From the air, the ground looked nothing like the maps of Israel they'd learned to draw in school: the coastal plain with a bump for Haifa; the desert in the south; to the east, the Sea of Galilee and the Dead Sea, connected by a straight line, each border carefully labeled: Lebanon. Syria. Jordan. Egypt. The word for leaving Israel and not coming back is *yerida,* descent. It's such a small country. Every body counts.

Later, Osnat's mother cried while Osnat pretended to sleep, her head in her mother's lap. She could tell her mother was crying by the way she took a long breath, held it, and then let it out slowly. One of her tears landed on Osnat's right earlobe. It was wet and warm and felt like something that belonged inside her.

When her father told Osnat they were moving to Michigan, he said it would be into a house with wall-to-wall carpeting and a private backyard. He didn't tell her the carpeting would be yellow and stained and ugly or that the backyard would be soggy with rain. He didn't tell her there would be heating vents in the floor, full of cobwebs. He didn't tell her the house would be made out of wood and that the floors would creak and the walls would shake if you shut a door too hard. He didn't say there would be a lightning rod on the roof.

"What's that?" Osnat asked, pointing at the white thing on the ceiling with the red blinking eye.

"A smoke detector," her father said.

In the kitchen sink, there was a garbage disposal. Osnat's mother shoved slice after slice of bread in there, and she and Osnat watched the drain suck them down. You weren't supposed to go after things that fell in the garbage disposal. It was dangerous.

The second night in the house, Osnat's father brought home a TV. It had color and twenty stations. On one of them, a man was climbing a fence while other men were trying to shoot him down. In the driveway, outside their house, there was a pale yellow station wagon with wood paneling on the sides. You weren't supposed to drive with the back window open because of carbon monoxide. People died that way. That was something Osnat wasn't supposed to know, just as she wasn't supposed to know that one of the trustees from the local university had jumped off the university's bell tower. But she knew, just like she knew—even though she'd only seen him for a second—that the man on TV wouldn't make it over the fence.

Osnat. Osnat. Osnat. Osnat.

The kids in Osnat's new school were pasty white, with thick arms and legs and big shiny teeth which they bared when they passed one another in the hallway. Next to them Osnat felt small and brown and fragile. When the bell rang for first period, she headed for the desk behind the only boy in the entire class whose skin was darker than hers. The boy, Mrs. Sherwood announced when she was taking attendance, was named Sanjay, and he was from India. "We have quite the international group this year!" she said. "India *and* Israel! No wonder this is Social Studies!"

Sanjay raised his hand. "I've been here since eighty-one."

"Three whole years!" Mrs. Sherwood said. "How lovely!"

Later, at lunch, Osnat sat next to Sanjay and across from a girl named Sharon who ate ketchup straight out of the packet. "So," Sharon said, "you're Jewish. I'm Jewish too." She squeezed the ketchup packet carefully from bottom to top, like a tube of toothpaste. "There's five of us in the whole school, you know. You, me, Brent Silverstein, Avery Roth, and Joel Cohen."

"At least there are other Jews," Sanjay said. "There's only one of me."

"There's Mohammed," Sharon said.

"He's Pakistani," Sanjay said. "It's not the same."

"Oh, Mark Green is also Jewish," Sharon said. "But he's older—in eighth grade—and has acne real bad."

"What's acne?" Osnat asked.

"You know," Sharon said. "Pimples. Whiteheads. Zits. Acne." She tore into another packet. "So," she said, "why are you named after mucus?"

"Mucus?" Osnat asked.

"You know." Sharon licked some ketchup off her right index finger. "The stuff up your nose. Snot."

"Jesus," Sanjay said. "Are you always so disgusting?"

"Jesus," Sharon said right back. "Are you always so rude?" Still, she stood up and started clearing her tray. Compared to Sanjay's precise vowels and tight *t*s, her English seemed loose and flappy, as if she had a hot potato rolling around in her mouth.

In America, at the university, Osnat's father had a corner office with a computer. On the door there was a plaque with his name on it: Dr. Marvin Greenberg. When people saw him in the hallway, they nodded and said, "Doctor," and he nodded and said, "Doctor" back. There was a picture of him in the university paper, with his name printed underneath. In it, his eyes were black and shiny, and he was smiling an openmouthed smile. This was the new Marvin Greenberg, the happy one who showed off all his teeth and took Osnat out in the backyard to toss around a football made of sponge.

Inside, Osnat's mother fried up chicken schnitzel, but nothing tasted right. "It's this meat," she said. "It isn't kosher."

"You could salt it," Osnat's father said.

"No," Osnat's mother said. "*You* can salt it."

Even the cucumbers were different. They were large, with waxy skin, and they tasted like water.

"You didn't tell me the food would be bad," Osnat's mother said, putting her fork down. "You could have told me."

"Come on, Efi," Osnat's father said, "I did tell you." But Osnat's mother was already halfway up the stairs. Osnat's father pushed back his chair, shrugged, and winked. "Wish me luck."

While she waited, Osnat cleared the table and scraped the cucumbers into the garbage disposal. Everything upstairs was quiet. That was the thing about America. It was too quiet. You couldn't even hear the traffic going by outside. At least in Israel, when her father locked himself up in the bathroom, there were twenty-three other apartments Osnat could visit. Or she could ride up and down in the elevator until her parents were done yelling. In America, the house creaked and creaked, and you couldn't even get an aerogramme out of the desk drawer without the floorboards signaling your location.

After she washed the dishes, Osnat wrote a letter to her grandmother—no, her aunt—no, her grandmother. She left the first line blank until she could figure out who the letter was for. "It didn't work," she wrote. "They're still fighting. I think they're going to get a divorce." Upstairs she heard her parents' bedroom door open and close and open and close, and feet padding along the hallway. Then she heard the water go on in the shower. She put down her pen and went to assess the damage. The bedroom was empty. In the bathroom, she could hear her father singing "Li VeLach" and her mother saying, "Shh . . . the neighbors."

"This is America!" her father hollered. "We have no neighbors!"

Back in the dining room, Osnat crossed out everything she had written and ripped the aerogramme into small pieces. Then her father was standing over her in his shorts, his hair wet.

"What are you doing?" he said. "Don't you know aerogrammes cost money?"

Calling was expensive, so Osnat's grandmother wrote them every Friday instead. "Hugs and kisses," she wrote. "I have new dentures. Wait until you see them. They're blinding."

On Saturdays, Osnat's mother wrote back: "It's raining again. Osnat is doing well. Marvin is very happy." She took long breaks between sentences, tapping her pen against her chin.

"Maybe I'll make things up," she told Osnat's father. "You would think that in a country where money grows on trees, it wouldn't be so hard to find a job."

"Ha ha," said Osnat's father. He had a job, after all. He always had a job.

"No, really," Osnat's mother said.

On Sundays, Osnat's father woke up early and bought the *Detroit Free Press* and the *Ann Arbor News.* While he waited for the water to boil, he went through the classifieds and circled the jobs he thought made sense. Then Osnat's mother made coffee, sat down with a cup in her left hand and a pen in her right, and crossed out every one of the circles. "Day care assistant? I'm done changing diapers. Kmart greeter? You've got to be kidding. Florist? Aren't there any jobs where you get to think?"

Osnat could tell her father was trying. He blew his nose and cleaned his glasses and traced invisible patterns on the table with his right index finger. Still, sooner or later, he always ended up saying it: "You need good English to get those. You know that."

This was Osnat's signal go upstairs and get ready for Hebrew school. She didn't really like Hebrew school, but she was glad to get out of the house. She already knew the fight script by heart, including the long pauses for the eye-rolling and dramatic sighs.

She waited in her room until one of her parents knocked on her door and drove her to the synagogue. On the way over, whoever it was asked her where she wanted to eat when Hebrew school was over. "How about McDonald's? Does Burger King sound nice?" This was part of the script too. Once there, whoever it was would order her a large fries and watch her eat as if she were a small child who might begin choking at any moment. "So," whoever it was would ask her, "does that girl, Sharon, still like to eat her ketchup straight?"

Sharon also went to Hebrew school, greasy and bleary-eyed. During breaks, she asked Osnat to teach her curse words in Hebrew.

"Zayin," said Osnat. *"Zona."*

In return, Sharon taught her *asshole, dick, cunt, whore, screw.* Osnat took careful notes on a sheet of paper. Her favorite word was *fuck.* There was something satisfying about her teeth against her lips, her throat closing on the hard *k* sound. "You fucker," Osnat told Sanjay at school on Monday. "Don't fuck with me."

"Fuck you too," Sanjay said. "What did I do?"

There were parts in Osnat's grandmother's letters that were just for Osnat, and parts that were just for her mother. She wrote in black ink on sheets of paper that seemed impossibly thin. Then she folded the two parts of the letter separately and taped them shut. You had to use a knife to open them, or else the paper ripped. In Osnat's part, her grandmother wrote things like: "You'll grow thick arms and thick legs of your own. And once winter starts, you too will grow pale." In the margins, she drew pictures of chickens and palm trees. To Osnat's mother, she wrote: "Don't think I don't know you're not telling me the truth. That's okay. I've discovered where your sister keeps the letters you send her." Osnat's mother kept her parts of the letters in her underwear drawer, but Osnat found them anyway, along with the letters from her aunt: "If I never see another banana again, it'll be too soon. She refuses to throw them away even when they're completely black. The house smells like rotting fruit. There are flies everywhere."

The bananas in Michigan were much bigger than the ones in Israel, and they were bright green. Osnat's mother didn't buy them. She also didn't buy red peppers because they were $4.99 per pound. While Osnat was in school, her mother did things like make the beds and figure out how to mow the lawn. At 2:45, when Osnat came home, her mother was already waiting just behind the doors, car keys in hand. After the first month, she stopped going places by herself. There were always so many questions that needed asking, and so many words with *r*s in them: *ruler, razor, self-rising flour, regular rice, where.*

When Osnat's mother called Osnat's father at work, she had to spell his name over and over before the secretary would transfer her. "G-R-E-E-N-B-E-R-G. Yes. G-R. No. R. R." If Osnat was home, she made her do the phoning. "That woman must know my voice by now," she told Osnat's father. "She hates me."

"You're exaggerating," Osnat's father said. "Just give it time."

"It's been ages," Osnat's mother said. "And I'm not exaggerating. It's the accent. They hate foreigners in this country."

"It's a conspiracy," Osnat's father said. "Is that what you're saying?" He shrugged and winked at Osnat.

"Don't shrug me off," Osnat's mother said. "I didn't shrug you off when you were unhappy in Israel. I didn't shrug you off when you thought everyone was robbing us blind."

"They *were* robbing us blind."

"Only because we let them."

"You're right," Osnat's father said. "It's my fault Israelis are pigs."

"Yes," Osnat's mother said. "That's exactly what I'm saying."

Osnat wrote her grandmother: "Don't forget to clean your teeth every night, or maybe they'll turn yellow." She chewed the top of her pen for a while. "Maybe we need to live somewhere halfway, like Switzerland."

"Don't chew your pen," Osnat's mother said. "It'll make your teeth crooked."

Osnat scratched out the part about Switzerland.

"I keep telling you and telling you," her father said. "Write it out in pencil first."

Osnat was the only girl in the seventh grade who braided her hair. Mr. Quimby, the shop teacher, said braids were a good thing. Loose hair was a safety hazard. If a girl leaned too far over, her hair could get caught in the lathe, and her scalp could rip right off. It had happened before, and—if they weren't careful—it would happen again. He walked over to where Osnat was sitting and tugged on one of her braids. "Watch and learn, girls," he said. "See what other cultures have to teach us." He said, "When you come from a country torn apart by war, you don't have time to blow-dry your hair."

In school, they had tornado drills. The alarm went off and then you were supposed to line up and walk down to the gym in an orderly fashion, and sit against the wall with your head between your knees. If you were at home when the sirens went off, you were supposed to go down to the basement. Osnat's father went down, but Osnat's mother liked to stand on the front porch and watch the blowing wind and the green sky.

"We had bomb drills in Israel," Osnat told Sanjay. "We had a bomb shelter right outside the school."

"Bombs. Tornadoes." Sanjay wasn't impressed. "Every place has something wrong with it. That's what my father says."

But it wasn't the place. It was her. Osnat knew she looked all wrong. Her jeans were embroidered instead of acid-washed, and—no matter how hard she tried—she couldn't get her socks to bunch up so that they looked like the other girls' leg warmers. Plus, even though she was getting paler, the dark hairs on her arms made her look like a boy.

In the locker room, changing for gym, Sharon said, "You should wear looser clothes, you know. You should wear a bra. You look like a slut."

"Fuck you," Osnat told her. "What's a slut?" She knew Sharon was right. Her T-shirts *were* too tight. All the other girls wore loose-fitting inside-out sweatshirts, with the washing instructions sticking out for everyone to see.

At the mall, the saleswomen, their eyes glassy with boredom, kept asking Osnat and her mother how they were without really wanting to know the answer.

"And they say Americans are nice," Osnat's mother said while Osnat tried on a bra. It was saggy and it pinched under her arms, and she couldn't figure out how to work the straps.

"Does it fit?" Osnat's mother asked. Before Osnat could say that it didn't, her mother said, "Great! Let's go."

Outside, it was raining again. The parking lot stretched for kilometers in every direction. All the cars looked the same.

"My God," Osnat's mother said. She spun around in a slow circle. "It's so big here. Everything's just so big."

After a while, it turned out there were worse things than teaching Hebrew. Being home all day, for example.

"But you don't want to teach Hebrew," Osnat reminded her mother.

"That was then," Osnat's mother said. "Now I just want to work." She put on some lipstick and made Osnat put on clean jeans. "Anyway," she said, "this is America. Jews have to stick together."

And they did stick together. The synagogue receptionist, when she heard the accent, stopped filing her nails and poured two cups of tea. "What a lovely country," she said. "Is your husband studying at the university?"

"He works there," Osnat's mother explained. "He's American. He didn't like Israel."

"No," said the receptionist. "Of course not, with all those wars." She lowered her voice. "You know, marrying Jewish is very important, but—believe me—I'd rather my son marry a Christian than an Israeli any day. Don't get me wrong," she said. "I'll gladly give Israel all my money, no problem. But my son? Am I crazy?"

Osnat's mother smiled and nodded. "She *is* crazy," she whispered to Osnat through her teeth in Hebrew.

The receptionist pursed her lips. "It's a crazy country," she said. "And I know Hebrew too."

"Oh well," Osnat's mother said later, over dinner. "Maybe it's a sign. Maybe God doesn't want me to work."

"You don't believe in God," Osnat's father pointed out.

"Well," said Osnat's mother, "maybe I should start."

"You could take up a hobby," Osnat said. "Sanjay likes birdwatching."

"I do have a hobby," Osnat's mother told her. "It's called waiting for the mail."

Osnat's grandmother wrote Osnat: "The lemon is a yellow and very useful fruit. Lemon juice will make your hair turn blond. And, when you're older, you can wax your arms with wax made of lemon and sugar. I did it myself, you know, in Poland." She wrote Osnat's mother: "Your sister is driving me crazy. She throws away perfectly good bananas and keeps switching off the gas. Please write her to stop it. I am not a little girl. I raised you two and three thousand chickens. I do know some things, and you both would do well to listen." That was the part her mother read out loud. The rest went into her underwear drawer.

On the cable box, if you pressed 23 and 27 down at the same time, you could get the Playboy Channel. It was squiggly at the edges, but sometimes—especially after thunderstorms—you could catch a clear glimpse of a breast or a behind. If those women wore bras, they didn't keep them on for long.

"So what?" said Sanjay, when Osnat showed him. "My sister has sex with the guy across the street. He can unhook her bra with one hand."

"How do you know?" Osnat asked.

"He never pulls down the blinds."

"I don't believe you," Osnat said. "No one can undo a bra with one hand."

"I can," said Sanjay. "All guys can."

Sanjay was shorter than Osnat, but he had long fingers and slender hands. Osnat leaned back into the couch. She could feel the spot where the hook pressed into her spine. She knew he could do it. At school, the boys were forever running down the hallways in packs, shooting spitballs and snapping bra straps. She would have to get a bra that closed in front. Or one that didn't have hooks at all.

"You shouldn't date Indians," Sharon warned Osnat in Hebrew school. "They worship cows, and anyway, they aren't circumcised."

"I'm not dating anyone," Osnat told her. And when Sharon kept looking at her, she added, "I don't even like Sanjay."

Sharon sighed. "You shouldn't lie in the synagogue." She was watching Osnat carefully, as if taking notes so she could report back to everyone at school. "Everybody knows you like him."

"God," Osnat said. "Why are you always such a bitch?"

"I see I've created a monster," Sharon said. "And you're going to hell for sure."

"You slut," Osnat said. "Jews don't believe in hell."

Still, when Osnat got home, her mother was lying in bed with the covers pulled up so high only her face was showing. Her hair was stringy and her eyes were closed.

"Mom," Osnat said. "Mom?"

Osnat's mother opened her eyes. They were red. "Go get Dad," she said. "Your grandmother's died."

After they dropped Osnat's mother off at the airport, Osnat's father said, "So, where do you want to eat? Burger King or McDonald's?"

"McDonald's," Osnat said. "No, Burger King. No, McDonald's." She ordered a large fries and peeled the pickles off her hamburger. She swallowed twice, but that didn't make things any easier. She cleared her throat. "Was it the gas?"

Osnat's father stopped chewing. "Yes," he said, "it was."

"Did she blow up?"

"God, Osnat," her father said. "No. Of course not."

Osnat's grandmother wasn't very old for a grandmother when she died. She was fifty-eight. In Osnat's parents' bedroom there was a picture of her from when she was young. Back then, she had long lashes and smooth skin, and there was a sparkly barrette in her hair. Then she moved to Israel—before it was even Israel—and went crazy.

"I don't know," Osnat told her father. "She didn't seem so crazy to me."

"Well," he said, "she used to be a lot more crazy before she went to the hospital. But you were little then. You don't remember." He picked up one of Osnat's discarded pickles with his fingers. "She had a very hard life, you know. She was supposed to live in the city and have nice clothes. She wasn't supposed to dry swamps and milk cows. Plus, she had to raise your mother and your aunt alone. It's hard to raise children when you're alone."

And maybe it was, but still, her father was a lot nicer with her mother gone. When they got home he let her watch *The A-Team* and didn't get mad when she asked for help with her homework.

"My grandmother in Israel is dead," Osnat told Sanjay the next day, during lunch. "She forgot to turn off the oven. She was crazy."

"Everyone's grandmother is crazy," Sanjay said.

"Not like mine," Osnat said. "Mine was bananas."

During the shiva for her grandmother, Osnat's mother called from Israel every other day. "I miss you," she said. "All your cousins are here and they're getting so big. They miss you too."

On Friday, there was a letter from her grandmother. Osnat knew it was from before she died, but she hoped anyway that it wasn't. Osnat's father wasn't home when the mail came, so she took the letter up to her room. In her part of the letter, her grandmother wrote: "I am getting quite good at popping my teeth out and then in again. I went down to the schoolyard today and took them out for the children and thought about you. By the time you come visit, I should be able to do it without using my hands." In the part for Osnat's mother, she wrote: "Husbands leave their families all the time. They give up and go to South America, and no one stops them. Always be the first to go, Efrat. You won't be allowed to be second."

Osnat called up Sanjay. "What's in South America?" she asked.

"I don't know," Sanjay said. "Summer. What kind of clothes did your mother pack?"

In her parents' closet, all of her mother's clothes were missing.

It was November, and she had taken her sandals. Over in Israel it was already almost midnight, but Osnat called anyway. "When are you coming back?" she asked. "Are you coming back?" She waited for her mother to say that of course she was, but she didn't. Instead she said, "I need time to think."

"What?" said Osnat. "You need *what*?"

She hung up and waited. The phone was silent for a few minutes, and then it rang. It was Osnat's father. "Don't move," he said. "I'll be right there." There was no way he hadn't known. After all, in their closet, his shirts were already elbowing their way into her mother's half.

More time passed and Osnat heard the station wagon pulling up and then her father opening the front door. She heard the stairs creaking under his weight. She could hear him breathe and she could hear him swallow. She could hear his pulse. She could hear his stubble rubbing against the air. She had super hearing. She listened to him standing next to her, waiting. She listened to him shift from one foot to the other. *Let him wait,* she thought. *Let him wait.*

Later, long after she was supposed to be asleep, Osnat heard her father sniffling in his bedroom. It wasn't right. Everyone was giving up too easily. There were things you could do in case of an emergency. You could stock up on water and canned goods. You could line up and head down to the gym. You could note the nearest exit. You weren't supposed to just curl up right there, in your bedroom. You weren't supposed to leave your daughter in a foreign country. You could figure out where your father put his wallet and take his cash and his credit cards when he wasn't looking. You could find your passport in the filing cabinet and pack your clothes instead of your books, and go off to school as if nothing were different. You could offer a taxi driver fifty dollars to take you to the airport. It was one thing to run away from your family and then say you needed time to think. It was another to have to look them in the eye. This was what Osnat tried to explain to the woman at the airport ticket counter, but the woman, who wore a purple uniform and lots of purple mascara, wasn't convinced.

"Do you want me to call your father?" she asked. "Are you sure you don't want me to call him?" She took Osnat upstairs, into one of the offices. "I can find out your number," she said. "Your father's name is right here in your passport. All I have to do is call Information and ask."

Osnat hoped her father would show up with a suitcase and his passport, but he didn't even bother to change out of his sweats. It took thirty-five minutes to get home from the airport. It was enough time to bite all your nails and push down all your cuticles and check your hair for split ends. The main thing was to avoid eye contact. If you could make it all the way home without talking, you'd never have to talk about it again.

In Sanjay's house there was a father who graded papers at the kitchen table and a mother who sang along with the radio while she cooked. On Tuesdays and Thursdays at 4 p.m., the boy across the street measured his thing with a ruler and jotted down his findings in a spiral notebook. Other times he did chin-ups on a special bar that he wedged in the door frame. If she watched him through Sanjay's bird-watching binoculars, Osnat could see the veins popping up across his biceps. His skin was very smooth, and sometimes it gleamed.

"I don't know why my sister likes him," Sanjay told Osnat. "He's an idiot."

Sanjay's sister had long black hair she wore pulled back into a ponytail. She watched soaps while she waited for her boyfriend to come over. Now she yelled, "Don't think I can't hear you!"

In Israel, the sun had been so bright the Mediterranean sometimes disappeared behind it. If you didn't close the blinds in the afternoon, it faded all your furniture. In America, if you were lucky, the sun came out for maybe two hours. Sanjay's room faced west, and between four thirty and five, the sun shone right on his bed. Osnat liked to lie in the warm spot while Sanjay told her stories about India. In India, he said, on sunny days everyone went up on their roofs and flew kites. If you were clever, you coated your kite string with a mixture of glue and glass, and then you could cut loose other people's kites when they weren't paying attention. Osnat closed her eyes and imagined the freed kites flying away like balloons. Sanjay's voice was low and gravelly, like a whisper.

"I don't want to go home," Osnat said.

For a while, Sanjay was silent. Then he said, "You could stay here. Who would know?"

On TV, it was time for *The Brady Bunch*. On the couch, Sanjay's sister and her boyfriend were kissing with tongue. Their mouths glistened with saliva. When they came up for air, a thin strand of spittle stretched between them. It was disgusting. Osnat elbowed Sanjay. "Check them out," she whispered, but Sanjay was already looking. She waited for him to make a face or roll his eyes, but instead he grabbed her shoulders and pressed his lips against her chin. "Oops," he said. And then he pressed his lips against her mouth. They were warm and wet and nothing like his voice. Osnat closed her eyes. It was what you were supposed to do when someone kissed you.

The Brady Bunch ended and *CHiPs* came on, but Osnat couldn't hear the theme music. Sanjay was breathing too hard, in short puffs that went straight up her nose. His weight on top of her was heavier than she expected, but it felt nice. He was radiating heat through his clothes. On the couch, Sanjay's sister was sighing, and then, suddenly, Sanjay's father was yelling, "What is this? An orgy?"

Osnat's father made scrambled eggs for dinner. He sliced four pieces of bread and put them on a plate, and then he put the plate on the table. Osnat wasn't hungry, but she ate anyway.

"Why make this harder than it has to be?" her father asked her. "Kissing boys and acting all wild isn't going to make her come back any sooner. All she needs is a little time to get over this."

"You didn't get over it," Osnat said.

"I lived in Israel for thirteen years, not three months," her father said. "There's no comparison. Be rational." He closed his eyes and put his head down on the table. He breathed in and out, and in and out, and then he got very quiet. "Don't you see this is hard for me too?" he asked. "Can't you help me out just a little?"

"Call her," Osnat said. "Come on. Make her come back. Call her. Call her right now. Pick up the phone. Call her. Call her. Pick up the phone. Call her. Call her. Come on. Call her."

"Quit it with the calling already," her father said.

"No," Osnat said. "Call her. Make her come back. Call her. Call her. Call her right now. Call her."

"Osnat," her father said. "Osnat."

When she still didn't stop, he picked her up and carried her upstairs. Osnat struggled against him, but he was too strong. He held her wrists in one hand and her ankles in the other. "Shhh . . ." he said. "Shhh . . ."

"Why won't you call her?" Osnat shrieked. "Call her. Come on. Call her. Call her."

For a while, Osnat thought she was going crazy. Maybe that was what happened when you changed countries. The air was different, or the maybe the water, and it just threw you off. She lay in bed and stared at the wall and waited. If you stared at the wall closely enough, you could see that the paint made small hills and valleys. In the corners of the room there were spiderwebs and spiders. They didn't move much, and neither did she. Even if she didn't go crazy, at least she would starve to death, and then they'd be sorry. After three days, her plan started working. There was blood in her underwear and everything.

"You see," she told her father. "Now I'm going to die."

Her father turned red and made a choking noise. He covered his face with his hands, and his shoulders shook. He was taking it a lot harder than Osnat thought he would.

"Oh, Osnat," he said. "You're not dying. You just got your period."

"No," Osnat said. "I'm dying." She had to be dying. Her stomach hurt, and her back hurt, and she felt like she couldn't breathe.

"No," her father said again. "You're not dying."

After that, she didn't talk to him anymore. The spiders in the corners were patient, and so was she. Her father checked in on her before he left for work and again when he came back. He sat next to her and tried to make her eat. Then finally, finally, she heard him on the phone with her mother. "Come back," he was saying. "I don't know what to do." He sounded sad, but Osnat didn't care. Her mother was coming back. She got up and moved all her father's shirts back to his side of the closet.

In school, Sanjay was acting funny. He kept pulling on his hair and clenching his hands into fists. Even though Mrs. Sherwood was talking, he kept turning around and looking at Osnat.

"I was worried," he whispered. "Are you in big trouble?"

"My mother's coming back," Osnat said. "I had to get everything ready."

"She's coming back?" Sanjay asked. "For real? She has a ticket and everything?"

Osnat nodded. She waited for Sanjay to turn away, but he didn't. He just kept clenching and unclenching his hands. "What?" she said. "What do you want?"

Sanjay cleared his throat and wiped his hands on his pants. "About what happened—" he started, but Osnat interrupted him.

"No, really," she said, "she's coming back. I swear. My dad told me."

When she came back, Osnat's mother brought Bamba, lemon wafers, *shkedei marak,* and Bazooka with the comics in Hebrew. After all the hugging and kissing was done, Osnat could hear her father singing to her mother all the way down in the kitchen. They went to McDonald's for lunch and to Bill Knapp's for dinner, and they even ordered chocolate cake.

"Jesus," Sanjay said in shop class, while everyone was lining up to get safety goggles. "What's going on with you? Why are you ignoring me?" He said it too loudly and Osnat saw Sharon raise her eyebrows.

"I don't know," Osnat said. "I guess I have more important things to worry about."

"Like what," asked Sanjay, "your parents?" He waited for Osnat to say something, but she didn't. He grabbed her hand. "Don't you get it?" he said. "This has nothing to do with you. They'll do whatever they want to anyway. Don't you know that?" His hand was all sweaty, but he wouldn't let go. "No matter how much they tell you that kids are the most important thing, they're not. In the end, parents do what they want."

"God," Osnat said. "Why are you so angry?"

Sanjay shrugged and let go of her hand. He was looking at her as if she were something small and disgusting. "Why don't you think about other people for a change?"

"Jesus," Osnat said, "that's all I ever do."

"Is it?" Sanjay asked. "Is it really?"

When Osnat came home from school, her mother was lying on her back on the front porch. "I hit a patch of ice," she said. "Help me up." Inside, she took off her pants and rubbed her right hip. She stood with her back to the mirror and tried to get a look at her legs. "That's going to bruise," she said. "I hate winter."

At night, Osnat heard her mother crying in the bathroom. It was 11:32 p.m. If she didn't stop by 11:45, Osnat figured, she would go in and talk to her. At 11:36, she heard her parents' bedroom door open and the floorboards in the hallway creaking. Then she heard her father's deep whisper, followed by her mother's sniffles. She gave them two minutes, but that was it. Too much time alone was dangerous. Who knew what they'd decide to do.

"Osnat," her father said when he saw her. "Why aren't you in bed?"

Osnat ignored him. "Are you leaving again?" she asked her mother. "Is that why you're crying?"

Osnat's mother blew her nose into a piece of toilet paper. Her eyes were red and puffy. "No," she said. "I'm staying."

"Then why aren't you happy?" Osnat asked. "Why aren't we enough for you?"

Her mother tore off another strip of toilet paper and folded it neatly into a square. "I don't know," she said finally.

There they were, Osnat's parents, barefoot and in pajamas and hunched over on the bathroom floor. They looked like lost little children, holding hands and shivering in the cold. They were never going to be happy.

"You know," Osnat said, "you should have thought about all this before you got married."

Sanjay's mother, when she opened the door, was wearing a pink and orange bathrobe. Her hair was parted down the middle and twisted into two braids.

"Osnat," she said, "your parents called. They said you were probably on your way over."

"Please," Osnat told her, "I have to see Sanjay."

"Okay," Sanjay's mother said. "But not in his room."

Osnat waited in the kitchen. On the table, there was an issue of *TV Guide* and a basket full of oranges. When Sanjay came down, he was wearing striped blue pajamas. Osnat covered her face with her hands. Her knees were shaking. She didn't know what to do.

"It's okay," Sanjay said. "Ignore them." He touched her hair, and when she didn't move, he started stroking it.

"They'll never be happy," Osnat told him.

"So what?" Sanjay said. "That doesn't mean you can't be."

"But they're my parents."

Sanjay sighed. "Fuck them."

Osnat sighed too. She opened her eyes. On the cover of *TV Guide,* the girls from *The Facts of Life* were standing shoulder to shoulder, smiling. They looked happy, as if they knew what was going to happen tomorrow, and the next day, and the day after that.

"I'll never look like that," she told Sanjay.

"That's okay," he said. "You look fine to me." It wasn't what Osnat meant, but it was good enough. "Anyway," Sanjay said, "those aren't real people." He walked over to the window behind the kitchen sink. "Come here," he said. "Look." Some of the houses across the street were dark, but some were lit up from inside. In his room, Sanjay's sister's boyfriend was still doing chin-ups. In the living room, his father was drinking a beer and watching TV. "Look," Sanjay said. "This is what real people look like."

How to Clean Up Any Stain

If there's a simple, logical explanation for everything—or, at least, an elegant one—then somewhere in Ann Arbor another man was running around with Marvin's name. There was plenty of support for this theory: people Marvin had never spoken to kept telling him they were so glad to hear from him again; letters from the library complained that he'd hung on too long to books with titles like *How to Clean Up Any Stain* and *Dinner for One*; and, to cap it all off, the dentist told him she'd been expecting someone else before pointing at the spittoon. "Rinse," she ordered. "I haven't seen teeth like that since they started fluoridating water."

No wonder, then, that Marvin had trouble smiling. And if there was comfort in numbers, it wasn't much: his daughter and wife had cavities too.

"So we had a bad dentist in Tel Aviv," Efrat told him. "It isn't a sign, you know."

But to Marvin, it seemed like a close call, evidence that moving back to the States had been necessary: hadn't he only narrowly managed to whisk Efrat and Osnat away before their teeth rotted out completely? He stood in front of the mirror in the men's room and bared his teeth in what looked like a snarl. They seemed more crowded than he remembered, his incisors worn down, as if he'd spent an inordinate amount of time gnawing on something: A bone? A stick? A chew toy?

Back in his office, he pulled out the university phone directory and looked himself up. There he was: Marvin Greenberg, Mathematics. And there he was again: Marvin A. Greenberg, Statistics. What were the odds? He consulted a map and discovered that the statistics department was across campus, tucked in with computer science and operations research. And somewhere over there was another Marvin Greenberg, one with perfect teeth and a middle name that started with *A*, who spent his evenings learning to cook dinners for one while his library fines kept right on accumulating.

On the way home, Marvin stopped at the Village Corner and bought himself a can of Sprite. He loved Sprite. In Israel, it came in glass bottles that exploded if they got too hot, so he never bought any: he didn't want Osnat's possible disfigurement on his conscience. Instead, he had Sprite only in secret, when the speech therapist he visited in order to lose his American accent had him gargle to practice his *r*s. Not that it helped—he may as well have walked around with "rich and gullible" scrawled on his forehead, the way Israelis tried to take him for every lira he had. He had put in thirteen hot, difficult years drinking noncarbonated, vile grapefruit Mitz Paz—because, to tell the truth, he didn't trust the water—and now he was paying the price with three cavities and the ridicule of his dentist. (No doubt Marvin A. Greenberg had perfect teeth, without even a hint of yellow.) Still, as some sort of acknowledgment of Efrat's misery, and of the fact that everything tasted different here—even yogurt, even cheese—he continued to avoid drinking Sprite at home, even though in Michigan it came in cans or plastic bottles. It was asking a lot, moving them all here, he knew. But hadn't she asked a lot too? And even if she hadn't, technically, hadn't he done a lot anyway? Besides, it was a warm day, and how would Efrat ever find out?

When Marvin got home, Efrat was on the phone to her sister

in Israel. She called her sister every week, sometimes twice. "Uh huh," she was saying. "Uh huh . . . uh huh . . ." There was no telling what they were talking about—sometimes, after watching Efrat nod vigorously for up to twenty minutes, she would finally say something and Marvin would realize that all they were talking about was the weather, or a recipe for *pashtida*. It seemed like a waste. Phone calls were expensive. It seemed to Marvin that if all you were going to do was nod and say uh huh, it was more economical to write a letter.

In the living room, things weren't much better: Osnat was watching a documentary on the fortieth anniversary of the bombing of Hiroshima and taking notes in preparation for the nuclear war she was sure was upon them.

"Maybe we could build a pool," she told Marvin when she saw him. "The people who happened to be swimming in Hiroshima didn't get hurt as bad. Or maybe just being in the bathtub would work."

Marvin didn't know where Osnat got her paranoia. He and Efrat had tried to explain to her that a nuclear holocaust was unlikely, and that, even if it wasn't, the Soviets would be satisfied taking out only New York and Washington, D.C., both of which were hundreds of miles away. But Osnat didn't seem convinced. "What about the radiation?" she'd ask. "What about the nuclear winter?" It was as if she didn't know what to do with all the vigilance she'd learned living in Israel, where billboards repeatedly admonished you to keep a lookout for suspicious persons and objects, and turned it instead against the sky, constantly gauging its color and appraising the changes in the weather: Were clouds really supposed to look green? Was that thunder or a fighter jet?

In Osnat's yearbook, kid after kid had written, "Have a great summer, and try not to worry about the nukes." Not that she listened. Instead, she fired off weekly missives to Ronald Reagan urging him to practice moderation: "Don't we have enough bombs already? What if someone makes a mistake?" There was something pathetic about her diligence. Sure, there had been that girl, Samantha Smith, who got a trip to the Soviet Union out of it, but she had written only one letter, and she had sent it to Andropov, and she had been ten and not nearly fourteen, like Osnat. Still, it wasn't as if Marvin's heart were made of stone. After the third form letter, he started intercepting the replies from the White House and swapping in his own: "Thanks so much for writing. I'm doing all I can for world peace, so please don't worry so much about nuclear war. Concentrate on getting good grades instead." It was surprisingly easy to write letters as Ronald Reagan, and by the sixth or seventh he was including little details about Nancy renovating the Oval Office, trips to the National Zoo, and descriptions of state meals that included disgusting foods like snails and frog legs. He'd hand Osnat the latest letter and ask her what was new with the Commander in Chief, but if Osnat was excited to hear about reupholstering the chair Lincoln had sat in, she sure did a good job of hiding it. Instead she rolled her eyes as if there was nobody on earth more boring than Marvin, and she did it so convincingly that sometimes he found himself worrying that maybe she was right.

Okay, so Marvin had been lax about getting them all to a dentist. They'd been in Ann Arbor nearly two years, renting a house in a neighborhood near the stadium. There really was no excuse for waiting so long, except that he was busy at work—thank God for the modem, or he'd never be home at all. Anyway, it was easy to forget your teeth when they didn't hurt, and when you had forty exams to grade, eight dissertations to go through, three lectures to prepare, and two grants to write. But now it was August, and Saturday, and summer, and—at least on the home front—he was finally catching up: dentist, oil change, lawn mower, storm windows. With all the chores done, there was no good reason not to do the one other thing he'd been meaning to do: go looking for the other Marvin Greenberg. He would take Efrat and Osnat, and they would all wear low-brimmed hats and dark glasses and make an afternoon of it. He might even bring along the binoculars.

"I don't think so," Efrat said when he finally tracked her down in the backyard. "I don't know if I can take all the excitement." She was crouched in the grass, holding out a handful of nuts to a couple of squirrels who were watching her suspiciously from the top of the fence.

"You really shouldn't do that," Marvin told her. "They might have rabies."

"You've got your projects," Efrat said, "and I have mine. Anyway, you don't want me to come with you. What if I see the other Marvin and like him better?"

"The man's learning to cook from a library book," Marvin said.

"Not a bad idea," Efrat said. "Maybe you should try it."

It was hard to tell when she was joking, especially since Marvin *had* been doing most of the cooking ever since Efrat announced that not being able to find a job didn't make her a maid. Maybe it didn't, and maybe he owed her that much, but surely she had better things to do with her time than trying to tame squirrels: she could still be working ahead in her ESL workbooks or reading through the classifieds, couldn't she? Not that there was any point getting into it right then. Instead, Marvin invited Osnat to come along and together they walked over to Marvin A. Greenberg's building, which was covered with sheets of ivy that rustled with birds getting ready for the long trip south. Inside, the hallways were tiled and neutral, like something out of a hospital. Marvin pointed at Marvin A. Greenberg's name on the building directory in the lobby. "There's another man here with my name," he told Osnat. "Only he's a statistician." When Osnat didn't look impressed, he added, "What are the odds?" She didn't get it.

They took the elevator to the third floor, and walked up and down the hallway, reading the names on the offices. No one was in, and Marvin A. Greenberg's door, when they found it, was locked. Still, there were plenty of clues: the door was covered with cartoons about dogs, of all things, and alternate lyrics to Frank Sinatra: "Bayesians in the night, assessing chances, we'll be sharing risk before the night is through. . . ." Marvin groaned.

"Ma?" Osnat asked.

"Speak English," Marvin told her. She needed the practice, and anyway, English was easier for Marvin—he'd almost forgotten how easy. There were thousands of words in English: all he had to do was open his mouth and there they were.

"What?" Osnat asked again.

"Bayesians are a type of statistician—they figure out probabilities," Marvin explained. "Maybe three people in the world get this joke."

"So he *is* like you," Osnat said, then scurried out of reach so that he wouldn't swat her.

"Actually," Marvin said, "my jokes are much funnier. You'll discover that once your English gets better."

In the city phone book—what luck—the other Marvin Greenberg had no problem with listing his full name: Marvin Alvin Greenberg, as if Marvin and Greenberg together didn't already invoke massive amounts of nostril hair, golf pants, and game after game of shuffleboard. The other Marvin Greenberg's brazenness made Marvin, who was careful to keep his own middle name—Sheldon—under wraps, a little nervous. Over the years, he had developed a theory that in any group of people there was a finite set of naturally occurring roles. Usually, he found this oddly comforting, a kind of catchall explanation for why certain things worked and others didn't: someone had to be the best, and someone had to be new, and someone had to be the idiot. All you had to do was figure out who had occupied your position before you to see where you were going to end up. It was how he stayed focused, able to believe that all Efrat and Osnat needed was time, that eventually they'd realize he wasn't asking too much, only doing what others in his same position had done before him.

Take the group of Israelis he and Efrat occasionally met for dinner: Israeli women and their American, academic husbands who kept stumbling over the gendered nouns in Hebrew. They always nodded when their wives talked longingly about tomatoes and cucumbers, even though really, deep down, they were glad—ecstatic even—to be back in the States, throwing big, bloody slabs of meat on the backyard barbecue and eating them in front of a color TV. It wasn't anything they said, but he could see it anyway—their relief was something palpable, like sweat or body odor. And it wasn't as though he and Efrat particularly liked any of them—he certainly would have never chosen to be friends with any of the men—but being with them was a lot like checking your reflection in the mirror. The wives, despite their griping, seemed content, their skin rosy and free of worry lines, their nails neatly manicured rather than bitten down to nubs like Efrat's. They laughed freely, exchanged phone numbers for masseuses and maids, and patted their husbands' backs with affection. Clearly, they'd survived the move to Michigan intact, even if it had taken them a while, and Marvin found their complacency comforting: if your reflection seemed fine, he told himself, then you'd probably end up fine too.

Of course, he was well aware that all this was abstraction, mere speculation, and nothing compared to the startling concreteness of another man who possessed your name, an occupation that was a more practical variation of your own, and the kind of self-confidence you only wished you had. And who topped it all off with cavity-free teeth.

"It only costs fifty dollars to pull a tooth," Marvin told Efrat after they brushed their teeth that night. "It's cheaper than a filling."

"Are you crazy?" Efrat said. "I'm keeping all my teeth."

"Not you," Marvin said. "Me." He wiped his mouth with a towel. "Who would know? They're way back there."

"I'd know," Efrat said. "You're going to get fillings, like a normal person."

"Or maybe a gold tooth. Then we could cash it in when I retire and move to Florida."

Marvin could tell Efrat was getting mad by the way she screwed the cap back on the toothpaste tube without wiping off the excess toothpaste. Still, he kept going:

"Then I could be the Marvin Greenberg with the gold tooth."

"Or the one without a wife," Efrat said.

"He doesn't have a wife," Marvin said. "He's cooking for one, not for two."

"Maybe she's on a diet," Efrat said. Then she sighed. "Anyway, I thought we were going back to Israel when we retire."

"We are," Marvin said. "Of course we are. Why wouldn't we?"

About six months before they'd moved to Michigan, Efrat and Marvin had gone to a conference in Niagara Falls, just the two of them, leaving Osnat with Efrat's sister. By the third day there, Marvin had stopped attending the sessions, opting instead to spend mornings in bed with Efrat, the curtains pulled wide open so that while he and Efrat made love, he could look down at the falls and feel as if he were flying. He took his time on those mornings, marveling at the pressure of Efrat's hands on his back, at the way her hair fanned out over the cool, white sheets, at the private, unmarred terrain of her body. After, when they were done, they'd sit in the heart-shaped tub and eat pancakes ordered from room service, or French toast, or waffles. "See," he told her again and again, "now this is real maple syrup." In the afternoons, they'd walk along the promenade and watch tourists posing for photos in front of the falls. "Here," Marvin would say, sidling up to the various fathers fiddling with the focus on their cameras, "let me do it. Don't you want to be in the picture too?" And the men would obediently hand over their equipment and go link arms with their families so Marvin could take a picture of them grinning in the mist.

"Everyone's so happy here," Efrat told him on their fifth day together. "It's a little creepy. And it's not just them. You're different too."

"Different how?"

"I don't know." She shrugged. "More relaxed. Not so serious. And then there's all the sex."

"Well," Marvin said, "we don't have to have it."

"That's just it," Efrat said. "I think we do." She sighed wistfully. "I wish you were like this all the time."

Now it was Marvin's turn to shrug. "We can put a lock on the bedroom door," he offered, but he knew that wasn't what she meant. As the time of their flight back to Israel drew near, he could feel himself tensing up. It had been days since he'd seen anyone in military uniform, or heard anyone yelling or honking, or smelled the sooty exhaust of city buses. Whenever he made eye contact with people, they smiled. The streets were swept, the hedges a lush green, the houses brightly painted with sloped, shingled roofs and basketball hoops over the garages. He could take baths without worrying about wasting water. Even the toilets were different, quieter, the flush less angry. "You made your choice," he reminded himself whenever his breathing grew shallow and he could feel himself starting to sweat. "Now live with it." Still, on the plane, he had to clench his jaw tight so that he wouldn't accidentally start to cry. He was turning into a ninny and Efrat knew it. When the captain turned off the Fasten Seat Belts sign, she reached over and squeezed his hand. He expected her to tell him to buck up, but instead she whispered, "I'm sorry. I'm so sorry," and a few weeks later, when it was time for him to submit a proposal for his sabbatical, she said, "Maybe you should look for a position in the States."

Another letter had arrived from the White House, thanking Osnat for sharing her concerns and assuring her that though a more personal reply was not possible, Ronald Reagan was doing his best for the country. After dropping Efrat off at the dentist, Marvin drove into work to borrow his secretary's typewriter. When Marvin first started writing the letters, he'd worried about not having anything that could pass as official White House stationery, but then he figured that his version of Ronald Reagan would use his own personal stash of paper anyway—it was more intimate. "Dear Osnat," he wrote. "With fall semester starting soon, Nancy and I hope you will do your part to make trickle-down economics work by going back-to-school shopping with your mother." Sometimes he really cracked himself up; he hoped Osnat was saving the letters somewhere. Sure, if Samantha Smith hadn't gotten there first and written Andropov, it could have been the three of them touring Red Square and writing best-selling books about how the Soviets are people too, but wasn't this letter exchange meaningful in its own, more private, way? Wouldn't Osnat look back one day and think, "Boy, my father really must have loved me to intercept all that mail"?

Efrat was in a bad mood when he picked her up from the dentist. "Am I drooling?" she kept asking. "I feel like I'm drooling." She squeezed her bottom lip between her thumb and index finger. "Nothing," she reported.

"So it didn't hurt?" Marvin asked, hopeful.

"Are you crazy? Of course it hurt." She tugged at her lip. "I feel like a cow," she said. "Give me some hay or something."

"I wrote Osnat another letter," Marvin said.

Efrat sighed. "You know I wish you wouldn't do that."

"Come on," Marvin said. "It's fun."

Maybe he was imagining it, but Efrat rolled her eyes. "It's misleading," she said. "Dishonest, even. We don't live in a world where Ronald Reagan has time to write little girls, and there's no reason to pretend we do. Sometimes it's better to just know the truth."

"Sometimes," Marvin agreed, "but Osnat's still young. She needs something to believe in."

"Is that why you haven't introduced yourself to the other Marvin Greenberg?"

Marvin could feel his face grow warm. "What does that have to do with anything?"

"Don't think I haven't noticed you staring at his name in the phone book," Efrat continued. When Marvin looked over at her, she added, "See? *I* pay attention. I'm the one who sees things for what they are." She leaned back in her seat and sighed again.

Marvin concentrated on his hands on the steering wheel. They had traded the used station wagon they bought when they first arrived for a nice sedan with automatic transmission and power windows and locks. "America?" he had said to Efrat before driving it off the lot, and she had answered, "America," maybe even with an exclamation mark at the end. Now it was all Marvin could do to stop himself from saying, "I pay attention too." All he ever did anymore was pay attention. He wasn't stupid. The problem wasn't that he couldn't see what was going on, but that no one trusted his judgment, no one listened. No matter how often he tried to explain the odds, Osnat refused to believe him that nuclear war was unlikely. And why should she trust him on matters of life and death when Efrat refused to even consider that the move to Michigan—which, if anything, upped their chances for stress-free survival—had been the right thing to do? As humiliating as it was dealing with irate bank tellers impatient with your accent, at least no one was whisking Efrat off to basic training with a bunch of eighteen-year-olds who stole your blankets every time you went out for a piss, and then expected you to fight to the death for a country whose citizens were so tense they only narrowly missed running you over every time you went outside.

"I'm sorry," Efrat said, reaching over to pat Marvin's thigh. "You know how much I hate dentists. But I also don't know why you're so obsessed about this guy. It's just a name. It doesn't mean you'll have anything else in common."

At home, Osnat was in the living room, watching TV. "Did it hurt?" she asked Efrat.

"Not one bit," Marvin said quickly. Osnat's appointment was scheduled for Monday. He imagined her sitting in the dentist's waiting room, staring at all the Polaroids of the other, smiling kids who were in the No Cavities Club, and wringing her hands. He tried to signal to Efrat to play along, but she didn't: "Well, maybe it didn't hurt your father," she said. "But it did hurt."

"A lot?"

"Of course not," Marvin said.

Osnat looked skeptical.

"It only hurts for a few seconds," Efrat said. "Then you go numb."

Marvin fished into his backpack and pulled out the letter from Ronald Reagan, which he'd resealed into its original envelope. "Look," he said. "You've got mail."

Later, while they were eating a dinner comprised entirely of easy-to-chew food—scrambled eggs, cottage cheese, soft white bread—it was hard not to notice how old they all were getting. There was Osnat with arms and legs and a face that were all bony and out of proportion, and Efrat with laugh lines and wrinkles on her neck and coarse silver hairs that insisted on standing up and declaring themselves. And here he was, responsible for them, *providing,* for God's sake, and all they could talk about was Efrat's sister's new color TV, as if they hadn't had color television for two whole years. "I can't believe they made him pink," Osnat was saying about some cartoon character, and Efrat was agreeing: "I thought he was brown."

"All right, so he's pink," he said finally. "Anything new outside the world of television?"

Osnat mopped up what was left of her eggs with a piece of bread. "So," she said, "I was thinking that maybe when football starts, I could sell cookies. I bet Lizzy makes lots of money."

Lizzy was the ten-year-old who lived down the block. Rumor had it she'd been selling cookies to fans heading to the football stadium since before she could talk. You had to admire that kind of business initiative from a toddler.

"If she makes any money," Marvin said, "it's because her parents pay for the ingredients." He pulled a pen out of his shirt pocket and flattened out the napkin he'd been using. "Let's see. How much is a bag of chocolate chips?" Efrat and Osnat exchanged looks. He knew he wasn't supposed to have seen them, but he had. “Anyway,” he said, “I don’t know if the market can bear another girl selling cookies. Lizzy has the advantage of being first, and of being younger and cuter.”

“Fine,” Osnat said. And Efrat said, “Marvin.”

“What?” Marvin said, ignoring Efrat’s glare. “I’m not saying Osnat isn’t cute. I’m saying she’s thirteen and Lizzy’s only ten.”

“What does that have to do with anything?” Efrat asked, but Osnat interrupted her: “Fine,” she said again. “I won’t sell cookies.” She stood up and started stacking the dinner plates.

Marvin tried to explain—“I was just being honest”—but across the table, Efrat exhaled sharply, exasperated, as if once again Marvin just didn’t get it. But he did get it—he could clearly see Osnat sitting behind a too small table on their front lawn, a batch of uneaten, unsold cookies on a plate before her, watching grimly as Lizzy pocketed quarter after quarter five houses down. Kiddie entrepreneurship was like treat-or-treating: it was only cute if you didn’t have acne or breasts; if you did, you were too old. Why couldn’t Efrat see that? Still, he was obviously missing something yet again, because here was Osnat reaching for his silverware, her lips pressed into a straight, flat line, as if someone had ironed all the expression out of her face: a two-dimensional girl in a three-dimensional body.

“Hey,” he said. “Don’t worry about the dishes. I’ll do them.”

“That’s okay,” Osnat said. “I got it.”

“No, really.”

Osnat shrugged. “Fine,” she said. “Suit yourself.”

Although he knew that any man walking by on the street could be the other Marvin Greenberg, Marvin found himself favoring tall, middle-aged white men with dark hair—no one would name a blond, blue-eyed baby Marvin, would they? He imagined the other Marvin Greenberg talking on the phone and stroking a well-kept, bushy beard. When Marvin had tried growing a beard in his twenties, it had sprouted scraggly and sparse. The other Marvin Greenberg—virile, hairy, and vigorous—would have no such problems. Perhaps he even played football in high school rather than chess.

"All right," Efrat said. "That's it. This has gone on long enough. We're going right up to his house and ringing his doorbell. Next you'll start imagining he's some kind of bodybuilder—"

"With no back hair," Marvin said. "Maybe I'll start waxing."

"If he's virile," Efrat said, "he has back hair. And anyway, if he's such a demigod, why is he a statistician?"

Marvin played it out in his head: first he'd finish washing the dishes, and then they'd watch *Wheel of Fortune,* and then they'd all get in the car and drive over to what would no doubt be the other Marvin Greenberg's mansion, complete with a hot tub and a live-in maid. Then what?

"I don't know," he said, rinsing out the dishcloth.

"Marvin," Efrat said. "Enough already. There are more important things to worry about."

"Like what?"

"Like Osnat," Efrat said. "Like me."

Even though she was smiling, her eyes were hard and wet. Marvin focused on the fine lines around her mouth. "But don't you see?" he said. "You're all I worry about. Why don't you think I worry about you?" He reached for her hands, which felt cool and limp like old celery, as if Efrat couldn't be bothered to use her muscles. "God, Efi," he said, "what is it?"

Efrat pulled her hands away from his. "Why shouldn't Osnat try to sell cookies?"

"I just don't want to see her disappointed."

"Well, you're going to have to," Efrat said matter-of-factly. "This isn't a fairy tale. There's no happily ever after. I keep telling you, but you won't listen."

Marvin knew his cue when he heard it. "No," he said. "You're the one who won't listen. I'm the one who keeps telling you we're going back."

Suddenly Osnat was standing in front of them. "Are you fighting?" she asked. Behind her, Marvin could hear the applause of a studio audience, and the opening strains of the *Wheel of Fortune* theme.

"We're discussing—" Efrat started to say, but Marvin interrupted her: "Of course we're not fighting."

"Because it's not important about the cookies," Osnat said. "It was just a thought."

It was Marvin who took Osnat to the dentist on Monday after Efrat begged off, saying it was too soon and that she could still smell that burning tooth smell from the drill.

"They don't burn your teeth," Marvin said.

"You know what I mean," Efrat said. "You take her."

Of course, they would have eventually heard the news, but that morning Marvin felt unprepared for the shock of it: there she was, Samantha Smith, grinning at them from every newspaper box, as if reproaching Marvin and Osnat with her own fine fluoridated-from-birth teeth. He'd recognized her picture right away, and even started to say, "Now what?" when the headline registered and he realized that she was dead, that she and her father had been killed in a plane crash in Maine the night before. He turned away quickly, hoping Osnat wouldn't notice, but she had. "Wow," she said. Then she shrugged and made her pronouncement: "Bummer."

Marvin waited for her to say something else, but she didn't. "Don't you want to talk about it?" he asked.

Osnat shrugged again. "It isn't like I knew her."

In the waiting room, while Osnat was in with the dentist, he studied Samantha's picture on the front page: the freckles, the side part, the wide smile. In addition to the trip to the Soviet Union, the TV special, and the book contract, she had recently taken up acting. If you ignored her untimely death for a moment, it seemed unfair to get so much in return for one letter. Timing really was everything.

"On the bright side," he told a numbed and drooling Osnat during the drive home, "if she hadn't written that letter, she never would have been on that plane. Life in the public eye involves a certain amount of risk. It's the same with the Kennedys, you know."

"Who?" said Osnat.

"Anyway," Marvin said, "you have that nice correspondence going with the President. It's probably good that Samantha Smith got there first." He could feel an apology bubbling up from somewhere deep inside him, but he wasn't sure what he wanted to apologize for. At least they were all still alive, he wanted to say. At least they were all still together. He tried to imagine Samantha Smith's father up on that plane with the engines failing—had he had any idea what was coming? Had he understood this was it? "You know I love you," Marvin told Osnat, "right?"

Osnat rolled her eyes in exasperation—like mother, like daughter, Marvin found himself thinking. "Of course you love me," Osnat said. "You're my dad."

It was a hot day, and the students were already beginning to trickle back into town. Even with the air-conditioning, it was hard to concentrate. Over lunch, Marvin bought a can of Sprite from the vending machine on the first floor of the other Marvin Greenberg's building and then parked himself on a bench across from the entrance: that way, he'd be sure to see him leaving for lunch. He was curious to see whether the other Marvin Greenberg would trigger some sort of signal—goose bumps, chills, a ringing in the ears—the kind long-lost siblings reported feeling right before finding each other, but man after man left the building without even glancing at him, and not one of them felt familiar. Samantha Smith leered at him from the newspaper boxes that lined the corner.

Back at the office, he called Efrat. "I'm just worried about this whole Samantha Smith thing," he said. "I mean, they're practically the same age, and she writes all those letters. I thought she'd be more upset. Why isn't she more upset?"

"Marvin," Efrat said, "it's not like they actually knew each other."

"Why does everyone keep saying that?" Marvin asked. "So what if they didn't know each other? It's still a connection."

"Enough," Efrat said. "Enough. God, how many times do I have to say it? Enough. I know you have this elaborate theory, but Marvin, it isn't fooling anybody."

"I'm not trying to fool anyone."

Efrat sighed. "You think Osnat doesn't know you're the one writing all those letters? You think she doesn't know we fight? She's thirteen. She's not stupid. And neither am I."

"I never thought you were."

"Then why do you do it?" Efrat asked. "Why do you keep pretending we might go back to Israel, when you sure as hell know you won't?"

The truth was Marvin knew no such thing. Sure, his sabbatical was coming to a close and he had accepted an indefinite extension, and sure, they had two more years of car payments in front of them, and sure, he sometimes ducked into open houses on Sunday afternoons on his way to or from the office so he could get a sense of their real estate options, but none of those facts added up to *never.* If anyone was keeping track, which he wasn't of course, then the truth was that Efrat decided they weren't going back to Israel long before they'd even made the move. "The money will be too good," she told Marvin. "The people will be too nice. We'll grow fat and spoiled and fall in love with the squirrels."

"So we should sell the apartment?" he asked.

"Yes," Efrat told him. "No. Of course not. Are you crazy?" Still, as they made round after round of good-bye visits, she clung to friends and family as if she would never see them again. "If only we were moving to New York," she would tell Marvin, "or L.A. No one will visit us in Michigan."

"Of course they will," Marvin said. "And we'll visit them. It's not like we're leaving for good. We're just going to see how it goes."

But Efrat didn't believe him: "I know how it goes. I watch TV."

Then why'd you suggest it in the first place? Marvin wanted to ask her. Their plane tickets were already purchased, their furniture stowed away in one of the bedrooms for safekeeping while they rented out their apartment. It was too late to back out, wasn't it? He lay in bed and listened to Efrat toss and turn, and realized he had to at least offer. "Do you want us to cancel?" he said, careful to keep his voice neutral. He held his breath waiting for her to answer, but he could feel his heart drumming against his rib cage. *Be a man,* he told himself. *Whatever she says, you be the man.*

After a long silence, Efrat spoke: "We already have renters." Even though it was a muggy night, she slid up next to him and hoisted her left leg over his hips. "Just for a minute," she said. "I know it's too hot." Already, the area where their skins touched grew damp and uncomfortable, but neither of them moved. Efrat sighed. "I've never lived anywhere else," she said.

"It's not so bad," Marvin said. "People do it all the time. I did it."

"I know," Efrat said. "And look how happy you are."

"I'm fine."

"Well, then." Efrat moved her leg away. "I'll be fine too."

And Marvin had believed her, although now, looking back, he wondered if he should have. Sometimes it was hard not to feel like an idiot. He'd spent thirteen years in Israel and had never felt at home. Whatever made him think Efrat would feel at home in less than two? Fool, he thought. Moron. But then he took a deep breath and waited for his heart to slow. It wasn't the same, he reminded himself. Israel was no America, Ann Arbor no Tel Aviv. And at least he'd tried. He'd dutifully gone to Hebrew classes and reserves duty and speech therapy, gladly suffering through too high taxes and terror and sweat. He hadn't stayed at home and wept and refused to cook or clean. He'd tried hard. For thirteen years. When you really thought about it, he reflected, there truly was no comparison.

On the news, they replayed clips of Samantha Smith's visit to the Soviet Union. Osnat sat on the couch, knees tucked up under her chin. She had dark hair, like Samantha's, but Osnat's was wavy, and her skin was too sallow for freckles. Whatever wholesome, all-American quality it was that Samantha Smith radiated as she toured Red Square, Osnat didn't have it. Still, as wrong as it was, Marvin couldn't shake the strange feeling of relief that, somehow, he had only narrowly avoided a great disaster.

"So," he said during a commercial break, "Mom told me you found out about the letters." He didn't know if he should look at Osnat or at the TV screen, so instead he concentrated on picking a loose thread from the couch cushion. "Are you mad?"

Osnat shrugged. "I'm almost fourteen," she said. "I know Ronald Reagan is too busy to write back."

"So why didn't you say something?"

"I don't know," Osnat said. "I guess I figured it wasn't hurting anything."

She sounded so resigned Marvin felt frightened. Where was all that youthful optimism everyone always talked about? "I just hate it that you're so worried about nuclear war," he said. "You weren't this scared in Israel."

Osnat rolled her eyes. "Dad," she said, as if he should have known better, as if he really didn't understand her one bit, "when the world ends, it won't matter where we live. It won't matter at all."

Every imaginary conversation Marvin had with Efrat ended with her packing her bags and leaving, sometimes taking Osnat and telling him it was for good, and other times going alone and pretending she just needed a break. Either way, Marvin's evenings stretched out long and empty before him, filled with stacks of canned soup and frozen dinners eaten in front of the TV. This was what happened when you strayed from careful planning and fell in love with the natives in a country you were only visiting for its archeological artifacts. It was easy to get swept up in the novelty of it all: the sun, the heat, the contested borders. Everywhere you looked there were Jews—buying groceries, writing out parking tickets, emptying garbage cans—and that deceptive blank-slate feeling of new neighborhoods rising in the sand and drip irrigation turning the desert green. And he loved Efrat, who picked him over hairier men with calloused hands and combat experience, and who didn't mind that he sang in the shower and was nervous around anything with an exoskeleton. He was young and believed the Beatles that love was all you needed, and now here he was, fifteen years later, and it turned out he needed more: a job worth going to, a language in which he could tell jokes, snow. Even worse, he realized now, his family needed more too. And who was he to choose his own happiness over theirs?

Efrat was outside, setting up a trail of cocktail-mix nuts in the backyard that led from the fence to the patio, trying to impress the squirrels with salted and roasted cashews and macadamias. It's never going to work, he wanted to tell her. Squirrels are squirrels—they aren't dogs, they aren't pets. Then again, what was the point? She was outside. She was busy. She was even humming a little under her breath. And there was still an hour of daylight left. Marvin decided there was only one thing he could do. It was time to seek a greater wisdom.

"All right," he announced from the back porch. "I'm doing it. I'm going to see the other Marvin Greenberg."

Marvin walked briskly, swinging his arms and concentrating on the way each foot rolled forward from heel to toe. The other Marvin Greenberg, he had noted with little surprise, lived on the other end of his very same neighborhood, on a shady street that boasted large brick houses with two-car garages. It was exactly the kind of street Marvin would have chosen for himself if he already had tenure: America.

Now that the air was starting to cool, people were outside, sitting on front-porch swings and watching Marvin walk as if he were a parade of one. Marvin stared straight ahead, hoping it would make him seem more purposeful. He could hear children shooting baskets off garage doors. *Hello,* he thought, imagining himself marching right up the front walk and ringing the doorbell. *Hello, I'm Marvin Greenberg. Hello there, I'm Marvin. Hi. Hello.*

But when he finally got to the right house, there was a man on the front lawn, large and sweaty and steaming mad, cursing a lawn mower that was lying on its side. "Damn it," he was saying. "Damn it. Damn it." Marvin kept right on walking, but when he reached the edge of the lawn, he stopped. He wanted a better look.

"Need some help?" he asked, even though it was Efrat who was normally in charge of the mowing.

"Thanks," the man answered, "but no thanks. It's a heap of junk, this machine." He looked nothing like Marvin had expected: he was shorter, for one thing, and nearly bald. There were grass stains on his pants and he was wearing a white T-shirt that was brittle and yellow under the arms. No wonder he was still hanging on to the book about stain removal. "What I need," the man announced, "is a riding mower."

"I'm Marvin," Marvin said, extending his hand. "I'm new here."

"Marvin?" the man said. "I'm Marvin too. Marvin Greenberg."

Marvin braced himself for a bone-crushing handshake, but when it came, it was nothing special. "Huh," he said. "My last name is Greenberg too."

"What are the odds?" the other Marvin said. Then he laughed. "I've been saving that up for weeks. You're the one in mathematics, right? Hang on a sec. I have a bunch of your mail." He disappeared into the house, and came out holding two beers and a small stack of envelopes. "I kept meaning to stop by, but you know how it goes," he said, handing Marvin a can.

"Yeah," Marvin said. "I know exactly."

Later, after Osnat was asleep, Marvin lay in bed and watched Efrat give herself a manicure. She cut her nails square and close, then trimmed her cuticles. Earlier, with the other Marvin Greenberg, it had been so simple to sum up the essentials of his life: a wife, a child, a clean shot at tenure, thirteen years in Israel and now some time in America, where, by all objective, quantifiable standards, life was easier. No one could argue with that. Bringing your family back to America was a no-brainer, in the same way that no one questioned families who moved from the city to the suburbs. Compared to the other Marvin Greenberg, with his estranged wife and broken lawn mower, Marvin's life seemed full, exciting even, garnished with danger and exotic locales.

Now, though, with Efrat on the edge of the bed, rubbing lotion into her hands, Marvin knew—he *knew*—that the last thing they needed was to talk everything over yet again. These things took time, but you got used to them: the lush, green lawns; the clean streets; the big cars; the way people smiled and asked about your day. A body could resist for only so long, and then it had to adjust, the same as it did to the local water and cooler temperatures until suddenly you were sweating when it was only 45 degrees. What Marvin needed was patience, and Efrat and Osnat would begin to see things the way they actually were: how tired everyone looks in Israel, the way everybody yells, how there's nothing natural about hennaed hair.

"So," Efrat said, "fat and balding, you say?"

Marvin nodded. He lifted up the covers so Efrat could climb in, then pressed his mouth against the warm skin between her shoulder blades. It tasted like soap. "But he knows how to do laundry."

Efrat snorted. "Anyone can do laundry." She was quiet for a moment, and then she took a breath. "Marvin—"

"Efi," Marvin interrupted her, "let's not talk about it. Let's not talk about it tonight." What he really wanted to say was, Trust me.

Trust me to do what's best. But here it was, his life: his wife stopped at the beginning of a sentence, all that breath waiting to be exhaled, and him pressed against her, hoping she wouldn't continue, hoping she'd forget exactly what it was she wanted to say.

Running

In English they were reading the short version of the play based on Anne Frank's diary. The play didn't show the Nazis coming to get Anne and her family. Harriet told Jennifer that this was where the real diary ended too. She had spent lunch in the library flipping through it, and all it was were people hiding out in an attic. The real stuff, according to Harriet, happened after, when there was no time for writing, or at least no paper to write on. She showed Jennifer the picture of Anne Frank on the diary's cover. Anne Frank had dark frizzy hair, like Harriet, only she looked happy.

"She didn't know what was coming," Harriet said.

Their homework was to write an alternate diary—it could be from one of the other characters' point of view, or it could be a sequel. You had to make it look as if it had been found in someone's trunk, or under the floorboards of someone's kitchen. It wasn't hard to make paper look old. You just soaked it in some coffee, and it dried brown and crinkly. Jennifer wrote a version of Peter's journal. In it, she described how the Nazis were burning the Jews alive in the infirmaries. She got a C. Mrs. Lincoln had taken points off for confusing "infirmary" with "crematorium," and more points off for saying the Jews had been burned alive.

"The very idea," Mrs. Lincoln told Jennifer. "They were killed in the gas chambers, and *only then* were their bodies burned."

Harriet didn't do the assignment, but she didn't get in trouble.

When they were through reading the play, she had raised her hand and announced, "My mother was in the Holocaust." Harriet's last name was Shapiro and she had a big nose. Anyway, it wasn't as if you could call up Harriet's mother and ask if it was true. Some things are better off ignored.

The town in Indiana where Harriet and Jennifer lived was crisscrossed by railroad tracks. Sometimes cars had to stop in the middle of the road to let trains go by. The trains never had any windows. It was a small town, and Harriet was new, having just arrived from Michigan. Every day, after school, she made Jennifer watch the 4:05 and the 4:27. Jennifer was fat; she couldn't afford to be picky. The other girls called her the Welcome Wagon. She showed new girls around until they got their bearings and moved on to better tables in the cafeteria. Usually, the whole process took maybe two weeks. Jennifer kept waiting for Harriet to make the announcement. They were going into week four.

On the last day of the Anne Frank unit, Mrs. Lincoln took them outside and made them stand in a circle, as if they were still in grade school. In daylight, she looked sallow. Her gray hair, it turned out, was frosted with blond. She clapped twice and told everyone to take ten giant steps backward. She cupped her hands around her mouth and hollered, "Look at the grass." They looked. It was green and spotted with dandelions.

Back inside, Mrs. Lincoln explained that they had circled about a million blades of grass. "Just think," she said, "that's how many Jewish children died in the Holocaust. Anne and Margot and Peter were just three."

Everyone put on their best somber faces.

That Saturday, the one between week four and week five, Jennifer invited Harriet to sleep over. At the grocery store, she made her mom buy Oreos and chocolate ice cream. She wasn't supposed to have either, but it was a special occasion. Once a week she went to a meeting with all the other fat kids in town and listened to a skinny woman with big hair lecture about the importance of eating enough fruits and vegetables. In the bathroom, during break, Jennifer traded colored pencils for chocolate bars. She had no choice. Her parents had stopped giving her an allowance when they discovered the stash of candy in her sock drawer.

Before the pizza arrived, they did makeovers in the bathroom. Harriet put on lipstick and Jennifer put on blush. Harriet put on eye shadow and Jennifer put on eyeliner. Then they traded. When they were done, Harriet said to Jennifer, "Guess who I am." She had brushed her hair and parted it on the side. It curled out at the tips. The lipstick made her lips look full.

"I don't know," said Jennifer.

"I'll give you a hint," Harriet said. She turned her left arm so it faced Jennifer. Halfway between her wrist and her elbow, she had scrawled a bunch of numbers with the eye pencil.

"I'm Anne Frank," she said. She flipped her hair and folded her arms one over the other, just like Anne in the photo on the cover of the diary. She smiled. "I'm Anne Frank after the camps."

They took off the makeup with cold cream, but Harriet didn't wash off the numbers. Jennifer knew her mother would notice because her mother always noticed. Even before they finished passing out slices of pizza, Jennifer's mother pointed at Harriet's forearm and asked, "What are those?" By then, the numbers had begun to blur. The eights looked like nines, and the twos looked like fives.

"Is that a phone number?" Jennifer's mother asked.

"They're concentration camp numbers," said Harriet.

Jennifer saw her mother and her father exchange glances. Her father raised his eyebrows and her mother cleared her throat.

"Well," said Jennifer's father. "Maybe you should wash those off."

"That's okay," Harriet said.

"Come on," said Jennifer's father. "It'll only take a minute." He pushed his chair back and stood up.

"Really, it's fine," Harriet said. She reached for another slice of pizza. Jennifer reached for one too.

"Jennifer," said her mother.

Jennifer thought about putting the slice back, but she didn't want to. Instead she said, "Harriet's mother was in the Holocaust."

Jennifer's parents slept with their bedroom door open. They liked being able to hear what was going on in the house. It was how they had discovered Jennifer's stash—by the crackling noise the wrappers made in the middle of the night. Jennifer ripped the package of Oreos wide open so that later, after Harriet fell asleep, she would be able to eat as many as she wanted without making noise. Just their smell made her light-headed. She watched Harriet change into her nightshirt. She was bony and flat, and you could see all her ribs. You couldn't see Jennifer's ribs even when she stretched her arms straight up over her head and inhaled. She turned out the bedside light, making sure the Oreos were within reach.

"You have a night-light," Harriet said.

"Don't you?" asked Jennifer.

"No," Harriet said. "I'm trying to develop my night vision."

"Oh," said Jennifer.

She heard Harriet shift in her sleeping bag and take a big breath. Jennifer reached for an Oreo and popped it whole into her mouth. Chewing made too much noise, but she could suck on it until it dissolved. She reached for a tissue and spread it out on her pillow. The last thing she needed was to drool chocolate. It would be a sure giveaway. She lay back, the Oreo in her mouth, and tried to breathe as quietly as possible. She always made so much noise. Breathing, swallowing, digesting—could other people hear the saliva swishing in her mouth? Could she hear Harriet's? She froze and tried to listen. She heard nothing. Then Harriet gasped and started panting, as if she'd just been underwater.

Jennifer swallowed the rest of her cookie. "Are you okay?"

"Just doing my exercises," Harriet said.

"In bed?"

"They're breathing exercises," Harriet said. "For the gas chamber. If I hold my breath long enough, maybe I won't die."

"What gas chamber?" Jennifer asked.

Harriet didn't believe there were a million blades of grass in the entire schoolyard. It took more than that to get to a million. She lay in the sleeping bag at the foot of Jennifer's bed and counted off the people she knew. In her family there were three and in Jennifer's family there were three. Six. Next door there were five. Eleven. There were twenty-eight people in her homeroom, including Mrs. Lincoln, and thirty in the other homeroom. Sixty-four. Sixty-two if you didn't count Harriet and Jennifer twice. There were three grades at the middle school. One hundred and ninety. There were five clerks in the grocery store. Ninety-five. Two at Baskin Robbins. Ninety-seven. Four crossing guards on the way home. Two hundred and one. On football Saturdays in Ann Arbor, the town where Harriet had lived in Michigan, there were over one hundred thousand people in the stadium, so many that even though all her friends were there, she never saw anyone she knew.

Harriet counted off in a low campfire voice, the kind that turns every falling leaf into a one-armed killer. Jennifer felt her fingers go numb. It took three tries before she could turn on the bedside light.

"You'll never reach a million that way," she said.

"You have a better idea?"

Jennifer stepped over Harriet and got a notebook and a couple of pencils from her desk. She ripped out a page for herself and another for Harriet.

"We could write it," she said. "We'll get there twice as fast." She started writing out numbers. Her fingers left Oreo smudges on the paper, but she didn't notice. She didn't even notice when Harriet fell asleep somewhere around four thousand. She kept thinking how her parents would be surprised at the way she counted to a million all by herself.

1 2 3 4 5 6 7 8 9 10 11 12 13 14 15 16 17 18 19 20 21
22 23 24 25 26 27 28 29 30 31 32 33 34 35 36 37 38 39
40 41 42 43 44 45 46 47 48 49 50 51 52 53 54 55 56 57
58 59 60 61 62 63 64 65 66 67 68 69 60 61 62 63 64 65
66 67 68 69 70 71 72 73 74 75 76 77 78 79 80 81 82 83
84 85 86 87 88 89 90 91 92 93 94 95 96 97 98 99 100 1 2
3 4 5 6 7 8 9 10 11 12 13 14 15 16 17 18 19 20 21 22
23 24 25 26 27 28 29 30 31 32 33 34 35 36 37 38 39 40
41 42 43 44 45 46 47 48 49 50 51 52 53 54 55 56 57 58
59 60 61 62 63 64 65 66 67 68 69 60 61 62 63 64 65 66
67 68 69 70 71 72 73 74 75 76 77 78 79 80 81 82 83 84
85 86 87 88 89 90 91 92 93 94 95 96 97 98 99 200 1 2
3 4 5 6 7 8 9 10 11 12 13 14 15 16 17 18 19 20 21 22 23
24 25 26 27 28 29 30 31 32 33 34 35 36 37 38 39 40 41 4
2 43 44 45 46 47 48 49 50 51 52 53 54 55 56 57 58 59
60 61 62 63 64 65 66 67 68 69 60 61 62 63 64 65 66 67
68 69 70 71 72 73 74 75 76 77 78 79 80 81 82 83 84 85
86 87 88 89 90 91 92 93 94 95 96 97 98 99 300 1 2 3 4

5 6 7 8 9 10 11 12 13 14 15 16 17 18 19 20 21 22 23 24
25 26 27 28 29 30 31 32 33 34 35 36 37 38 39 40 41 42
43 44 45 46 47 48 49 50 51 52 53 54 55 56 57 58 59 60
61 62 63 64 65 66 67 68 69 60 61 62 63 64 65 66 67 68
69 70 71 72 73 74 75 76 77 78 79 80 81 82 83 84 85 86
87 88 89 90 91 92 93 94 95 96 97 98 99 400 1 2 3 4 5
6 7 8 9 10 11 12 13 14 15 16 17 18 19 20 21 22 23 24 25
26 27 28 29 30 31 32 33 34 35 36 37 38 39 40 41 42 43
44 45 46 47 48 49 50 51 52 53 54 55 56 57 58 59 60 61
62 63 64 65 66 67 68 69 60 61 62 63 64 65 66 67 68 69
70 71 72 73 74 75 76 77 78 79 80 81 82 83 84 85 86 87
88 89 90 91 92 93 94 95 96 97 98 99 500 1 2 3 4 5 6 7
8 9 10 11 12 13 14 15 16 17 18 19 20 21 22 23 24 25 26
27 28 29 30 31 32 33 34 35 36 37 38 39 40 41 42 43 44
45 46 47 48 49 50 51 52 53 54 55 56 57 58 59 60 61 62
63 64 65 66 67 68 69 60 61 62 63 64 65 66 67 68 69 70
71 72 73 74 75 76 77 78 79 80 81 82 83 84 85 86 87 88
89 90 91 92 93 94 95 96 97 98 99 600 1 2 3 4 5 6 7 8 9
10 11 12 13 14 15 16 17 18 19 20 21 22 23 24 25 26 27
28 29 30 31 32 33 34 35 36 37 38 39 40 41 42 43 44 45
46 47 48 49 50 51 52 53 54 55 56 57 58 59 60 61 62 63
64 65 66 67 68 69 60 61 62 63 64 65 66 67 68 69 70 71
72 73 74 75 76 77 78 79 80 81 82 83 84 85 86 87 88 89
90 91 92 93 94 95 96 97 98 99 700 1 2 3 4 5 6 7 8 9 10
11 12 13 14 15 16 17 18 19 20 21 22 23 24 25 26 27 28
29 30 31 32 33 34 35 36 37 38 39 40 41 42 43 44 45 46
47 48 49 50 51 52 53 54 55 56 57 58 59 60 61 62 63 64
65 66 67 68 69 60 61 62 63 64 65 66 67 68 69 70 71 72
73 74 75 76 77 78 79 80 81 82 83 84 85 86 87 88 89 90
91 92 93 94 95 96 97 98 99 800 1 2 3 4 5 6 7 8 9 10 11
12 13 14 15 16 17 18 19 20 21 22 23 24 25 26 27 28 29
30 31 32 33 34 35 36 37 38 39 40 41 42 43 44 45 46 47

48 49 50 51 52 53 54 55 56 57 58 59 60 61 62 63 64 65 66 67 68 69 60 61 62 63 64 65 66 67 68 69 70 71 72 73 74 75 76 77 78 79 80 81 82 83 84 85 86 87 88 89 90 91 92 93 94 95 96 97 98 99 900 1 2 3 4 5 6 7 8 9 10 11 12 13 14 15 16 17 18 19 20 21 22 23 24 25 26 27 28 29 30 31 32 33 34 35 36 37 38 39 40 41 42 43 44 45 46 47 48 49 50 51 52 53 54 55 56 57 58 59 60 61 62 63 64 65 66 67 68 69 60 61 62 63 64 65 66 67 68 69 70 71 72 73 74 75 76 77 78 79 80 81 82 83 84 85 86 87 88 89 90 91 92 93 94 95 96 97 98 99 1000

She fell asleep on the floor, her back pressed into Harriet's. In the morning, her mother found her drooling chocolate onto sheets of notebook paper scrawled with numbers, a pencil in her fist. She had only made it to 6250. Her mother knelt down next to her and patted her back.

"Come on, Jen," she whispered. "You're too big for me to lift."

When Jennifer stood up, the parts of her that had touched Harriet felt empty. In her bed, the sheets were cold and impersonal against her skin.

For breakfast, Jennifer's mother made heart-shaped pancakes and scooped out orange balls from a cantaloupe. Harriet looked impressed.

"At our house, we eat cantaloupe in slices," she told Jennifer's mother. "It's more efficient."

"What do you mean?" Jennifer's mother asked.

"It wastes less," Harriet said. "You can eat right down to the rind."

Jennifer's mother was wearing a bathrobe over her pajamas, and now she pulled the belt in tight and double-knotted it. "Well," she said. "To each his own, I guess."

Jennifer could tell her mother hated Harriet. She was smiling too much and too widely. When Harriet announced, "She's here," and ran out to her mother's car, Jennifer's mother locked the door behind her.

"Wow," she said to Jennifer's father, who was standing next to the kitchen window, watching Harriet's mother's car back out of the driveway. "What a morbid little girl."

"What's morbid?" asked Jennifer.

"What were you doing last night?" her mother asked, changing the subject. "What were all those numbers?"

"We were trying to find out how much is a million," Jennifer said.

She waited for her parents to ask her why, but they didn't. Instead her father sat down at the kitchen table and started scooping cantaloupe directly out of the peel with a spoon. Jennifer could hear it when he chewed, and she could hear it when he swallowed. When there was no more cantaloupe left to scrape, he said, "Maybe it would be good if you two didn't spend so much time together."

Later, when her parents were watching football in the TV room, Jennifer called Harriet. Her mother answered the phone. She had a slight accent. Jennifer had never seen Harriet's mother up close. She worked late as a beautician. Harriet's parents' bedroom smelled like the perfume counter at Sears, and there were always fresh flowers on the vanity. Jennifer's parents' bedroom smelled like lemon Pledge and the only mirror was the one in the closet.

Harriet took in the news as if she'd been expecting it. "Yeah," she said, "that always happens. It's because they can't face the facts."

"What facts?" asked Jennifer.

"They think there's no reason to get ready," said Harriet. "But they're wrong. You've got to be ready. You don't know who they'll come after next time."

Jennifer knew Harriet was right. Some days at school, the popular girls ignored her. Other days they wrote "Fat Cow" on her desk and flushed her lunch down the toilet.

During recess, Harriet coached Jennifer on sprinting. She had a watch with a timer. She stood at the far end of the schoolyard and measured how long it took Jennifer to reach her. Jennifer hated running. She couldn't breathe. It made her sweat. For the rest of the day, she kept her arms close to her sides and her legs crossed so that no one would accuse her of smelling.

"Too slow," Harriet always said. Or else, "You'll die for sure."

For the first few days, the other kids lined up and watched her go. Sometimes they ran beside her, arms flapping, legs flailing. They hollered one-liners about earthquakes and heart attacks. They clutched their chests and made jokes about jog bras. They dangled cookies and potato chips in front of her and yelled, "Come and get it."

"They'll get bored," said Harriet, and eventually they did.

After Jennifer finished the sprints, she and Harriet did three laps around the playground. As they ran, Jennifer imagined how, when it happened again, she would lead her parents into the woods on the west side of town. Her mother would be crying and her father would be pale. They would say things like, "What will become of us?" and "What will we do?" Then they would reach a clearing and Jennifer would take them to a tree that looked ordinary but was really a hideout. There would be enough room for them and for Harriet's family, and enough food to last them weeks. Her parents would be impressed by her resourcefulness, by the way she could produce fire by rubbing two sticks together and hunt pigeons with a slingshot. "We were so scared," her mother would tell her, "but we should have known you'd come through. You always were extraordinarily gifted. And I'm not saying that because I'm your mom."

In their history book, in the chapter about World War II, there were three paragraphs about the Holocaust. On page 242, there was a picture of Jews behind barbed wire. They were wearing black. The men had stubble. The women wore kerchiefs tied around their heads. Everyone looked old—even the children—and everyone was thin. Jennifer couldn't imagine being that thin. The Jews in the picture were even thinner than the skinny woman who led the weekly nutrition meetings. During week seven of her friendship with Harriet, the woman made Jennifer stand up while everyone applauded her for losing ten pounds.

"So, Jennifer," the woman had said, "what's your secret?"

"Running," Jennifer said.

The woman put her hands on her hips and made a what-do-you-know face.

"You see, kids," she said. "Exercise. It'll do it every time. That, and drinking lots of water."

That night, Jennifer's mother sat on the edge of Jennifer's bed and stroked her hair. It was something she hadn't done in years. Jennifer closed her eyes. *Don't stop,* she thought. *Don't stop. Don't stop.*

"I'm so proud of you," her mother said. "I didn't even know you ran. And when you lose the rest of that weight, there'll be no stopping you." She sighed, but Jennifer could tell it was a happy sigh. "I knew that friendship with Harriet was holding you back." Her mother's fingers smelled clean, like lotion.

Don't stop, thought Jennifer. *Don't stop.*

. . .

Jennifer could hold her breath for forty-five seconds. Harriet could hold hers for a minute. In the best-case scenario, you had to be able not to breathe for three minutes. Plus you had to be careful not to be trampled. Gas was heavier than air.

After school, Jennifer's father took her to buy running shoes because plain sneakers weren't good enough anymore.

"If you joined the track team," he said, "you wouldn't have to run all alone." On the way home he asked her, "You want to stop for ice cream?"

"No," said Jennifer. "Chocolate." Chocolate lasted longer. She ate one square so that her father wouldn't get suspicious. Later, in her room, she wrapped the rest in Saran Wrap. Not having an allowance was a problem. They needed supplies. Jennifer's mother didn't like buying canned food. She claimed you could always taste the metal. Plus, she was bound to notice things were missing from the pantry. She noticed everything.

"Three more pounds!" she said. "Good girl!" She bought Jennifer a belt. Then she bought her new jeans. Then she bought her a shirt.

Until they could find a hiding place, Jennifer kept the food out behind the garage. There was a space, overgrown with weeds, between the garage's back wall and the fence that separated Jennifer's family from their neighbors. It was too narrow for the lawn mower.

"Don't forget a can opener," Harriet said. "It won't do us any good if we can't open it." She told Jennifer that she hid her own supplies down in the basement, next to the furnace. Under her bed, she kept an emergency backpack. In it was all her money, bandages, a Swiss army knife, beef jerky, the earrings her father's mother had given her when she'd turned ten—for trading—and a German-English dictionary.

"Of course," Harriet said, "they might not be German this

time. But still, they might need a translator." She gave Jennifer a Russian-English pocket dictionary of her own. "You should have an emergency backpack too, you know."

"I don't even have an allowance," Jennifer said. "They think I'm still stealing food."

"Well," Harriet said, "you are."

Out in the woods on the west side, most of the trees were still young. Jennifer could wrap her arms around their trunks and feel them swaying in the wind. No matter how far you went, you could still hear the highway on one side and see the trains passing on the other.

"We need camouflage," Harriet said.

As they walked, twigs snapped and popped under their feet. Squirrels scurried for cover. Birds called out in alarm.

"It's no good," Harriet said. "They'd hear us for sure."

They watched the 4:05 train go by and then the 4:27. There was nowhere to hide. Except for the woods on the west side, the town was all mowed lawns and shrubbery and houses with aluminum siding. Two miles in any direction, you ended up neck deep in corn.

At the town they had lived in before, Harriet told Jennifer, there had been plenty of hiding places. There was an arboretum thick with trees next to a river and a junkyard that wasn't guarded by dogs. There was a wilderness area ten miles away, and Detroit with its broken-down, abandoned houses. Best of all, there were trailer parks with homes people could just hitch up to their cars. One day they'd be there, and then the next they'd vanish.

Running: once you settled into the breathing, there was no reason to stop. At night Jennifer stood in front of the mirror, flexing and pointing her feet. She could see her calf muscles tighten and relax. She was aware of the ways her legs were put together: bone, muscle, cartilage, balls and sockets, hinges. She loved long strides, the part after one foot left the ground and before the other foot landed. She loved how when you ran fast enough, you could make your own wind. She imagined joining the track team. There were hurdles. There was the pole vault. There were so many ways of flying.

At school, Mrs. Lincoln said she didn't like the dark circles under Harriet's eyes. "You feeling all right?" she asked. "You want to go see Mr. Vaughn?"

"No," said Harriet.

"Jennifer," said Mrs. Lincoln, "walk Harriet down to the nurse's office, will you?"

Mr. Vaughn, the school nurse, was a large man with a gap between his front teeth. He could whistle without puckering. Rumor had it he had a lie detector built right into the blood pressure gauge. When he wasn't in the nurse's office, he taught gym.

"Don't leave me," Harriet said to Jennifer. "I don't trust doctors."

"I heard that," said Mr. Vaughn, "but don't worry, my feelings aren't hurt." He looked at Jennifer and whistled. "You've lost some weight. Good for you!" But to Harriet he said, "If you get any skinnier, the wind will blow you away. You want me to call your mother?"

"I'm fine," Harriet said.

"It would be an excused absence," he pointed out. "You could lie around and watch TV."

"My mother was in the Holocaust," Harriet said.

"Oh," Mr. Vaughn said. He made a clucking noise. "Bad luck."

"No," Harriet said. "Luck has nothing to do with it."

"Is that what your mom says?"

"It's what I say," Harriet said. The moment they were out of the office, she added, "Moron."

"He'll hear you," Jennifer said. "He'll call your mom."

"He won't," Harriet said. "They never do."

She stopped walking and looked around as if she couldn't remember where they were going. Jennifer patted her shoulder. Harriet's skin radiated heat through the fabric of her shirt.

"Everything will be better once we find a hideout," Harriet said. "What kind of town is this, anyway?"

The 4:05 train went by, followed by the 4:27. The boxcars were black, or green, or dark blue, labeled with white or yellow numbers. In Art, they made drawings using penciled-in grid lines as guides for perspective. Harriet was assigned to draw the post office, Jennifer the supermarket. They taped the pictures along the hallway, a miniature paper town. Above their drawings, the custodians hung a sign: "Welcome Parents!" There were no trains in the pictures. There weren't even railroad tracks.

"We could always jump a train," Jennifer suggested. "Some of those boxcars are empty. They just don't bother closing the doors."

Harriet glared at her. "Don't you know anything?" she said. "Can't you think for yourself for even one second?"

She stomped off toward the swings, kicking up dirt with her shoes. Jennifer counted the weeks on her fingers. They were coming up on week eleven. She took a deep breath. Everyone around her looked busy. Some of the boys were playing soccer, and the popular girls were perched on top of the monkey bars, swinging their legs. She headed back inside, but the kid who was hall monitor asked to see her pass.

"Recess isn't over," he said.

"You let Stacey and them come in whenever they want to," Jennifer said.

"That's different." The boy shrugged. "You know the rules."

Before they went home for the day, Mrs. Lincoln handed out name tags. They wrote out their names in Magic Markers and taped the tags to their desks.

"Once your parents see this classroom," Mrs. Lincoln said, "they'll know you're no longer in elementary school. For one thing, your desks are full-size."

And they were. Jennifer looked over at Harriet, but Harriet was busy putting markers back in their box. The moment the bell rang, Harriet was out of there. Jennifer ran up Poplar and down Maple. She waited by the tracks at their usual spot. It would be ages before another new girl moved to town. If she was lucky, there would be one in January. Halfway up Elm, Jennifer stopped running. How many friends could one person make? Her legs felt thick and heavy, as if they were filled with water. When it happened again, she realized, she'd have to survive all by herself.

Later, when Jennifer got out of the shower, her mother was waiting in her bedroom with her arms folded across her chest.

"Been to the garage lately?" she asked.

Outside, ants were marching in long lines across the driveway and out toward the fence. Jennifer's father was leaning on the back of the Buick, watching them, still in his suit and tie.

"We thought you were done stashing food," he said without looking at her.

"I am," Jennifer said.

"Then what's with the chocolate?"

Jennifer shifted her weight from one foot to the other. "Harriet—"

Her father crossed his arms. "I thought you two weren't friends anymore."

"No," Jennifer said. Then she swallowed. "How will we know when it's time to run away?"

"Run away?" her father echoed.

"From the Holocaust."

"God, Jennifer," her father said. "The Holocaust has been over for a long time. Nobody has to run away because of it. Besides, we're not even Jewish."

"But what if the Nazis think we're Jewish?"

Her father stood up and brushed off the back of his suit. "Why would they?" he said. "I mean, there aren't even that many Nazis around anymore."

"But what if there were?" Jennifer insisted.

"There aren't," her father said. "There's no point worrying about it."

Everything felt like a trap. The backseat of the car. The seat belt. The child safety locks. Her mother drove and her father sat in the passenger seat. They didn't talk. Jennifer curled and flexed her fingers. Her knuckles changed colors from pink to white to pink again.

Inside, the school glowed yellow and you couldn't see anything but night out the windows. Everywhere you looked, there were parents: wandering in the hallway, ducking into the bathrooms, stopping to drink from the water fountain.

"Which one's your locker?" Jennifer's mother asked. "Which one's your drawing?"

In Mrs. Lincoln's class, the parents admired the desks and the textbooks. They drank cherry soda from small paper cups. They talked about the weather and what their other kids were doing. They laughed too long and too loudly and checked their watches when they thought no one was looking. Still, when Harriet's mother walked in, they all got quiet.

"Is this it?" she asked Harriet, and when Harriet nodded, she said, "Hello, I'm Harriet's mother."

She looked nothing like the pictures of Holocaust survivors. She wasn't wrinkled and her face didn't droop. When she took off her jacket, even the parents stopped breathing. She was wearing a bright purple T-shirt and three silver bracelets. Her arms were long and thin and freckled, and by the time she was finished shaking everybody's hand, Jennifer knew it for sure: she didn't have any numbers.

"So you're Jennifer," Harriet's mother said, bending down. Up close, she smelled like gardenias. Her bracelets jangled. She didn't have any numbers. "Harriet told me you had a fight."

"No, I didn't," Harriet said.

"Well, I can tell anyway," Harriet's mother said. She straightened up and smiled at Jennifer's parents. "Harriet's got quite a temper," she said. She didn't have any numbers.

"So," Jennifer's mother said, "Harriet tells us you're from Europe."

Harriet's mother laughed. "Oh, not me. I'm from Oswego. But my parents immigrated from Prague."

There were no Oreos anywhere in the house. There were ants in the chocolate and the can opener had rusted through. Jennifer lay in bed flipping through Harriet's Russian-English dictionary.

She looked up *liar.* She looked up *moron.* She looked up *scumbag.*

In the living room, her mother was on the phone with Harriet's mother. "I just thought you should know," Jennifer could hear her saying. "I knew you'd understand." When she was finished, she came into Jennifer's bedroom and sat on the edge of her bed.

Jennifer looked up *idiot.* She looked up *bitch.*

"Think about something else," her mother said. "Think about running. Think about how far you've come."

The next day, in gym, they played prison ball. Harriet and Stacey were captains. Jennifer knew Harriet wouldn't pick her and Harriet didn't. She waited for one of the popular kids to say something but they didn't. Once the game started, she lobbed red rubber balls at Harriet as fast as she could pick them up. She didn't stop even after she felt something bounce off her hip.

"You're out!" Harriet screamed. "Cheater! You're out!"

Mr. Vaughn whistled through the gap between his teeth and pulled them aside. "I thought you were best friends," he said. "What happened?"

"She told," Harriet said, and Jennifer said, "She lied to me."

"No, I didn't," said Harriet. "She could have been in the Holocaust."

"But she wasn't," said Jennifer.

"But she could have been," Harriet said again, pausing after every word.

"Make up," said Mr. Vaughn. "Right now." He had a thick hairy neck and thick hairy forearms. His T-shirt sleeves were tight around his biceps. He was wider across than the two girls standing side by side. The basketball backboard framed his head like a halo.

"Right now," he repeated. "I'm counting to ten."

Hands Across America

The spring Osnat was in ninth grade, her parents forced her to go on an endless rotation of Saturday-morning Bar and Bat Mitzvah ceremonies. Her mother had gotten a job—finally—in the synagogue gift shop, but after she ordered a set of greeting cards that suggested that the best thing about turning thirteen was that you were only three years away from a coveted driver's license, Mrs. Klein, her manager, had given her a talk about keeping up appearances.

"I know all about the Israeli cynicism," Mrs. Klein said, "but that's the privilege of growing up in a theocracy. This is a synagogue. We respect religious tradition. If they want wit, they can buy their cards at the mall." Then she suggested that it might behoove Osnat's mother to show up at Shabbat services every once in a while. "We're not just a gift shop," she said. "We're part of the congregation."

Osnat's mother knew a warning when she heard one. And she already knew all about the mall: she had spent the previous three months under the Gap's fluorescent lights, folding clothes and taking orders from teenage girls who smelled like bubble gum and nail polish. It was much easier to take orders from Mrs. Klein, who had wrinkles and wore rings on every finger, and who decorated the cash register with photos of herself shaking hands with various pillars of the Jewish community.

Still, that Saturday morning, Osnat's mother stood staring into her bedroom closet as if it were empty. "What am I supposed to wear?" she asked Osnat and Osnat's father, who were both sitting on the bed, watching her. "Is Mrs. Klein going to give me a clothing allowance? Can I file a complaint?"

"At least you're going into this with the right attitude," Osnat's father commented.

Osnat's mother's face darkened and Osnat stood up. Sometimes she couldn't see the fights coming, but this time she could. In Israel, her mother had been a real estate agent who sold luxury apartments with Mediterranean views, but in Michigan it had taken her nearly two years and three ESL classes just to get that job at the Gap. Even if you took the employee discount into consideration, there was still no comparison. Maybe Osnat's mother wasn't cleaning houses or working at Kroger, but there was still something unsettling about seeing her dressed in clothes intended for girls with no hips or gray hair, smiling and telling other women's daughters how cute they looked. It was as if Osnat's mother had somehow never made it out of high school and was left to pound erasers in the back of the classroom while everybody else graduated and went off to college. If there was a right attitude toward being left back over and over again, Osnat didn't know what it was. Still, empathy aside, Osnat's trying to leave the room right then turned out to be a mistake. Both parents homed in on her, glad for the distraction.

"I know," Osnat's father said to her mother. "Why don't you take Osnat with you?"

"Me?" Osnat said. "Why not you?"

"Because I'm already a hardened atheist," her father said, "and you're still young and impressionable. Besides, it's Bar Mitzvah season. You might make some new friends."

"But I'll be older than everyone," Osnat said. Her own Bat

Mitzvah had taken place in Israel shortly after she'd turned twelve. Her parents had thrown her a party at her aunt's house, which had a lawn, and Osnat's grandmother had worked for three weeks straight, baking *rugelach* and *bourekas* and arranging them in circles on brightly colored plastic trays. Then she spent the entire party pressing the guests to have some. "Have a *bourekas,*" she'd say to anyone who would listen. "Have one. Just a small one. They're homemade. They're good for you. Have one. Have one. Come on. Have one." Later, when Osnat was helping pick up crumpled napkins off the grass, she found half-eaten pastries tucked under the hedge, no doubt left there by people too polite to say no to her grandmother, and she'd imagined the geckos and chameleons holding their own celebration once everyone had gone home, then climbing up the walls of her aunt's house using their suction-cup feet, their bellies full of chocolate and mashed potatoes, smacking their lips and looking for more. After that, Osnat's family had moved to Michigan and it turned out that in America, girls didn't just have parties for their Bat Mitzvahs, they had full-blown ceremonies, just like the boys, where they read the Torah and gave little speeches. Osnat had considered asking her parents for a do-over when she'd turned thirteen—American girls had their Bat Mitzvahs at thirteen, not twelve—but there seemed to be little point. It would have been the same as saying that the American way was better, which of course it wasn't; or if it was, you certainly weren't supposed to say so, especially when it was so clear that the American way was making your mother miserable. Anyway, Osnat reminded herself now, even if her parents had agreed to a second Bat Mitzvah, who exactly would she have invited?

But Osnat's father was already slapping his knees and standing up, a sure sign that he'd made his decision and was determined to see it through. "So what if you're a little bit older?" he said to

Osnat. "The developmental gap between thirteen and fourteen just isn't that big."

Osnat's mother smoothed a pair of slacks against her hips. "I think it's a great idea," she said. "You could use some new friends."

"But I have friends," Osnat said, raising her voice so that her parents wouldn't hear it tremble. "I have Sanjay."

"That's exactly it." Osnat's father shook his head. "You have *one* friend. That isn't enough. You need some friends you don't make out with."

So maybe Osnat did make out with Sanjay, but they only did it sometimes, during lunch, in the C-wing stairwell of her junior high, especially if it was a day they were serving fish. Really, it was their only chance. After school, Osnat's and Sanjay's parents took turns supervising as if neither could be trusted to keep their clothes on.

"They think it'll keep us from having sex," Sanjay said, "but it won't."

"How do you know?" Osnat asked.

"It doesn't stop anybody else."

That part was true. The high school, which they'd toured in preparation for the following fall, had an entire wing devoted to pregnant girls, where they took classes in child care basics and typing. "Pay attention in sex ed," said the teacher who was guiding the tour as he led them past classrooms in which enormous girls squeezed into tiny desks were rubbing their bellies, "especially if you hope to one day go to college. You won't believe how much having a kid interferes with doing homework. And you can forget all about advanced placement, you know." As if to prove his point, the Pregnant Girl wing opened into the Special Ed wing, which, in turn, opened into a special parking lot where short buses picked up their passengers in privacy or in secret, depending on how you looked at it.

Sanjay rolled his eyes at the tour guide's caution, maybe because his father was a sex researcher at the university. When he'd first told Osnat what his father did, Osnat had imagined Sanjay's father wearing a white lab coat and holding a clipboard on which he jotted notes about couples he watched having sex. Osnat didn't know where he found these couples. Sometimes, when she and Sanjay made out, she'd wonder what Sanjay's father would think if he could see them. Would he approve of the way Sanjay seemed to know exactly how long to kiss her before sliding a warm hand under her shirt, only to veer off to the side mere millimeters before reaching her bra, or would he begin shouting out instructions like "Go for the breast, son!" or "Use more saliva!"? And what would he say about the way Osnat could feel her body opening under Sanjay's touch, the fine hairs on her belly bristling as if trying to guide his fingers with a will of their own?

After a while, though, it was clear that whatever kind of research Sanjay's father did, it wasn't pleasant and didn't involve sex so much as its consequences. On nights Osnat came over for dinner, he often told long, involved stories that ended up with recitations of statistics. "Imagine their horror," he'd conclude, "when they learned condoms were, given typical use, only ninety percent effective." Then, as if Osnat and Sanjay weren't both already taking geometry, he'd add, "That means that condoms fail one in ten times."

"Oh, Patag," Sanjay's mother would say, "can we talk about something else?" And Sanjay's father would change topics, but not before earnestly declaring, "These kids, they're living in dangerous times, and it's our job to prepare them." At this, he would cast a meaningful glance at Sanjay's older sister, who was already on her third boyfriend that month. "No pregnancy or VD for my kids," Sanjay's father would remind them. "At least not before they're done with medical school." And Osnat would look down at her plate, afraid that if she looked at Sanjay she'd break into nervous laughter.

Sometimes, Osnat tried to imagine having sex with Sanjay, but despite everything she'd seen in the movies and on the late-night scrambled Playboy channel, she couldn't quite see it happening. As private as the C-wing stairwell was, leading as it did from the furnace room in the basement to the exit behind the Dumpsters where the custodians liked to go on their cigarette breaks, it also seemed cold and dirty, as if it hadn't been properly mopped in ages.

"Don't worry," Sanjay whispered as if he could read Osnat's mind. "The average teenager doesn't lose his virginity until age sixteen. It's even later for girls."

"But that's years from now," Osnat said.

"So what?" Sanjay's breath was hot in her ear. "We've got plenty of time." But then he slid his hand back under Osnat's shirt, and suddenly she wasn't so sure.

The rabbi at the synagogue where Osnat's mother worked was a short man with kinky hair and a broad mustache sprinkled with silver. While the cantor sang, he would rock back and forth on his heels, smiling and staring at the ceiling, periodically readjusting his prayer shawl. "Thank you," he'd say when the cantor was finished. "Very nice. That was lovely." Then he'd look at his watch. "Don't worry, folks," he'd say. "We'll still be out of here at twelve bells." And they always were, no matter how long that week's Torah portion happened to be, which was why the congregation loved him, at least according to Mrs. Klein. By the third week, she was saving Osnat and her mother seats, dismissing Osnat's mother's preference to sit in the back of the sanctuary. "Nonsense," she said briskly. "No one will see you there." Which was, of course, the whole point.

What this meant was that Osnat was positioned right in the sights of the Bar Mitzvah kids, who would struggle bravely through the weekly Torah portion and then through the haftarah, rushing and slurring their words so that Osnat had no idea what they were actually saying, maybe because they didn't either. Then, eventually, they'd finish, and their parents, more often than not, would breathe an audible sigh of relief before settling back in their pews to dab their damp foreheads with handkerchiefs embroidered especially for the occasion and to listen to the speech portion of the ceremony. It was the speeches that really drove Osnat crazy, maybe because the Bar Mitzvah kids seemed to deliver them straight at her: "Today, I am a man, blah blah, adult, blah, world peace, blah, community service, blah blah, responsibility." Then, the following Monday at school, she'd see them in their new wristwatches and Star of David necklaces, eating bacon cheeseburgers in the cafeteria and acting as if they hadn't spent the past Saturday morning staring directly at her with eyes wide with fear, and as if she hadn't stared right back at them and sent them encouraging thoughts like *You can do it, you're almost there,* because the desperation they were feeling seemed so palpable she couldn't just sit there and let them flounder. There was something intense about all that eye contact, and it didn't seem right that after all that, instead of seeking Osnat out in the crowd of well-wishers rushing up to congratulate them, the Bar Mitzvah kids would resume being awkward, gawky thirteen-year-olds with braces and acne, wanting nothing more than to move to the reception hall on the second floor, turn up the music, and P-A-R-T-Y.

"But the fact is, they don't know you," Sanjay pointed out when Osnat tried to explain to him over lunch how awful the Bar

Mitzvahs were. "They're just seventh-grade babies. And anyway, you eat bacon cheeseburgers all the time. Aren't you eating one right now?"

He was right, of course. There was no arguing that he wasn't, but still, Osnat tried. "Okay," she said, "but I didn't stand up before God and everybody and promise that I wouldn't." Sometimes she wondered if she was becoming an atheist like her father, but then, when it was time to go back to class, she'd find herself praying, *Please, God, please, don't let there be a pop quiz today,* and when school was over, she'd find herself praying, *Please, God, please, let no one be home,* or *Please, God, please, let them be in a good mood,* and then when she watched TV, she'd find herself praying, *Please, God, please, don't let there be a nuclear war.* And sometimes her prayers worked, and the nuclear holocaust would be averted, at least temporarily, and her father would be in the kitchen, humming and chopping vegetables for dinner and wanting to hear all about Osnat's day.

Before Mrs. Klein opened the synagogue gift shop, she'd raised four strapping young Jews whom she then sent to law or medical school, or at least to college where they became accountants. "And every holiday it was the same," she said, smiling across the table at the Rabbi, whom Osnat's mother had also invited for dinner. "I had to drive to Southfield just to buy some Hanukkah gelt. Ann Arbor then wasn't like Ann Arbor now—we have more and more Jews every year."

"Very true," the Rabbi agreed, nodding wisely.

"And so many babies," Mrs. Klein continued. She had eaten off most of her lipstick along with the appetizers, and it was all Osnat could do not to stare at her mouth, which looked like a wound that had only recently scabbed over. "The little baby yarmulkes sell out as quickly as I can get them in."

The Rabbi continued nodding. "We Jews are all about the procreation. It's a mitzvah, you know."

"But only if you're married," Osnat's father added quickly, looking pointedly at Osnat.

Mrs. Klein looked shocked. "But she's so young!" she exclaimed, as if Osnat weren't sitting right across from her and hadn't just handed her the breadbasket. "She already has a boyfriend?"

Osnat opened her mouth to answer, but her father sighed loudly, drowning her out. "What can you do?" he said. "She's going to be a heartbreaker like her mother."

"And it's spring outside," the Rabbi said. "Even the kindergartners are in love. Just yesterday I had to give little Joshua Brenner a talk about hair-pulling."

But Mrs. Klein wouldn't be distracted. "So who's this boyfriend?" she asked Osnat's father. "Are his parents members?"

"Members?"

"Of the synagogue."

"They're Indian," Osnat blurted out. This time, she beat her father to it. She could see the tips of his ears turning red, but then again, he deserved a little embarrassment. If anyone was going around breaking hearts, it was him acting like everything was a joke: Sanjay, Mrs. Klein, her mother's job. "Jews, Jews, Jews," he'd said earlier in the kitchen when he was opening another bottle of wine. "Jews, Jews, Jews!" He waved the corkscrew in the air, as if it were a gavel. "There's more to life than being Jewish," he announced.

"Shh . . ." Osnat had whispered. "They'll hear."

"They won't," her father had said. "And if they do, they'll be too polite to let us know."

And if they had heard, there was no way of telling. Still, Osnat imagined Mrs. Klein asking her mother to wash the windows or wipe down the display case as punishment, her lips pressed into a thin, disapproving line, and her mother getting upset and quitting, and then sitting at home, where she would have more than enough time to fantasize about leaving Osnat and her father and going back to Israel. There was no way Osnat would be able to watch her all day long, as she had over the summer, making sure to need something just as her mother got too sad—a slice of watermelon, a ride to the mall, someone to go see movies with.

But now Mrs. Klein cleared her throat awkwardly. "If they're Indian, then I'm thinking probably not." She took a sip of water. "Although you should know that many Jewish parents forbid dating outside the religion. There are just too many Christians around."

"Sanjay isn't Christian," Osnat corrected.

For the first time that night, Mrs. Klein looked directly at her. She had pale blue eyes that looked as if the pigment in her irises had been diluted. They weren't the eyes of an old woman. "Maybe not," she said, "but your parents know what I mean."

From his seat next to Mrs. Klein, the Rabbi nodded agreeably, as if the conversation couldn't have been more pleasant, but what he said was, "Intermarriage is the biggest danger facing Jews today, more so than anti-Semitism."

For a moment, everyone sat in silence, as if to contemplate the threat Osnat posed to the survival of the Jews. Then her mother said, "Well, Mrs. Klein, as you said, she's only fourteen. And as nice as the boy's family is, they're moving to Texas in June."

There was the chance, of course, that Osnat's mother was wrong. Her English wasn't strong, and Sanjay's parents also spoke with an accent. Maybe she'd misunderstood—*Please, God, please, let this be a misunderstanding,* Osnat prayed—but it turned out that she hadn't. Sanjay's father, when he opened the door for Osnat, had taken one look at her stricken face before sighing in exasperation. "I was hoping to avoid hysterics," he said. "I was waiting until the end of the school year to tell them so that it wouldn't interfere with their studies. Moving is quite stressful, as I'm sure you know." When Osnat still didn't say anything, he waved her away. "For God's sake," he said, "you'll still be able to write letters. There's no better way to test a relationship. Many of the world's greatest love affairs were carried out through correspondence. Abelard and Héloïse are just one example, and that was back in the Middle Ages. Look them up, why don't you?"

But Osnat didn't want to look anything up. She didn't want letters. When her family had first moved to Michigan, she sometimes got aerogrammes from her friends in Israel complaining about how boring school was and inquiring if she'd spotted any movie stars and whether she had her own private pool to swim in. From far away, her friends had seemed provincial and naïve, foolish for believing everything they saw on TV. Not that Osnat hadn't been just like them, expecting America to be full of witty banter and a laugh track, shiny furniture, and fluffy snow that came just in time for Christmas and then neatly disappeared. But life in America, she quickly realized, wasn't all that different from life in Israel, except that the winters were colder, and instead of terror, you had to worry about nuclear war, which, although less likely to happen, was also potentially much more devastating. Even worse: if Osnat's father had been the unhappy parent in Israel, at least he'd had an office and a full-time job to keep him busy; now it was Osnat's mother who moped and sulked, often spending entire days in bed. But when Osnat tried to write about her new understanding to her friends, she couldn't. It would have been like breaking some kind of promise. So after a while, she'd stopped writing, and so did they, and these days she didn't even think about them all that much anymore. If that was what was going to happen with Sanjay, Osnat wasn't interested. She needed Sanjay here, beside her in the cafeteria or in the C-wing stairwell, not in Texas surrounded by oil wells and cattle. He'd moved to the U.S. only two years before she had, and he never laughed when she pronounced the *h* in *herb* or didn't know what a blow job was. Instead, he was always ready to explain whatever it was she didn't understand, using illustrations when she was being especially clueless. Then, in the locker room after gym, when girls talked about Aunt Flo and sixty-nines, Osnat could nod or giggle as appropriate. It was important to blend in, Osnat knew, and she couldn't do it on her own. Sanjay taught her to put pennies in her loafers and to wear them without socks, and to carefully roll up her T-shirt sleeves if they were too long. And when Osnat would wake up some mornings to find her mother's eyes puffy, her nose red from crying, it was Sanjay who would reassure her that his mother had cried too those first couple years, that his parents had also spent hours whispering furiously behind closed doors, but that this was the nature of homesickness, and it too would pass.

Now, standing in front of Sanjay's father, Osnat didn't know what to say. "Is it the sex?" she asked finally, and then, when she saw the horrified look on his face, she quickly added, "Because we're not having any. Sanjay can still go to college and everything."

Sanjay's father sighed. "You kids," he said, bending down toward her even though he was only a couple of inches taller. He had thick, dark lashes, like Sanjay, and Osnat could feel herself blushing. "Not everything is about you, you know. Sometimes parents do things for their own reasons."

But wasn't that the problem? Osnat wanted to ask. Wasn't that exactly the problem right there? But instead of asking, she nodded, then turned around and went home so Sanjay's father could tell Sanjay and his sister the news in private.

. . .

It didn't seem fair to get such bad news just when it was finally nice outside. The trees that lined Osnat's way to school were flowering so aggressively that even Osnat's mother had to admit spring in Michigan had its merits. In the C-wing stairwell, Sanjay picked crab apple petals out of Osnat's hair before kissing her, even though Osnat didn't know what the point was in kissing anymore.

"Well," Sanjay said, "for one thing, it feels nice."

But it didn't really, now that he was leaving. It was easy to imagine Sanjay finding another girl to kiss in Texas, a blond one who wore a cowboy hat with rhinestones, one who would teach him to talk with a drawl.

"I think we should stop," Osnat said, even though Sanjay was already fingering the hem of her T-shirt, sending goose bumps up and down her rib cage.

"Why?" Sanjay whispered into her neck, and then his right hand was on her belly.

Osnat clapped her own hands down on top of his, through her T-shirt, blocking his path. She could imagine him pressing her against the wall, her arching her back to give him better access and wrapping her legs around him like she'd seen done in the movies. He wouldn't forget her if she was his first. She let go of his hand and tried not to shudder when suddenly he was touching her left breast, his fingers wiggling under the elastic of her bra, straining to reach her nipple, which, as if in fear, seemed to be shrinking down into nothing more than a wrinkled nub.

"Osnat," Sanjay was whispering, "Osnat," as if it were the most lovely name in the world.

"Don't go," she wanted to tell him. "Don't leave me." But she knew that if she said anything, she would start crying, so instead she said, "I don't feel good. I've got a headache. I think I need to go see the nurse." Then, alone on the green vinyl cot in the nurse's office, the curtains drawn around her for privacy, she lay flat on her back, breathing deeply and listening to the locker doors slam open and shut in the hallway like metallic applause congratulating her on her steely resolve. Meanwhile, on the phone, the nurse was saying, "And how far apart are the contractions?"

On Saturdays, Osnat's mother had taken to positioning Osnat between her and Mrs. Klein. Up close, Mrs. Klein smelled sharply of mouthwash and of a mustiness Osnat associated with basements. "You're the one who works with her," Osnat had complained once she realized what her mother was up to, but her mother had just said, "My point exactly," before conveniently dropping back to get a drink from the water fountain. "Go on in. I'll be right there."

Usually, Mrs. Klein would ask Osnat how school was going and how her week had been, but this time she screwed her face into a sorrowful expression and whispered, "Hanging in there?" Osnat nodded, and Mrs. Klein added, "Just barely, I see."

"Oh, she's fine," Osnat's mother said, sliding into the pew after Osnat. "What's a little letter-writing between friends?"

"It's a comfort, of course," Mrs. Klein said, "but it's hardly the same."

Osnat could feel her mother stiffen. "Don't you think I know that?" she said.

"Of course you do," Mrs. Klein said soothingly. "But Osnat's still a child. She doesn't have all your experience."

"And a good thing, too." Osnat's mother laughed, a little too brightly, and the man sitting in the pew in front of her turned around to give her a look of warning.

"Shh . . ." he said. "It's about to begin."

On the stage, the Torah scrolls were being unrolled while that week's Bar Mitzvah boy looked on. He was olive-skinned with thick, dark eyebrows that met over his nose. In the right light, there was a shadow over his upper lip, as if a mustache were lurking under the surface and waiting for the right moment to emerge. Osnat could feel her neck prickling in anticipation, but it wasn't until the boy started reading that she understood why: he was Israeli. His consonants came out hard, the *ch*s phlegmy, the vowels sharp. He knew when to pause between sentences. He didn't wear a tie.

"Who is that?" Osnat's mother whispered to Mrs. Klein.

"That's Arnon Kessler," Mrs. Klein whispered back.

"Is he new?" Osnat asked. Inside, she felt a flutter of something like hope. If Arnon was new, maybe she could show him around and teach him the kind of stuff Sanjay was always teaching her: not just sleeve-rolling and euphemisms, but also how to time his appearance in the cafeteria so he wouldn't have to stand in line and how to skip assembly without getting caught. Even though he was too young for her personally, she could show him the C-wing stairwell so he could get some practice making out with the eighth-grade girls. Then, after he would hit puberty and grow tall and thick-limbed and move on to the high school, he'd finally work up the nerve to confess his love for Osnat, which, it would turn out, he'd felt pretty much from the first time he saw her, nodding encouragingly at him during the speech portion of his Bar Mitzvah.

Except that, according to Mrs. Klein, Arnon wasn't really all that new. "They've been here two, maybe three years," she told Osnat. "I'm surprised you don't know each other. He's cute, isn't he? And Jewish. You might consider him when you're ready to move on."

Osnat could feel herself turning red. "He's too short," she said.

Mrs. Klein patted her knee reassuringly. "They all start out that way."

Osnat sat up straight, shoulders back, and waited for Arnon to spot her, for her chance to smile and nod. But Arnon apparently didn't need her support. He seemed self-assured, relaxed, happy to spend his speech cataloging the differences between Israel and the United States. "And I'm not just talking snow," he was saying. "There's also the matter of sports. Soccer is the real football. Just ask the rest of the world." The congregation laughed appreciatively. "On a more serious note," he continued, "the lesson I will take with me to Israel when my father's sabbatical ends this summer is how to speak English fluently and ace my matriculation exams. Just kidding. The lesson I will take back is that despite our differences, we are all people. Deep down, Jew or Christian or Muslim, we are all the same."

"Well said," Mrs. Klein murmured. "Too bad his going back to Israel rules him out as boyfriend material."

Osnat glanced at her mother, but now that the Kesslers were leaving Michigan, she was busy flipping through the prayer book and counting the pages left until the end of the service. It was what she did every week, as if despite all evidence to the contrary, she continued to doubt the Rabbi's ability to stick to the schedule. Then, once they were safely home, she would report back to Osnat's dad: "We got out at eleven fifty-nine. Right down to the wire today," and Osnat's father would say, "Phewf. Close one."

That Saturday, they got out at 11:54, even though they had to push their way through the crowd of seventh graders slapping Arnon on the back. "Excuse me," Osnat's mother said, shoving past them. "Excuse. Me." Then, in Hebrew, she said to Osnat, "Doesn't anyone have manners anymore?" She said it loudly, and Osnat could see Arnon freeze in the middle of his congratulatory huddle and look their way. She shrugged at him as if to say, "Parents, what can you do?" but by then a woman who had to be Arnon's mother was barreling toward them. She had the same long eyebrows as Arnon, only hers were slanted and angry-looking, lined with blue eye shadow.

"Lady," she said when she reached Osnat's mother, "*savlanut.* Patience. What's wrong with a little happiness? Did you leave the stove on?"

"Yes," Osnat's mother said. "And the iron, too." Then she grabbed Osnat's arm and pulled her out of there. "What do I care?" she said as they marched out to the parking lot. "They're the ones leaving in a month, lucky bastards."

In the car on the way home, Osnat imagined lecturing her mother on her behavior. "You're not a little kid," she imagined telling her. "There's no need to be rude." Once she got started, the platitudes just seemed to pop into her head: "No one promised you a rose garden," she imagined saying, and "If life hands you lemons, make lemonade!" But whenever Osnat looked at her mother, her mouth would go dry. Her mother was sitting low in the driver's seat, her shoulders hunched toward the steering wheel as if she were practicing to become the kind of little old lady who spent afternoons brushing her cats and shooing children away from her mulberry bushes. Next thing Osnat knew, her mother would start forgetting to turn off the stove and insist on eating only yellow foods like her own mother—Osnat's grandmother—had done before she died. It wasn't fair. Her mother wasn't even forty, and Osnat wasn't even fifteen, and yet here they were, in America, alone in a way that even Osnat's father couldn't understand. Maybe somewhere deep down Osnat's mother wanted it that way, but Osnat sure didn't. Still, if she said anything, she knew her mother would accuse her of becoming one of *them,* one of the many superficial Americans who made small talk and offered unasked-for advice as if they had any idea what she was going through, as if moving to Michigan from Indiana was at all comparable to moving to Michigan from Israel. And maybe she was right, at least about the superficiality. Hadn't Osnat betrayed Sanjay that very morning without even a qualm the very second Arnon presented himself? What could she possibly know about relationships and real feelings? And at least Osnat got to go to school. What did her mother get? To sell bumper stickers that said *Michigan* in Hebrew to those Israelis lucky enough to leave, and who invited her to call when she herself returned so they could get together for coffee and reminisce about the good old Michigan days, "As if that would ever happen," Osnat's mother liked to say. "As if we're ever going back."

"Of course we're going back," Osnat's father would reassure her.

"When?"

"I don't know."

"That's because we're not."

And those conversations never ended well. Sometimes, Osnat reflected, they didn't end at all.

"I don't want to go to synagogue anymore," Osnat told her father later, after they'd all eaten lunch and her mother had gone upstairs for an afternoon nap. Then she rephrased. "I'm not going to synagogue anymore." She'd practiced saying it inside her head the whole way home, but when she said it out loud, her voice still wavered.

Osnat's father was scraping leftover rice into a Tupperware container, but now he stopped. "But your mother needs you there," he said. "For moral support."

"She makes me sit between her and Mrs. Klein."

"So?"

"She counts the pages left until the service is over."

Osnat's father chuckled, but he stopped when Osnat glared at him. "Look," he said, "sometimes you have to do a thing over and over before its meaning becomes apparent to you. The meaning comes through the action. That's why ritual is such an important part of being Jewish."

Osnat considered this for a moment. "Then how come you're an atheist?"

Osnat's father turned around and put the rice in the fridge, then wiped his hands dry on a towel. He took a deep breath. "What is this really about?" he asked. "Is this about Sanjay?"

"God," Osnat said, "not everything is about Sanjay."

"Then what's going on?"

Osnat shrugged. "I don't know."

"So it is about Sanjay."

"Dad," Osnat said, "you're not listening."

"Of course I'm listening."

"You're not!"

"Shh . . ." Osnat's father said. "Your mother is trying to sleep."

And she was. When Osnat looked in on her, her mother was lying flat on her back, her arms spread out to the sides, her hands curled into claws. Her nail polish was chipping and her eyeliner was smudged. She was breathing heavily through her mouth. Maybe later, Osnat thought, she could convince her mother to take her to the mall and get a manicure, or even an entire makeover. If meaning came through ritual, makeovers seemed a lot more promising than going to synagogue. At the very least, they had visible results. Still, to be on the safe side, she also prayed: *Please, God, please, let the makeover work.*

"The Bar Mitzvah boy today was Israeli," Osnat told Sanjay when she met him at the movies that night. They were seeing *Top Gun,* or at least they were supposed to, but they sat in the last row, and as soon as the lights dimmed they started making out. "I might show him the C-wing stairwell."

"He's too young for you," Sanjay said, unimpressed. "Don't be mean."

But Osnat wanted to be mean. She'd been mean throughout dinner, to her mother for not cheering up after the makeover and to her father for not understanding. "Perk up, will you?" her mother had said finally when she was dropping Osnat off outside the theater, and Osnat had meanly rolled her eyes and turned her back to her. Her mother grabbed her arm. "Look," she said, "I know you're upset, but don't take it out on me."

But you take it out on me, Osnat wanted to say. Instead she said, "I'm not taking it out on you."

Her mother continued as if Osnat hadn't said a thing: "We're here because it's the best thing for your father and the best thing for you. But even good decisions have a price. It's a big country and people move around a lot and far away. It's not like in Israel, where the whole country could fit into Lake Michigan and you can't get away from anybody. Friendships just aren't as deep here. The sooner you get used to it, the better."

"Fine," Osnat muttered, and got out of the car. And now, here was Sanjay kissing her as if earlier that day she hadn't already moved on to Arnon, albeit briefly, and all she could do was kiss Sanjay back and wait for some kind of insight. This time, when Sanjay pushed up the armrest between them and slid his hand under her shirt, she didn't even flinch. Stomach or breast, what did it matter? They were both parts of her body.

"He looked older than thirteen," she whispered now.

Sanjay stopped kissing her, but his hand kept stroking her nipple. "Who?"

"The Bar Mitzvah boy."

"You're not supposed to talk about other guys when we make out," Sanjay reminded her. Then he put his hot mouth on her neck, and she could feel it happening again, her body opening up as if it were telling her, *Let me go. Let me go. I know what to do.* It was disgusting. She had no control.

Sanjay pulled back. "What?" he said. "What is it?"

Osnat took a deep breath. Who was she to complain? She was as superficial as the next person. "Nothing," she said, pulling Sanjay back toward her, then reaching down between his legs to cup what she figured had to be his penis. In the flickering of the air-fight explosions taking place on-screen, she could see that Sanjay's face had gone soft, that he had withdrawn inward and was concentrating on pushing back against her hand, the fabric of his jeans rough against her palm. She held firm and looked into his eyes, which were half-open, blurry, unfocused. It was hard not to hate him. He was gone already.

She washed her hands carefully after the movie and Sanjay untucked his shirt, and if his father's sex-researcher instincts detected what had happened, he didn't ask any questions beyond what they thought of the movie.

"I don't know," Sanjay said. "It was kind of hard to follow."

Back at her house, Osnat's parents' door was already shut for the night, although she could hear them whispering. If anything, their voices made her feel lonelier. They had each other, but who did she have?

She awoke to the smell of pancakes, and to her father humming in the kitchen. When her mother shuffled downstairs in her bathrobe, he paused. "If it isn't Grumpy McGrump!" he said, serving her from the stack he'd been keeping warm in the oven.

"Quit it, Marvin," Osnat's mother said, but Osnat's father wasn't biting.

"Yes, sir," he said, "it's a veritable black cloud here today. Good thing I have a plan." They were, he announced, going to drive down to Toledo. "It's time we engaged in some unbridled optimism," he said.

"You're thinking of some other family," Osnat's mother said. "There are no optimists here."

Osnat's father put down the ladle he was using to pour more batter into the pan. "Look," he said, his voice serious, "I've had it with all the moping. Americans may be different than Israelis, and they might talk a lot about things you don't care about, but that doesn't make them bad. When people want to get to know each other, they have to start somewhere. We had to start somewhere, remember?"

Osnat saw her opening. "Where did you start?"

Her plan worked. Her father smiled. "By asking your mom for directions to the bus stop, and then asking where to get groceries—"

"And then asking what kind of cottage cheese to buy," Osnat's mother continued. "It's a wonder we got together at all."

"Well, I am very handsome," Osnat's father said. "You didn't have much choice."

Osnat felt herself relax. She reached for some sugar to sprinkle on her pancakes.

"So Toledo," her father said. "Here we come."

The reason they were going to Toledo, Osnat's father explained once they were on US-23 heading south, was because that very afternoon, at 3 p.m., millions of people were going to hold hands and form a human chain that would stretch out across the nation. They would sing "America the Beautiful" and sway back and forth in unison, and then they'd pull out their wallets and donate money to help the homeless and the hungry. "Isn't that something?" Osnat's father said. "We're going to be part of history."

"Which interestingly won't be passing through Michigan at all," Osnat's mother noted.

Even from the backseat Osnat could see her father's jaw clench. "Give it a chance, Efrat, will you?" he said. "It isn't my fault Michigan is surrounded by water. It's the gesture that counts, okay?"

Outside the car, there was nothing to look at except the occasional gas station. The freeway was wide, the land on either side grassy and flat, dotted with clumps of trees. *Please, God, please,* Osnat prayed, *don't let them fight.* Then, to distract herself, she tried to remember the words to "America the Beautiful," which she had heard sung plenty of times in school but had never bothered to learn. Would all the other people in line notice if she merely hummed along?

They ended up on a two-lane highway a few miles outside Toledo, in what Osnat's father said was the Michigan portion of the line. There were already plenty of cars parked along the shoulder, and lots of people were standing on the side of the road, smiling and waving at them as they looked for a place to pull over.

"Wow," Osnat's mother said at first, sounding impressed, but then she said, "Oh God. Duck!" and slid down in her seat.

Osnat obeyed, but not before seeing Mrs. Klein and the Rabbi standing side by side, wearing "Jews Across America" T-shirts emblazoned with huge Stars of David.

"Too late," Osnat's father said. "There's a whole synagogue contingent."

"We didn't drive all the way to Ohio so I could hold hands with Mrs. Klein," Osnat's mother muttered.

Osnat's father ignored her. "Maybe they have extra T-shirts," he said. He drove a little further, then parallel-parked between a rusted-out pickup truck with a "Go Blue" bumper sticker and a station wagon with wood paneling. "It's two fifty-five," he said, opening the car door. "I don't care who you hold hands with, but you've got to hold hands with someone." When Osnat's mother hesitated, he shrugged. "Come on, Osnat," he said. "Let's go." Then, once Osnat was out of the car, he said, "You pick. We can hold hands with whoever you want."

Osnat looked around. It was a warm spring day, and most of the people were wearing shorts. Many of them had sweat stains under their armpits and rolls of fat behind their pale, fleshy knees. Their hands, she imagined, would be hot and moist, unpleasant.

"Two minutes," Osnat's father said.

There was no way Osnat could choose that quickly. She took a deep breath and headed toward the nearest cluster of people. At first it looked as if there wouldn't be room for her and her father—everyone was already linking arms—but then a bearded man with crooked teeth smiled at her and let go of the hand of the woman next to him. "Don't be shy," he said. "There's plenty of room for everybody." His hand, when Osnat took it, was large and cool. If anyone's hands were clammy, they were Osnat's. She wiped them dry on her jeans.

"It's time," someone yelled and turned up the volume on his car radio. For a moment, everyone got quiet, as if not sure what to do next, but then the man next to Osnat let out a whoop. "America, baby!" he shouted, drowning out the opening strains of music and pumping his fist in the air. Then he launched into song, swaying lightly from side to side. "Come on now," he told Osnat. "Don't you know the words?"

Osnat shook her head.

"That's okay," he said. "Fake it."

Osnat looked over at her father, who was watching her. He nodded. "You've got to start somewhere," he said.

All around them, people were singing and smiling, their voices fervent and off-key. A little way down the line, Mrs. Klein had her arm around the Rabbi's shoulders. Their eyes were closed and they rocked back and forth together as if praying. Osnat closed her eyes too, but then she thought about her mother, and opened them. She glanced behind her shoulder, and sure enough, her mother was still buckled into the passenger seat, dark sunglasses hiding her eyes, her expression blank. She looked so small and alone, abandoned. Osnat couldn't leave her there like that, could she? Beside her, her father was singing loudly, oblivious, as if this line of Americans was where he belonged. And maybe he did. When she let go of his hand, he nodded as if to say, "Suit yourself, but I'm staying."

If her mother saw Osnat coming, she didn't react—she didn't even turn her head when Osnat slid into the driver's seat and reached for her hand. For a moment, Osnat didn't think her mother would respond even to this gesture, but then her mother curled her fingers around Osnat's.

"I'm sorry I didn't join you," Osnat's mother said finally. "I didn't see you. You blended right into the crowd and I was afraid I'd get lost."

Looking out at the chain of people, Osnat could see what her mother meant. The place where Osnat had stood had been swallowed up by the line as if she'd never been there in the first place, and it took her a few minutes to spot her father, who was now holding the bearded man's hand. Even so, she only recognized him because he was wearing sandals instead of sneakers—from behind, he could have been any balding, lanky man in khaki shorts. She squeezed her mother's hand. "That's okay," she said. "I came back. I'm right here." She could feel the heat radiating out from their palms into their fingers, warming them both until she couldn't tell where her hand ended and her mother's hand began. "I'm right here."

Her mother sighed and leaned her head back on the headrest as if exhausted. "I know you are, Osnat," she said. "Believe me. I know."

The Dangers of Salmonella

Sometime after Harriet loaded up the station wagon, but before she arrived at her freshman-year dorm, her parents decided they were getting a divorce. "You're out of the house now," her mother explained when Harriet called to let her parents know she'd got there safely. "Less trauma for everyone involved."

"But I've only been gone three hours," Harriet said. She had chosen to attend Northcrest, a small college in southern Michigan, mainly because it wasn't in Indiana, where the women were either blond or dyed their hair blond and where people referred to Harriet as "you know, the dark one," and also because an admissions officer named Ruth had sent her a high-quality crimson and ivory sweatshirt along with a note inviting her for a visit. Then, when Harriet did visit, every student she met—some of whom had brown hair—seemed to be wearing T-shirts boasting slogans like "Literature Is for Lovers: Northcrest College English Department" and "Swim with the Fishes: Northcrest College 12th Annual Biology Retreat." Not only that, but a man in the bookstore was handing out free razors designed for sensitive skin, along with shaving lotion that smelled like berries. Harriet loved free gifts, and she imagined herself sitting out on the quad, wearing a different free T-shirt every day, her legs smooth and well moisturized. It was only after she'd arrived on campus that she learned that you were expected to pay for your own T-shirts, and that the razors had been a onetime promotion.

"Really, Harriet," her mother told her over the phone. "Who ever heard of a school that supplies its students with razors?"

But Harriet was feeling stupid already. "If your roommate kills herself," she said, "you get an automatic A for the semester."

"That's only in the Ivy League," Harriet's mother informed her. Harriet resented her cheerfulness. As far as she could tell, her mother wasn't moping around or drunk-dialing her father the way newly separated women did on TV. Instead, she went on and on about how nice it was to drink coffee without anybody tsk-tsking, and how good it felt to finally be able to take down that awful painting of the dogs playing poker. "And I'm thinking of dyeing my hair pink," she announced in a way that made Harriet suspect the divorce had been mainly her mother's idea.

Harriet cleared her throat. "Have you heard from Dad?"

Her mother didn't even have the dignity to sound flustered. "Nope," she said lightly. "Why would I? That's what being separated *means.*"

Of course, Harriet wasn't surprised by the divorce. Her parents didn't fight, but they were champions of silence. After they'd moved to Indiana, when Harriet was eleven, they began to work in shifts—her father, a dentist, worked during the day, and her mother, a beautician, worked afternoons and evenings, and Saturdays too. This way, they explained, someone would always be home for Harriet, even after she entered high school and got her driver's license and an after-school job manning the register at Arby's because you had to be eighteen to use the slicer.

"We just want to be prepared," Harriet's father liked to say, "in case you need us." And who could blame him? Every six months, he sat Harriet down and reminded her exactly where she could find his will and a list of his various bank accounts, along with the spare key to his office. "If the house burns down," he instructed, "there are duplicate forms in the locked file cabinet in the records room."

"But where are you going to be?" Harriet had asked him the first time he'd walked her through the drill.

"Dead, of course," her father said as if this were obvious. "Why else would you need the papers?" And if the office burned down too in some freak fire that consumed both their house and the dental office and the seven blocks in between, then there were also copies in the safety deposit box at the bank across town.

"But I don't want you to die," Harriet had said.

"That's why we have smoke detectors in every bedroom, honey," her father said. "But everybody dies eventually. We just want to be prepared."

So Harriet was prepared for the divorce long before her parents were having trouble, back when her father would still pull her mother away from her post by the oven or the kitchen sink and her mother would cross her arms across her chest and allow him to squeeze her breathless. "Not you," Harriet's father told Harriet when she approached him with her own arms crossed. "You're going to know how to hug back." He was a broad man, and tall, and Harriet couldn't close her arms around him or get enough traction against the wool V-neck sweaters he liked to wear. No matter how far she stretched, he'd slip slowly out of her grasp, leaving her hair and clothes clingy with static. Or maybe that was already the first sign of trouble, and she'd been too young to know it. Anyway, it was soon followed by other signs, like Harriet's father buying a second TV dedicated to football and a mini-fridge all his own, both of which started out in the basement but then moved to Examination Room 5 in his office suite because, he claimed, the dentist chair saved him from having to buy a recliner too. And these signs were followed by more, like Harriet's mother training for a marathon, which got her up early in the mornings and kept her outside for hours, then shut her up in the bathroom soaking in the tub or doubled over from stomach cramps.

"Jesus," Harriet's father complained when he reached for her mother, "you're as hard as a rock. And those veins on your arms—Jesus."

But Harriet liked the raised veins on her mother's arms—she liked pushing on them and watching her mother's flesh turn white under the pressure from Harriet's fingers. Sometimes she held her mother's right arm across her own body and strummed the veins, a makeshift guitar. "Her name is Rio," she sang, "and she dances on the sand."

"Stop it," Harriet's father said. To her mother, he said, "That's disgusting. We are not living in a famine. For God's sake, Donna, eat something. No woman's arms should look like that."

By the second week of school, Lisa, Harriet's roommate and, of course, a blonde, was dating a boy named Tomer. He was from Israel and he played the French horn. Harriet figured he was at Northcrest because he wasn't good enough to go to a school with a real music program. At least that's what she told herself late at night, when she lay in bed and listened to the wet smacking noises coming from across the room. But during the day she had to admit that there was something about him. He was older, for one thing—he'd been in the Israeli army for three years before starting school—and muscular, and he had a mole tucked under his right nostril and enough hair on his chest that it sometimes poked through his T-shirt, and occasionally Harriet would find it on her bedspread and know that he'd been lying there. Most of the time, though, he lay on Lisa's bed wearing nothing but striped boxer shorts, and after a while the room took on that musty smell that Harriet eventually associated with all guys: a combination of sweat, semen, and damp socks. She considered saying something to Lisa, but she didn't want to be a prude. Her high school class motto had been, "Love is fine, sex is great, we're the class of eighty-eight," but she'd assumed it was all just talk until the class president had gotten pregnant and was forced to resign two weeks before graduation.

Now, in college, Harriet stood in the communal showers and sneaked peeks at the other girls, with their full breasts and bikini waxes, and felt flat-chested and downy, like a thirteen-year-old boy. She thought about the thin strip of hair that led from Tomer's belly button to the waistband of his boxers. She had a similar strip on her own belly, which she was careful to shave off whenever nobody was looking, just like she was careful to pluck the hairs that grew in around her areolas. She didn't think she'd be having sex soon, but you never knew. Sometimes, in the middle of the night, she could swear she saw a dark reflection in Tomer's eyes, as if he were lying awake in Lisa's bed and staring at her. And maybe he was staring at her, because one morning, while Lisa was off brushing her teeth, he asked Harriet, "Are you going home for Rosh Hashanah?"

Harriet swallowed hard and folded her arms across her bony chest. "How'd you know I was Jewish?"

Tomer laughed. "Are you kidding me? Have you looked in a mirror?" Then, when Harriet didn't say anything, he said, "So . . . are you going to invite me for Rosh Hashanah or not?"

It wasn't that Harriet was ashamed of being Jewish, or that she was even hiding it. At least, she hadn't thought she was hiding it, instead assuming that her newly developed craving for pork products, which she piled high on her tray at every dining hall meal, pointed to some kind of vitamin deficiency. You had to listen to your body, right? And she wasn't the only Jew on campus, of course. There was a girl named Abby who lived on the third floor of Harriet's dorm who flaunted her Chosen People status by wearing a gold Star of David around her neck and wrinkling her nose at the pineapple and Canadian bacon pizzas the resident advisers insisted on ordering for dorm meetings.

"Just pick the meat off," one the guys who lived in the triple on the fifth floor had advised Abby. "If you blot the cheese with a paper towel, it'll be good as new."

"You're kidding, right?" Abby had said. She'd locked eyes with Harriet and raised her eyebrows, but Harriet had shrugged unhelpfully, careful to keep her own expression neutral. And it was a good thing, too, because the guy from the triple was watching.

"Girls." He sighed. "They're so picky about what they eat."

"Not me," Harriet told him. She ran thirty-five miles a week, sometimes more. She could eat whatever she wanted. She took a second slice.

"Right on." The guy gave her a thumbs-up and then later showed up drunk at her room and challenged her to arm wrestling. "Your biceps," he said, "they're something else." His own arms were pale and flabby, but he'd still beaten her. Guys were just strong like that sometimes. It wasn't fair. Harriet stood up. "You know you're going bald, right?" she said.

"Man," he said. "Such a sore loser." To Lisa he said, "Have fun with this one."

Lisa rolled her eyes. "I've got a boyfriend."

"Of course you do," the guy said. "We hear you all the way up on the fifth floor."

He was a charmer, all right, and for the next few days Harriet was careful to watch her back. Someone in the dorm was scrawling "I hate fags" on the dry-erase message boards on people's doors, and the resident advisers called meeting after meeting to discuss the need for tolerance and understanding, one time even turning off the lights so that people would feel free to express their feelings. Harriet sat in the dark, nibbling carefully on her pizza, and listened to everyone else chewing around her. Someone in the back of the room sneezed, and someone else burped so impressively that everyone laughed. "Nasty," one girl said. "I can smell that all the way over here."

"Concentrate, people," the first-floor RA reminded them. "What if instead of writing 'I hate fags,' this guy had written 'I hate blacks' or 'I hate Jews'?"

"I believe the term you're looking for is African Americans," the third-floor RA corrected her.

Even though it was dark, Harriet thought she could hear everyone's eyelashes fluttering as they rolled their eyes. Until that moment, she hadn't realized that everyone living in the dorm was white. And wasn't that how it always happened? You walked around feeling safe until one day you discovered you weren't, that you'd never been safe at all.

Back in junior high, when she first realized her parents were in trouble, Harriet had studied the children of divorced parents that she knew. They seemed normal enough—their faces clean, their clothes freshly laundered. At night, she made lists of her belongings, trying to decide what she'd keep at her mother's, what she'd take to her father's. "Is it true about the two sets of presents?" she'd asked a girl named Cindy whose mother and father had gotten divorced in eighth grade. Now, driving home for Rosh Hashanah with Tomer in the passenger seat, his lips still glistening with Lisa's lip gloss administered during one last sloppy French-kiss good-bye, Harriet tried to recall Cindy's answer, but the main thing she remembered was Cindy's nails, which were so uniform in shape and length that in retrospect Harriet wondered if they were real or yet another concession to the divorce itself. Not that Rosh Hashanah was a gift-giving holiday, but it was still important, nearly as important as Christmas, a holiday where you got together with family and ate apples dipped in honey to ensure a sweet new year. And yet here were Harriet's parents, at best lukewarm about her visit, never mind Tomer's: "I didn't realize you'd be coming home," her mother had said when Harriet had called to finalize arrangements, but at least she'd cleared her throat and tried again, trilling, "Can't wait to see you!" before hanging up. Harriet's father, on the other hand, was quick to declare his new apartment too small for overnight guests, too small, he claimed, even for Harriet. "I'm paying rent, a mortgage, and college tuition," her father told her. "If anyone's sleeping over, it has to be in my bed."

"Ew," Harriet had said.

Her father ignored this. "Your mother has four bedrooms and two baths," he'd continued. "She has a treadmill in the basement. She has a recently remodeled kitchen and a fridge with an ice maker. I'm the one stuck eating gefilte fish from a jar." Then, when Harriet pointed out that they always ate gefilte fish from a jar, he'd said, "I'm newly separated. Let me be bitter, at least for a little while, okay?"

After that conversation, Harriet had considered faking an illness, something to keep her under the covers, locked in her dorm room, with Lisa bringing her meals from the dining hall in leaky Styrofoam containers, except that then Harriet would still have had to hear Lisa having sex with Tomer, who preferred their double and Lisa's all-cotton sheets to his messy quad and polyblend pillowcases, and who would instantly recognize that Harriet's cough was forced, and that her clenched teeth and balled fists had nothing to do with cramps, menstrual or otherwise. So here they were, in her station wagon, listening to ad after ad touting two-for-the-price-of-one breast enhancement surgeries, driving south on I-69, the irony of which wasn't lost on Harriet, even if it was, she could only hope, lost on Tomer, heading toward her parents and God knows what. She was fully prepared to deal with her parents together—quiet, civil, discreetly unhappy—but, she was realizing, she had no idea how to even begin to prepare for what they were like apart.

Harriet's mother was in the living room when they arrived, her hair, much to Harriet's relief, the same ashy blond it had been when she had left for college, although now it was shorn so short that her mother's face was all sharp cheekbones and thick, dark eyebrows. "Myrna at the salon did it," Harriet's mother explained. "It's wash and wear and doesn't get in my face when I run." She stretched one calf and then the other, her legs lean in running shorts, her muscles sliding smoothly as she pointed and flexed her toes. When she was done, she cracked her neck twice, first left, then right, and then she looked Tomer over for one long, awful moment. He was wearing rumpled khakis and a white T-shirt that read "Northcrest College Symphonic Band: Kiss My Brass." The hair on the back of his neck was bristly and too long. He was wearing scuffed sandals. Harriet should have never brought him home.

Finally, Harriet's mother said, "You need a haircut," and Tomer, without missing a beat, said, "Maybe Myrna can do it."

The three of them stood in silence eyeing each other. Harriet could feel herself flushing. *Stupid,* she told herself. *Stupid, stupid.* But then her mother laughed. "Come on," she said. "Let's order a pizza. Pepperoni and mushroom okay?" It wasn't pineapple and Canadian bacon, but it might as well have been. Either way, Harriet's father would have never allowed it: not kosher, he would have protested, and just think of all that grease pooling in your arteries. And he certainly wouldn't have allowed them to eat the pizza in the living room, on the matching white couch and recliner he and Harriet's mother had purchased when Harriet had turned sixteen because sixteen-year-olds were practically adults—the state trusted them to drive, after all—and therefore could be expected to keep things clean.

As if reading Harriet's mind, her mother said, "Don't worry. It's Scotchgarded." Then she balanced her plate on her stomach, tucked her can of beer between her knees, and pointed the remote at the TV in so practiced a gesture that Harriet was sure this was something she did every night. And Scotchgard or not, already there was a yellow stain on the armrest of the recliner and a spray of pink droplets along the seam of one of the couch cushions.

"Ooh," Harriet wanted to say, "Dad's going to *kill* you," but of course she didn't. Upstairs, her mother had moved the bed from the room she'd shared with Harriet's father to the room that used to be the office. The new room was smaller, and even though her mother had positioned the bed flush against the wall, you still couldn't open the door all the way. The family photo taken at Harriet's high school graduation that used to hang in the hallway—her father smiling broadly, her mother squinting in the sun—had been removed, the nail hole filled in with putty and painted over. There were candles in the bathroom, and matches, and a frilly fabric shower curtain that felt like cotton. There was a throw rug on the landing at the top of the stairs. It was as if her mother had never heard of fire hazards, or of slips and falls, or of keeping your escape routes open; it was as if she'd never heard of couples that fought, and separated, and even filed papers and went to court, only to wake up one morning and realize that they'd been wrong all along, and that they did belong together after all.

. . .

In the morning, Harriet's mother was waiting for her in the kitchen just like Harriet knew she would be, a glass of orange juice in one hand, a granola bar in the other. Tomer stood at the kitchen counter behind her, pouring himself a bowl of cornflakes. "You brought your shoes, right?" Harriet's mother asked.

Harriet had brought her shoes, and her jog bra and shorts too, but right at that moment she realized she couldn't do it, she couldn't go running with her mother and make small talk as if her father were still at home whipping up pancakes and waiting for them to return, or—even worse—listen to her mother talk about her plans to tear out the wall-to-wall carpeting and refinish the floors herself in preparation for selling the house, which she'd no doubt end up doing once the divorce was final, just before packing up and moving to another town with more beauty salons and fewer dentists. If Harriet's mother was going to pretend the divorce was simply a matter of rearranging furniture and systematically erasing her husband's presence, Harriet wasn't going to have any part in it. There were limits. She shook her head and tried to keep her voice measured. "I don't run anymore," she said. "Who has the time?"

Harriet's mother looked surprised. "You're not serious." Behind her, Tomer raised his eyebrows meaningfully. He knew Harriet was lying.

Harriet shrugged. "I'm taking five classes," she told her mother. "This is college, you know."

Her mother hadn't gone to college, hadn't even taken the SATs. When it had been time for Harriet to apply, it was her father who had studied the rankings and made recommendations. "If only your GPA was two-tenths of a point higher," he'd lamented. "If only you were in the top ten percent of your class." But how could Harriet have known that puberty, when it finally arrived the summer before her senior year of high school, would knock her right out of contention for a Division I athletic scholarship? She'd seen it happening with some of the other girls on the cross-country team, but she'd thought she had her body beat, that she'd always be narrow-hipped and light on her feet, that running would always be easy, effortless even, all air and wind and steady breath. Then, one June morning it seemed, she woke up twenty pounds heavier, just about all of it in her hips and thighs, hardly any of it in her breasts—which was just her luck, of course—and, on *good* days, nearly two minutes over her personal best. And all the studying she did that fall couldn't make up for the studying she hadn't done in previous years, when she'd been too busy training, "because," her father liked to say, "there are just so many star Jewish athletes out there, let alone Jewish runners, so why not play those odds?" Other times, he'd watch Harriet lace up her shoes and remind her that "Jews are about the brains, not the brawn." But when she didn't make varsity her senior year, he'd put his arm around her and kept it there until she was done crying, and never once came close to saying he'd told her so. And when she'd quit running for six weeks in the middle of October and instead spent her afternoons on the white couch, sulking and watching TV, he didn't say anything other than, "Don't forget to take off your shoes," which was exactly what she needed to hear, not the nagging her mother insisted on doing, complete with platitudes like "Use it or lose it" and "One day at a time," even though, back then, her mother wasn't running yet, not even going for walks, just standing all day in the salon, blowing out bangs and teasing hair to new heights as if it didn't matter that it would deflate long before her customers made it home.

Now Harriet's mother shifted her weight from her heels to the balls of her feet. "But don't you miss the running?" she asked. "Don't you miss it?"

"No," Harriet said. "Of course not."

"But—"

Tomer set his bowl of cereal on the kitchen table. He cleared his throat. "I'll go with you, Donna"—*Donna,* Harriet thought. *Donna?*—"if you want the company."

"I didn't know you run," Harriet said.

"I don't," Tomer admitted. "But that doesn't mean I shouldn't."

"Harriet's the one who got me hooked on running," Harriet's mother said. "Best thing I've ever done."

From her bedroom window, Harriet watched the two of them head out. Tomer's arms were all over the place, and before he'd gone ten steps she could tell he pronated. He'd last two blocks, she thought, maybe three: if a side stitch didn't get him, his knees would. After he and her mother rounded the corner, she went back downstairs and opened the refrigerator and cabinets, taking stock: frozen lasagna, frozen ravioli, frozen high-fiber bread, a half-empty jug of skim milk, and a half-eaten bag of plain M&M's. There was no chicken waiting to be dressed, no potato kugel, no challah, no gefilte fish in a jar. There weren't even any apples to dip in honey. She found a pen and a piece of paper and started making a shopping list. She didn't want Tomer telling it all over Northcrest that her family was falling apart.

By the time Harriet had made it back from the supermarket, both Tomer and her mother were showered, and her mother had a shirtless Tomer sitting in the middle of the kitchen, newspapers lining the floor underneath his chair, that strip of hair under his belly button pointing like an arrow to his crotch. "Okay," she was saying, "now bow your head forward." The casual way that she patted Tomer's back irritated Harriet—it was unseemly. Your parents weren't supposed to touch your friends—okay, acquaintances, but the fact that Harriet knew what Tomer sounded like having sex had to count for something—unless it was to remove a splinter or administer the Heimlich in times of emergency. And Tomer just made matters worse: "Will you scratch?" he asked. "Yes. Yes. Right there!"

"So it was a good run," Harriet said, putting down the grocery bags.

Harriet's mother busied herself with the clippers. "He's a natural."

"Pssh . . ." Tomer said modestly. "Not really."

"I ran out of breath before he did."

"It's the French horn," Tomer explained. "Lung capacity is very important for playing, you know, so we do exercises. I can hold my breath for three minutes, ten seconds."

Harriet couldn't help but be impressed. "That's enough to survive the gas chambers," she said, "assuming you didn't get trampled." The longest she'd ever managed to hold her breath was one minute forty-five seconds, and that was back when she was thirteen. She glanced at the clock on the microwave and gulped down some air.

"Good to know, I guess," Tomer said. Then he reached for Harriet's mother's right wrist, wrapping his thumb and index finger around it to form a bony handcuff. Even his fingers were hairy. "Don't forget, Donna," he said. "Not too short. I'm a civilian now."

"Aye-aye, sir." Harriet's mother saluted. Really, it was enough to make anyone lose focus and exhale, no matter that only twenty seconds had gone by. Plus, there was all that raw chicken to refrigerate.

"Geez," Harriet's mother said. "I'm only one person. Who's going to eat all that?"

. . .

Usually Harriet's family drove all the way to Indianapolis to go to synagogue on the High Holidays. It wasn't that they were the only Jews in their town—there were enough that on the High Holidays the United Methodist Church on the corner of Seventh let them use their rec room for services—but after the time that someone slit the station wagon's tires on Yom Kippur, Harriet's father decided that Indy was safer, if only for the fact that the congregation there had enough money to hire security guards to check people's IDs and patrol the parking lot. "Three gallons of gas and peace of mind are much less expensive than replacing four tires," he argued whenever Harriet's mother complained about having to eat dinner at four so that they'd have enough time to drive to evening services.

"Not this year," Harriet's mother told Harriet. She was watching Harriet scrape the fat off chicken thighs with a small paring knife while Tomer diced tomatoes. "I'm not making the trek to Indy just to stare at the back of your father's head, and I'm certainly not going to sit in some church basement and be pitied by all the Jews in this town. I can be Jewish just fine at home. I hope that doesn't offend you, Tomer."

Tomer laughed. "In Israel, synagogue is just for the Orthodox. Do I look Orthodox to you?"

"Not with the haircut I gave you," Harriet's mother said. "Now you just look mysterious, smoldering even. Lisa better watch out."

"Mom!" Harriet protested, never mind that Tomer did look smoldering. Her mother had layered his hair so it framed his dark eyes, and she'd cleaned up his sideburns and neck. His ears, newly revealed, looked soft and pink, practically edible. "Control yourself."

"My daughter, the fuddy-duddy," Harriet's mother said. "What's wrong with being proud of my work?"

Harriet didn't answer. Instead, she collected the discarded chicken fat and threw it in the trash. It left her hands slimy, her fingers slick, and she had to wash them with dishwashing detergent three times before her skin felt like it belonged to her again. She dried her hands, picked up the phone, and dialed her father. If she put the chicken in the oven in the next ten minutes, she'd have enough time to run some over to his place and watch him eat before it was time to leave for services. Except that her father wasn't going to services either, at least not to ones at the synagogue in Indy: "I can walk to United Methodist from where I live now," he told Harriet, "so no worries about the car. But I'll definitely take some chicken, if you've got extra."

"Mom's not going at all," Harriet said. She switched off the oven, which was already preheating. "Maybe I won't go either."

"Well," her father said, "you're an adult. You can make your own decisions. But don't forget the chicken, okay?"

And so Harriet, her mother, and Tomer sat down to dinner at six o'clock like normal Jews, and at six forty-five Harriet drove herself to United Methodist because, really, it didn't seem right not to, especially given that she was missing school. On the way over, she debated whether to pull into the church lot or park a couple of blocks away, opting finally to park across the street. Anyway, it wasn't as if her car had any distinguishing Jewish marks: an "I'm a Jew!" bumper sticker, a circumcised tailpipe. There was, of course, the chicken she'd promised her father, but it was sealed in Tupperware and could easily fit under her seat.

On the church's front steps, the other Jewish families in town were busy exchanging air kisses and admiring each other's holiday finery. Even without their yarmulkes, Harriet realized, you could tell these were Jews: dark-haired, sallow, small boned, pinched-looking—not all of them, of course, but enough, especially when you remembered that this was Indiana, where just about everybody's hair was stick-straight and blond, or else stick-straight and so light a shade of brown it might as well have been blond, and where the faces were wide-open, earnest, the eyes pale and watery. Harriet's father was nowhere to be seen, and Harriet soon found herself surrounded by a group of older, fluffy-haired women—her mother's longtime clients—who insisted on squeezing her hands and saying how sorry they were to hear about her parents. "At least they waited until you were all grown up," a woman with frosted pink lipstick consoled her. "You're one of the lucky ones."

Harriet shrugged. "I guess."

When the church bell rang seven, everybody filed inside and Harriet followed, hoping that her father had arrived early and gone straight in, and it turned out he had—there he was, sitting in the third row of folding chairs between the Levis and the Waldmans, right in front of a giant cross someone had draped a sheet over—but he hadn't remembered to save her a seat.

"Just grab one and bring it over," he mouthed at her as the Rabbi opened services, pointing at the chairs stacked against the back wall of the rec room. "We'll make room."

Harriet eyed the pile of chairs warily, or at least that's what she told herself later, after the first chair slipped from her grip and sent all the other chairs toppling over right as everyone started singing the Shema. Of course, everyone stopped singing and turned around to look at her, and Harriet knew—she just *knew*—that they were pitying her, first the divorce and now this. Poor, clumsy Harriet with the father who didn't even bother to save her a seat, and who, when he realized what was happening, turned away from her and stared straight ahead at the covered cross with all the devotion of a recent convert.

"I'm sorry," Harriet said.

"Well," said the Rabbi from his improvised bima at the front of the room, "today does mark the beginning of the Ten Days of Awe, a time for introspection and repentance. . . ." When no one laughed, he said, "It's a joke, people. . . ."

Harriet could feel her face burning. She reached for one of the chairs, but there was no way to pick it up without sending even more sliding.

"Leave them," the Rabbi said. "We have to be out of here by eight anyway."

"I could give you a ride home," Harriet told her father after services were over. Outside, the sun was setting and the sky was red. Something about the light and the suit her father was wearing—the way it bunched under his arms—made him look like someone out to sell her a used car. All around them, the trees were raining leaves.

"That's okay," Harriet's father said. "It really is only a couple of blocks, and the walk will do me good. I've been walking a lot lately."

The street lamps flickered on. Harriet shifted her weight from one leg to the other. She wasn't sure exactly what she was supposed to do next. "Well," she said finally, "I brought you that chicken."

"You did?"

"It's in the car."

Harriet's father made a face. "Who leaves chicken in the car? Did you at least put it in a cooler?"

Harriet shook her head. She didn't know why she hadn't even considered salmonella. She was slipping. "There's more at home."

Her father pursed his lips as if to ask, *Whose home?*

Harriet could feel herself starting to get annoyed. Or maybe she was already annoyed. She took a deep breath. "I can bring you some chicken later," she offered. Her father shrugged noncommittally, and Harriet realized that she wasn't just annoyed, she was angry. Her fingers, if she sniffed them carefully, still smelled like raw chicken. "You could have saved me a seat, you know," she said.

"I didn't know you were coming."

"Well," Harriet said, "I'm your daughter. You should have."

Back at home, back at *her mother's house,* Harriet's mother and Tomer were eating ice-cream sundaes in the kitchen and giggling, although they stopped as soon as Harriet walked into the room.

"Check this out!" Harriet's mother said before Harriet even got a chance to set down the chicken. She stretched out her right arm to Harriet, wrist side up. "Look!" About two inches above her wrist, there was a painting of a sneaker with wings. "Just like Mercury!"

"You got a tattoo?" Harriet swallowed hard.

Harriet's mother nodded. "It hardly even hurt."

"Your mother's a real trouper!" Tomer confirmed.

"Shut up," Harriet told him. To her mother she said, "What were you thinking? Tattoos are for life. They're permanent. And on your forearm? Of all places?" Jews didn't get tattoos on their forearms, at least not by choice. It was insensitive. Disgusting, even.

Harriet's mother and Tomer exchanged looks, which was how Harriet knew that she wasn't paranoid and that they *had* been talking about her—extensively—and saying nothing good. She turned her back to them and propped open the garbage can.

"What are you doing?" her mother asked.

"Dad didn't want the chicken after it sat in the car all night."

"That's perfectly good chicken," her mother said.

"Fine." Harriet slammed the tray of chicken back down on the counter. "Then *you* eat it and *you* get sick."

Harriet's mother sighed. "Harriet," she said, sounding tired, "look at me." When Harriet did, her mother moistened the tip of her index finger and rubbed the tattoo. It smeared. "It's just one of those temporary ones," she said. "We thought it would be funny. A joke."

"Ha," Harriet said. "Ha ha ha." She grabbed a drumstick out of the tray and bit into it. She would get sick and spend the rest of Rosh Hashanah in the emergency room. That would show them.

Harriet's mother turned to Tomer. "Other people's kids do drugs to rebel. Mine eats suspect chicken."

"We all have our troubles," Tomer conceded. "Can you pass the chocolate syrup?"

Of course Harriet didn't get sick. Instead, she lay in bed, sniffing her fingers—she could still smell the chicken, she was sure of it—and listened to her mother and Tomer murmuring in the living room below. She tried to imagine having to explain to Lisa that her boyfriend was cheating on her with a woman old enough to be her mother. Or at least Harriet's mother. It wasn't fair. Not that Harriet wanted Tomer, but if he was going to hit on someone in her house, you'd think it would have been on her and not her mom.

Later, after her mother and Tomer retreated into their respective rooms—Tomer to her parents' old bedroom, her mother to the room that used to be the office—because even they apparently had limits, Harriet knocked on Tomer's door. Inside, he was lying in bed, his chest hairy and bare, the rest of him naked except for boxers, although Harriet had to assume this last part because he was already under the covers. "What's up?" he asked.

Harriet stood in the doorway awkwardly. She imagined her mother in her new bedroom, her ear pressed against the door, listening expectantly for what Harriet was going to say next, or maybe waiting for Harriet to leave so that she could tiptoe over to Tomer's room—her old bedroom . . . and then what? "Can I come in?"

Once inside, though, the door closed behind her, there was no place to sit other than on the bed itself. Harriet could feel herself flushing, and she crossed her arms over her chest. This had to be, she imagined, what Little Red Riding Hood felt when she first saw the wolf in her grandmother's bed, looking both at home and out of place at the same time. She cleared her throat. "Listen," she told Tomer, "you already have a girlfriend."

"Yes," Tomer agreed.

"Then what are you doing?"

"Well," Tomer said, "I'm going to sleep."

"I'm not talking about that," Harriet said. "I'm talking about the flirting. Stop flirting with my mother."

Tomer laughed. "You're talking to the wrong person," he said. "She's the one flirting with me."

"This isn't funny," Harriet said. "And you don't have to encourage her."

Tomer pulled himself up so that the blanket fell to his waist. Not that Harriet was looking or anything, and not, of course, that she hadn't seen it all before. "Actually," he said, "I'm doing her a favor. Because that's the thing about flirting. It makes people feel good. It makes them feel wanted. Isn't that why you do it?"

"Me?"

"You're doing it right now."

Harriet didn't know what he was talking about. She wasn't flirting. She was standing stiffly, her face stony, her knees braced.

"Don't give me that look," Tomer said. "I know better."

"You hardly know me at all."

"So what?" Under the sheet, Tomer crossed his legs. "I've been in this country long enough to know that I'm irresistible to Jewish women. No exceptions. Not even you." Harriet opened her mouth to protest, but Tomer kept right on talking: "I'm not being arrogant. It's just how it is when you're Israeli. It's like a curse."

"Are you hearing anything you're saying?" Harriet asked.

"Yes, because *I'm* the self-deluded one," Tomer said. "It's just flirting, you know. It happens. And your mom moving on, well, even though it won't be with me, that's going to happen too. It's not a disaster. That's the problem with you Americans. You have no sense of perspective. You worry and worry about all the wrong things."

After that, Harriet went running. So what if it was dark? She'd run along these streets so many times that her feet had memorized the potholes. There was a big hole at the intersection of Elm and Main, and a bigger one at Miranda and Fourth, where her mother had twisted her ankle the first time she'd gone out alone. "I don't know what I was looking at," she'd said. And Harriet had said, "Not at your feet, obviously." Harriet had thought that would be the end of it, the end of her mother running. None of the other mothers ran, that was certain, although some did aerobics in front of their VCRs after work, wearing shiny leotards and leg warmers and terry-cloth sweatbands. Harriet occasionally caught glimpses of their high kicks and air punches when she ran past their houses, but that was before she'd gone from being district champ to junior varsity to quitting the team entirely—it was hard to imagine those mothers going on with their workouts, oblivious, and even harder to imagine her mother deciding right then, of all possible times, to take up running herself. But three days after twisting her ankle, there she was, her mother, in an old pair of Harriet's sneakers, limping only slightly and blocking the television screen. "Come on," she'd told Harriet. "Let's go." This was a couple of weeks before the Thanksgiving of Harriet's senior year, and by this time Harriet hadn't been running long enough that she no longer felt caged and restless in the evenings.

"Fine," her mother had said. "Then it's on you if I break my ankle, and don't think I won't tell it all over town."

Harriet had rolled her eyes and sighed dramatically, but when her mother had started stretching—incorrectly, Harriet noted—she'd gotten up off the couch, given her mother her good running shoes, put on the old ones herself, and jogged dutifully beside her praying that no one would see them. For the first mile, her mother had gasped for breath, barely able to nod and smile when Harriet asked her if she was doing okay. But then her mother had found her rhythm, and it was all steady breathing and pounding feet and cool wind, and Harriet had almost started crying right then, that was how much she'd been missing running without even knowing it, never mind her slow times and hippy hips. And when they'd gotten home, instead of saying, "I told you so," Harriet's mother had said, "Let's run that Turkey Trot 5K on Thanksgiving," and when they'd trained and run that one, she'd said, "Let's run that Winter Wonderland 10K in December," and then, "Let's run the Love Ain't for Sissies 15K in February," and so on, one race each month, while Harriet's father huddled in his coat on the sidelines, cheering them on, yes, but also complaining about the way the entrance fees and T-shirts were adding up. "No woman needs eleven T-shirts," he'd told them, the poor fool, not realizing that Harriet's mother wasn't just running, that she was running away, and that Harriet, without fully knowing it even, was helping her go: "Let's do that half marathon in Indy, that marathon in Chicago." Each race was farther from home, and Harriet's mother, when she crossed each new finish line, would raise her arms high in the air, as if gratefully acknowledging applause only she could hear, while Harriet slowed down to a jog and tried to catch her breath, wondering when, exactly, her mother had become so good.

Harriet hopped on the sidewalk to dodge that pothole on Miranda and Fourth only to discover that it had been paved over. On both sides of the street, the houses were mostly dark, the blue light of the television flickering in some upstairs windows. No one, she guessed, was doing aerobics right then. She turned right onto Cherry, then remembered that this was her father's new street, that he lived on the first floor of a house that had been split up into apartments. She slowed down to a walk and looked for his car, which turned out to be parked in front of a large, rambling Victorian whose lawn needed raking. And there he was, her father, standing in front of one of the windows in a brightly lit room, looking straight at her, except that he wasn't, he was looking at his own reflection, and after a moment he shook his head as if waking up from a trance, turned around, and disappeared.

Harriet hesitated, but then she gingerly stepped on the lawn, hoping that her father wouldn't hear the leaves crunching under her feet, and crept up to the window to look in. She wasn't sure what to expect: Her father watching the evening news? Doing crossword puzzles? Talking on the phone with that blond hygienist, since didn't all dentists have affairs with their hygienists? But when she looked in, her father was doing none of these things. He was sitting on the couch, his head tilted back, his eyes closed, his hands on his knees, palms wide open. He looked stubbly and tired, and for a moment Harriet's heart contracted the same way it did when she saw puppies or other newborn animals. She leaned in for a closer look, her hand already raised to knock on the glass, ready to rush in there and comfort him, when something about the room gave her pause. It took her a moment to figure out what it was, but then she didn't know how she could have missed it: her father was sitting on their old yellow corduroy couch, the one they'd replaced when Harriet had turned sixteen, in front of their old coffee table. She blinked, but even from that distance, she could see the ink stain on the couch's right armrest from the time she'd fallen asleep doing homework with her pen uncapped.

Her father sat up and opened his eyes. This time she knew he saw her—he gasped and clutched his chest, pausing to take a few deep breaths before standing up and walking over to the window and sliding it open.

"My God, Harriet," he said. "I nearly had a heart attack."

"That's our old couch," Harriet told him.

"My pulse is racing." He offered her his wrist. "Feel it."

"I thought we gave it to the Salvation Army."

Her father shrugged. "We were going to, but then I changed my mind. Now are you going to come inside? It's late. You shouldn't be out alone."

"But that was two years ago," Harriet said. "More than that, even. Where was it all this time?"

"In storage, of course," Harriet's father said as if it were a dumb question.

"In storage," Harriet repeated.

"Yes." Her father was starting to get irritated.

"But why? Why keep it?"

"What's the big deal?" Harriet's father asked. "I kept it because you never know when you're going to need a couch."

But Harriet suddenly understood that he did know, that he had known for years, that if she were to walk into his bedroom she'd find her parents' old headboard, replaced when she'd been thirteen, and her parents' old mattress, replaced the following year. All this time, her father had been slowly accumulating furniture even as Harriet wrote out Happy Anniversary cards and served her parents increasingly complex breakfasts in bed hoping to keep them there, because according to the magazines at the salon where her mother worked, happy couples spent lots of time in bed, doing things like getting in touch with their feelings and reconnecting. Not that her plan worked: her parents would pick at the meals she'd prepared for a few moments before heading out into the kitchen for bowls of bran cereal: "You know I don't like green peppers," her mother would say. Or "I'm allergic to strawberries." "And scones are so fattening," her father would add, "not that we don't appreciate the gesture." Which, of course, they didn't, because why would they when they'd already made up their minds, when all they were doing was biding their time and waiting for her to grow up, move out, and—finally, at long last—set them free.

Back home—back at Harriet's mother's house—her mother was in the kitchen, picking at a chicken breast with her fingers. "It's even good cold," she told Harriet. "Want some?" When Harriet shook her head no, she added, "I'd guessed you were out running. But maybe next time you could leave a note."

Harriet poured herself a glass of water. She could feel droplets of sweat at the base of her neck and along her hairline. "Okay."

Her mother chewed thoughtfully for a moment. On her forearm, the smudged temporary tattoo looked like a bruise. "Why did you tell me you quit?" she asked.

"I don't know." Harriet tried to keep her voice light.

"Well," Harriet's mother continued, "that's a load off my mind. It was hard enough getting you off that couch last year, and that was without you living six hours away."

"What are you talking about?"

Harriet's mother laughed. "Don't get me wrong—running's the best thing I've got going these days. But I never would have started if you hadn't quit the team. There's only so much moping a mother can take."

Harriet felt stupid. Nothing was the way she thought it was. Later, she stood in the shower, the water as hot as she could bear it, and practiced not breathing, monitoring her progress using the second hand on the clock that hung on the wall across from the toilet. Thirty. Forty-five. Fifty seconds. Tomer had been right: she did worry about the wrong things. Or she worried about the right things, but incorrectly. How could she have allowed herself to be caught so off guard, and not just by one event, but by a whole slew: the divorce, college, even puberty. Even worse: it wasn't that she hadn't thought about these things, that she hadn't planned or prepared, but that she had, and she'd still ended up so far off base. She took another breath and held it. After thirty seconds, she could feel her heart pounding against her ribs, the pressure rising in her chest. How did she allow herself to get so out of shape? Fifty seconds. Fifty-three. Fifty-five. She turned off the water and exhaled.

The thought of going to sleep in her childhood bed, surrounded by walls scarred by the yellowing Scotch tape from when she'd taken down all the newspaper clippings about her running, seemed unbearable to Harriet. She stood in the hallway, wrapped in her robe, and worked on not crying. Except for her breathing, everything was silent. She waited, even though she wasn't sure for what: Tomer to decide he wanted her after all? Her mother to come find her? She rocked back and forth on her toes lightly, waiting, waiting, but the only thing that happened was that Tomer started snoring behind the door to her parents' room, sound asleep as if he belonged there. Harriet envied him. Not only could he go back to Northcrest and forget all about Harriet and her mother if he wanted to, but he could leave America entirely and go back to Israel, where no one would have to know that he spent his time abroad sleeping with blondes and flirting with other people's mothers. He was visible and invisible at the same time. He wasn't like Harriet, exposed. What had she been thinking, bringing him home?

"Harriet?"

Harriet jumped. Somehow, without her hearing it, her mother had opened the door to her room.

"What's going on?" her mother asked.

"I don't know. I can't sleep."

"Tell me about it," her mother said. "Well, come on then." She waved Harriet inside her room. "I've got cable and everything now. Which side of the bed do you want?"

Harriet shrugged. It wasn't a fair question. She waited until her mom got in on the right side—the side she'd always slept on—before crawling in on the left. She lay there for a moment, waiting for her mother to say something. When she didn't, Harriet said, "Dad has the old couch. And the old coffee table."

She expected her mother to look stunned, but her mother just pointed the remote at the TV she'd set up on the dresser. "I know. I guess at least this way they're getting some use. Now what are we going to watch? There's a horror movie on channel three."

And just like that, her mother was done talking about the divorce. Harriet felt something like admiration. She didn't know how she could have underestimated her mother, underestimated both her parents, and yet she clearly had: here they were, both of them with lives she knew nothing about. And if Harriet knew so little about her parents, what could she possibly know about the rest of the world, which now loomed dark and ominous, full of dangers she couldn't foresee? She would have to pay more attention. She would have to learn to observe with more care. She could no longer afford to get distracted by free T-shirts and razors, blond hair, guys who stared at you from someone else's bed. The news was full of people who hadn't seen things coming, people who installed smoke detectors in every bedroom only to be killed by a tornado or a freak flash flood. And that was before you considered man-made disasters, like Chernobyl or the Holocaust. Wars, fires, salmonella, love affairs. Harriet wouldn't be caught off guard again. She couldn't be. She checked her mother's bedside clock and waited for the second hand to cycle back to the 12. She took a deep breath and held it, wondering how long she could go.

Entebbe

My dog, I swear, was a racist. At first I thought it was only Arabs, but no, she also hated the Romanian who cleaned the lobby of our apartment building, the construction crew of Nigerians that worked down the block, and the woman from Thailand who took care of Mrs. Friedman in 22. As for Mrs. Friedman, her family had been in Israel for nine generations, so naturally the dog had no problems with her: whenever we passed her parked in her wheelchair outside the grocery store on Arlozorov, waiting for the Thai woman to bring her chocolate milk in a Baggie, the dog would act all charming in that charming-dog way of hers, slobbering all over Mrs. Friedman's hands. But then the Thai woman would return and the dog would lose it, showing her teeth, growling, the whole works. One time she even took a nip at the Thai woman's thigh, which made Mrs. Friedman start muttering about lawsuits, even though I always held the elevator door open for her, and despite the fact that she wasn't the one who'd been bitten.

By then, I was already dragging my feet. I was twenty-eight, and single, and tired of spending a full month each year eating sand in the army, especially after what happened last time. With Mrs. Friedman making speeches about the inherent goyishness of living with dogs and threatening to mobilize her son-in-law lawyer, I figured, why not move? Moving seemed simple enough:

you held a moving sale, packed up the leftovers, and got on a plane. The last part, of course, wasn't easy—I hated planes—but I was desperate to leave before my next reserves notice came around from the army. Twelve hours on a plane was nothing if you ended up in New York, where—if you believed the hype—the shops on Broadway were full of Israelis getting rich selling off-brand camcorders to tourists; and where, if you lived in the right part of town, you didn't even have to learn English. Even better: as long as the dog was vaccinated and could be stowed as luggage, I could bring her with me. I knew my mother would have been disappointed, but she'd been dead two years, and my father, who already had a new girlfriend, was in no position to do anything but offer to drive me to the airport despite the 2 a.m. departure time, then stand around while I took deep breaths in preparation for going through security.

"*Yallah,* Noam," he said. "Be a man."

I stood up straight and squared my shoulders, but it didn't help—the flight was still awful. I kept thinking I could hear the dog howling from somewhere deep inside the belly of the plane, and worrying that maybe they put her in a place that wasn't heated or pressurized, and she was slowly freezing to death. You heard about that kind of thing happening all the time, about people ending up in a new town with a dog Popsicle instead of a dog. On top of that, and on top of the fact that the Dramamine and acupuncture bracelet weren't working, there was something wrong with one of the wing flaps, and we had to land in Athens. That just about killed me. I swear, I started praying to God. I clasped my hands and closed my eyes and made promises—solemn oaths, even—to stop voting left and start lobbying for a Whole Land of Israel complete with Jerusalem and the Jordan River, and every other place mentioned in the Bible, and I also reminded God of all the times I was assigned to escort settlers' children back and forth from school and only complained a little bit, and definitely within reason. Then, even bargaining got to be too much and I needed all my concentration just to keep on breathing. And for the rest of the time we were in Athens, and for the eight hours after that it took to get to New York, all I could think was, *Now inhale. Now exhale. Now inhale. Now exhale.*

The dog, of course, was fine, exhibiting no signs of frostbite, nice and warm against my hands. I rented a car and bought a map of Manhattan, thinking we'd head straight for Times Square and all those other Israelis, but the first thing I saw when I got off the highway was a man on the sidewalk beating a woman with a dead fish that was as long as his arm. The woman was cowering and covering her eyes, but you could see her wet open mouth and all her missing teeth. The dog was going crazy, barking and fogging up the window, and I could see what any other man would have done—stopped the car, grabbed the fish, made sure the woman had some nice soft food to chew on—but all I could think about was that, between this and Athens, the signs were too obvious to miss. I'd made a mistake leaving Israel, and now I was trapped—there was no way I was getting on another plane. So instead of getting out of the car, I got back on the highway and kept driving. Outside, it was raining, and nothing looked right: the trees and the soil, the lines on the freeway, the other drivers in their cars, their faces blank as cardboard. But the thing I really couldn't get over was the sky, which stretched out in every direction, so low you could feel its weight pressing down on everything, not hard, but steady, so that I wouldn't have been surprised if the sheer force of it ended up wedging the car into the freeway, and me and the dog along with it.

It wasn't until halfway through Pennsylvania, when I was almost out of gas, that I could finally think clearly enough to get a map. I climbed into the backseat and locked all the doors and traced I-90 heading west. The only familiar place was Chicago, and that was another big city. I was having a hard time breathing again, so I let the dog lick my hand until we both fell asleep and I ended up drooling all over Lake Michigan. I knew it was another sign, but I didn't know for what until I got there and it was something straight out of the movies: the rain stopped and the sun broke through the clouds, and, when I rolled down the windows, the birds were singing. And even though the water was fresh and not salty, and the beach was cleaner than any beach I'd ever seen, something about it felt familiar and right, and I thought maybe it was someplace I could stay.

In Israel, I'd been a driving instructor. It was easy work, and if your pupils paid you cash, you didn't have to report all your income. But here was the thing: every time they started blowing up buses again, you got all these scared women who couldn't even afford the high price of gas signing up for lessons. They took the test maybe thirty times before they passed, or until things calmed down and they could start taking the bus again. If you stopped to consider all the people dying in regular traffic accidents, it didn't make sense, but that kind of thing never makes sense, and I wasn't above that sort of logic either. So what if flying a plane was a million times safer than driving? At least in a car you didn't end up in *Athens* of all places. Anyway, for me, the terror was cash city, and I wasn't crazy. I was already thinking of leaving, and I needed the money, same as them.

The town I ended up in was maybe three blocks long, with forty-eight ice cream parlors and a marina full of yachts so big you needed three eyefuls to take them all in. Except for the people serving food and rinsing off the decks, everyone else seemed to be on vacation, strutting around with a glass of chardonnay in one hand, an ice cream cone in the other. It was how I imagined heaven: pink sunsets, lobster dinners, ice cream scoops the size of your fist. In the evening, everyone changed into high heels and glitzy dresses and ties just to walk back and forth along the same three blocks they'd walked along all day. The lights on the yachts came on, and inside you could see men in Hawaiian-print shirts mixing drinks behind shiny black marble bars. The air was chilly, so I bought a sweatshirt with "Yes! Michigan!" printed on the front, and really, it was how I felt. Even the dog seemed like a calmer, more accepting dog, content with inspecting light poles and fire hydrants and sniffing up the dirt on American dogs, and not even wincing when complete strangers—tanned and sturdy, with mouths full of teeth—knelt down beside her and shouted, "Now who's a good doggy? Who?" As far as I could tell, we were maybe the only Israelis ever to set foot in this place: three blocks, twelve churches, not even one synagogue. But then we turned down a side street and the dog snapped out of it and lunged at a man hauling a large bag of garbage to a Dumpster. Naturally, the man started swinging his bag at us, back and forth, back and forth, knocking over garbage cans and making a lot more noise than necessary. Then the bag broke, spraying everything with fish bones and potato peels and cabbage, and the man lost his balance. He wasn't a big man, and now he lay on the ground, cursing in Spanish, confirming the dog's suspicion that he, just like us, didn't belong there in the first place.

"José!" a man yelled from a nearby doorway. "José! What the hell's going on?"

José pointed at the dog, who was eating scraps off the ground. "That dog attacked me," he said.

The man in the doorway surveyed the damage as if considering his options. He was as big as José was small, maybe two meters tall, with a rosy, round face and three chins. Behind him, I could make out what looked like the kitchen of a restaurant, all steam and banging pots and flaring grease fires. "You see," he said, "that's why I keep saying, no dogs. You tell your friend there, no dogs." When José didn't say anything, the fat man turned to me. "No dogs," he said. "No work either. José, you tell your friend, no work."

José shrugged. "He's not my friend," he told the fat man. "He's not even Mexican."

"Then what is he?" the fat man said. "What are you?" and I said, "Israeli. You know, from Israel." That shut the fat man right up. "No kidding," he finally said. "From Israel?" I nodded. "No kidding," he said again. "You don't look Israeli." Then he said, "Does Sid know you're here?"

Sid, it turned out, was the only Jew in town. He had three daughters and a wife who wasn't Jewish herself. This was what the fat man, whose name was Larry, told me while I brushed the garbage off my clothes. "That's love for you," he explained. "Or so they say." He reached over and picked a piece of wilted lettuce out of my hair, then stepped back to admire his work. "A real Israeli," he said. "Sid's going to be thrilled. He sounded thrilled on the phone." He patted the dog, and the dog let him.

But when we got to Sid's house, which was nothing special on the outside except for a birdbath in the front yard, Sid didn't look thrilled. He was maybe ten years older than me, and, if anything, he looked embarrassed and a little scared, maybe because the dog took an instant dislike to him and growled every time he glanced at her. After looking around, though, I thought maybe I understood why the dog was getting so upset. On every wall, there were pictures of Orthodox Jews: Orthodox women braiding bread, Orthodox men praying at the Western Wall. Orthodox children playing hopscotch on a street paved with Jerusalem stone. There was a fireplace, brick and everything, which I'd only seen on TV until then, and which would have been exciting, except that the mantel was crowded with menorahs and candlesticks and souvenir dreidels made out of glass—of all things!—and which you could tell were designed to look expensive but not to actually spin.

"From my mother," Sid said by way of explanation, and Larry added with a wink, "Sid's mother's not a big fan of the shikas bride."

"Shiksa," Sid corrected. To me he said, "She's just trying to give the girls a sense of identity." He pointed to a *tzedakah* box next to the doorway. "Twenty percent of their allowance goes straight to Israel."

He was expecting me to say something approving, maybe thank him for his support, but instead I smiled at the three little girls who were watching me wide-eyed from where they sat on the couch. The littlest one kept trying to stick her pinky up her nose, but the middle one kept swatting her hand down. She was so much faster that the little one had no chance.

"I give money to Israel too, you know," Larry said. "To help the Jews."

I knelt down in front of the littlest girl and she stopped moving, except for the booger that fluttered like a small yellow insect every time she breathed. The next thing I knew, I reached out with my own pinky and, just like that, brushed it away. The littlest girl sneezed. And she didn't cover her mouth either.

"Ilana!" Sid said. "Get your sister a tissue." The two older girls looked confused. "Ilana!" Sid said again. Then he said, "Jenny," and the middle girl sprang into action, in and out of the room in under three seconds, waving a white Kleenex like a flag. Sid smiled apologetically. "Sometimes they don't remember their Hebrew names."

After that, Sid's wife came home from the drugstore where she worked the evening shift. She was so blond she had no eyebrows, and right away she stooped over to pat the dog, who already loved her so much that she'd rolled over and exposed her belly.

"Smart dog," Larry said. "It knows who's in charge."

"Yes," I said. "The blondes."

"True," Larry said. "Only you've got to be careful. We've got some good hair dye here in America. Not that anyone needs it in this house."

"That's right," Sid's wife said.

"No mousy brown wife for Sid," Larry said.

Sid rolled his eyes. "I didn't marry Cindy for her hair."

"No," Sid's wife said. "You didn't." She stood up, wiped the dog residue off her hands, and flipped a switch on the wall. Within seconds, a gas log was burning cheerfully in the fireplace, and, as if on cue, the dog lay down in front of it and all three girls got busy brushing her fur and decorating it with barrettes. "Martini?" Sid's wife asked.

"Now this," Sid said, spearing an olive with a toothpick, "is why I married her."

"Yes," Larry agreed. "It's why any one of us would've married her." He sighed wistfully.

We sat around in silence for a few minutes, and then Sid looked at his watch and said, "Well, I'd invite you to stay for dinner, but we don't keep kosher. You have to drive to Chicago or Detroit for kosher meat around here."

"Hell," Larry said, "you have to drive all the way to Grand Rapids just to go to temple."

"That's okay about the meat," I said. "I don't mind."

"That's nice of you," Sid said. "But it's also leftover night."

"I have an idea," Larry said. "You and Noam should come to the restaurant for dinner. Noam already met one of the Mexicans, you know. It's why my guacamole tastes so good—real Mexicans in the kitchen."

"I don't know," Sid said. He looked at his wife. "What do you think?"

"She thinks it's a great idea," Larry said. "Come on, Sid. How often do you get to hang out with your own people?"

It was my second day in the States. I was tired and hungry and a little disoriented, and there was Sid, watching me and wringing his hands as if I were an officer of some international Federation of Jews coming to see how he was holding up in the middle of the Diaspora. I thought about leaving, just standing up and walking out while Sid and his wife went back and forth about her staying behind with the kids and the dog: "But you just got home," Sid was protesting, but his wife kept insisting she was fine, he should go, no worries, et cetera. But what it all came down to was that the more Sid wanted me gone, the more I wanted to stay. The dog knew her stuff. Sid didn't belong in this town any more than I did, and still, here he was, with his blond wife and blond daughters and strange birds I'd never seen splashing in the birdbath out front. And all this despite his shifty eyes and white skin and pale, hairless legs. I was tan and strong and had plenty of hair on my chest. If someone like Sid could have all this, I wanted to know what was out there for me.

Larry's restaurant was wedged in between two ice cream parlors, across the street from the marina. Inside, the menus were written on Styrofoam surfboards, and you could order drinks in a coconut shell decorated with tiny toothpick umbrellas.

"Nice, huh?" Larry said about the umbrellas. "I bet you don't have these in Israel." It was what he said about everything—the Mexican-style cheeseburgers, the Mexican-style fries, the Mexican-style milk shakes, as if Israel didn't have both McDonald's and Burger King.

"Larry," Sid said finally. "Give it up, will you?" Up until then, he'd been busy arranging the sugar packets into a complicated geometric design on his place mat, but now he pushed them aside and looked up.

"No," Larry said. "Don't you see? Israel's not so different. Your girls can still have Happy Meals and play with Barbies, it sounds like."

I was used to religious people coming with visible warning signs, like black coats or a *kippah,* so I wasn't prepared for what came next, which was Larry grabbing one of Sid's hands and earnestly declaring, "Sid, I love you, I really do. But it says right in the Bible that the Jews belong in Israel, that the Messiah won't come before that. And now here's your chance to find out what it's really like over there, and all you're doing is sulking."

"I'm not sulking." Sid pulled his hand free. "We've talked about this a million times. It's not like I'm personally holding up the Second Coming. When the rest of the Jews go, I'll go too." He turned to me. "That's Larry for you. Welcome to America, now leave." Larry started to protest, but Sid continued talking right over him. "Anyway," he said, "if Israel's such a land of milk and honey, why does it seem like such a mess on the news?"

It was a good question, and I was interested to hear Larry's explanation, except that suddenly they were both looking at me.

"Yes, Noam," Larry said. "The truth now."

"Yes," said Sid. "Is it really as bad as it looks on TV?"

There were four stories I liked telling about the army. I was practiced at telling them too: they made for good small talk, distracting new drivers just enough so they didn't overthink lane changes and traffic circles. The first story was about being so bored one weekend that some of the guys started poisoning the stray cats that roamed the base and betting on how they'd leap from the pain. It wasn't something I was proud of, but it made for a good story if you could do the caterwauling convincingly, which I could. The second story was about a friend of mine, an officer, who spent the last week of every course he taught working his way through the female troops. He was a good-looking guy—he'd done some modeling—but he attributed his success to the residue of authority coupled with lots of eye contact. This story was especially good when told in a public place, where your listeners could practice staring at attractive strangers. The third story was about the time they forgot me on sentry duty until I had no choice but to crap in the bushes, which is when—go figure—my CO showed up and nailed me for leaving my post; this was another good one for sound effects and facial contortions. The last story was about the time my father came to visit me on check-post duty and started handing out baked goods to the Palestinians who were lined up for processing. You could have knocked those Palestinians over with a stick when this little Iraqi Jew started chitchatting with them in Arabic and passing out sesame cookies.

I started going through the stories, but from the way Sid and Larry kept looking at each other, these weren't the stories they wanted. They were horrified anyone would ever poison cats out of boredom. "But you have a dog," Sid said to me. "You'd poison your dog?" They laughed a little at the story about the model, but it was a polite laugh, as if sex didn't belong in the army, as if sex weren't the natural consequence of sticking thousands of horny eighteen-year-olds together in close quarters. After that, I decided they wouldn't appreciate the crapping story, so I went straight to my father's visit, and that's when Larry leaned forward and started squinting at my face and cocking his head from side to side like some pasty, overweight bird.

"No wonder," he said finally. "No wonder I mistook you for a Mexican. I mean, look at you. You look nothing like Sid, and you got the skin and hair and hooked nose that Arabs have. I mean, it's a wonder no one at the check post was detaining you." Then he turned to Sid and said, "Isn't that right, Sid? Isn't he a regular Arab? We could drop him off in the middle of Dearborn and no one would give him a second look."

By then even Sid was looking uncomfortable. "Now, Larry," he said. "I wouldn't call him an Arab. I certainly wouldn't."

"Well, why not?" Larry said. "He's practically from Iraq, isn't he?"

The whole exchange was making me want to leave, but the dog was still at Sid's house getting a makeover, and I needed to get her back without traumatizing those little girls, who were no doubt so in love with the dog by now that Sid would have to promise them a puppy just so they'd let her go home. It's a mistake to leave small children with a dog.

"Larry," Sid said, "he's a Jew. A Jew can't be an Arab."

"Sure he can." Larry slapped his thighs so hard I could feel my own palms tingle. "If you can have a Christian Arab and a Muslim Arab, why can't you have a Jewish Arab? I mean, if Sammy Davis Jr. can be a Jew, couldn't—I don't know—Saddam Hussein?"

"Come on, Larry," Sid said. "Change the subject, will you?"

"I just don't get it," Larry said, shaking his head. "What are you getting so upset about?"

Sid looked at me meaningfully in some kind of secret Jew-to-Jew code for "Can you believe this goy?" but I wasn't playing. I looked down at my Mexican-style onion rings.

"I saw that, Sid," Larry said. "Fine. Be all defensive. I don't need this half-assed conversation anyway."

"I'm not being defensive," Sid said.

"Then why do you keep changing the subject?"

"Because it's pointless," Sid said.

"No," Larry said. "There's nothing pointless about understanding your place in the world. At least the Bible tells you Jews where you belong. What about the rest of us?"

Even before the dog nipped Mrs. Friedman's Thai woman, I was already practicing leaving. When I had a couple of hours between driving lessons, I'd drive down to Lod, to the airport, and watch people make their way from the security screening, to the baggage check-in, to the escalator that led to the departure gates. If they were scared, I couldn't tell. If anything, they looked determined, grim even, the same way the dog used to before she learned to heel and was always straining against her leash. I'd heard that the upstairs of the airport, the departure area, was a different world from the downstairs, with its long lines and border police. Upstairs came complete with duty-free chocolates, stereo systems, and washers and dryers you could purchase and which would wait patiently, like a prize, for your return. Once you made it up the escalators, rumor had it, you were already halfway to gone. And that was maybe the only part of my trip that was exactly the way it was supposed to be. I surrendered the dog at the baggage claim, and suddenly I was alone with my carry-on and travelers' checks, clutching my ticket and wandering among all those brightly lit appliances. I could have disappeared right there, but I didn't. I got on the plane and had to sit next to an old Arab man with lots of nose hair whose hands shook so much he had trouble opening the soda can the stewardess handed to him. *Here,* I thought. *Here, let me do it,* but being on the plane made me selfish: the last thing I wanted was to talk, and even if the old man had been Jewish, I wouldn't have wanted to talk to him. What was there to talk about? Besides, my hands were shaking too, and I knew he knew it, because after we were on our way and the pilot announced we were being diverted to Athens, the old Arab man patted my shoulder as if I were the one who needed help. Luckily, this was something I had practiced for too and I shrugged him off like a pro. So maybe we could have gotten along, become best friends even. So what?

This was why I couldn't understand what was going on with Sid and Larry. There were maybe thirty million different kinds of Jews in Israel, and sure, everyone could tell where your parents were from just by sizing up your cheekbones and skin tone, but you could do a lot worse than being born Iraqi. At least Iraqis were known for being good with numbers and skilled merchants, and not for being thieves and wife beaters like Moroccans, or for wasting their lives away playing backgammon and chewing khat like Yemenites. And even if some parents still didn't like their daughters dating Sephardic Jews, these days Russians married Ethiopians all the time without making the evening news. There was no point in debating whether Arabs could be Jewish or not. They weren't because they didn't want to be, and that was all there was to it.

I excused myself to go to the bathroom, which was labeled Dudes and had a picture of a cowboy hat on the door. I washed my hands, and my face, and my hands again, and thought about the dog back at Sid's. Maybe she was happier there, lounging in front of a fireplace, surrounded by Aryans, whom I was beginning to suspect she preferred. It was probably only a matter of time before she turned on me too, most likely in the middle of the night, when I'd be too busy snoring to notice.

The door swung open, and Sid walked in, so I switched off the faucet and reached for a paper towel.

"Listen," Sid said, "I can't move to Israel. I'm not even considering it."

I shrugged. "I don't care where you live."

"I go to synagogue twice a year."

"That's more than me."

"I married a shiksa."

"It happens," I said. "But you really shouldn't call her that."

"You can't help who you love."

"Yes," I said, "you can."

Sid put his hands in his pockets, then took them back out, as if he didn't know what to do with them. "That's what Larry says too," he admitted. "But too late now."

"I suppose."

"How am I going to live in a Jewish country with a Christian wife?"

We were both silent for a moment, eyeing each other through the bathroom mirror, Sid looking all hopeful as if I were somehow closer to God and could explain his special circumstances to Him. Really, if I'd let it, it could've been a heartwarming moment, but all that potential for sentimentality made me jealous: where was my own own personal absolver of sins? But then I thought, *Why not?* What did I care? If I didn't say it, he'd eventually find someone else who would. I shrugged and turned to face him. "Israel's not right for everyone," I said, not sounding a bit like I was reciting. "The economy's bad and it's dangerous, with the terrorism and the car accidents. Your daughters are safer here—even Larry knows that. Family comes first in Judaism. And even Israelis sometimes leave Israel. Look at me."

Sid sighed and smiled a big, dimpled, tooth-baring smile. "Thanks," he said. "Thanks, Noam. I mean, that's what I figured, but it's good to hear it from someone who really knows. I try not to pay attention to Larry—he means well, but sometimes it gets a little overwhelming, between him and Christmas and being the only Jew."

"I can imagine," I said. "You have to live where the jobs are."

"Yes!" Sid looked relieved. "Exactly! I knew you'd understand."

Back at our table, Larry had ordered another round of beers. He offered us each a bottle and said, "Peace?" and now that we were best friends, Sid and I said "Peace" back. It was late and most of the other tables were empty. Two of the waiters were sitting in a booth near the kitchen, rolling silverware up in napkins, and another waiter was getting out a broom.

"Ah," Larry sighed. "That's good stuff." He raised his bottle in the air. "To Noam!" and Sid echoed, "To Noam!" and added, "What Israel needs is more brave men like you!" I was sure he was joking, but when I looked at him, his face was so earnest and open that, for a second, I was afraid he was going to stand up and start singing "Hatikvah" or some old pioneer song about building and being built in the land of Israel.

"Oh no," I said. "Not men like me."

"Exactly men like you," Sid insisted. "Don't be shy. Larry can tell you how every time we hear the news, I tell him that what Israel needs is some reasonable men—"

"Like you too, Sid," Larry interrupted.

But Sid ignored him and continued. "—who won't lose their heads every time children throw stones. That's the thing that's killing Israel, you know, shooting those children."

"That's right," Larry said. "If they'd stop shooting children, the rest of the world would shut up about a Palestinian state. I mean, everybody was behind you, you know, until you started shooting children."

Even when I got a chance to think about it later, I couldn't come up with one single response. Not that a response would have made a difference anyway. Clearly, clearly, no one had ever thrown rocks at Sid and Larry, or at least not very many. At the time, though, I was too busy worrying about the ringing in my ears. It was all I could do to push my chair back from the table and stumble toward the door so that I didn't collapse and start flopping right there, in the middle of the floor. The last thing I needed to think about was children with rocks, especially after going through Athens to get away from them.

By the time I got back to Sid's place, the girls were in pajamas and the dog was under a blanket, and they were reading her stories and patting her head. But that wasn't my problem. I called the dog, and the good thing about her was that, secret racist or not, she could always tell when I was serious. I could hear the littlest girl wailing all the way to the end of the block, but I didn't care. You just couldn't afford to get upset over every little thing.

I checked the dog and me into the Happy Trails motel a couple of kilometers outside of town. It was nothing special, but there were three hundred channels on TV, and flipping through them gave me something to do. I knew I had to leave town, but there was no place else I wanted to go, and that was maybe the first time that ever happened. I mean, *this* was the place I had always wanted to go whenever I dreamed of leaving the place where I was, which had always been Israel. Suddenly, I was afraid that meeting Sid and Larry was yet another in a series of signs that God was trying to tell me something, and that if I hadn't stopped going to synagogue after my Bar Mitzvah, I would have known how to interpret the clues. Even so, I was beginning to suspect that what God really wanted was for me to go back to Israel. Just the thought made me want to cry, and that was before even considering the flight. I wanted to talk to somebody, but I couldn't think of anybody to call. In Israel, it was 4 a.m. and everyone was asleep. My father was probably over at his girlfriend's. Not that it mattered. He probably would have just asked if this was about my mother, which was what the grief-management counselor said you were supposed to ask your kids, no matter how old they were, and which really, it wasn't.

By this time, the dog was curled up on the bed snoring, and I could hear the crickets and owls going at it outside. Then, on TV, as if God couldn't leave me alone, they started showing pictures of an old Air France plane with propellers, and of a white terminal in the middle of nowhere, and it all seemed so familiar that I turned up the volume. It was a documentary about Entebbe, of all things, as if being diverted through Athens weren't enough, and now I actually had to watch a documentary about a plane that had been hijacked from there to really get the full picture. The coincidence made me want to crawl right under the bed, but instead I sat there watching and wondering whether I could get back to Israel by ship, and if ships allowed dogs. On-screen, the former hostages took turns describing how they had tried not to think too much about the fact that everyone who wasn't Jewish or Israeli had been sent home, when something one of the men was saying really made me stop and listen. The man was a relative of one of the people who'd been taken hostage, or maybe he'd been a hostage himself—the caption flashed by too quickly for me to read. But what this man was saying was that for years, for years after the hijacking, all that the former hostage—his relative—had tried to do was figure out what the hijacking meant. Surely something that big didn't happen to you just so you could go on living your life and worrying about bills and buying groceries and changing the oil in your car. There had to be something greater at work, a big lesson or moral, some kind of new understanding or enlightenment, or else what was the point? It was something the former hostage struggled with to this day. But the thing was, the man said, there was no hidden meaning. These things just happened. And if you had the bad luck to be on the plane at the time, and these things happened to you, then they still didn't mean anything. There was no lesson. There was no enlightenment. These things happened, and if you survived them, you had no choice but to go on living your life, knowing no more and no less than the rest of us.

I turned off the TV and lay in bed, trying to match my breathing to the dog's. I could hear someone running water in another room, but except for that, there was nothing: just the crickets and the owls and the air going in and out of the dog's lungs, and in and out of my own. I could feel my body pressing down on the sheets, and the sheets down on the mattress, and the mattress on the bed frame, and the frame on the floor, and the floor on the pipes, and the pipes on the earth, which was pushing back against all that weight so that nothing collapsed or went flying. People died every day from boarding planes and riding buses, and sometimes they were your relatives and sometimes they weren't, and sometimes they were your mother and sometimes they weren't, and there was nothing you could do about it except miss them and hope it didn't happen again. And there was nothing to do after it happened except put one foot in front of the other and keep moving. Because you had to go somewhere, and that somewhere was forward, and there was no choice about that part. No choice at all.

Thanksgiving

The night after the Israeli Prime Minister was shot, Osnat dreamt one of the Chrises was shaving his legs in her mother's shower. She couldn't tell which Chris it was. She was on her seventh, but he hadn't wanted to come with her to visit her parents that weekend, and anyway, he was blond, and the Chris in the dream was standing in a puddle of black hairs, his skinny legs striped white with shaving lotion. He was using Osnat's mother's pink razor.

"What are you doing?" Osnat asked.

"It's because of the war," the Chris said, "so I won't get caught in the weeds."

"What war?" asked Osnat. "Is there a war?"

The Prime Minister was shot on a college-football Saturday. It was an important game. Osnat's father had just bought a big-screen TV, and here was reason to use it. He split the screen in two and watched the game on one half, CNN on the other. The offense set up in shotgun formation, sweating in the afternoon sun, while in Tel Aviv's nighttime darkness, people covered their mouths in disbelief.

"Should we tell Mom?" Osnat asked.

"Not yet," her father said. "Maybe at halftime."

The TV room was in the basement, and Osnat could hear her

mother's footsteps in the kitchen above her, where she was making soup. She imagined going upstairs and breaking the news to her—she could feel the words rolling around in her mouth. It was what always happened when she found out about disasters—the space shuttle, the Gulf War—as if it wasn't *really* a tragedy until someone you knew started weeping. It was disgusting. Even though the Prime Minister didn't die until well into the fourth quarter, already she could hear herself telling the current Chris all about it: "It was hard. My mother was devastated. She cried all night."

"Well," Osnat's father said when the game was over. "That's that."

On TV, CNN was looping its broadcast and replaying the Israeli government's press conference at regular intervals. Every time the official announced the Prime Minister's death, the people in the room with him cried, "No!" as if it were news. It took Osnat's father—up in the kitchen—maybe two and a half loops to tell her mother what had happened, and then they both came downstairs and sat on the sofa, Osnat's mother clutching Osnat's father and crying into his shoulder. Her father kept saying, "Shhh . . . Shhh . . ." Osnat sat in the rocking chair and watched them. She watched her mother wipe her nose against her father's shirt. She watched her father blink. She watched them both carefully, as if watching a filmstrip on the etiquette of grief. Her mother *was* devastated. She *did* cry all night. But although Osnat checked and checked, and kept on checking, as far as she could tell, she—Osnat—didn't feel anything at all.

Back in the Chicago suburb where Osnat had lived ever since she'd graduated from college—because you had to live in a city after college, or at least close by, and Chicago was cheaper than New York, and the suburbs cheaper than downtown—the seventh Chris was as hairy and blond as ever. Usually, Osnat had a hard time saying no to sex with any of the Chrises, which made things awkward with her colleagues, who were older and married, and liked to set Osnat up with friends of friends of friends and then wink at her knowingly in the break room the next day. Luckily, though, Osnat had met this Chris on her own—he lived in her apartment complex—and he was so short and skinny that early on she'd told him that she didn't believe in sex without love. She thought it was a good line, that it had integrity.

Still, this Chris was unfazed. "In the end you'll love me," he'd said. He knew he was seventh, and thought this meant he was the lucky one. That Monday—the Monday after the assassination—Osnat wasn't home five minutes before he called. She knew it was him even though she didn't answer the phone and he didn't leave a message.

Osnat's mother was sure Osnat was dating this Chris on purpose, just like she was sure that Osnat was living in Chicago's southwest suburbs instead of the northern ones—the ones with the Jews—on purpose, never mind that the company Osnat worked for writing HR brochures had its offices in Hinsdale instead of downtown. Not that it ultimately mattered where Osnat lived: blind dates or no, Chrises were much easier to find than Jews in any given suburb, and as an added bonus, they thought she was exotic. Plus, this way, she never had to worry about getting their names mixed up, which was a good thing, since already some of them were beginning to blur—which Chris was it who gave her the necklace, and did he give her a teddy bear as well? That was the other nice thing about the Chrises. They all came bearing gifts.

For a while, before the Prime Minister was assassinated, it had looked as if peace were breaking out. Every time you turned to

CNN, there he was: signing treaties, making speeches, shaking hands with the Chairman. Or there he was: sitting under a tree holding binoculars, watching the King of Jordan fly over Jerusalem and talking to him on the phone, saying, "I can see you. I can see you."

Each time, Osnat's mother called her to remind her to watch, then called her again after to make sure she did. "Did you see them?" she'd ask, her voice breaking. "Did you see them touch?"

"They didn't *touch,*" Osnat said. "They shook hands."

"Well," Osnat's mother said, "you have to start somewhere."

Osnat looked at the wall. She looked at her hands. She couldn't imagine it—peace—or what it meant. She hadn't been to Israel in years, not since she'd been old enough to choose not to go. Still, she knew her mother was right. All the Chrises started out with handshakes too. And once you touched them, it was hard to back out.

The Prime Minister wasn't the only one with binoculars—Osnat had a pair too. When she used them, she turned off the lights in her apartment so that her neighbors—if they happened to look out—wouldn't be able to tell she was monitoring their movements. To be extra careful, she kept the blinds closed and watched them through a gap in the slats.

She had forgotten all about the binoculars until she'd started dating this Chris. The telescope in his hall closet was what reminded her. Sure, he had taped a star chart above his bed, and there was a solar system mobile in his bathroom, but Osnat knew this was just a way to make it *appear* that he had a genuine interest in astronomy. Truth was, people didn't watch stars. They watched each other.

It turned out that when he was alone, what this Chris did was spend his evenings shifting furniture around and hanging up different holiday decorations. For Halloween, he had dressed up his couch as a ghost and the recliner as a jack-o'-lantern. He had strung chains of candy corn across the room and then hosted a party in which his guests raced each other to see who could chew his way to the kitchen first. Now he was redoing his apartment for Thanksgiving: already he had made a tail out of a bouquet of dusters for the recliner and was hard at work glue-gunning feathers to the armrests. Osnat imagined that he had a turkey defrosting in the bathtub. Osnat's family didn't celebrate Thanksgiving. They didn't even like turkey, and anyway, it felt silly, going through all that fuss for three people. She picked up the phone and dialed, then watched Chris drop the glue gun, startled.

"I'm back," she told him. "It was hard. My mother was devastated. She cried all night."

She waited for Chris to extend his condolences, but all he said was, "What? Why?"

"You know," Osnat said. "The assassination? In Israel?"

"Oh yeah," Chris said. "I heard about that."

He nestled the phone between his neck and shoulder, and picked up the glue gun and a handful of feathers. It was outrageous, the way people thought you wouldn't be able to tell they weren't paying attention.

"Hey," Osnat said, "stop that. This is serious."

"Stop what?"

"Doing something else while you're talking to me."

"Sorry," Chris said. He repositioned the phone so that Osnat could hear him breathing, but he didn't put down the glue gun. "I'm all yours."

"Put down the gun," Osnat said in her best TV cop voice.

"I knew it," Chris said. "You're spying on me." He stood up and walked over to his living-room window. "You're using your binoculars."

Even though it was impossible, magnified by the binoculars Chris seemed to be looking right at her. Osnat hung up, but he didn't look away. Instead he raised his right hand as if he was about to take a pledge, not really waving, not really signaling her to stop.

But the Prime Minister was still dead. On NPR, commentators went over his achievements: peace, peace, and more peace. Now it was unclear whether all that peace would continue. Of course Osnat wanted peace—didn't she have five million relatives in Israel, all of them riding buses and shopping in malls? And weren't there new McDonald's branches popping up everywhere, and a Dunkin' Donuts right there, in downtown Tel Aviv? That, at least, was what Osnat's aunt had reported when she had come to visit that summer. "A regular America," she'd said, with plenty of American companies to work for, all looking for employees with "English mother tongue," some of them even offering their workers dishwashers—dishwashers!—and portable stereos as gifts for Passover.

Osnat had been twelve when her family left Israel. By then, she was old enough to know that what they were doing was wrong. So what if there were no wars and better jobs somewhere else? You couldn't leave the living and dying to other people. You had to do some of it yourself. To make matters worse, Osnat kept getting hung up on what she knew were small, senseless matters, like the giant roaches that crawled all over Tel Aviv's sidewalks at night. Sometimes they flew indoors, their wings noisy like small helicopters, and settled down on various windowsills and lamp shades where they waited patiently to scare you, one even hiding inside Osnat's shoe, where she didn't find it until it wriggled under her bare toes. Now, whenever Osnat went back for a visit, she moved her bed away from the wall: maybe that way they would leave her alone. One time, on the El, an Israeli student from Northwestern asked her why she didn't go back—"You're old enough now," he'd said—and Osnat had told him the truth. "My God," he'd said, repulsed. "There are roaches everywhere." At the next stop he'd moved over to sit by someone else. Not that it mattered—Israelis were never interested in Osnat, and she couldn't blame them. Nobody wanted to date a coward.

It was still early, there was nothing on TV, and—even though she was sure he would—Chris still hadn't called her back, as if she weren't the same woman that, just last week, he'd lain on top of while his couch watched them with its ghostly, glue-gunned, Halloween eyes. If she lay flat, arms and legs straight out, he could fit inside her as if she were his chalk outline at a murder scene: her body a little too wide at the torso, her arms and legs a little too long. It made her feel large and gelatinous, and glad that she was nowhere near falling in love. Still, Chris hadn't seemed to notice: "Why won't you sleep with me?" he'd said. "I have condoms, so why won't you sleep with me?"

Outside, the streetlights were just coming on. For a while, Osnat drove up and down Ogden Avenue. It was an ugly street, all strip malls and apartment complexes, and the only people around were the ones in the cars driving nearby. Osnat turned off onto a side street and followed it as it became narrower, the houses larger. Pretty soon, she was lost in a neighborhood where the garages were so large you could stack them two or three deep with cars. She heard an engine, and after a few seconds, realized it was an airplane, but instead of moving away, it kept getting closer. She tried to see where it was coming from but she couldn't. It seemed to be flying right over her. It was going to crash. She knew it. That was what planes did. When she was in seventh grade, a small plane had crashed into a house near the elementary school in her neighborhood. It was trying to make an emergency landing in the playground, but then the bell rang and all the children came rushing out. The pilot had no choice but to ram the plane into a nearby house. He died. There were body parts everywhere, but Osnat's mother wouldn't let her go with the other children to watch the police clean up. Now it was all catching up with her. She would have to pick up detached limbs and then find ice to keep them fresh. Osnat stopped the car, leaned forward, and covered her head with her arms, waiting for the explosion. There was none. The plane's engine got weaker, slowed down, and then stopped. Someone was honking. Osnat looked up and saw that she was blocking an intersection. On the corner, a yellow sign warned, "Danger. Low-flying Aircraft." On the left, she saw a grass runway, lined with blue lights, and a man climbing out of a small red plane. The big garages, it turned out, were plane hangars. The car behind her honked again. She thought maybe she would cry right then, but she didn't. Her hands weren't even shaking.

The last time Osnat had been to Israel, she'd been sixteen and tired. The first Chris had just broken up with her—mere days after presenting her with a chocolate bunny for Easter—because a senior girl had asked him to the prom. He wasn't anything special, but dating him had pissed off Osnat's parents, and right then (and for a long time afterward), that was exactly what she had wanted to do. It wasn't so much that Osnat's parents were upset that the Chrises weren't Jewish; they were upset at their failure to imagine the logical conclusion of uprooting your child and moving her to a country where being Jewish translated into sometimes missing school and refusing to participate in the annual Christmas pageant. "You lived in Israel?" the other Jewish kids asked her when they found out. "Weren't you *scared?*" Not that kids Osnat saw when she visited Israel were any better: "Have you met Michael Jackson? Who shot J.R.? Why are you so pale?"

Still, her parents hadn't been entirely wrong. Whenever Osnat got tired of a Chris, all she had to say was "I want my children to be Jewish" to send him scurrying for cover. If he argued—"You're the least religious person I know"—she'd pull out the ace: "So were all those Jews in 1939 Germany." The Chris she dated in college had been skeptical—"Come on, that was *ages* ago"—but most of the Chrises didn't put up a fight.

In retrospect, Osnat's parents signing her up for a tour that promised inner-tubing down the Jordan River and hiking in the desert with boys who had names like David, Brett, or Jonah—and certainly not names like Chris—seemed sweetly naïve and optimistic. It took Osnat maybe three days to realize that she hated every single person in her group, and that they hated her back: when they went on shoplifting expeditions or took turns making out with soldiers in exchange for their uniforms, they didn't invite her along. Instead, Osnat spent her time talking with the different tour guides, skinny guys in their early twenties who were nice enough but always ended up asking her when she was moving back: "You'll be eighteen soon. You can do what you want." They always did this at dramatic moments: as they watched the sun rise over a misty Dead Sea, or as the Wailing Wall first came into view with its throngs of swaying men in black. It was hard to resist, and sometimes Osnat tried to imagine it, coming back, but the heat made her crazy, and so did the smell of urine that seemed to be everywhere. And so did the roaches. And so did the plain truth that even though it had only been four years since she moved to America, she still had maybe only two friends—both of them from other countries as well. And now this trip too was a failure. The bottom line, Osnat realized, was that she was afraid that if she moved to Israel, she'd discover that really, the problem wasn't the place she'd been taken without being asked, but that the problem was her—there was something wrong with her.

If you thought about all of it long enough, it was hard not to feel sorry for yourself. Here was the Prime Minister, dead, and even though it really had nothing to do with Osnat, it still felt as if it did. She was too old for the army now, but she was single and doing nothing special with her life. Her aunt was right. There was no reason she needed to be in the United States. If she had been in Israel, she probably would have been at the peace rally where the Prime Minister was shot. She might even have heard the gun go off. Either way, she would have been doing something more important than watching football and not even bothering to turn off the game because that's exactly how unaffected she was.

After she found her way back to Ogden, Osnat still didn't want to go home. Instead, she pulled into one of the strip malls. There was a Jewel-Osco, a dry cleaner, and—on the very end—a small Middle Eastern restaurant called Ali Baba's. Suddenly, Osnat was starving.

Inside, there were palm trees painted on the walls. There were wood camels with embroidered saddles and brass *nargilas* lined up on black shelves. In one corner, a television was tuned to *Roseanne.* The place was empty except for a man with a black mustache who stood behind the cash register and arranged coins into little piles. He waved to Osnat.

"Sit anywhere," he said. Then he called out, "Noam!"

Osnat chose a table near the television. It was the episode of *Roseanne* where Darlene gets her period. Roseanne was explaining to Darlene that the news wasn't all bad, and that three good things had come from Roseanne getting her own period: Becky, D.J., and Darlene, her children. For a minute, Osnat felt weepy, but then she concentrated on unwrapping her silverware and she was fine again.

Then Noam came out of what must have been the kitchen. She recognized him immediately. She always recognized Israelis. Every hair on her body pointed in his direction. He was tall and thin and tan, with a crew cut and a halfhearted attempt at a goatee.

"Yes," he said. "What do you want?"

She couldn't look at him directly. She stared at the menu he handed her, but the humming she was convinced his body was making kept distracting her. She couldn't make out the letters.

"I don't know," she said.

"Chicken *tawook,*" Noam told her. "And some tabouleh." He didn't wait to see if she agreed. "Ahmed," he said to the man next to the cash register, "*tawook* and tabouleh." Ahmed nodded. "Ahmed's the cook," Noam told Osnat. "I'm just the help."

Ahmed stopped counting the change and disappeared into the kitchen. On television, Darlene decided not to throw out her baseball glove after all.

"Touching, eh?" said Noam.

He looked at Osnat, and Osnat looked away. He switched channels and sat down at the table next to hers. On TV, a little boat was making its way down a river. Everything was silent, and then there was fire from both banks. The screen was white with smoke. When it cleared, one of the GIs on the boat was dead. Another couldn't find his dog. Some of the GIs were crying, and Noam was saying something under his breath that Osnat couldn't make out. He had pushed up his T-shirt and was rubbing his belly. There were scars on his stomach. They were like firebreaks across the curly black hair. They were still a little red. Osnat looked and looked and kept on looking.

When she was done, she said, "You'll only catch fire in sections," and Noam, startled, pulled down his shirt and said, "I guess I already did."

Osnat thought about telling Noam that she was from Israel—it had been a while since she'd thought of herself as Israeli—but she didn't know how to bring it up. Real Israelis always started talking to each other in Hebrew. Osnat had already lost her *r*s and her *l*s, and anyway, how would she introduce herself? To the Israelis she met, it seemed, there was nothing interesting about another ex-Israeli. American Jews didn't know any better, but ex-Israelis had deliberately left Israel and chosen not to return. Plus, most American Jews thought Israelis were brave, that they risked their lives every moment of every single day. Wasn't that what happened in wartime?

Still, time was running out. Who knew how long it would take Ahmed to make the chicken? Osnat wiped her hands on her skirt. She wanted Noam to see beyond her pasty skin, but she didn't know how to make him look at her. She cleared her throat and opened her mouth, and waited for the words to come to her. When they did, they weren't what she expected: "Can I touch them?"

"What?" said Noam. He turned to look at her, and she realized one of his eyes was brown, the other green.

"Can I touch your scars?"

Noam shrugged.

"Will it hurt?" Osnat asked. "I won't do it if it'll hurt."

"No," Noam said. "They're pretty much healed."

Osnat scooted her chair closer to him. She reached out with her right hand, but she didn't know what to do next. Was he waiting for her to lift up his shirt?

"Here," Noam said.

He took her hand in his and—in one smooth motion—tucked

it under his T-shirt and against his belly. His scars, when she touched them, were warm and dry. They felt like plastic. Noam shifted in his seat, and Osnat saw that he was hard. She cleared her throat again. "You want to go somewhere?"

They didn't even wait for her food. Noam followed Osnat out to her car. "Can we go to your place?" she asked. Noam shook his head no. She didn't know where to go instead. She didn't want Chris to see them. Finally she drove around behind the Jewel-Osco—Noam's hand clammy on her thigh—and parked in the dark corner of the parking lot. They didn't bother with kissing. Noam unbuttoned Osnat's blouse, and she pulled up his T-shirt and traced his scars with her index finger.

"Can you tell when it's scar and when it's not?" she asked.

Noam didn't answer. He adjusted the seat back and pulled her on top of him. He rolled up the skirt she was wearing and undid his pants. Osnat watched him kiss her breasts. His eyes were closed, and he was pumping away, and there she was, on top of him, parked behind a supermarket. It didn't seem real. Even his grunts, his hot breath on her skin seemed fake.

"Ken," said Noam. *"Ken."* He thrust one last time, and then he stopped moving. Osnat could feel him pulsing inside her.

"Shhh," she said. *"Ze beseder."*

Noam opened his eyes. "What?" he said. "What did you say?" When she didn't answer, he asked, "Are you Jewish?"

"Israeli," she said.

"Oh," said Noam. "A *yoredet.*"

There was no point pretending. Noam had called her the thing she was: a person who had left a higher plane of existence for a lower one. You were worthless if you didn't go back. She pulled away and moved over to the driver's seat.

"What?" Noam said.

Back when she was sixteen and spending the summer in Israel, the tour guide had taken them to Ben Yehuda Street in Jerusalem. When Osnat stopped to look at some earrings, the vendor, a dark man with smooth cheeks, had said to her in Hebrew, "You like them?" Next thing she knew, she was telling him how much she hated the tour. The other girls were standing right beside her, and they didn't understand a word. The vendor listened and rubbed alcohol onto her earlobes. Right before piercing them, he said, "I can sense things about you. You aren't like other girls." Back then, she had thought this was a good thing, that she was somehow special. But three nights later, when they'd returned, the vendor didn't remember her, and anyway, he'd been wrong: she was just like all those other Israelis in limbo who refused to admit they were in the U.S. to stay. Even Osnat's parents, when asked, still mumbled something about retiring to Tel Aviv.

And now, sitting in her car with Noam beside her, the Prime Minister dead, and all that peace about to end, the one thing Osnat wanted was for Noam to absolve her. She'd had sex with him—wasn't that worth something? Hadn't she done her part for Israel, however indirectly, by lifting the spirits of a battle-scarred soldier? He'd given his body, and now she'd given hers. It was so noble that for a brief moment, Osnat could almost imagine it as her life's work: fucking soldiers. She would meet them at the airport as they deplaned and take them straight to bed. They would go back to Israel and tell their friends about her, and knowing she was out there, waiting for them, would give them hope. And it would give her a reason to stay.

"I'm sorry," she said, but Noam misunderstood her. *"Shtuyot,"* he said. Nonsense. "These things happen."

She dropped him off at Ali Baba's, and even though he didn't ask for her number, he did ask if she still wanted her food. She didn't. She wanted to go home. Her thighs, under her skirt, were wet and sticky, and she was dripping. She was afraid she would never get the smell out of her car. She rolled down all four windows. It was cold out—November—but the wind felt good, like a slap.

Back at her apartment complex, she pulled the car into her parking spot and looked up at Chris's living room window. It was dark. Still, she went over there and knocked on his door. He'd glued a picture of a turkey onto his knocker. If he saw her, surely he wouldn't want her to love him, not the way she was, smelling of another man, in a skirt stained and wrinkled by someone else. She felt as if she were watching a movie of her own life. What did she have in common with this woman standing in front of Chris's door? What control did she have over this woman's actions? This woman would go in or she wouldn't. Chris would get angry or he wouldn't. And Osnat would watch the two of them. She would watch and watch, and feel nothing at all.

But then Chris, in striped pajama bottoms and a black T-shirt, threw the door open and pulled Osnat inside. The air was downy with duster feathers, but the recliner turkey was finished, complete with a red wattle made from a rubber glove. It was ridiculous. Osnat stood in front of it and scowled.

"Don't start," Chris said. "People who live in glass houses . . ." Osnat didn't say anything, so he added, "You look like you haven't bathed in days." He led her to the bathroom, handed her a towel, and pointed at his robe. "Put that on, and then we'll talk." When Osnat didn't move, he began to undress her. He unbuttoned her shirt and pulled it off one sleeve at a time. He stood behind her and unhooked her bra. He knelt in front of her and pulled her skirt down and then her damp panties. Osnat held her breath—surely he'd recoil in disgust—but he remained quiet, efficient, businesslike. He turned on the water and adjusted the temperature. Then he nudged Osnat into the tub. She watched his pale hands on her skin. He had long, slender fingers, and the hair on his knuckles was curly and thick. She stood under the shower and waited. Chris waited too.

"You'll have to do the rest yourself," he said finally. He reached for her right hand and put a bar of soap in it. It was a brand-new bar. It smelled like lavender.

"It doesn't make a difference," Osnat said. "I still won't have sex with you."

Chris looked at her. "Fine then," he said. "Don't." He turned to go.

"Wait," Osnat said. "What if I don't ever feel anything ever again?"

"Osnat, Jesus," Chris said, before closing the door behind him. "All you're feeling is nothing but sorry for yourself."

When she was done showering, Osnat found Chris in the kitchen, making spaghetti sauce out of ketchup.

"I'm making some special Secret Love Sauce," he said. "You'll fall for me now, for sure."

He chopped onions, fried them, and stirred in the Heinz. One by one, he removed small jars from the large spice rack on the wall and unscrewed the caps. Gently, he sniffed out what the sauce needed: cinnamon yes, garlic no, dill yes, oregano yes.

"My mother's from Uruguay, you know," he told Osnat between sniffs. "She's three times your age, and I can tell you from watching her—this is just how things are. There is no right place, except inside your body. You're not the only one who feels this way."

"But you're blond," Osnat said, surprised.

Chris shrugged. "Sometimes that happens too."

When it was ready, they ate the spaghetti in front of the TV.

They sat in Chris's dark living room, on the couch that was on its way to looking like a corncob, and watched the *Late Late Show.* The host kept smiling at the camera as if there were only good news in the world. Osnat didn't even like ketchup, but the cinnamon, it turned out, was key. It wasn't exactly the thing she was looking for, but right then, at that moment, it was close enough. She finished her plate.

Ask for a Convertible

The psychic on Walnut in Hinsdale, Madame Rita, was having a sale: palm readings for only ten dollars. She lived in a small white house, with green shutters and a red neon sign that boasted 97 percent accuracy.

"Now that's what I like in a psychic," Chris said. "Honesty."

It was maybe nine thirty at night on a Thursday, and they had nothing better to do, so they stopped. Anyway, they'd been dating for more than a year, and Osnat figured it was time to get an outside opinion.

"What for?" Chris said. "You know we're getting married just as soon as you say yes."

Even though they could make out the sound of a television underneath all the humming neon, the house seemed strangely still. The door was cracked open, and through it, they could see a woman lying on a couch, her mouth lax with sleep. She was wearing blue jeans and white sneakers, and had greasy, thin brown hair. She looked like someone you'd expect to find scanning groceries at Jewel-Osco, or driving her children to soccer practice, not like someone you'd expect to have otherworldly connections.

"Should we knock?" Chris asked.

"I don't know," Osnat said. "She looks so tired." After they'd tiptoed back to the car, she added, "Strange that she didn't know we were coming."

"Ha ha," Chris said.

Still, Osnat was surprised to discover she felt disappointed. She wondered if this was some sort of sign, a psychic who didn't pick you up on her radar. No wonder all the black cats in the neighborhood insisted on crossing the street when they saw Osnat coming.

"Give me a break," Chris said. "The Dumpsters are on that side of the road."

"Fine," Osnat said. "Fine, I'll marry you." She'd been practicing saying it for weeks, and each time, the words came more easily. This time they felt so natural she was almost convinced herself.

Chris believed in making lists of pros and cons, and he made Osnat do them too. If she refused, he did them for her. Earlier that week, before she'd said yes, he'd made her a list detailing the pros and cons of marrying him:

Owns microwave	Sheds
Cooks	Nostril hair
Handy with a glue gun	Snores
Twice as many holidays	Snorts
Sexy as all hell	Sneezes in sunlight
Loves you	Keeps reupholstering the couch
You'll never wear heels again	Not very tall

"Which column is the pros?" Osnat had asked. But she knew he was telling the truth. He was sexy as all hell, for a midget, and he did love her, and he certainly did snore.

Now that it was official, she took down the list from her refrigerator and stowed it away in one of her desk drawers, next to the ring Chris had purchased for her on clearance at Wal-Mart so she could practice feeling engaged. It was December, and Chris was busy making gifts for his family back in Wisconsin. This year he was knitting his parents hooded brown sweaters, to which he planned to attach antlers he'd pieced together out of wire and plush black velvet so they could all go caroling as reindeer. He was a quick knitter, and there was something soothing about the plastic clacking of the needles, the way the sweaters grew from balls of yarn into panels and pockets and sleeves. Osnat's job was to sew on the buttons. This way, the sweaters could be from both of them. Somewhere in Wisconsin, she knew, there was a stocking waiting just for her, and—Chris assured her—someone had already snuck her name onto Santa's list. "It's the Jewish Girlfriend Exception Clause," he told her. Plus, Chris's mother was making turkey instead of ham. It was the least you could do when a Jew was coming over. "And we *love* ham," Chris said. "Mmmm . . . ham . . ."

"So have the ham," Osnat said. "I don't mind starving."

"Oh no," Chris said. "We're going to stuff you until you're fat, and then we're going to eat you up, gingerbread house and all."

Really, there was no reason to be nervous. Osnat knew how Christmas worked—she'd been watching TV all her life. You went to church, you opened presents, you ate sugar cookies shaped like bells and Christmas trees. If your family was dysfunctional, then you ended up fighting and slamming a door or two, but then someone—usually one of the younger children—brought home a homeless person, or at the very least a puppy, and this indirectly taught you all about the true meaning of Christmas. After that, if you happened to take a breather from all the hugging and kissing to glance outside, you'd see one star in the sky shining brighter than the rest, or maybe even shooting across the horizon. And you knew: God was up there, watching you, and surely wouldn't mind one bit if the next day you took back those ugly shoes and traded them for kick-ass boots.

Even if that wasn't quite right, Osnat figured it had to be better than the hunkering down her family usually did over the holidays. On December 20, they turned off the television and didn't turn it back on until the 26th. In the meantime, Osnat's father sorted through the year's receipts and calculated his income tax, and Osnat's mother rearranged the paintings on the walls. They were always finished by Christmas Eve and, after they took Osnat on a grand tour of the newly decorated living room, the three of them joined the rest of the town's Israelis who were too cool to go to the local synagogue for the annual Hanukkah bazaar and all-ages *Sound of Music* sing-along. Why would they? *They* were hardly so insecure that they needed to reaffirm their Judaism by eating lukewarm potato pancakes and singing along with a nun, of all people, even if she *was* being chased across the border by Nazis. Instead, they went to a Chinese buffet where they ate egg rolls and crab rangoon—Hanukkah *was* all about oily foods—and everyone complained about their married children who were off celebrating Christmas with their spouses' families: "You turn your back for just one moment, and the next thing you know, they're sucked right in." After that, they went to the movies with all the Asian university students who didn't have enough money to fly home over winter break, and watched stupid comedies in which successful but jaded businessmen woke up to discover that it still wasn't too late to lead a happy life. Pshaw. Christmas. The only thing good about it was the after-Christmas sales.

But even though she knew all of this, Osnat still kept having nightmares in which she knocked over fully decorated Christmas trees and stepped on Baby Jesus figurines, and ended up having sex with Chris's father because, really, it would have been rude to say no.

At work, when she was supposed to be copyediting a pamphlet

about appropriate health practices for flu season—"Don't spit in the water fountain" was one tip—Osnat made a list of the pros and cons of purposely contracting botulism (Pro: no Christmas in Wisconsin. Con: hospital not well staffed during holidays).

"Why are you making such a big deal out of this?" asked Jeannie, the technical writer who worked in the cube across from Osnat's, when she saw what Osnat was doing. "These days, Christmas is pretty much a secular holiday. You don't have to have sex with anyone, unless you want to."

"You're making fun," Osnat said. Jeannie was a new hire—she specialized in memos—and Osnat wasn't sure what to think of her. Her first day at work, she'd stood by the window and scowled at the view, which was pretty much all freeway and parking lot.

"The last place I worked looked out on Lake Michigan," she'd said. "One time I even saw a plane go down in it."

"No, you didn't," Osnat had said.

"It was a small plane," Jeannie had said. "Okay, it was a model plane. But small plane sounds more dramatic." Then she'd smiled at Osnat and said, "I always have candy in my top right-hand desk drawer."

Now Jeannie told Osnat, "I'm not making fun. It's just that sex with future in-laws shouldn't be taken lightly. The worst-case scenario," she continued, "is that you'll end up with a Christmas sweater with flashing lights. Anyway, no one leaves their Jesus figurines where you can step on them."

Jeannie *was* making fun. Osnat knew it. There was nothing secular about Christmas. If you took Jesus out of it, there would hardly be anything left to sing. Even Osnat's parents were nervous.

"When you go to church, remember to bring small bills for the collection," her father advised her. "They like to collect money in church. Oh, and don't wear a short skirt because there's all that standing up and kneeling."

Her mother was listening in on the extension. "It must be pretty serious," she said, "if you're going to church together. On Christmas."

"It is pretty serious," Osnat agreed. She was still practicing telling them she was engaged, but every time she tried saying it for real, her throat closed up.

"Well," her mother said, "he seems nice enough."

"That's because he *is* nice," Osnat said. "He's knitting his parents reindeer sweaters for when they go caroling."

"They go caroling?" her father asked.

"Huh," Osnat's mother said. "I thought that was just on TV."

Chris was maybe one of three people in his family who had actually left Wisconsin, and he'd only gone as far as Chicago. Once he was done with the reindeer sweaters, he whipped up some flash cards for Osnat so she'd be able to tell who was who. He had thirty million relatives and, even worse, they all turned out to be blonds, even Chris's mother, who was from Uruguay, and whom Osnat expected would somehow be easier to spot.

"Nope," Chris said. "She's even lost her accent."

"Not my mother," Osnat said.

"Your mother hasn't been here as long."

"It's not that," Osnat said. "She doesn't want to."

Chris shrugged.

"What?" Osnat said. "Admit you hate it. Admit you hate the way she keeps slipping into Hebrew even when you're around."

"Look," Chris said. "You're nervous about this trip, so I'm not going to fight with you. This isn't about your mother. My family's going to like you."

At work, Jeannie brought sugar cookies shaped like snowmen and Christmas trees to the break room. Later, after the staff meeting, she brought gingersnaps shaped like Stars of David and others shaped like dreidels to Osnat's cube.

"No one can say I'm not inclusive," she announced. "I made ones shaped like dragons for Maxine."

"But she's Japanese," Osnat said.

"In that case, I guess I offended her," Jeannie said. For a moment, she looked worried, but then she smiled. "Well," she said, "I just won't tell her I made them special."

Osnat laughed—she *did* like Jeannie, she decided—but then she looked at her cookies. The stars were frosted in yellow. All that was missing was the *Juden* in black lettering. She imagined pinning one onto her shirt. And this was Chicago, she thought. Who knew what could happen in Wisconsin, when she wasn't busy tripping over Jesus figurines or having sex with Chris's father? Maybe it would be like all those movies where the guy brings home a girl he handpicked expressly to piss his parents off. Her father, Osnat knew, had once pulled the same trick and brought home a Catholic woman, but he'd just wanted money for a convertible. He was nineteen, and this strategy had worked for two of his friends, he'd told Osnat. It didn't for him. His mother—Osnat's grandmother—had simply taken the girl's coat and fed her some brisket and some apple pie. "You're not mad?" Osnat's father had asked her afterward, and she'd said, "Do you think I'm blind? Or maybe you think I'm stupid?" Then she added, "My son, the pimp." This always made Osnat's father laugh. "And this is why you should never blackmail," he liked to say. "You want a convertible? Ask for a convertible." And when Osnat finally did, he told her to get a job like everyone else. "This is Michigan," he'd said. "You don't need a convertible."

On the way home, Osnat drove by Madame Rita's. The neon sign was on, but part of the seven was burnt out. Just like that,

Madame Rita was down to 91 percent accuracy. The star, the neon sign, they had to be an omen, but Osnat didn't know for what.

Swaddled in flannel, their faces blotchy from the cold, Chris's relatives looked nothing like the ones in the flash cards, and they all seemed to have dogs with names like Bo, Bob, Birdie, and Buford, who were busy chasing each other around the living room or trying to wriggle out of their own dog-sized sweaters.

"After a while, you just run out of gift ideas," Chris's mother explained. "So one Christmas, we all got dogs, and now presents are never a problem." She motioned Osnat to follow her into the bathroom, and showed her a small pile of rawhide chewies she was keeping on the upper shelf of the linen closet. "For their stockings," she said. "Dogs love Christmas too."

She was a small woman, maybe five feet tall, and Chris was right: there really was no way to tell she was from Uruguay if you didn't know to look for the dark roots on her head, and the fine, dark hairs on her arms, and even those revealed nothing if you really stopped to think about it.

Back in the kitchen, Chris's grandmother was busy peeling sweet potatoes over a trash can. She was rosy and large, and quick with a knife. When Chris introduced her, she leaned forward and wrapped her arms around Osnat, and Osnat could feel the knife's handle pressing into her spine. When Chris's grandmother let go, she said, "We're making turkey, you know. In addition to the ham." She smiled. "That's the great thing about Christmas: there are never too many main dishes." She hacked the tip off a sweet potato, and it shot out past Osnat and rolled behind the refrigerator.

"I think your grandmother's trying to off me," Osnat told Chris.

"You're probably right," he agreed. "Keep your back to the wall."

And she did. She leaned right up against it and watched Chris and one of his brothers slide the refrigerator out of its spot and retrieve the potato nub. It was startling how similar they looked from behind. They had the same stringy blond hair, the same side part, the same narrow back. It was easy to get confused.

"You know," Osnat said, "Chris, I think you need a haircut."

"More than one, probably," said Chris's brother. And Chris said, "Ha ha."

Outside, a Santa made of fairy lights was busy whipping his reindeer on the front lawn. Some of the reindeer were already in the air, but others were still on the ground, frozen midstride, the whip hovering only inches above their backs. Not that it mattered—even if they did achieve takeoff, it was obvious they had no chance of clearing the large evergreen on the edge of the property.

Between the dogs and the cousins, it was hard not to be jealous. Most of Osnat's relatives were in Israel—except for Osnat's father's mother, who lived in a nursing home in Miami and was convinced the attendants were trying to poison her, and some of her father's cousins, who lived in New York and thought Michigan was just a place you stopped to change planes. Family, Osnat soon learned, was all about location, not blood. If you lived somewhere interesting, like Los Angeles or Orlando, they came to visit. Otherwise, they didn't. And anyway, the New York cousins had maybe fifteen children between them, so there was no reason to go looking for more in Michigan. It was like economics: supply and demand. You had lots of children, you stayed put and waited, and thirty years later, there it was: voilà, a clan.

They slept in Chris's old room, squeezed together on his twin bed, glow-in-the-dark constellations fading on the ceiling above them. The air smelled faintly of dust and old sweat socks, and Osnat could hear Chris's grandmother snoring in the next room. Then Chris was asleep too, and no matter how hard she stared at him, he wouldn't wake up. He had to be faking. Gently, she pried one of his eyelids open and watched his pupil travel from right to left, unseeing. It was unfair. Weren't you supposed to have furtive, silent sex at your boyfriend's—your fiancé's—parents' house? Not that Osnat wanted to have sex, but she wanted Chris to want to, to be—at least for a little while—someone other than a son visiting home. What was this place, with dogs panting at every doorway, a grandmother who passed out dry bedtime pecks on the cheek, and a mother who spoke in perfect English and could play "O Come All Ye Faithful" on the piano without even glancing at the sheet music? The Hallmark commercials, apparently, *were* true. Norman Rockwell *wasn't* making things up. There were millions of Americans asleep all over the United States *at this very moment* who had spent the day decorating Christmas trees and baking cookies and building human pyramids, all of it without a drop of irony. They weren't hunkering down and waiting for Christmas to pass like some annual kidney stone. They were wishing Christmas would never end.

"Chris," Osnat said. "Chris." She shook him, but when he finally woke up, she didn't know what it was she could say: Please don't enjoy the holidays too much? I can't stand all the joy? Instead she clutched her stomach and said, "Too many sugar cookies."

"No problem," Chris said. "I'll get the Tums."

On the morning of Christmas Eve, Chris's mother sat in the kitchen and phoned her family back in Uruguay. She was louder in Spanish, and no matter how carefully Osnat listened, she couldn't tell where one word ended and the next began. Meanwhile,

Chris's grandmother held court in the living room, where she watched the daytime soap families exchange gifts, and—during the commercials—offered whatever grandchild happened to be nearest a nickel for a Christmas kiss.

"Save your money, Grandma, and buy some mistletoe," said a pimply fourteen-year-old boy. "This isn't the Great Depression." It was the same boy who earlier had fake-sneezed into his hand, and then held out his palm and said, shocked, "Oh snot!" Even though more than seven years had passed since high school, Osnat still didn't have a comeback. She felt exposed. "Congratulations!" she told him. "You're the first to ever come up with that one! Ever!" She hated teenagers. She was planning on sending her own children away preemptively the moment they turned twelve.

Chris's grandmother, it turned out, was much better at snappy retorts than Osnat. "Smarty-pants," she told the boy. "Maybe your kisses aren't worth more than that."

On TV, a dark-skinned Gypsy woman was warning one of the soap families that the upcoming year would bring discord and mayhem. "Now there's a news flash," Chris's grandmother said. "Look at her—that's not even the right way to read palms."

"Grandma reads the horoscopes," Chris explained. "That makes her an expert."

Chris's grandmother smiled. "Better safe than sorry," she said. "And the good news is that, according to *Good Housekeeping,* you two are going to be very happy together."

"Hear that?" Chris said to Osnat, squeezing her hand.

Chris's grandmother kept right on smiling, her smile stretching wider and wider until suddenly it looked as if her skull were trying to break out of her skin. She reached into her mouth and popped her teeth back into place. "Darn this bridge," she said. "It's always coming loose, like it's possessed or something."

And maybe it *was* possessed. Hadn't Osnat's own grandmother—

her mom's mom—gotten dentures only a short time before she died? And didn't she amuse the neighborhood children by popping them in and out of her mouth? Maybe now she was trying to communicate through Chris's grandmother's bridgework.

"I don't know," said Chris when Osnat proposed this idea to him. "I thought the undead communicated through cold breezes and slamming doors." Then he said, "You do realize you're being ridiculous, right?"

Osnat counted out the evidence on her fingers: Madame Rita's, the black cats, the *Juden* cookie, the teeth. There was no denying it was all adding up to something, and she wasn't even superstitious.

Back in the kitchen, Chris's mother was done with the phone and busy scooping heaping spoonfuls of Crisco out of the can and into a bowl. "For the stuffing," she told Osnat, rolling the *r* in *for.* Then she looked embarrassed. "Sorry," she said. "Sometimes I forget."

"I can't roll my *r*s at all," Osnat said.

"It's better that way," Chris's mother said. "It took me forever to lose my accent. It's bad enough that I still count in Spanish."

"My mom does that too," Osnat said, "only in Hebrew. And she still has an accent."

"Yes," Chris's mother said. "Chris told me." She turned her attention back to the Crisco. "Now I lost count," she said matter-of-factly. "You think that's seven or eight tablespoons?" When Osnat didn't know, Chris's mother shrugged and started ladling the shortening back into the can.

Later, Chris scrounged up a pair of clippers, and they shut themselves in the basement bathroom so that Osnat could give him a trim without worrying about Barry or Birdie jumping up on her lap.

"Maybe we'll go shorter," Osnat said. "Okay?"

The more time she spent with Chris's family, the less she felt she could tell everyone apart. They were like slightly distorted reflections of each other, their noses and mouths and eyes blurring together as if at some point, the original pattern had been copied so many times it had started to fade. There were so many of them, and they knew so much about each other, even the wives and husbands who were Nordic rather than German, with higher cheekbones and pinker skins—they all seemed to be participating in some unknown ritual, not Christmas itself, but what comes before it, the knowing without asking who was responsible for defrosting the turkey and who was supposed to watch and make sure the baby didn't get trampled by all those dogs.

Maybe that was why Osnat set the clippers to number 2—no one in the family had a buzz cut—and once she started, it was too late to go back. Even worse, the buzz cut only made everything more obvious: Chris's scalp shone pink through his stubble, his eyes seemed larger, and there was no doubt he was descended from Germans. All that was missing was a uniform and some shiny black boots. *"Sieg heil,"* Osnat said when she was finished. She saluted Chris, clicking her heels together. "Will the trains be running on time?" Of course it wasn't funny, but it felt good, as if they were done pretending she belonged. Chris's mother would see what she'd done and kick her out. It was hard enough to maintain your own disguise without a future daughter-in-law dressing up your son as a Nazi.

"My God," Chris said. "Who knew my hairline went so far back?" He rubbed his hand against his scalp, and it made a bristling noise. "I'll never hear the end of this."

And he didn't hear the end of it. Instead, cousin after cousin cracked jokes about cue balls, and although Chris's mother pursed her lips—Osnat was sure she did—his grandmother loved it and pulled out photographs of her husband, Chris's grandfather, from

1942, when he too had been nearly bald and fresh-faced, and glad for the chance to kick Nazi butt.

After lunch, they took the dogs for a walk, careful to keep them from urinating around Santa's sleigh and electrocuting themselves. Then Chris's father, instead of propositioning her, sat Osnat down and showed her home videos of Christmases past.

"If you're going to be part of the family," he said, "you have to pay the price, you know." He stood next to the TV and pointed out the important details. "Coming up is the time that Buford knocked over the eggnog. And here's the angel we used to put on top of the tree before my mother accidentally stepped on it." In the early videos, Chris's mother's hair was black, but then it started getting lighter—brown, then red, then strawberry blond—until finally it disappeared altogether, turning so white that the camera couldn't handle the glare.

"Oh yeah," Chris's father said. "That was the year of the tragic bleach incident." He chuckled and fast-forwarded to the next Christmas, when Chris's mother's hair was back, this time a honeyed yellow arranged in soft puffs around her neck. "That's the good thing about hair," Chris's father said. "It always grows back."

By sundown, there was no avoiding it. It was Christmas Eve, and tomorrow would be Christmas Day, and Osnat was in Wisconsin, with a bunch of Catholics who were getting ready to go to Mass and expected her to go with them.

"Your first Christmas!" Chris's grandmother exclaimed, clasping her hands together. "Yours and the baby's!" She was holding the baby in her lap, where it was busy drooling and gnawing on its hand, oblivious.

"The first of many," Chris's father said. He raised a cup of eggnog. "Welcome to the family!"

"Hear, hear," said Chris's mother. Around her neck, she was

wearing a small gold crucifix, and now it swung back and forth, as if in agreement.

"Maybe I shouldn't go," Osnat told Chris while they were getting their coats. She didn't know why she was so nervous. She'd been in churches plenty of times, but they'd been empty, and she'd been there only to look at the stained-glass windows and the murals.

"What's going on?" Chris said. "I thought you wanted to."

"I have a headache," Osnat said. When Chris looked skeptical, she added, "Maybe it's botulism." She waited for him to say something, but he just stood there, looking at her. "And I'm not supposed to bow down in front of other gods."

"I want you to go," Chris said. "It's important to me that you go."

"I know," Osnat said. "But I'm scared. And I have a headache. And I have botulism. You'll have a better time without me."

"I want you to go," Chris said again. "Go."

The church—St. Agnes—was a big one, and there was a line of cars just waiting to drop grandparents off on the steps so that they wouldn't have to walk across the icy parking lot in their fancy dress shoes. Chris's grandmother got out too, and the crowd immediately closed in around her until she disappeared in the throng of old ladies in red and green suits.

Osnat felt weepy, the way she often did at weddings and at the end of particularly melodramatic novels. Everyone seemed to be in such a good mood, hugging and kissing and shaking hands, marveling at how tall the children were getting. It was hard to resist all the excitement. The choir was singing in the balcony, and no matter where they turned, someone knew Chris, and he kept introducing her as his fiancée, his fiancée, and everyone kept saying, "Congratulations!" and "How lovely!" and shaking her hand as if they somehow thought she belonged there, in church, on Christmas, with Chris and his mother, who they probably thought was from Kenosha, because why would she be from anywhere else?

They pushed their way through the crowd only to be flagged down by Chris's grandmother, who was saving them seats toward the back. "Christmas Catholics," she whispered, nodding her head toward a family with four daughters sporting identical bowl haircuts and red velvet ribbons. "Those people hog our pew every year. It's because we're never on time."

"Come on, Ma," Chris's father said. "They haven't rung the bells yet."

"They're going to ring the bells?" Osnat asked Chris. It *was* just like *The Sound of Music.* There were even nuns sitting up front, near the altar. She braced herself for the tolling, expecting the pews to tremble and the chandeliers to shake, but when the bells finally rang, they sounded distant, muffled. She twisted the candle one of the ushers had given her between her hands. She was going to cry. She knew it. Either that, or she was going to pee, right there, in the pew, and everyone would be so shocked they'd pretend not to notice. Then the lights went off, and everyone grew silent, and Chris nudged her. "Relax," he whispered. By then, the priest was making his way up the aisle, carrying a large candle. When he reached the front of the church, he said something—Osnat couldn't make out what exactly—and lit the candles of the people on the ends of the front pews. It was like nothing Osnat had ever seen. The people with lit candles turned to those next to them, and lit their candles, and then those people turned to their neighbors and lit *their* candles. Men and women and children emerged from the shadow and into the light, their faces glowing. The flames made their hair shimmer and their eyes sparkle. There were, apparently, no ugly Catholics. Osnat felt her breath catch.

How was she supposed to resist this, this spreading light racing toward her? It would consume her, she knew, and there would be no going back, and here she was, stuck between Chris and his mother, the light like a snake wriggling toward her, and there was nothing she could do but take it, then pass it on. And if that weren't bad enough, the choir burst out in song, accompanied by organ and brass and tympani, and everything—the incense, the light, the music—was so much bigger than anything she'd imagined. She wanted to crawl under the pew, but she knew she wouldn't fit, and anyway, this thing, it was too large. There was no point in resisting: you could only stand back and hold your breath and wait for it to subside.

After Mass, they went home and watched the news. The weatherman kept interrupting to report on Santa's progress from the North Pole. Outside it was cloudy, but there was no reason to think Santa wouldn't be able to make all his deliveries. In Bethlehem, people were already gathering for morning prayers. Even though she'd never been to Bethlehem, just hearing it mentioned made Osnat homesick. She wanted to ask Chris's mom how she did it, but what was the point? His mom had made her choice years ago, and looking at her now, there was no easy telling who she was. With her blond hair and flat Midwestern English, she could have been just about anyone. And truth was, so could Osnat. The only thing different about her anymore was her name, and how many times had she thought about changing it to something less phlegmy? Every day in junior high, and every other day since. But she hadn't, because even though she was twenty-five, and a technical writer, and engaged to be married, who would she be without her name?

Later, after everyone was asleep—even the dogs—Osnat snuck downstairs and called her parents. It was well after midnight, and they were asleep, but she knew that she was overreacting, and that what she needed was for someone to tell her to stop. Sure, her mother hadn't married a Christian, but she'd married an American, and she'd had to leave her family, and maybe it wasn't always easy, but she'd managed, and now she was happy, or at least content, and she was still herself, wasn't she? But her mother, once she woke up and sorted out everything Osnat was trying to tell her, didn't say any of those things. Instead she said, "You always end up losing a part of yourself. You just have to choose which part."

Back in Chris's room, Chris was awake and waiting for her. "Are you all right?" he asked her. She climbed on top of him and kissed him, then kissed him harder. Somehow, she would have to get through opening presents the next morning, and through dinner—the turkey—the next afternoon. She pressed her full weight against Chris, feeling the way her arms and legs stretched beyond his. He was so small underneath her.

"Osnat," Chris whispered. "What's going on?"

"Nothing," Osnat told him. She imagined the list of pros and cons for marrying Chris that she'd make once they got back to Chicago. There would be maybe two hundred things under the pros, and it still wouldn't make a difference. Some things you just couldn't reason through.

"Nothing," she said again. "Nothing. I'm fine."

On Being French

On the morning of my tenth anniversary of working at Fantasy Bridal, the owner, Lucille, presented me with a can of Diet Coke. "Tenth anniversary is aluminum," she announced. "Congratulations, *ma chérie*!"

It was June, and things were slow. The brides were taking a breather between the spring and fall collections, so I was spending entire days in the back room, steaming the wrinkles out of silk organza, surrounded by wedding gowns so stiff they often stood up by themselves. Right then, it was only the two of us working since Lucille had recently fired Ruby, the bookkeeper, because she was going through a divorce and kept muttering things like, "*Fantasy* is right," or "Have you noticed that *bridal* and *bridle* sound exactly the same?" whenever she saw the Fantasy Bridal logo. She had been married eleven months and three days.

"Here at Fantasy Bridal, we're all about the optimism," Lucille offered by way of explanation; really, she was making sure Ruby didn't steal the stapler or any ballpoint pens while she gathered her belongings. "Here at Fantasy Bridal, the *D* word does not exist. Nor does the *A* word."

"The *A* word?" Ruby had asked. "Accounting?"

"Annulment. Adultery. Affairs. Alcoholism. Take your pick."

"Easy for you to say," Ruby muttered. "Your husband's dead."

Lucille pursed her lips. "Well," she said, "good luck to you,

Ruby. Perhaps they need someone at the Vanderberg Funeral Home."

But Ruby was the one who had the last word: "I hope so. I'd love to see you again someday. Soon."

And then she was gone, and it was just Lucille and me and the can of Diet Coke, which ended up, perhaps not coincidentally, being so warm and flat it was nearly undrinkable, a word that begins with neither *A* nor *D*.

"That's it," Lucille said. "From now on, on I'm hiring either singles or people who have been married more than twenty years. Or, of course, widows."

And she was true to her word: she hired Harriet, who was single, twenty-six—the same age as my daughter, Osnat—and studying for a master's in accounting at the university because, she explained, "Everyone needs accountants." And who could argue with that? Accordingly, perhaps, Harriet looked tough, no-nonsense, solid on her feet. Even her shoes were sensible: blue leather, low-heeled pumps.

"That girl isn't getting married," Lucille said after the initial interview. Then, even though the shop was empty at the time, she lowered her voice. "I bet she has cats. She just looks like a cat person, don't you think? I just hope she doesn't get fur all over the dresses."

Despite Lucille's rules, it was hard to avoid the *A* word that summer. At the weekly Hooray for Hebrew lunch at the JCC, over kosher egg salad sandwiches, Malka, the other Israeli, updated me on her affair with the cantor, a man whose baritone was so lovely that even his grunts during climax were musical—"lilting and soulful" was how Malka described them. In the two months since the affair had begun, Malka had learned the following facts: sex didn't have to happen at night, in bed, with the door closed. It could happen in broad daylight, with the windows open, at fancy conference hotels, if the occasion was right, or at roadside motels. It could happen in kitchens and bathrooms, in cars and in vans. Malka was thirty-nine. I was fifty-one. Just about everyone else at the lunch was well into their seventies and eighties, their Hebrew so poor they had trouble asking for the salt, which most of them weren't supposed to have anyway. *"Melach,"* Malka would pause to enunciate. *"Meh. Lach."* Then she'd turn back to me and keep right on going: "On a plane," she'd say in Hebrew. "In that little tiny restroom."

And Malka wasn't the only one. "I think I'm going to seduce the electrician," my sister, Gila, told me over the phone the previous night. "I am. I'm really going to this time. I know it." It was 1 a.m. and my husband, Marvin, was snoring in the next room, where he had fallen asleep in front of the TV. In Israel, though, it was eight in the morning, and Gila was sitting on the 601 on her way to work, the bus's starts and stops punctuating our conversation like sighs. "When it comes to home repair," Gila continued, "you have to go with your gut." As evidence she cited a long list of homely plumbers, painters, and carpenters who had done her wrong through the years, leaving her with cracked toilet bowls, dripping faucets, doors painted shut. "But not this one," she said. "He even fixed the short in the bathroom. And he's cute. And he's young."

"And you're not," I'd said, which pretty much ended the conversation right there. Now I sprinkled more salt on my egg salad sandwich and told Malka, "My sister's thinking of having an affair too."

"It is the summer of our marital discontent," Malka pronounced solemnly, this time in English—just because she was Israeli didn't mean she wasn't well-read. "I'm guessing you're next."

"No," I said. "Not me. I need to stay married to keep my job."

"That's ridiculous," Malka said. "Jobs can't depend on marital status. It's illegal."

For a moment, I imagined Lucille and me facing off in court—"But why do you care?" the judge would question me. "Aren't *you* happily married?"—and then I thought better of it. My job wasn't interesting, but it hadn't been easy to find, and Lucille, it seemed, was the one person in America who didn't mind my accent, still strong despite years and years of swallowed *r*s and softened *l*s—"Strong on purpose," Marvin would no doubt add, convinced this was another sign of my refusal to adapt to life in Michigan, although, I swear, it really wasn't.

For Lucille, though, the accent was a plus. "What we need around here," she'd said when she hired me, "is a nice European accent for that sense of haute couture."

"But I'm Israeli," I'd said.

"Maybe in the outside world," Lucille had said. "Here at Fantasy Bridal, you're French. Unless, of course, the bride is French—or do you think you could learn the language?"

"Mais oui," I'd said, convinced she was kidding. "I've had several layovers at Charles de Gaulle."

But Lucille had clasped her hands and smiled a smile that was all gums and no teeth. "Excellent! You're practically a native!" That was Lucille for you: she took the fantasy part of Fantasy Bridal seriously. And what did I know? Maybe she was right. Really, there was no reason I couldn't have been French, one of those Frenchwomen with cool hands and creamy white skin. That first week, I even checked some French language tapes out of the library. *"Où est la robe?"* I practiced saying. *"Où sont les chaussures? Où est le mari?"*

Marvin liked to say that working at Fantasy Bridal wasn't so different from what I'd done in Israel, which was selling houses, at least not when you reduced each transaction to its essentials: making families, making homes. For a while, he'd even pretended that selling wedding dresses would somehow lead me back to real estate. "Look," he'd say, flipping through the paper while I made eggs and Osnat poured juice, "there are classes starting up at the community college. You could have a license before the end of the year." On Sundays, he'd hold up the classifieds section and point out open houses in our neighborhood. "Fifteen hundred eighty square feet, four bedrooms, two baths. We could go, the three of us. You could make contacts, and we could see if there's anything we like."

"But we're not looking for a house," I'd remind him. "We already own a place." And we did: in Tel Aviv, sixth floor, 92 m^2, a view of the Mediterranean, and two balconies.

"You of all people should know that real estate is a good investment," Marvin said.

Investment in what? I wanted to ask but didn't. Still, when Marvin wasn't looking, I'd study the photographs of the real estate agents that accompanied the ads, glassy-eyed men and women with large, white teeth and shiny hair shellacked to the tops of their heads. I didn't know who Marvin thought he was kidding. People only made major purchases from others who looked and sounded just like them, and I looked nothing like these real estate agents. My own hair tended toward frizziness and my face was long, my lips so thin they disappeared without lipstick; there was nothing moony or peasantish about me, which, I pointed out to Marvin, wasn't ultimately my fault, but rather theirs, some of them less than one generation removed from wanting to murder me, Marvin, and Osnat too.

"Jesus," said Marvin. "Now there's a cheerful thought."

That, to me, was America in a nutshell: Opportunity, justice, blah blah blah—for all that to work, you had to ignore history again and again and keep trudging forward, sloughing off bygones like layers of dead skin. I knew what these real estate agents would say without even talking to them: "So your husband's American and you're Israeli? And he hates Israel and you hate Michigan? Ha ha! How very quaint! Just like this house, with its imported Italian tile and red, white, and blue bathroom! Besides, what's a thirty-year mortgage between you, me, and the bank? After all, time flies!"

And time did fly. But here it was, my one strength: I could get used to anything and like it. I was nothing like Lucille or Malka or my husband, who—if you came right down to it—believed they were owed something better: a never-ending, perfect, white, gauzy wedding; a dignified, perfumed, musical lover who laughed at your jokes; a place to live that felt nothing but familiar.

And time kept right on flying. It was Harriet's first day at work, and Lucille was busy laying down the rules: "Here at Fantasy Bridal, we never look better than the bride," she said. "If she's old, you be older. If she's fat, you be fatter." She demonstrated by pulling up her shirt to reveal a quilted belly. "Beware," she said. "Beware the wrath of a dissatisfied bride." Then she told Harriet about the different wedding packages: Barbie Wedding, Renaissance Wedding, Spring Is Eternal Wedding, Cowboy Wedding, Gypsy Wedding. In the back room, each theme had its own rack of sample costumes: peasant dresses, Starfleet uniforms, tasseled boots that could be dyed to match the flowers. "Here at Fantasy Bridal, we don't judge," Lucille said. "We enable."

Harriet listened, nodding at the appropriate intervals. She was still wearing her sensible pumps, but that day she was carrying a sensible briefcase as well, and you had to look closely to see that the leather was dry and cracking near the seams. With the exception of my daughter, Osnat, I didn't know many people in their twenties, and, if pressed, I didn't know Osnat all that well either. Now that she was no longer living with us, only checking in periodically—"Osnat's on the phone for her debriefing," Marvin liked to call out—who knew what she was really up to? She was living in Chicago, far enough away that sometimes it made more sense to fly than to drive to see her, and she was spending her free time dating Christian boys more or less exclusively, then crying for weeks when things didn't work out. Or maybe that was only how things seemed from a distance. Either way, it was hard to imagine her looking calm and attentive like Harriet, her nails manicured, her hair pulled back into a neat ponytail, the very picture of professional, if short-on-cash, competence.

When I came home, Marvin was watching the soap opera he was addicted to. He used to watch it with Osnat before she grew up and left, and now he still taped it every day, ostensibly so he could provide her with updates when they spoke. As it was, now our dinners went something like this: I would tell Marvin about what Lucille brought for lunch—salami and peanut butter sandwiches! Cream cheese and bacon baguettes!—and then he would update me on what was happening to the woman who was possessed by the devil on daytime TV. Usually it wasn't much, but some days the woman levitated while napping. This was something I liked to think about late at night, after Marvin was asleep: what it would feel like to press against nothing, your nightgown hanging down around you—not so much a free fall as a free float. It made time go by faster and more pleasantly, even though, on bad nights, I still found myself counting down: *Now in Israel it's five o'clock in the morning. Now it's six.* Once it hit seven, I could call Gila, a morning person through and through, and a woman not easily impressed by flat Coke, sensible blue pumps, or other people's cantors.

"So he has a nice voice," Gila would say. Or, "So she levitates.

But does she know how to install a circuit breaker like my sweet, sweet electrician?"

At the end of each month, Marvin would scrutinize the phone bills: "Still not sleeping, huh?" Of course I wasn't sleeping, which was something he would have known if he ever stayed awake past ten. So there we were, me dreaming about levitation and Marvin using the phone bill as a diagnostic tool: "Maybe you could try some hot milk? Exercise might help too." Then it would be time for Hooray for Hebrew, where the future was on display for anyone who cared to look: false teeth, walkers, hearing aids that emitted high-pitched whistles. No wonder Malka had been driven straight into the cantor's vigorous, open arms: at least he jogged three miles every morning, rain or shine.

"Okay, Efi," Gila would instruct me over the phone, "you need to relax. Focus on the now." Or, if she was in a bad mood, which sometimes happened, she would say, "Listen to yourself. I told you it was a mistake to leave Israel. You want to end up like Mother?"

We were moody, Gila and I, just like our mother had been moody.

Gila scoffed. "Moody?" she said. "Is that what you're calling it? We're moody like other families are diabetic."

We *were* moody, but this was an argument we'd had before. I changed the subject. "There's a new bookkeeper at Fantasy Bridal," I told Gila. "She's Jewish. The customers ask us if we're mother and daughter."

"I hope you say no," Gila said.

But I didn't say no, at least not anymore, because Lucille thought that a mother-daughter team working at Fantasy Bridal could be an extra selling point—didn't most brides go shopping with their mothers? "I'd be Harriet's mother myself," she'd said, "but physically we're nothing alike. Fair women like me don't have dark babies. Besides, if you can be French, you can certainly be Harriet's mother."

"I knew you weren't French!" Harriet exclaimed from where she was sorting receipts into different piles.

"She's from Israel," Lucille said. "And even though she seems straight off the boat, she's been in Michigan for years."

"For years," I repeated now to Gila. "With me standing right there. Can you imagine?"

"I don't have to imagine," Gila said. "She was telling the truth."

"If you're going to be my daughter," I told Harriet the next morning, "you need to get new shoes. No daughter of mine would wear shoes like that."

"If you're my mother," Harriet said without missing a beat, "you'll pay for a new pair."

"If you're my daughter," I said, "you'll earn the money for the shoes yourself."

Harriet laughed. "It's just as well. I have really big feet. With crooked toes. And calluses."

And that was how we ended up in my kitchen with Harriet soaking her feet in a small plastic tub. "My mom's a beautician," she told me. "She'd be scandalized if she knew what shape my feet are in."

Then, while Harriet waited for the polish on her toes to dry, I lent her a pair of Osnat's flip-flops (too small, of course) and showed her some photographs from Israel: Gila and I standing in front of the lemon tree in our mother's yard; eleven-year-old Osnat and her cousins in their bathing suits, eating Popsicles; the view from our apartment, all sand and sea and blue, blue sky.

Harriet sighed. "It's beautiful," she said.

Marvin, who by this time had come home and was getting himself some orange juice from the refrigerator, tsk-tsked. "That's just one part of the view," he said. "What you don't see is the power station with the great, huge smokestack a little off to the left."

"It wasn't that big," I corrected him, but he ignored me and continued: "Or the construction waste in the sand, rusted barbed wire, slabs of concrete, stuff like that."

Later, after Harriet had gone home, I said, "So what if there was construction waste? The view was still something special."

Marvin shrugged. "You can't just focus on one part of it and ignore the rest," he said, as if that wasn't pretty much what everyone did all day long about matters large and small. "You need to look at the big picture."

It was hard not to get irritated, but I took first one deep breath, and then another.

"Listen, Efi," he went on, sounding like the college professor he was. "Maybe it's just as well that we're having this conversation, because there's something I need to tell you."

He wasn't smiling, and I felt a hard and hot knot push its way into my throat. "Oh God," I said. "Oh God. Don't tell me you're having an affair too."

"Jesus," Marvin said. "Of course not. Who's having an affair?"

"Malka," I said. "Gila. Probably Harriet. Maybe even Osnat, for all we know."

"Okay, Efi, focus," Marvin said. "This has nothing to do with an affair. What it does have to do with is the house."

"What house?"

"Well, not just one specific house, necessarily," Marvin said, "but there's one over on Oakwood with a For Sale sign. You know, the red brick one on the corner." He was talking faster and faster, but I thought I could see where he was going, except that, of course, I couldn't. "It's a really nice house," Marvin went on breathlessly, "wood floors, screened-in porch, lots of light. I think we should look at it."

I was slow, but then I caught up. "You mean *I* should look at it."

Marvin grimaced. "There's a fireplace in the living room and another in the basement. The real estate agent said—"

"The real estate agent?" I interrupted, and for a moment we stood there staring at each other wide-eyed. It wasn't, of course, anything like finding out that Marvin was having an affair, except for all the ways in which it was.

"My God, Marvin," I said finally, and the words came as if I'd been rehearsing them all my life. "How could you?"

"If you marry the cantor," I told Malka at the next Hooray for Hebrew lunch, "I could set you up with the Old Country Wedding. It's supposed to be Italian, but it could also pass for Fiddler on the Roof. It comes with props, dishes made out of sugar that you can smash on the floor without worrying about injuries."

Malka laughed. "I'm already married," she said. "And even if we got divorced, I wouldn't marry the cantor. I mean, he's done it with half the congregants."

"He has?"

Malka patted my hand. "Come on, Efrat, don't be so naïve," she said. "Sometimes it's good to get a little perspective, you know. All these years together and you stop appreciating what you have. You start thinking the hair on his back is a big deal. So you get right up close with some age spots and saggy ear cartilage, and it knocks the sense right back into you."

I hid my own age-spotted hands under the table and tried to smile. It was hard not to think Malka was an idiot, but luckily, I was good at keeping up appearances. "Oh," I said. "I see."

But a little perspective was right, I reminded myself later. You could get used to anything and like it, especially if you remembered that most people didn't have a choice. Every night, Marvin and I watched other countries falling apart on the evening news. Worrying about the phone bill or whether the cantor was sleeping around were luxuries. Marvin, of course, disagreed. "I notice *your* worries aren't as luxurious," he said.

"It's the American in him," I told Gila. "It's like always having a mother to come running home to. A mother who bakes cookies."

"Isn't his mother in a nursing home in Florida?"

"So what?" I said. "At least she's alive. And she still recognizes him half the time."

"Efrat," Gila said, "you like it that he's American."

And I did. But that was when he was an American in Israel. In Michigan there were plenty of Americans already, all of them operating according to some secret code they'd been sworn never to divulge, pretending that their smiles and their apple pies somehow disguised the fact that they actually wanted nothing to do with you, that they were afraid they'd catch your accent like a disease.

"It's not that I don't want to get used to it," I told Gila. "I mean, I'm trying—"

But Gila interrupted me: "Give me a break. You've been against America from day one."

She was exaggerating, of course: it wasn't like that at all. I was happy to move, really, even though the move wasn't anything I'd imagined doing.

"Well," Gila said, "you should have imagined it. It's always the same with Americans who come to Israel: one foot here, one foot there, always sitting on the fence and wondering why it's so uncomfortable. So I'm telling you again: fences aren't made for sitting."

"Don't tell *me,*" I said. "I'm not American. Not yet."

Gila exhaled sharply. "Stop kidding yourself. You're an American citizen. What more do you want?"

"Marvin insisted—"

"But you're the one who took the test. You, Efrat, not him."

I could hear Marvin stirring in the next room, so I lowered my voice. "How can you say that?" I said. "This isn't even about America. It's about Marvin being happy. Everything's easier when he's happy."

And everything *was* easier when it came to Marvin. He was grateful in that enthusiastic, bounding way dogs were grateful when you rescued them from the shelter. He grew tomatoes in the backyard. When Osnat was younger, he taught her to throw a football, and later, when she was older, he showed her how to change the oil in her car. He was always squeezing and hugging and tousling whichever one of us was nearby, as if we were precious or on the verge of disappearing, as if his touch was what kept us here beside him. And no matter how hot or stuffy it got, summer or winter, inside or out, he no longer complained that he couldn't breathe.

I could hear Gila clinking a spoon against a glass. "I'm late for work," she said.

Even though it was 3 a.m., back in our room Marvin was awake, his breath sour and heavy with sleep. "You okay?"

"See?" I said. "This is why you need to brush your teeth after dinner."

"I did brush," Marvin said, but he rolled away to his side of the bed. "Is that better? Or can you still smell me from here?"

"Marvin called three times while you were out," Lucille told me when I got back to Fantasy Bridal. "You have a fight or something?" She was sitting with Harriet by the desk where she did her ordering, studying pie charts illustrating that, without a doubt, most brides preferred the Princess for a Day wedding with the groom in a tuxedo instead of in britches.

I shrugged. "He wants us to buy a house."

Lucille clapped as if this were good news. "You've finally arrived!" she exclaimed. Then she added, "I can't believe you've been renting all this time. It's like throwing away money. Isn't your husband a mathematician?"

"He watches *Days of Our Lives,*" I said. "What does he know?"

Harriet laughed, but Lucille kept right on talking: "That's a good one," she said. "There's a woman on that show who's possessed by the devil. Her eyes glow red and she sounds like a man with laryngitis. You normally don't see that kind of thing on daytime television."

"Okay," I said, "but you know they're going to exorcise that demon and that she'll be just fine. Isn't that what always happens?"

"Her boyfriend thinks the reason she's so pale is because her iron is low," Lucille continued. "People see what they want to see, I guess."

Which was the truth. I saw it every day at the salon, outfitting people for weddings so lavish and ceremonies so elaborate that you knew they had to be covering something up, that all that tulle and beadwork only had one function: to obscure and distract. All the same, it wasn't my job to point this out. It was my job to get out the tape measure. Not every marriage ended in divorce. Some people had affairs.

"That's why my ex isn't in the ceremony," one groom's father explained that very afternoon while Lucille filled out his order form. "She went off to the Bahamas with the dentist, and my son is still angry. He'd already set the date for the wedding. She could have waited six months and left then."

Lucille tsk-tsked and wrapped the tape measure around his waist. "Forty-two," she said. The man sucked in his belly. "Uh-uh," Lucille said. "Relax. You don't want the wedding cake to give you heartburn."

The man was nearly bald, his head shiny under the fluorescent lights. He would look terrible in the maize and blue suits that were part of the School Spirit Wedding the bride had selected. She had been a cheerleader, one of the girls who did a backflip for every point the football team scored. The pep band was going to play at the reception.

"Still," the man said while I rang up his total, "it's a hard thing, this wedding. I wish my wife had waited six months too."

"Lies and all?" I asked him.

"Lies and all," he said. Then he cocked his head and narrowed his eyes. "What are you, French?"

"Yes," I said. "Sure, I'm French."

"No, you aren't"—he squinted at my name tag—"Efrat," only he said it *Ef-rat*. He held out his hand. "I'm Walter. Walter Stevens." To Lucille he said, "You really should be offering some kind of wedding escort service for the newly divorced." Then, when he saw Lucille's horrified expression, he blushed, stuttering, "Without the sex, of course. Imagine if I showed up at the wedding with a Frenchwoman. What dentist can top that?"

He was still holding my hand, but I was good at dealing with the unexpected. "That sounds lovely," I said. I squeezed his fingers and then let go. "Nice to meet you, Winston—"

"Walter."

"Walter. Good luck to you."

"Now really, Efrat," Lucille said once he'd left. "Here at Fantasy Bridal we remember our customers' names." It was Harriet, though, who made a low whistling sound and announced, "Somebody *likes* you!"

"He didn't like me," I said. "He liked my accent."

"Doesn't matter," Harriet said. "You would have been recorded for posterity in all the wedding photos. Just think of that."

I tried to imagine it—me in pink, Walter in maize and blue;

who'd be able to tell that we hadn't always been together?—but already Walter's features were starting to blur. Who knew what he looked like? Still, for a man whose wife had recently left him, Walter had seemed fine, not like someone who spent nights crying into his pillow. I knew this much: Marvin wouldn't have been so blasé. If I left him, he'd be on the next plane, right there behind me, wild-eyed, luggage-less, unshaven.

"You don't know that," Lucille said. "That's one of those things you can't know until it happens."

"Very true," Gila agreed later, when I filled her in over the phone, "but in this case, you do know."

"Exactly," I agreed. Of course I knew. Marvin and I had been together nearly thirty years and, if nothing else, I knew him in all the ways that counted. Besides, our shocker, our big test, had already happened, and we'd survived: we were here together, despite the clouds and snow and homesickness.

"Wait," Gila said. "Wait a second." For a moment I was afraid she'd ask how I knew we'd survived, but instead she said, "Who said you only get one test?" And then she said, "And anyway, that wasn't what I meant. What I meant was that he didn't come after you before."

"Before?"

Gila sighed. "Before," she said, enunciating each word clearly. "When you left him."

"I never left him."

"Right," Gila said. "You keep telling yourself that."

It was important to stay focused, to not allow yourself to feel trapped. This wasn't how I'd imagined my life, how I'd imagined things would be decided. I'd imagined long discussions and much hand-wringing. Marvin would say, "It's only fair. I put in all those years in Israel, and now it's your turn," and I would argue that this wasn't about fair, that I had never signed up for fair. Fair would have been Marvin declaring his intentions up front, over a bagel at the Yaffo bakery where he proposed: "I want to be with you but I can't live here." If this was a discussion we'd had, I didn't remember it. What happened instead was Marvin lying awake most nights, sometimes pale and sweating, wanting more air despite the fans and the breeze from the sea. So we'd packed up and moved—temporarily, just for a year or two, a brief rest. Except that every August Marvin would place the following year's lease in front of me and say, "Or should we look into buying?" and I'd pretend to think about it before saying, "I don't know." And then I'd sign and that would be that. Our fourth year here, the packing boxes we'd kept in the basement got wet and started rotting until Marvin finally threw them away. "We'll get more if we need them," he'd said. *If?* I wanted to ask but didn't. *If?*

Now, though, maybe for the first time in our married lives, we were teetering on the verge of fairness: I'd been in America as long as Marvin had been in Israel. And still we were locked in what felt like a game of Chicken. How could either of us admit that our own individual happiness was more important than the other's? We weren't monsters. We weren't even like Malka and her husband, or Gila and the electrician, or like Walter and his wife and the dentist. We weren't bored or flighty. It wasn't that we wanted someone better. Really, if you stopped to think about it, this wasn't even about us. It was about where we could live together. And it wasn't even about that, because somewhere along the line, that had been decided too. Now it was just a matter of getting used to things, and that was easy. That was playing to my strengths.

And what did Marvin know about all this? Not much. "Have you thought about the house on Oakwood?" he asked me after work on Tuesday, and then again on Wednesday. On Thursday, I brought Harriet home with me and set her to work pounding chicken breasts for schnitzel. "Don't be afraid," I told her. "Pound hard."

"I had a crush on an Israeli boy when I was in college," Harriet told me while she worked. "Maybe because he was older."

"Israeli men tend to be better-looking than average," I said. "It's a scientific fact."

Marvin came into the kitchen. "Now when the devil woman floats, she moves to the living room and back," he reported. Then he grabbed a carrot stick and left.

"Israeli men don't watch soaps," I told Harriet.

"I think it's cute," Harriet said. "He's like a sensitive man of the nineties."

I changed the subject. "So what happened to your Israeli?" I asked.

"He went back to Israel, of course."

I dipped the chicken breasts in egg batter and then bread crumbs. "Well," I said, "there are more where he came from. Maybe I could even fix you up." I looked her over carefully, from sensible pumps to slicked-back ponytail. "Have you considered bangs?"

"No," Harriet said. "My mother says bangs always go out of style before you can grow them back, and she knows what she's talking about."

She was so sincere that I pulled out the ingredients for chocolate cake. And then ingredients for fruit salad. Anything to keep her there longer.

"It's late," I said when all the food was eaten, and the three of us were slumped around the dining-room table, our bellies stretched tight with too much food. "Do you want to spend the night?"

Harriet shook her head. "I only live a couple miles away." She stood up and smiled at both of us. "This was really nice."

"Okay," I said, "but let me drive you."

After I dropped her off, I drove up Murray and down Thaler, then up Glendale and down Abbot. It was hard to make the right turn onto Oakwood, but then I finally did. It was a narrow street, lined with ash trees and neat, trim lawns. The houses were brick and vinyl, their windows brightly lit. In front of one of them, an elderly couple was sitting on a porch swing and holding hands; in front of another, a man was watering geraniums with a hose. It was easy to see what Marvin liked about the area: the flower boxes, the backyard swing sets, the crickets. In the house that was for sale, a woman was washing dishes in front of the kitchen window. Her face was neutral, her expression blank. Behind her, I could make out the blue flicker of a TV set. I tried imagining living there, under the elderly couple's watchful gaze: "Now they're fighting again," the husband would tell the wife, and she would squeeze his hand tighter, glad that at least the two of them got along.

Back at home, I called Osnat. "Your father wants to buy a house," I told her.

"I know."

"You do?"

"He's wanted to buy one for years," Osnat said.

"He has?"

"Sometimes we went to open houses together," Osnat continued. "He let me pick out my room."

I imagined Osnat and Marvin wandering through other people's homes, peeking in closets, checking out the furnace. "Where was I in all this?" I wanted to know.

Osnat sounded tired. "I don't know. Working?"

"You went to open houses while I was at *work?*"

"Mom," Osnat said, "Mom, I've got to go."

"Where?" I asked her. "You have to go where?"

"Somewhere," Osnat said, suddenly sounding defeated. "I wish I knew." Then she started crying. "I miss Chris," she said. "I miss him. I don't know what to do with myself."

I listened to her sob for a couple minutes and busied myself with trying to untangle the phone cord, which had twisted around itself tightly, as if the phone wanted its receiver back safe in its cradle. "There, there," I said finally, because what else could I say? She was my daughter, and she was upset. "You'll find someone else soon."

Osnat stopped crying with a sharp intake of breath. "How would you feel," she asked, "if I said that to you?"

"Well?" Gila asked me later. "How *would* you feel?" But she didn't wait for an answer. "When you wake up tomorrow," she said, changing the subject, "send me good thoughts. I'm going to have a little talk with the electrician. I really am this time. I know it."

At Hooray for Hebrew, Malka was scooping tuna fish onto her plate. *"Tuna,"* she was telling a woman with hair so white it looked blue. *"Tu. Na. Too-nah!"* To me she said in Hebrew, "Thank God you're here. I'm so tired I can barely walk."

"I'm not sure I needed to know that," I said, busying myself by pouring water into paper cups. "The cantor?"

Malka shook her head. "My husband. I read in a magazine that the best thing you can do for a marriage is take the TV out of your bedroom, and it turns out it's true. Who knew it was so easy?"

"So that's that?" I asked. "The end of the affair?"

Now it was Malka's turn to shrug. "Not necessarily."

I looked around the table. Just about all of the seniors were wearing sweaters even though it was so hot outside I was still sweating. They were mainly women—only a couple of the regulars were men—and as far as I knew all of them were widowed. Still, for the most part, they seemed to be coping. Across from me, Mrs. Cohen was freshening up her lipstick and fluffing her hair with a comb that looked like a fork. "Enough," Mr. Katz was saying to her. "You already look lovely."

"In Hebrew!" trilled Malka. "You know the rules!" To me she said, "Last week he was in love with Mrs. Freed. Now look at the way she's scowling. So cute."

But there was nothing cute about the way Mrs. Freed was eyeing Mr. Katz, or about the way her hands shook when she brought her spoon to her mouth. She had a son in California, I knew, and a daughter in Texas, and here she was, in Michigan, eating a sandwich on soft white bread without crusts, her loneliness so palpable I thought I could smell it.

"This would have never happened in Israel," I told Malka. "You can't live so far away from your children in such a small country."

"We lived fifteen kilometers from my grandmother and only saw her twice a year," Malka said. "Israel has nothing to do with it."

"But at least you had the choice." I thought about Osnat alone in her apartment in Chicago, crying. If we were still in Israel, I could have come over with chicken soup, and it would still have been warm enough to eat when I arrived.

"If Israel's such a paradise," Malka said, "why are there so many Israelis living here?"

"Because of their husbands?" I offered.

Malka snorted. "He's your *husband,*" she said. "He's not God. He's not even a cantor." When she was done laughing at her own joke, she continued, "There are so many Israelis here because life is better. I don't know why everyone acts like all they're doing is counting the days until they go back. It's hypocrisy of the worst kind."

"But someone needs to live there," I said.

"Okay," Malka said. "But why should it be me? Or you, for that matter?"

She was an idiot and the daughter of an idiot. It was all I could do not to stare at her openmouthed. What could the cantor possibly see in her? What could her husband?

"Don't look at me like that," Malka said. "At least I'm happy. At least I know where I stand."

I was good at many things, but I wasn't good with witty comebacks. Back at work, between customers, Lucille, Harriet, and I tried to brainstorm replies.

"Where you stand?" Lucille said. "And here I thought you spent most of your time on your back."

"Not snappy enough," I said.

"At least you're happy?" Lucille tried again. "There's more to happiness than a man-sized vibrator."

"Okay," I said, "stop right there."

"See?" she said. "It would have shut her up. Not that I don't see her point."

"You do?"

"Sure," Lucille said. "Chosen people, holier than everybody, I get. But why do you Jews always have to be so miserable?"

"I guess it's the burden of running the world from behind the scenes," Harriet said. "I know it wears *me* down. It's hard clutching those purse strings all day long."

Lucille clapped her hands. "Speaking of purses, what do you think of this one?" She held up the catalog she'd been flipping through to a picture of a bride holding a beaded purse shaped like a champagne glass. "Too chintzy?"

"No," Harriet said. "Just right."

Still, for some reason, I spent the rest of the day feeling restless and riled, out of sorts. Every time a customer walked in, I jumped. I had trouble using the cash register. I pricked myself with a safety pin three separate times.

"You better not get blood on the dresses," Lucille warned me. "Here at Fantasy Bridal, we pride ourselves on dresses that are body fluid free."

"Yes," I said, sucking on my right index finger. "Of course."

"Here," said Harriet, digging through her briefcase. "I think I've got a Band-Aid." Then she said, "Are you okay? You look tired."

And I *was* tired, what with Malka's niggling and Marvin's seeing other real estate agents behind my back. It was enough to send any woman crawling into another man's bed. Already, I could see it unfolding like a daytime soap opera of my own life. Some man—Walter even—would come in for a fitting, and I would kneel at his feet and hem in his pant legs and act so foreign and alluring that he would think to himself, *This is what I need, my own version of a dentist.* There would be coffee, and lunch, and a rendezvous at one of the motels off US-23, and he would think, *This isn't my wife,* and I would think, *This isn't my husband.* Everything would be wrong—the smell, the taste, the texture—and we'd both lie there, staring at the ceiling and thinking, *Is this close enough?* I never believed in love at first sight. Love was something that crept up on you. You had to listen for it. You had to say, *Come here, you too skinny American mathematician, and wear me down until I can't remember life without you.* Housewives all over America would run for Kleenexes because they'd recognize my soap opera for what it was: the truth, no devil, no possession, no gimmicks.

"I don't know," I told Harriet. "I need a break, some time to think."

"Sounds like you need a vacation," she said. "To somewhere fabulous."

I tried to imagine it, Marvin and me in bathing suits, crashing surf on one side and palm trees on the other—we'd swing in hammocks while sipping drinks served by waiters in white linen suits—but I just couldn't see it. "The semester's starting soon," I said, "and Marvin's so busy."

"So what?" Harriet said. "Pack your bags. Buy a ticket. Go."

It was eleven o'clock at night in Israel, and if they weren't asleep already, Gila and Gabi were probably sitting in front of their TV, except that maybe today she was on the far end of the couch, where he couldn't put his arms around her. And although everything looked the same, there she was, in a new part of her life, the part made up of sneaking around and lies and confessions. And here I was, in Michigan, my suitcase packed, my boarding pass tucked into the outside pocket for easy access, waiting for Marvin to say something. Families were falling apart all around us, and instead of intuiting that something incredible was happening, instead of taking me into his arms and saying, "My God, I had no idea things were this bad," all Marvin could say was, "But it's hurricane season in the Bahamas."

I ignored him and headed to the bathroom with a toiletry bag. After a moment, Marvin followed and we stood side by side in front of the mirror, our skin creased, our eyes bifocaled, the flesh of our necks already loose and flabby. This is how close we were: When Marvin swallowed, my own throat constricted.

"Jesus," he said now. "Oh Jesus. I knew it. You're leaving me again."

Again? I wanted to ask. *When did I leave you before?* Instead I busied myself with packing up the toothbrush and toothpaste, even though by then I already knew it was all for show.

"Don't go," Marvin said, oblivious. "Don't leave. We'll cash in your ticket and go together for Christmas." In the mirror, his reflection looked gray, colorless, concerned. "It's only a couple months. Please."

"Okay," I said, "I won't go," because what else could I say? He was my husband. We'd been together nearly thirty years. We didn't need to play these games, at least not the way other people played them. Still, to save face, I added, "I mean now. I won't go *now.*"

Marvin reached for my hand and squeezed it. "That's good," he said. Then he said, "The Bahamas, huh? Why there?"

Later, Gila picked up the phone before it even had time to ring. "I knew it was you," she said.

"And?"

"What do you think?"

I didn't know if I was ready to place a bet. Instead I said, "Marvin and I are going to the Bahamas in December."

"Are you crying?" Gila said. "Why are you crying?"

"I'm not crying," I said, too loudly—in the next room, Marvin stopped midsnore. I lowered my voice. "It's just that I can't believe you did it. How could you? What kind of future will you have with an electrician?"

"Hey now," Gila said, "electricians make good money, and this one is twenty-six with nice muscles. Besides, I didn't go through with it."

I could feel the blood making its way back to my hands and feet. I swallowed, then swallowed again. "You really had me scared."

"Yes," she said. "I don't know how that bastard does it."

That was Gila for you: she never forgot anything, even though it had been years, and it had only happened one time, and Gabi hadn't done it since. But pointing this out only made her angry.

"A year and a half is not *years.*" Gila's voice was hard. "And how do you know he hasn't? *I* don't even know. Damn it, I should have . . ." she paused, searching for the right word, "*fucked* that electrician. Or I should have left Gabi. I probably will anyway, one of these days. Maybe we're just genetically programmed to fail at marriage."

"Come on," I said, "plenty of marriages work out."

"I'm not talking in general," Gila said. "I'm talking about you and me. First our father leaves and our mother goes crazy—"

"She was moody—"

"Oh, stop it," Gila said. "She was *crazy.* First our father leaves, and then our mother goes *crazy.* And then you leave Marvin. And now here's me."

She wasn't making sense. We both knew it. In the next room, the bedsprings creaked and Marvin sighed.

"Are you even listening?" Gila hissed. "I swear, the things you gloss over, Efrat. It's irresponsible."

"You don't have to be mean."

"I'm not being *mean.* I'm being *honest,* Miss I'm-French-Now-And-My-Mother-Was-Moody. Miss I-Love-My-Husband. Miss Let's-Pretend-America-Doesn't-Make-Me-Want-To-Wither-And-Die."

"What?" I said. "What?"

Here it was, the truth: our mother was *moody;* I never left Marvin, not *really,* and only for a few days for my mother's funeral, which hardly counted; there *were* worse things than being in America.

Gila and I could argue our way into phone-bill bankruptcy over these points, but sometimes you really just had to be there. I understood this, even if she didn't. Marvin and I didn't fight very often and, compared to Gila and Gabi, who were always screaming, we didn't fight at all. We were adults and I wasn't blind or heartless. Maybe Marvin was unhappy in Israel, but one of the things I loved about him was that he felt everything deeply. He was sensitive, and not just about soaps. He checked the phone bill for errors but didn't mention how much each call had cost. He noticed when the garbage can was full and the plants needed watering. He washed dishes. All these years of marriage and he only asked one thing, and he was even nice about that. "I can't stay here," he said, "but if you can't come with me, we'll work something out, see each other on vacations and over the summer." Why would I leave a man like that?

"Because now you're the unhappy one," Gila said. "Because you don't do ultimatums."

"My God, Gila," I said. "*What* are you talking about?"

"Efi," Gila said, "you can keep telling yourself these little stories, but aren't you worried? Aren't you worried you're going to forget something important?"

"Like what?"

"Like that you're better than selling dresses and wiping the drool off old Jews," she said. "Like that our mother was crazy. For God's sake, Efi, what if it's hereditary?"

I hung up then. It was a pointless conversation. Marvin was right. Selling dresses wasn't so different from selling houses. Gila would be angry for two days, and then we'd both forget about it and move on. Still, I was having a hard time catching my breath.

"Are you okay?" Suddenly Marvin was standing in front of me, glowing in the light from the hallway. I could distinguish every shimmering hair on his head, but his face, turned toward me, disappeared into darkness: my own private devil husband. "Did you and Gila have a fight?"

"Nope," I said. "I just have a headache."

And I did. It was all I could do to shuffle off to the bedroom, Marvin trailing behind me with a glass of water. I took two aspirin, and then two more, then lay down and stared at the ceiling. A former tenant had pasted glow-in-the-dark stars up there, and the landlord had painted them over so all you could see were their outlines. I closed my eyes. The air around us was close, heavy with summer heat, but Marvin pulled a sheet up over me anyway, and when he did, I thought about grabbing him, pulling him down on top of me. There was a lot I'd been saving up to tell him—about Malka and the cantor, about Gila, about renting and buying and wanting to leave—but suddenly I knew that, really, there was nothing to talk about. The worst thing we could do was discuss, analyze, overthink, start looking around and asking cantors and electricians and the newly divorced for their advice. We weren't like them. They couldn't help us. So I kept my eyes closed, and by 7 a.m. I was up and about, just like always. I had the headaches down to a science: you lay down, you waited, you got up and made breakfast. No big deal.

When I got downstairs, Marvin was outside, refilling the bird feeder. On the kitchen counter, there was a flyer from the house on Oakwood and another from a house on Birch. He wasn't going back. *We* weren't. We would buy a house, and we would install a porch swing, and we would be happy. There was no point in pretending we weren't. Still, I gave the flyers a wide berth, circling them as you might a dead animal.

Marvin came back inside and started the coffee. I opened the refrigerator and pulled out the milk. *Look at me giving this a chance,*

I wanted to tell him. *Here it is: my best effort.* But I didn't. Instead I put the bagels in the toaster and waited for them to toast.

"Got everything?" Marvin asked, sitting down at the table.

I looked down at my hands, at the coffee steaming in our mugs and the butter melting on our bagels. I could do this, I told myself. I wanted to. If I didn't, I'd be a fool.

"Yes," I said. "I think so."

Your Own Private America

The rains came early in Israel that year, and hard. It wasn't even February, and already yellowish gray watermarks sagged beneath the windows and decorative stonework of Osnat's apartment as if the building itself were sweating through its white stucco walls. All that wetness put Osnat's aunt, who had come prepared to dispense advice, in a bad mood. "View or no view," she told Osnat, "it was stupid of your father to buy an apartment on the top floor." She pulled a tissue out of her purse and blew her nose. Then she folded it back up into neat squares and said, "Let's go get some lunch." Because that's what people were supposed to do whenever there was any bad news: they were supposed to eat.

They went to the café by the main entrance to Tel Aviv University. It sat on the top of a hill that led all the way down to the Mediterranean, flat and blue in the distance. It wasn't as good a view as the one from Osnat's apartment, but at least here you could sit down and enjoy it over dessert, then leave well before the next storm rolled ashore. And these days, an easy exit was everything, wasn't it? Osnat's aunt sighed happily and ordered a piece of chocolate cake and two forks.

From where she was sitting, Osnat could watch students line up and unzip their backpacks for security inspection. Beyond the entrance gate, on the campus side of the fence, there were steps that led up to a sculpture that looked like a picture frame on a stick. If you stood next to it and looked west, it divided the view into street and sea, so you could focus on sand and water and ignore the boxy apartment buildings on either side. Osnat's father was the one who had shown her the sculpture. Back when they all still lived in Israel, he had worked at the university, and for thirteen years he had walked up the hill and up all those steps every morning to his office, which was on the east side of campus. Now that Osnat's parents lived in Michigan, he still had to walk up a hill to get to work even though Ann Arbor was mostly flat. "I guess that's what puts the *higher* in *higher learning,*" he liked to joke. Then he always added, "It's our family curse, walking up hills."

And maybe it was the family curse on her father's side. But on her mother's side, at least according to Osnat's aunt, their family curse was rain. Either there wasn't enough of it, and the crops failed, and Osnat's grandfather, distressed, jumped on a ship to South America, leaving her grandmother to slowly go crazy raising two young daughters, or else there was too much of it, and it seeped in through cracks and under moldings. And this was before you paused to consider all the wars.

Osnat knew historical context was important, but spending time with her aunt depressed her. Her aunt was shorter than her mother, and thinner, and her hair was hennaed into a hue between copper and rust. On weekends, she read the classifieds that listed apartments for sale in New York and Los Angeles, tsk-tsking in either disapproval or envy—Osnat wasn't sure which. Her aunt lived on the outskirts of the village where Osnat's grandmother's house still stood, in a nice three-bedroom house that stayed dry through the winter and came complete with a patio and a bomb shelter in the basement. On Saturdays, strangers drove right up to the front steps to ask if it happened to be for sale, and her aunt always said that it wasn't—land was something you didn't let go of, never mind that now it was just her and her husband, Osnat's uncle, living there. Her three daughters—Osnat's cousins, all girls around Osnat's age—were already married and living in houses of their own, busy being both successful lawyers and the kind of casserole-making dutiful daughters who stopped by their mother's once a week between court appearances so she could place her hands on their growing bellies and admire the progress of their respective pregnancies. Next to them, Osnat felt dowdy and very, very young. Although they all dipped in more or less the same gene pool, she was taller and broader, a lumbering corn-fed giant from the Midwest barely able to take care of her own soggy apartment, let alone manage a husband and an unborn set of twins. And here was her aunt—almost her mother and yet nothing like her—licking chocolate icing off her fork and saying things like, "Views and sunsets are all very well. But you're the one breathing in mold spores. Maybe your father won't scoff when you tell him *that,*" before sending Osnat home with a doggie bag and soggy premonitions of doom.

But Osnat's father did scoff. "Mideast tensions over water are *not* our private family curse," he said. "We are *not* the center of the world." But then Osnat's mother had said, "Did I tell you the sunroof in the car is leaking again?" And her father had sighed. "Fine," he said to Osnat. "Fine. Call in the waterproofers."

Before coming to Israel, Osnat had read a book about positive thinking. Even though over a year had passed since then, Osnat was still conscientious about doing her daily affirmations each morning. So far, she was sticking to the basics: "I will live in Israel for the rest of my life" and "I am a real Israeli" twenty times each. Someday soon, she knew, all that hard work would finally pay off and suddenly tourists would be stopping her on the street to ask for directions; or else she'd suddenly find herself sitting at a café surrounded by actual friends, laughing at their jokes—because she actually got them—and maybe even actually telling some of her own while she expertly scooped up hummus, *ful,* and hard-boiled egg with a piece of pita; or else suddenly she'd be able to look people in the eye without dropping her gaze and actually know, really *know,* if they were telling the truth or lying. And just like that, the transition part would be over, she'd have made it, she'd be here to stay. In the meantime, black mold or no, she had to keep moving forward, and besides, the waterproofing ads in the phone book gave her reason to hope: twelve full pages of handsome guys rappelling down the sides of buildings, grinning as they dangled over small print describing the ten-year limited warranty. And then, like a sign from God, a chunk of plaster fell from the ceiling right onto the illustration of a man in a harness who appeared to be gazing dreamily off into the distance. A coincidence like that had to mean something, didn't it?

"It means nothing," said Gary, Osnat's boss at the high-tech company where she worked as a copyeditor. It was Sunday and they were both getting their morning coffee. He was an Orthodox Jew from South Africa who now lived in the territories; he had no patience, he claimed, for superstition. "Don't put all your faith in ceiling plaster," he advised. "Make sure you ask for references."

And Gary was right, of course. The man who finally showed up at Osnat's apartment wasn't handsome. He wasn't even cute. He was short, sharp-featured and sharp-toothed, with sideburns that were carefully brushed and so glossy they appeared to be plastic, starting out wide at his cheekbones and tapering down to fine points at his jawline. Not only that, but he was weird too: although he was wearing blue overalls with his name, Avner, clearly stitched below the company logo, he introduced himself to Osnat as Elvis. "Yes," he said. "Elvis." And then he winked.

References, Osnat reminded herself. Ask for references. But then, as if reading her mind, the man sighed and his face went slack, and that's when, just for a second, she saw it, a tired, wistful look that, if you tried hard enough, you could easily mistake for dreamy. So at least the ad in the phone book had been accurate about that.

Maybe the whole Elvis thing made sense, Osnat reflected later, as she followed the waterproofer around her apartment and watched him touch the black mold on her bedroom wall with the tip of one finger and jot notes on a small clipboard. Elvis, real or not, would still need to earn a living after leaving all his worldly possessions back in Memphis years ago: rich man, eye of the needle, blah blah. Surely waterproofing was as reputable and symbolic a profession for the King as any. In fact, Osnat realized, if you squinted a little, the illusion was almost perfect, as long as you ignored the leathery skin and too thin lips, and—of course—the accent.

When Elvis had seen everything there was to see, he returned to the balcony and scowled at the Mediterranean sprawled out in front of them.

"The leak is the price you pay for the view," he said. Then he made the same kind of tsk-tsking sound Osnat's aunt liked to make. "There's always a price, you know—all that wind hitting you straight on. You couldn't pay me to live here."

"That's fine, I guess," Osnat said. "But how much will it cost to repair?"

"Of course, you're American," Elvis said. "That's who lives in this neighborhood: English speakers and rich people. There's even a soap opera about you on TV."

This part was true—Osnat watched the show every Friday night. When they weren't having sex with one another's spouses in the swimming pool or servants' quarters of their respective penthouses, the characters were forever backstabbing each other at a restaurant that was only a few blocks away from her building. There was no denying the facts, but Osnat tried to anyway. "I was born here," she pointed out reasonably, "and I'm not rich. It's not about me."

"Maybe," Elvis said, stroking his chin in an attempt, Osnat thought, to look mysterious. "Maybe not."

He climbed onto the balcony ledge and leaned over, swaying, checking out the wall beneath them. Watching him made Osnat nervous—she lived on the sixth floor, and it was a long way down. She positioned herself so that if he started to fall, she could grab the tail of his T-shirt, a move that came in handy when, a few seconds later, he tilted a little too far forward.

"Are you crazy?" Elvis said, shaking her off and climbing down from the ledge. "You could have killed me. Never touch a man balancing above the jaws of death."

"Aren't you supposed to use a harness or something?" Osnat asked.

"I'll tell you the truth," Elvis said. "The mold on your walls isn't just from this year. This whole building is crap, with all its fancy mosaic trim. Whoever sold you this apartment cheated you."

Osnat swallowed. "No one sold me this apartment. It's my parents'."

"Whatever." Elvis dismissed her with a wave. "One day, this wall will rot through completely. If you're smart, you'll wait until everything dries out in the summer, then paint over the mold and sell the place before next winter." Then he added, "That'll be two hundred dollars."

"For what?" Osnat said. "For standing on the ledge for two minutes?"

She steeled herself for the argument that would follow. She knew it was part of the script, like fighting with cabdrivers over whether their meter was truly broken, but she still wasn't used to all the yelling.

"Okay," Elvis said. "I'll tell you what. I can see you're upset. Two hundred dollars, and I'll paint over the mold for you."

"It was a mistake not to sell that place," Osnat's father said when Osnat called to tell her parents the news. "We should have sold it back in eighty-four."

"We didn't know we weren't coming back," Osnat's mother said. She was listening on the extension.

Osnat's father sighed. "Sure we did. You just didn't want to admit it."

"You said we'd go for a year and then decide."

It was an old argument, one that always ended badly. For years, Osnat's mother had refused to sell the apartment because maybe, just maybe, they would return—if not soon, then when they retired, which was when Osnat's father would have no choice but to start paying her mother back for sticking her in Michigan, of all places, where it was cloudy all year round and people asked how you were without really being interested in the answer. Fair was fair, and Osnat's father's turn was coming up quickly. And if it turned out that the sun in Israel was still too bright and all the yelling still bothered him, well, he could just get a hat and earplugs and suck it up. Usually, Osnat's father would listen to her mother's litany for a while, then have a go at it himself. "Yes," he'd agree. "Let's calculate exactly who's more miserable." It was enough to make Osnat want to hang up. She'd moved back to Israel. She'd done her part. Couldn't they work the rest of it out alone?

But this time, the argument just petered out, as if there was no question that Elvis was right and the apartment was a goner.

"What?" Osnat said. "What happened?"

She heard her mother take a deep breath. "There's just something about this family and rain—"

"Rain has nothing to do with it," Osnat's father interrupted. "Your aunt Gila wants to tear down your grandmother's house."

"She doesn't *want* to," Osnat's mother said. "She *has* to. She says it's barely standing up on its own."

"Huh," Osnat said. "She didn't say anything to me."

"Why would she?" Osnat's mother voice shook. "It wasn't your house."

"Are you crying?"

"She's been crying all week," Osnat's father said.

"I'm not crying," Osnat's mother said, although now she clearly was. "It's just that we won't have anything left. With the apartment sold, and your grandmother's house torn down, we won't have anything left at all."

If you stood on the roof of Osnat's grandmother's house, you could see across the highway all the way to the Mediterranean. In the front yard, there were trees that grew olives and avocados and lemons—at least that's what Osnat's aunt claimed. Osnat was terrible at recognizing trees.

The house, Osnat saw, had certainly been neglected since Osnat's grandmother died, which only made it look even more like the kind of place a crazy person might live. The stucco walls were crumbling, and, in the back, parts of what used to be the chicken coop lay rusting on the ground. Inside, there wasn't enough light and everything smelled musty. The furniture was gone, claimed by Osnat's cousins as each moved into her own home, but the main thing missing was the stove, which Osnat's mother and her aunt had taken straight to the junkyard the moment the shiva was over—it had seemed wrong to keep it.

"See?" Osnat's aunt said, pointing to places along the ceiling where the plaster was flaking. "At the very least, it needs a new roof, but I think the walls are going too." She was unusually brisk, guiding Osnat away from the kitchen, with the gas hose snaking across the empty space where the stove used to be, and into the living room from where, if you listened carefully, you could hear the old woman next door hollering on the phone. "What do you mean you were here this morning?" she was shouting.

"We could move the new house back a little," Osnat's aunt said, "away from Golda's. There will be plenty of room once we clear the coop."

"What new house?" Osnat asked.

"Didn't your mother tell you?" All morning, her aunt had been smiling a thin, polite smile, but now she pursed her lips in a way that made her look haggard, as if somebody had pricked her with a pin and she was slowly deflating. "She said she would tell you we were tearing it down."

Next door, Golda was still shouting away: "I'd remember my own son coming to visit," she yelled.

Osnat's aunt sighed, then resumed her smiling. "Golda took care of us, you know. When your grandmother was ill."

Ill, Osnat knew, was a euphemism for *crazy,* but neither her mother nor her aunt liked to call it that, at least not in front of the children. She wanted to ask her aunt exactly what illness her grandmother had suffered from, but her aunt was already busy closing the blinds and locking the place back up.

"So," Osnat's aunt said, turning the key in the front door, "did I pass inspection? Are my motives honorable?"

"This wasn't an inspection," Osnat said.

"Then why did she send you?"

"She didn't."

"Sure," Osnat's aunt said. "Anyway, it's a crappy house full of bad memories. I hated living here, and so did she. For years, for years, I told her the place needed new roof tiles, new paint, new gutters. But that stuff costs money, and I'm not the one living in America, where out of sight is out of mind and money grows on trees. I'm just the one who has to drive by this place each day."

Already, Israel had Osnat believing in genetics: it was strange how much her aunt smelled like her mother—eyes closed, she didn't know if she'd be able to tell them apart. Now, inside her grandmother's house, she realized that maybe she had gotten the scent all wrong. The air was bland, like bananas, damp and slightly sweet like bedsheets that needed washing. Osnat's mother and aunt, it turned out, didn't smell like each other: they smelled like their house. On the bus back to her apartment, Osnat kept sniffing her shirt—did she smell like it too? But under the detergent and deodorant and sweat, all she smelled was familiar.

In a way, the same was true of her neighborhood. In the fifteen years or so between the time Osnat's parents had packed up their belongings and left Israel (taking twelve-year-old Osnat with them) and the time twenty-seven-year-old Osnat came back, the building where they owned an apartment had been dwarfed by taller, fancier apartment buildings that came complete with central A/C and double-paned windows that kept the cooled air from escaping. Some had vacuum cleaners built into their walls (just plug a hose in and go!) and landscaped yards kept vibrant by automatic sprinklers. Each of the new buildings came with its own billboard: "America, right here in Israel!" or "America, right in your own home!" It was also what people said when Osnat told them where she lived—"Pssh . . . America!"—although she never quite knew if they were impressed or disgusted.

Even so, her neighborhood was like no America Osnat had

ever been to. At the tiny shopping center near her apartment, there was a vending machine that dispensed video rentals and a grocery store whose owner carefully knocked on each watermelon before selecting the one his fourteen-year-old son delivered to your house. You could buy chocolate milk in a baggie and tiramisu in a plastic cup. There were seventy kinds of hummus. One time, at the supermarket, Osnat saw the little girl who did TV commercials for peanut puffs—she wouldn't have recognized her if the cashier hadn't asked her to sing the jingle—and she was only one of the many flesh-and-blood celebrities who lived in the area, people like a former Miss Israel, a local mafia boss, and the widow of an MP, all with yippy apartment-sized dogs they didn't bother cleaning up after, distracted by their spectacular Mediterranean views.

But underneath and tucked away between all the new parts were the places Osnat remembered from before. Her grade school had gone into hiding behind two new apartment buildings and a country club, but the pizzeria on the boardwalk where her parents used to take her was still there, and the sun still felt the same, beating down on the concrete sidewalks and warming the air. If you closed your eyes and inhaled, even the newest neighborhood was reduced to its essence: hot asphalt, a trace of urine, cracked earth. All the whirring sprinklers and fashionable socialites strutting around couldn't mask that.

At work, Gary was busy planning what he would buy on his next business trip to the States. He always bought things so ordinary Osnat would have never thought of bringing them back—last time he'd passed out aluminum foil all around, claiming it was much cheaper in New York. "What do you think," he asked Osnat, "a car stereo? Or maybe some nonstick cookware for my wife?"

"I might need to move," Osnat told him. "My apartment is leaking. The waterproofer looked like Elvis."

"Did he sing?" Gary wanted to know.

"He didn't even hum."

"Well," Gary said. "I guess all that stuff is relative. I live in a trailer with three children, and we're still waiting for someone to come through and pave the streets."

It didn't seem at all related to Osnat—Gary choosing to live in the West Bank and her wanting to stay in her Tel Aviv neighborhood—but maybe it was. At least neither of them was stuck in a refugee camp. It was something she didn't like thinking about, in the same way that she didn't like thinking about those starving children in Africa. Even though the territories were only a few miles away, she'd been careful to avoid them—she didn't even go to Jerusalem if she could help it. Anyway, this wasn't about right and wrong, not really. She needed to live *somewhere,* didn't she? Still, here was Gary, saying the same exact thing: "I'm not any more land crazy than the next person. Everybody wants a place to live that feels like home."

But what Osnat kept coming back to was that there was no way she'd be able to afford another apartment as nice or so much like America—and America *was* nice, with its air conditioners and manicured lawns. No wonder her aunt tsk-tsked every time she looked through the classifieds, and she was nowhere near desperate either: in addition to her house, she owned a duplex in Holon and two apartments in Netanya, both willed to her husband, Osnat's uncle, by the elderly relatives who lately seemed to be dropping dead left and right, leaving behind peeling flowered wallpaper and stacks of embroidered pillows. If Osnat was selfish for wanting a view of the sea, what did that make her aunt?

. . .

As if he were taunting her, everywhere she went, Osnat saw Elvis zooming around in his little truck: there he was, at the gas station across from her bus stop, putting air in his tires; outside the Supersol, shoving a big bag of kitty litter into the passenger seat, driving past her when her arms were full of groceries and she could have really used the ride. How was it that she hadn't noticed him around before? And what right did he have to show himself off so flagrantly when he'd already determined her apartment was a lost cause?

"Listen," she said finally, the night she saw him smoking outside the bar on Ben Yehuda where they taught line dancing, "are you *sure* there's nothing you can do?"

Elvis raised his hands up in front of him, palms facing out. "Excuse me?" he said.

"Don't you remember?" Osnat asked. "You wanted two hundred dollars for a problem you couldn't fix."

"Ah," Elvis said, "now I remember. You're twisting the facts. Two hundred dollars for a paint job is a bargain." He lit another cigarette, then rolled the pack back up into the sleeve of his white T-shirt. He blew out the smoke in a long, steady stream.

"Oh," Osnat said. "Okay." She turned to walk away.

"I'm not the bad guy here," Elvis called after her. "You can't just fix your apartment without redoing the rest of the building too. Water's like that. You can't just seal up one crack and expect to stay dry."

For her part, Osnat's aunt didn't see the problem. "So sell," she said, "and move into one of the new buildings down that block."

There was something about the way her aunt was always urging her to buy, buy, *buy,* that made Osnat feel like the fat girl whose skinny friend kept encouraging her to eat and eat. "That's just how much stuff costs here," her aunt liked to say. Or, "Surely your parents can help you pay." It didn't matter that she had the same number of televisions and drove the same kind of car as Osnat's parents. There was simply no arguing with the spacious homes and glitzy automobiles you saw on TV. It was easier to believe in those than in the pasty, blubbery people who lived in trailer parks and sometimes came to blows on American talk shows. If one of these realities had to be rigged, then let it be the poor one.

"Maybe you should tell her you aren't rich," Osnat told her mother over the phone. So what if her parents had a big backyard and an attic? It wasn't their fault that land in Israel was so expensive.

But it didn't work that way. There were things you gave up when you left Israel, and one of them was the right to be pitied. That was strictly reserved for the people who stayed behind, the ones who were stuck dealing with inflation and exploding buses. Once you moved to the States, you were supposed to act concerned, periodically checking in to make sure everyone you knew was still alive, and feel a little guilty that you weren't out there too, doing your part to bring about a lasting peace.

Osnat's mother was well trained in the protocol of expatriation. "Come on," she told Osnat. "You know better. It's different living here."

"But have you seen the plans for the house she wants to build?" Osnat said. "Talk about America, it's going to have a hot tub on the roof and everything."

"What?" Osnat's mother said. "What house?"

The key to success, Osnat knew, was to keep going through the motions even when all you wanted to do was stay in bed. That was the theory behind the affirmations she did every morning—repeat them often enough and they'd become more than empty words—and this seemed to hold true for everyday living as well. Or at least it was supposed to. Plenty of people moved to Israel without an apartment waiting for them, and some of them even managed to stay. Clearly, the next step was to browse the real estate classifieds, maybe even make a couple of calls, visit a few places. She bought a paper on her way to work, and spent the bus ride circling ads for the apartments she could afford. Once she got to her cubicle, she even picked up the phone and dialed. She couldn't quite make it to the seventh digit, but no one could argue that it wasn't a start.

"Okay," Gary said when he found Osnat tearing up in front of her computer monitor, "you're taking this whole housing thing a little too seriously." He handed Osnat a tissue and waited patiently while she blew her nose. "This isn't a person you're crying over. It's just a place."

Osnat nodded, which Gary took as an invitation to pull up a chair and sit down.

"Look," he said, crossing one leg over the other. "You're twenty-seven and single. You should be renting a flat in south Tel Aviv and working your way up north like everyone else your age. No more special treatment for you."

But Osnat wasn't asking for special treatment, was she? When she'd been a little girl, it seemed as if every other book she'd read involved someone realizing there was no place like home, only home was always in Israel, where everyone greeted you with open arms and apple cake and small cups of steaming Turkish coffee, no matter how poor or malaria-ridden they happened to be. Of course, Osnat hadn't expected anyone to bake cakes and brew coffee to celebrate her return, but she also hadn't expected to be so thoroughly ignored. As far as she could tell, Israelis just didn't make friends with Americans. And why should they? Americans never stayed in Israel for long, and spent most of their time complaining and rolling their eyes in dismay over spots on their water glasses and waiters who didn't clear their plates the second they put down their forks. Who needed that kind of aggravation? Let them be friends with one another.

When she was little, Osnat's favorite story had been about a woman who worked as a spy for the British Army, helping to free Palestine from the Ottoman Empire, only to be caught and tortured until she had no choice but to shoot herself using a handgun she'd hidden under a loose tile in the bathroom of her parents' house. All that sacrificing, and for what? Sometimes Osnat caught herself marveling over how small everything seemed now that she was an adult—you could walk Tel Aviv north to south in less than an hour—but deep down she knew this nostalgia wasn't exclusive to her, or even to Israel. No one she knew got to live out their lives in the same exact space where they'd been children—it seemed an extravagant thing to want. It seemed almost like a mistake, as if, instead of moving forward, Osnat had decided on moving back.

Still, on Saturday mornings, Osnat liked to lie in bed in the same room where she'd slept as a child, half asleep, half listening to old folk songs on the radio. In those early hours, there was no language more beautiful than Hebrew. It was easy to imagine the pioneers sitting around campfires, playing the accordion, and making up songs about poppies and cyclamen, and how—if you really, truly believed—it wasn't just a dream. So what if they couldn't hit all the high notes? She imagined her grandmother, with her smooth skin, long lashes, and sparkly barrette, sitting with them, clapping her hands or maybe shaking a tambourine, even though she knew it was more likely that her grandmother had been off in some corner crying and wishing she were anywhere else but here, stuck taking care of a coop full of chickens and two squawky girls who—no matter how much attention you paid them—still wanted and needed more. She hadn't been free like Osnat to get up whenever she wanted, pack a lunch, and head for the beach. So what if at night cars lined up for prostitutes along the road leading down to the water? In the early mornings, a small tractor drove by, sweeping the sand and turning over the condoms, leaving the beach looking as if it had been combed. Old couples wearing straw hats walked on the packed sand next to the water. The waves rolled in and rolled back out, and Osnat, for once, could feel herself relaxing, as if the sea were a giant mother whispering shhh, shhh, shhh.

And there, outside the Supersol—again—was Elvis, this time handing out flyers to shoppers wheeling their carts out to the parking lot.

"It's the Elvis National Competition," he told Osnat. "The winner goes on to compete in the European Elvis trials for an all-expense paid trip to Graceland."

"How many of you are there?" Osnat asked.

"Seven full-time," Elvis said. "Maybe another twenty part-time. And more around Purim."

"But why do you do it?" Osnat asked. It seemed like so much work: the shaving, the rhinestones, all the grinding and gyrating. "Elvis wasn't even Jewish."

"So?" He gestured broadly at the parking lot around him. "Look around you," he said. "Now more than ever, what this country needs is the King."

At first, Osnat figured he was just being melodramatic. But later, walking home, she started thinking that maybe he was right, especially given all the bulldozed houses and stalled peace negotiations. You could imagine the real Elvis biding his time, lying low in a dingy one-bedroom walk-up in a neighborhood bordering the Old City, until the day both Palestinians and Israelis flung their hands up and looked to the heavens in despair, at which moment he would swoop down from a nearby roof, all agleam and aglitter in a white jumpsuit, his bell-bottoms working like parachutes to slow and cushion his landing, bearing a white dove in one hand and an olive branch in the other. "Thank you," he'd say. "Thank you very much," and the Israelis and Palestinians would close their astonished mouths and realize that if Elvis could make the ultimate sacrifice—faking his own death and leaving the luxury of Graceland's jungle room for this hot, dusty country that was downright inhospitable to polyester—well, then surely they could find some way to get along, to break fried kosher-bologna sandwiches with each other's families, to stop all the hound-dog accusations and opt—finally, at long last—to be each other's teddy bears.

The bulldozer was scheduled to come Tuesday morning. Osnat took the day off from work. She'd borrowed a video camera from Gary—it seemed like something that should be recorded—and taken the 6:40 bus north to her grandmother's village, even though it meant skipping her daily affirmations. She wanted to get there first—her mother, after recovering from the news, had asked her to save some of the blue and white bathroom tiles—but by the time she got there, the crew was already setting up.

"Can I help you?" the foreman asked Osnat. When she explained to him what she wanted, he lent her a trowel. "The grout's probably half rotted anyway," he said. Later, he stood next to her while the bulldozer made quick work of knocking down the walls. It was a small house. The whole thing took maybe ten minutes and made hardly any noise. There wasn't even enough time for Golda to come out of the neighboring house to watch.

"Wow," Osnat said.

"Practice makes perfect," the foreman said. He nodded at the man on top of the bulldozer. "Moti does this in the army too.

Learned from the best." He pulled out a pack of cigarettes from his shirt pocket and offered one to Osnat, shrugging when she refused. "This is a great location," he said between puffs. "One day, it'll be worth millions. And I mean dollars, not shekels."

"Really?" Osnat said.

"With a view of the Mediterranean?" the foreman said. "Are you crazy? You must be just off the plane."

"I was born here," Osnat said.

"Well," the foreman said, "you certainly didn't grow up here."

He was shorter than Osnat, and skinnier, and she could imagine belting him one, except that just then, a car pulled up behind them and Osnat's aunt came bolting out of the passenger side.

"Is it gone?" She came to a standstill next to Osnat. "Oh God. Is it gone already?" She covered her face with her hands, and her shoulders started shaking. But she deserved it, Osnat figured. Who did her aunt think she was, ordering her grandmother's house demolished? No Jacuzzi was going to make that okay. Anyway, it wasn't as if her aunt needed her: already her three daughters were around her, patting her back and squeezing her hands and handing her tissues. "Oh God," Osnat's aunt sobbed. "I didn't think it would feel like *this.*"

The foreman looked meaningfully at Osnat. "Don't worry," he said in a low voice. "This happens all the time, and people get over it just the same."

Back at her apartment, Osnat hooked the camera up to the television and watched the house collapse in both fast and slow motion. Once the walls buckled, it could have been any house, anywhere. The only thing left standing was the refrigerator, which the workers had hauled out earlier, and now it stood with its door swinging on its hinges, gaping like an open mouth. The tape ended with Osnat's aunt, off-camera, saying, "Is it gone?"

After that, Osnat had been too embarrassed to keep recording, and it was just as well. She couldn't come up with one good reason for showing the tape to her parents. Instead, she put it in a plastic case and tucked it into the back of her closet.

Outside, she could see clouds gathering over the Mediterranean, skewered by the occasional lightning bolt. About a kilometer off into the water, a tanker was unloading oil into an underwater pipeline. She walked from room to room, closing the shutters. It was nearly the end of February. There was maybe one more month of rain.

The phone rang, and Osnat considered not picking up, but then she did anyway. "I just wanted to let you know I'm all right," her aunt said. "In case you were worried." When Osnat didn't say anything, she added, "The rest will be easier, I hope. Have you talked to your mother?"

"No," Osnat said. She took a deep breath. "Was this just about money?"

"What?" her aunt said.

"The foreman told me the land was worth millions." Even though she tried to keep her voice neutral, she could tell the words had come out wrong, accusatory.

Her aunt sighed. "Look, Osnat," she said. "I'm going to tell you what I'm going to tell your mother—"

"I know," Osnat interrupted her. "You hated the house. You're glad it's gone."

"Not all of us can move to another country," her aunt said. "Some of us have to stay here."

"Okay," Osnat said. "I understand." The room around her was dark. She could hear drops of water starting to hit the outside walls.

"No," Osnat's aunt said. "You don't. You've had it all handed to you—a spiffy neighborhood, a view of the sea, America. I'm fifty-six," she said. "I've worked hard and been patient and raised three lawyers to boot. It's my turn now. I want some America too."

At the grocery store, the little girl who did commercials for peanut puffs was throwing a fit because her mother wouldn't buy her a lemon Popsicle. Puffy-faced and red-eyed, she looked nothing like the girl with the checkered bow and shiny Mary Janes who sang and danced with an animated elephant. Still, her crying did the trick, and her mother gave in. "Fine," she said, "go get one," and the little girl shot off toward the freezer section in the back of the store.

"I'm sorry," the girl's mother said to Osnat, who was standing in line behind her. "After a hard day, sometimes you just really need a Popsicle." Osnat nodded, and the mother smiled. "I think we live in the same building," she said. "You're on the sixth floor, right? Isn't the wetness this year something else?"

Osnat felt stupid. It had never occurred to her that the rain was seeping into every apartment, not just hers, even though the wet spots were there for anyone to see. "Yes," she said. "My mother thought it might be an old family curse."

"Then we must be related," the mother said. "On the bright side, winter's almost over, and soon enough we'll be praying for rain." To her daughter, who had returned and was fumbling with the Popsicle's wrapper, she said, "Took you long enough."

Outside, the sun was shining. In the light, Osnat's building looked old and tired, as if it had recently been weeping. Beyond it, the sea sparkled blue. The sidewalks looked clean, freshly washed. It was easy to feel optimistic, even if the walls in your bedroom were growing mold. There were twenty-five other apartments in Osnat's building. The people who lived in them weren't going anywhere, and neither was she.

. . .

On the first really hot day of summer, Elvis came by to patch over those places where the wet spots had dried into bubbly strips of dried plaster. "Our Elvis placed fifth in the European trials," he told Osnat. "Not bad for a Jew, although of course he's disappointed not to be going to Graceland."

"I've been there," Osnat said. "It's much smaller in real life, and they don't let you see the bedrooms."

"I tried to tell him, but you know how it goes: America, America, America," Elvis said, pulling off a chunk of wall. "I keep telling the others that we could never do what we're doing in America. I've seen shows about it on TV—they have thousands of Elvis impersonators, and those are just the ones who can sing. A short, skinny Israeli like me—like any of us—would be laughed right out of the country. Have you even heard my English? If you're a small fish, it's sometimes better to move from the pond to the fishbowl."

Osnat shrugged.

"No," Elvis said. "Don't deny it. It's why you came back. It's why all of you come back." Then he turned away from her and continued patching the wall.

Osnat wasn't sure if she should feel insulted—it *seemed* as if she should, but she didn't know what difference it would make. She had written maybe three notebooks full of affirmations, and still, here she was, in an apartment that leaked, taking advice from a short, skinny, Israeli Elvis and feeling as if *she* were the ridiculous one. But here she *was.* Wasn't that worth something? Everyone she knew was looking for their America, even if it was fishbowl-sized and located in Israel. And if her own private America happened to be a crappy apartment with a view of a beach that doubled as a red-light district, well then, so what? People moved from one end of the world to the other every day, and some of them went crazy, but more of them survived. Hadn't Osnat's own parents survived? Her mother, on occasion, even claimed to be content. All Osnat needed to do was wait, and her own Graceland would slowly reveal itself to her. She was patient, and she had time, and for now, that was good enough. For now, that was plenty.

Land of Ass and Honey

In the back of the local Tel Aviv paper, there were pictures of women spreading their legs and touching themselves, their private parts covered by red hearts, their heads dwarfed by thought bubbles that announced, "I'm bored! I'm wet! Call me!" In the adjoining columns, European men advertised for companions: good-looking women interested in discreet relationships that included rent and expenses. Osnat was still having trouble reading the news, but she had no trouble understanding the sex ads. The only problem was, she was twenty-eight, which was older than the European men wanted their mistresses, and she still had some self-respect—and this despite the fact that one of the mistresses had written a column arguing that at least, her way, she was getting the cash up front instead of in dinner-and-a-movie form. It was hard to argue with that kind of logic.

"Come visit," Osnat wrote her friend Jeannie. "Land of milk and honey, my ass. More like land of ass and honey." She'd been in Israel nearly a year and a half, and she wasn't bored, and she wasn't wet, but she was lonely. The only people she talked to were ones she was paying: the deli guy at the grocery store, the plumber, the guy who sold insurance outside the Secretary of Interior. They picked up the tab for dinner, and sometimes for dessert, and then they pulled up outside her apartment building and looked at her expectantly, as if she hadn't already paid them enough.

Osnat wasn't stupid. She'd read the travel books that warned women against Israeli men. "Avoid direct eye contact," they cautioned. "Never accept a cup of coffee from a stranger." In college, Osnat knew a woman so large she needed a cane to get around, and even she had been fair game in Israel. "It's the accent," this woman said when she returned sporting a suntan and camels carved out of wood. "Just make sure they hear you speak." She lowered her voice: "I liked it. It was nice." And it *was* nice. At the beach, men with potbellies strutted around in their underwear; women wore bikinis even if their thighs touched and their upper arms sagged. What you looked like didn't matter, as long as you couldn't roll your *r*s.

Jeannie wasn't Jewish, and she and Osnat weren't even close friends, but she'd once had sex with an Israeli guy named Dudi. "What is it with you Israelis naming people after things your body excretes?" she'd asked Osnat when they first introduced themselves. Of course, there were names worse than Dudi or Osnat, like the name of a TV anchorman that was pronounced Guy *Penis,* but the part that really didn't seem fair to Osnat was that Jeannie had slept with a real Israeli and actually enjoyed it. In fact, she enjoyed it so much that she was ready to give other Israelis a try. "Okay," she wrote Osnat. "People have spent more to get laid—like Robert Redford in that movie, or Charlie Sheen." Still, waiting for Jeannie at the airport, Osnat felt herself getting all misty-eyed: it wasn't everybody who spent eight hundred dollars on airfare just to come see her in a country with a travel advisory. This was way more than dinner and dessert.

When Osnat first arrived in Israel, she was armed with a long list of relatives and family friends, each of whom, once contacted, dutifully invited her to dinner, where they asked her why she moved back to Israel and if she was dating anybody. After dessert, they sometimes volunteered their own children, who were closer to Osnat's age, as tour guides and helpers, writing out their cell phone numbers so Osnat could call them if she needed anything. For a while, Osnat did try calling, but the whole meeting-people-your-own-age-for-coffee thing wasn't working the way she'd hoped. Blood was blood, but the small talk could bring you to tears. It felt just like dating, except that with relatives there was no prospect of sex. Instead, you were stripped down to bare essentials: lousy Hebrew, no army experience, no marriage prospects, no kids—for God's sake, Osnat didn't even have cable. "You know," cousin after cousin told her after they ran out of conversation, "I know the perfect guy for you." It made Osnat feel like a hot potato.

These days, the only person who still called Osnat was Pini, one of her mother's friends from college, and that was only because his own kids were mad at him for leaving their mother and moving into his own place. Not that Osnat minded. The only thing she remembered about Pini's boys was that back when she was thirteen and in Tel Aviv for a visit, the two of them had spent an afternoon trying to pull down her tank top so they could see her brand-new breasts. Although she knew they had probably grown up into decent people, she was glad to have Pini to herself, even if he was fifty-three. There were perks to hanging out with someone old enough to be your parent: he had a car, and cable, and always insisted on paying if you went out for coffee or to the movies. But the main thing about Pini was that he was newly lonely too and knew better than to talk about it. Instead, when she told him Jeannie was coming, he offered to drive Osnat out to the airport. And thank goodness: despite the fact that in the States she'd driven twelve years without a ticket and here she'd gone on three dates with her driving instructor, Osnat had still flunked the driving test for new immigrants.

Jeannie, when she finally emerged from the terminal, was all perk and dimples. She squealed when she saw Osnat. "Look at you!" she said. "You're so tan!" They hugged. "So guess what?" Jeannie said. "Two men hit on me on the plane."

"My God," Osnat said. "How efficient."

"It bodes well for this visit," Jeannie said. "Too bad they were married."

"Marriage isn't a wall," Osnat pointed out. It was what the driving instructor had said to her when she pointed to his ring. "You can get around it."

Jeannie laughed, a little too loudly. "Is that what you've been learning, here in the Holy Land?"

In Tel Aviv, where Osnat lived, there was a McDonald's on every other block, and a Dunkin' Donuts near Rabin Square, and still everything felt to Osnat as if it had been shifted a little—a smaller, dirtier, almost-America—as if someone had gone through her house and rearranged the furniture and all the closets so that she couldn't find her shoes. At the pool, people swam the breaststroke instead of the front crawl, and in fairy tales, the three little pigs were now little goats. Clearly, the rules weren't the same anymore. When guys excused themselves and didn't close the bathroom door behind them, Osnat gave them the benefit of the doubt: maybe it was a cultural difference. When they walked down the street, she tried not to stare if they stopped to urinate against trees and parked cars. One time, she saw a man peeing against the wall of a gas station, ten meters away from a restroom. Now, everywhere she went with Jeannie, the two of them stumbled onto naked men, sunbathers who decided to flip over right as they walked by, boys skinny-dipping at the beach. The bus stops reeked of urine.

"God," Jeannie said. "What *is* that smell?"

"You get used to it," Osnat said.

All around them, the tension was thick enough to touch. When they weren't running around naked, people looked angry and hot. The sun was fierce. Buses spewed black soot. The schools were fenced in. Signs warned you to be on the lookout for suspicious objects.

Jeannie wore her blond hair twisted into a knot at the nape of her neck. Her toenails were painted red. Even though she kept blotting the sweat off her face with a tissue, the sun made her shimmer. You could pick her out a mile away, in her white T-shirt and white sandals and pink, pink skin. She looked happy, plump, a tourist through and through.

Every morning, the news announcers tallied up the traffic casualties since the beginning of the year—they were already in the hundreds. Osnat could hear traffic accidents from her balcony: brakes squealing followed by shattering glass, followed by more squealing brakes as traffic backed up and people got out of their cars to yell at each other. She hadn't seen anyone die yet, but she once saw an accident where the driver had to be sawed out of his car and carried off on a stretcher.

"Jesus," Jeannie said. "So much for worrying about terrorists."

Downstairs, Pini was waiting for them in his Subaru. It was day two of Jeannie's visit, and he had volunteered to keep her company while Osnat went for another driving lesson. She was scheduled to take the test again the day Jeannie was leaving. If Osnat failed this time, she'd have to take the written version, and she was a terrible test taker: in college, she had majored in English just to avoid exams. She couldn't fail. Her American license had expired in March.

The driving instructor, Jackie, was in a good mood. Osnat figured that one of his other students must have put out, even if she hadn't.

"Who needs a student when you have a wife?" Jackie said when she asked him why he was so cheerful. "Anyway, don't think all driving instructors have it as good as I do. Most of them are just short and ugly, and have hair growing out of their ears. At least my wife trims my ear hair." He laughed and patted Osnat's right thigh. "Don't worry, sweetheart," he said. "You'll learn how to drive one of these days."

Osnat had given up on telling Jackie that she already knew how to drive. He always just waved her off. "That wasn't real driving," he said. "That was America, where everyone's polite." And he was right. Whenever Osnat was with him, she couldn't drive to save her life: her hands trembled so badly she had to clutch the steering wheel just to steady them. People died every day on this very highway while trying to avoid the mopeds and motorcycles and cars zooming from lane to lane, and they'd lived in Israel forever. What chance did she have?

"So," Jackie said. "Who's your friend? American, right? I can always tell."

"Can you tell about me?" Osnat asked.

"Just when you open your mouth," Jackie said, "but that's because there's something different about you." He narrowed his eyes meaningfully. "Something special." It was what Israeli guys always ended up saying to Osnat. Then they laid it on heavy with the eye contact.

On day three of Jeannie's visit, Pini drove them to the central bus station so they could catch a bus down to the desert. They were going to spend the night at a hostel below Masada, an ancient Roman fortress on a cliff overlooking the Dead Sea, and then hike up in the morning, when it was cool. The bus station was a monster of a building, all fluorescent lights, dirty tiles, and little shops where you could purchase souvenir T-shirts and bootleg

CDs. It was Sunday morning, so the place was full of bleary-eyed soldiers heading back to their bases, eating bagel toast and omelet sandwiches and drinking coffee, their rifles slung casually over their shoulders.

"Well," Jeannie said, "I must be getting old. They all look twelve to me, although there *is* something about that uniform."

She said it loudly, and the man sitting across from them in the waiting area looked up. "It's the gun," he said in English. "Not the uniform." He winked. Dark, curly chest hair poked through his shirt collar. "I'm Ron," he said. "And we are all soldiers in this country."

Jeannie laughed. She had a beautiful laugh, like a movie star's, and the gestures to go along with it: the tossed-back head, the exposed, creamy neck. Osnat's own neck was moist and sticky. When Jeannie was done laughing, she opened her eyes wide. "It must be difficult," she said. "Were you in danger? Were you scared?"

"Ah, danger." Ron waved his hand dismissively. "You're in danger here every time you get on the road. It's a hard, hard country to live in. If my wife and I could get green cards, we'd leave tomorrow."

"Not Osnat here," Jeannie said. "You should have seen our boss in America practically beg her to stay. He told me to bring her back with me, that's how much he misses her."

This was all news to Osnat, but she did her best to play along: "I miss you guys too."

"Then it's just a matter of time," Ron pronounced. "She'll be back before you know it."

"No," Jeannie said. "Not Osnat."

The bus station was located in an older part of Tel Aviv, and the ramp leading from the departure gate down to the street was so close to the surrounding buildings you could see straight into the tiny apartments where the Nigerian and Thai foreign workers lived, with all their peeling paint and moldy walls and bright laundry. Osnat hoped Jeannie wouldn't notice, or that at least she wouldn't say anything. Back on street level, the sidewalks around them seemed to blaze white with heat, and the edges of buildings looked burnt-out, overexposed. Stray cats lolled under parked cars. On one of the overpasses on the way out of town, someone had painted a huge portrait of Princess Diana, and written, "Buckle up."

For a moment, Jeannie seemed stunned into silence by the hideousness of it all, but then she recovered. "Here's the thing," she told Osnat. "People like talking about themselves, so you have to ask them questions."

"It's different for you," Osnat said. "You're a tourist. Real Israelis don't ask if being in the army is dangerous."

"Well," Jeannie said, "being tourists got us free goodies, didn't it?"

And it had gotten them free goodies: a half kilo of sunflower seeds, two chocolate bars, and a list of sites not to be missed, complete with directions, courtesy of Ron.

"I guess tourists just bring out the best in people," Jeannie continued. "They're just so easy to impress. You meet them, you buy them candy, and they think you're great. I mean, I think Ron is pretty great, for a guy who's married."

The thing was, Osnat didn't want to be a tourist. She wanted people to be nice to her even though she was staying and they could see her again. She wanted them to *want* to see her again. Suddenly, she was afraid that maybe the only reason Jeannie had come really had been to get laid, and now here they were, on the way to a hostel near the Dead Sea, in the middle of the desert, in the middle of the week, where the only other people would be tourists. At this rate, they were going to have to have sex with each other.

Outside, they crossed an invisible line in the landscape. North of it were fields of sunflowers raised for export. South of it was desert.

"Land of milk and honey," Jeannie muttered. "What were they thinking?"

At the hostel at the base of Masada, two backpackers from Australia were drinking beer and watching *Baywatch* on television. While Jeannie showered, Osnat called Pini, who had asked her to let him know when they arrived. "Someone has to check up on you," he liked to say, "and if your parents can't, then I guess it's my job." And maybe it was good that he did, because who knew how long it would take her corpse to start smelling so bad that the downstairs neighbors would notice it. Still, just in case, she was always careful to travel with her ID so that the police would be able to identify her body, or what was left of it.

When Osnat told Pini about Ron, instead of sounding disgusted, he made a *pshhh* noise, which, as far as Osnat knew, meant he was impressed. "That's sabra hospitality for you," he said.

"Or maybe he just wants to sleep with her," Osnat said.

"Give me a break," Pini said. "He's married. He was just being kind."

"Marriage isn't a wall," Osnat said. "And anyway, tourists bring out the best in people."

"I suppose," Pini said. "I mean, look at the way I drive you around, when I made my own kids take the bus everywhere."

"I'm not a tourist," Osnat said. "I just can't pass the driver's test." She thought about hanging up on Pini, but she wasn't sure it would bother him enough to make it worth her while. "And I'm not your daughter."

"You may as well be," Pini said. "At least while you're here."

"Yeah," Osnat said. "Why don't you ask your sons how they feel about that?" She could tell by the silence on the other end of the line that she got him. "I'm here to stay," she said. "I don't need special favors."

On TV, the *Baywatch* team was busy rescuing some kid dragged out by the undertow. For a while, it looked as if he was going to take Pamela Anderson down with him. One of the Australians said, "Drown her. Drown the bitch," and the other Australian said, "Hear, hear."

They woke up early, at 5 a.m., and took the Snake Path up to Masada in the dark. Below them, the Dead Sea was hazy, but then it was very blue. The hills around them changed color from brown to pink to gold. Inside the walls of the fortress, stray cats watched them eat breakfast, and they watched the Australians, who had made it up before them, and were now standing in what remained from the northern palace and shouting things over the edge of the terrace. The echo that rolled back at them multiplied their voices and made them sound like a mob, as if somewhere hundreds of men and women and children were calling for help.

"Creepy," Jeannie said, but she didn't say much except for that. Instead, she dashed from one patch of shade to the next, and fanned herself with the brochure that described what each structure was. Later, they hiked back down and took the bus over to the beach near Ein Gedi, where Osnat took pictures of Jeannie floating in the Dead Sea and reading a newspaper, and more pictures of Jeannie covered in mud. On the shore, there were green flies everywhere, biting Osnat through her clothing every time she got near the water's edge. And she wasn't the only one: the baseball cap of a man standing near her shimmered a crawling, coppery green. Osnat imagined herself running into the water, clawing at her face and neck, but she hated the Dead Sea, the way it appeared deceptively cool when really, it was warm like urine and smelled like sulfur.

On the drive back to Be'er Sheva the bus got stuck behind an army convoy—truck after truck carrying soldiers and some trucks carrying tanks. The roads wound and twisted through the hills, the bus's engine loud with effort.

"When we get back to Tel Aviv," Jeannie said, "we're going to get dressed up, and then we're going to go out and drink tropical drinks and pick up guys, soldiers even. So what if they're twelve?"

"This isn't the tropics," Osnat said, cringing the moment the words were out of her mouth.

Jeannie smiled brightly. "So what?" she said. "Surely someone somewhere serves drinks with little umbrellas." When Osnat didn't say anything, she added, "Look, Osnat, I'm really trying here. Why don't you give it a try too?"

Osnat felt her chest constrict. "What do you mean?"

"You're so quiet," Jeannie said. "You didn't used to be this quiet."

"Really?"

"Really," Jeannie said. "You used to talk all the time."

Osnat opened her mouth, but she couldn't think of a thing to say. She was out of practice. On dates, when Osnat said that the hardest thing about the move was not having women friends, the guys thought she was crazy. What did they know? They came fully equipped with male best friends with whom they watched soccer and went shopping and talked about their feelings. The only thing they didn't do with their best friends was have sex, at least not regularly. Somewhere, Osnat knew, there had to be single women her age, but she couldn't figure out where exactly that place might be. All her cousins were married, and there were babies everywhere, strollers parked in rows outside grocery stores. Besides, Osnat's dates reassured her, she didn't really want women friends. Women were always bickering over some guy, and then, once they got married, they disappeared. And who could blame them? Land was expensive. You needed two salaries to make a dent in your mortgage.

And here—finally and at long, long last—was Jeannie, captive and sweating, going nowhere, sitting right next to Osnat, and Osnat's mouth was so dry she could barely swallow, as if all the conversations she'd been saving all these months had simply shriveled up and disintegrated.

Back at the Tel Aviv bus station, Osnat went looking for the bathroom. Pini would be outside, waiting to drive them back to her apartment, and she needed to regroup. It was day four of Jeannie's visit. There were still three days to go.

The women's restroom was empty except for an old toothless woman in a babushka who was cleaning the floor with a mop. Osnat tried one of the stalls, but the door was locked. "You need a shekel," the woman informed her.

Osnat searched her pockets, but she didn't have any change. She gave her best pleading look to the woman. "Can't you just let me in one of them?"

"Why?" the woman said. "You're not sick. You're not here to use the bathroom."

"Yes, I am," Osnat said.

"Don't lie," the woman said. Osnat must have looked surprised, because the woman explained, "I tell fortunes. I have second sight. Ask me a question, and I'll answer."

Osnat could feel herself starting to sweat. She put her hands in her front pockets, and then in her back ones. What was it about her and all these so-called psychics? One time, when she had gone into a bakery to buy pita bread, the baker had offered to read her palm for an extra twenty shekels. "You're special," he had said. "I can tell that about you already," but Osnat couldn't do it. This wasn't America, and there was no guarantee the fortune-tellers would be nice. God knows nobody else went out of their way to make her feel good about herself. It was too risky.

The woman rolled her eyes. She was apparently tired of waiting. "You're in my way," she said. She dipped her mop in a pail of dirty water and slid it toward Osnat.

"Fine," Osnat said. "Fine." She tried to think of a good question, but all she could think of asking was if she'd ever be happy here, in Israel, and she was afraid the answer would be no. Instead, what she asked was, "Am I going to pass my driving test next week?"

The woman rolled her eyes again. "This is your question?"

"I really need to pass that test," Osnat said.

"Idiot," the woman said. "Passing the test isn't the right thing to care about."

"You call that an answer?" Osnat said, but secretly, she felt relieved. She stood next to the sink and ran her hands under the cold tap, trying to stop the trembling, until the attendant yelled at her for wasting water.

When Osnat first arrived in Israel, she started off each date by announcing that she wouldn't be having sex that night. But sex, it turned out, wasn't anything secret or special. You could bring your girlfriend home, and your mother would hand her a towel and make her breakfast in the morning. So Osnat took her cues from television, where she learned that the Israeli man was prickly on the outside and sweet on the inside. He wanted to say, "I love you," but three years of checkpoint duty left him embittered and closed off. His best buddy understood—he had been there too. The best thing about dating, it turned out, wasn't sex but the lovely parting gifts: a CD, a pair of parakeets, earrings. One guy had even offered Osnat his washing machine. For a while Osnat had been dazzled. Then she learned the script. "There's a short in the kitchen," she'd inform the guy she was dating. "Can you fix it?" Or else: "The toilet's backing up. Do you know what to do?" Still, the word in Hebrew for babe was a derivative of the word for cunt. The joke was: Why did God give women legs? So that they wouldn't leave a wet trail on the ground behind them.

Osnat figured Pini would be mad at her after their conversation, but he wasn't. He was right there, in his car, where he was supposed to be. "I know a place where the drinks come with little umbrellas," he told Osnat and Jeannie. "And the food isn't bad either."

"Now we're talking," Jeannie said.

Back at the apartment, Jeannie showered and switched into a pink sundress. Just looking at her made Osnat feel oily and drab. Dejected, she stood in front of the full-length mirror in the hallway. When had she started going gray? As if Jeannie knew what Osnat was thinking, she said, "You look fine," but somehow that made everything worse. Osnat could feel herself starting to tremble again.

"God, Jeannie," she said. "Look." She held up her hands so Jeannie could see the shaking.

Jeannie reached over and took Osnat's hands in her own. Her grip was strong, her hands surprisingly cool and dry. She squeezed Osnat's fingers and held on even when Osnat tried to pull back. "Relax," she said. "Your hands aren't going to shrivel up and fall off." Osnat took a deep breath, and Jeannie let go. "See?" she said. "Did that kill you?" She sighed. "You're wiping me out, Osnat. You're making me tired."

"What do you mean?" Osnat asked.

"Look," Jeannie said, "if you want people to lend you their car for the weekend, you have to ask. You have to give them a chance to say yes, Ms. I'm-Not-A-Tourist. And you have to give them something back in return."

"Like what?" Osnat said. "Jeannie, Jesus, all I've done since I've come here is have sex with people I don't like."

"That's your mistake, then," Jeannie said. "Try sex with people you like."

"Like who?"

"I don't know." Jeannie paused meaningfully. "Like Pini. It's obvious he likes you."

"Gross," Osnat said. "He's like my father."

"But he isn't," Jeannie said. "That's exactly it."

Osnat tried to imagine it, her and Pini. Sure, he was handsome—tall and slender, with curly salt-and-pepper hair and three dimples in his right cheek—but something about it didn't feel right. He knew her parents. When they had come to visit back in the winter, she had watched them tell jokes she didn't understand and laugh so hard her father had to whip out his inhaler. "Don't worry," Osnat's mother had said later. "A sense of humor is the last thing to come." And she was right: even though her Hebrew was getting better and better, Osnat still hadn't made one person smile since she'd been in Israel, if you didn't count the way guys laughed when she said she wasn't going to have sex with them. That usually got them going, her little speech, as if they could tell just by looking at her that it wasn't true.

They went to a fish restaurant down on the beach, close enough to the water that you could hear the waves crashing. They sat in a booth, Pini and Osnat on one side, and Jeannie on the other, and after a couple of glasses of wine, Osnat could feel Pini's thigh pressing into her own. It was something he'd done before, but she'd always assumed it was an accident, and even now, looking at the part of him that was above the table, she couldn't tell if it was on purpose. She moved her leg away, but he only spread his wider, and the truth was that the wind off the water was a little chilly, and he felt nice and warm against her, so she let things stay as they were. Across from her, Jeannie seemed oblivious, too busy flirting with the waiter to notice Pini's feet.

"So," she was saying, "was it dangerous in the army?" When the waiter left to get them more wine, she leaned forward and whispered, "Did you check out the size of his hands?"

"Oh, come on," Pini said. "You don't really buy that, do you?" He spread out the fingers of both his hands, and then closed them to form two large fists.

"Oh yeah?" Jeannie said. "Then why the elaborate display?"

"I'm a man," Pini said. "I've got to assert my masculinity."

"Gross," Osnat said. She moved her leg away from Pini's.

"That's Osnat for you," Jeannie said. "Always playing the prude." She winked and stood up. "Well, I'm off to pee."

They watched Jeannie make her way toward the back of the restaurant, and then Pini said, "I think I've had too much wine."

Osnat shook out her napkin and started refolding it. Pini's thigh was back against hers, and now his arm was hanging off the back of her chair. "So what's this?" she said, trying to sound casual. "Are you coming on to me?" It was a line she'd used before, with other men, and she could feel her face take on its just-try-to-ask-me-out expression, which always seemed to initiate the dating script. She hoped Pini would see through it, but he didn't.

"I don't know," he said. "Maybe."

The next line was supposed to be Osnat's—something along

the lines of "Well, which is it?" or "I don't understand Maybe," or "You know, I think you should"—which would be followed by Pini saying, "Okay, how about dinner?" Then they would go out on a first date—where Pini would tell her about his wife, and about how lonely it was to have your sons ignore you, and she would go down on him so that he wouldn't feel so sad—and on a second date—when he would offer to buy her a dishwasher or a car, and she would say no but sleep with him again after he told her she was special, she was different, and that he could see it right away—and on a third date—when she would realize that she could be anybody, anybody at all, as long as she had an accent and indulged his inner tour guide, who would offer to take her camping up north before asking for another fabulous blow job and suggesting that maybe, just maybe, the reason that *she* still didn't have any friends was because she'd never had any, ever, in the first place.

Osnat's hands were shaking again, so she sat on them. "Pini," she said. "You don't even know me."

"Sure I do," Pini said. "You've been here a year and a half already. I'd say I know you pretty well."

"This isn't me," Osnat said. "You can ask Jeannie, she'll tell you."

"Is it because I'm old?" Pini asked.

"No," Osnat said. "Can't we just keep on being friends?"

Now she knew she wasn't imagining it. Pini pulled his leg away. "I don't know," he said. "I already have friends."

Later, after Pini dropped them off, Osnat took Jeannie to see the dogs that guarded the air force base near her neighborhood. There was a full moon, so even though the base was dark, and most of the dogs were sleeping, here and there they could make out the glitter of their eyes and of the chains that kept them tied to their doghouses. In one of the watchtowers, they could see a soldier talking on a cell phone, leaning so far back in his seat that Osnat was afraid he'd tip over.

"I wonder if they jerk off in there," Jeannie said. "I bet the army is just one big hotbed of sex."

"I'm sorry you're not getting laid," Osnat said. "Maybe we'll find you someone tomorrow."

"You better." Jeannie laughed. "And if you don't, I have that waiter's phone number." She leaned against Osnat and nudged her gently. "I'm kidding, you know."

Osnat was feeling all weepy again. Already it seemed unbearable that Jeannie was going to leave, and all they'd done so far was bicker. She'd never come back at this rate, and Osnat would end up having sex with Pini, because she couldn't afford to lose him too, or at least not both of them at the same time.

Jeannie sighed. "Osnat," she said. "I think you should come back home. This place isn't good for you."

"But you were right about Pini," Osnat said. "Maybe I should try dating him."

"Sweetie," Jeannie said, "this isn't about finding a boyfriend."

Osnat didn't know what the matter was with her. She used to be much stronger—packing up, saying good-bye to everyone, and moving to Israel because, any way you looked at it, it was the right thing to do. And it wasn't as if she and Jeannie would live near each other for the rest of their lives: people in America were always moving around, and it was just a matter of time before you ended up alone. Wasn't that what had happened to her parents, aging and stuck in Michigan, all their friends retiring and moving south? And didn't it happen to Osnat herself again and again and again, when she finished college or every time she switched jobs? But here, in Israel, she had eight first cousins and forty-three second cousins, most of whom lived within an hour's drive, and who kept inviting her over for lunch on Saturdays but never offering to pick her up even though there was no bus service and she had no way of getting there.

And even supposing that she was meant to be alone, that there really was something wrong with her and she was a terrible person and a terrible friend, and ended up doing nothing with her life but working and paying taxes, then at least if she lived in Israel, where there were only six million people, she would matter in a way that she didn't in the United States. Unless she was doing something better with her life, something important—saving whales, curing cancer, training to be an astronaut—unless she was going to be someone extraordinary and not just a technical writer, or even just a teacher or a nurse or a banker or a doctor—then she might as well be doing it in Israel, where everybody celebrated the same holidays she did and no one asked her if a dreidel was a kind of cracker, and where just by going about her life she was making the statement that having your own country was important, and not just during times of emergency. So what if life was hard here? At least you felt you were *living.* Osnat had never been this exhausted back in Chicago.

By this time, Osnat was blubbering and getting snot all over Jeannie's shirt, and the soldier on watch duty had turned around and trained his binoculars on them.

"Girls," he said, using a bullhorn. "Girls, are you okay?"

Osnat sniffled and signaled to him that they were all right. "See," she told Jeannie. "No one cares about you like this in America."

On Jeannie's last night in Israel, they went to the beach and built a bonfire. Earlier that day, Jeannie had picked up the guide who led the walking tour of the Stations of the Cross in Jerusalem, and he had rounded up a friend who had then driven Osnat and Jeannie back to Tel Aviv. Now the guys were busy stomping on wooden platforms they had stolen from a construction site so they could use the boards for fuel, while Jeannie and Osnat wrapped onions and potatoes in aluminum foil for roasting. The tour guide, Ilan, was short and skinny, with big bushy eyebrows. His family had lived in Jerusalem for eight generations. His friend, Michael, was blond and from Haifa. His parents were Canadian.

"Really?" Jeannie said. "Are they happy here?"

"Of course they are," Michael said. "They just got a big-screen TV."

Later, when the fire died down, Jeannie sang sad Irish songs, and Osnat watched Michael and Ilan watch Jeannie, transfixed. Who could blame them? Behind Jeannie, her hair and skin rosy and reflecting the fire, the sea was a dark purple, and the only other lights were from an oil tanker a few kilometers offshore. Osnat didn't know how or when they decided which one of them would get Jeannie, but when she finished singing it was Michael who put his arm around her, and Ilan who made himself busy stirring the coals.

"Yeah," Ilan told Osnat when it was just the two of them, "he used to model swimsuits, so what can you do?" He flipped a board over, and the fire reignited. "But I think the potatoes are ready."

"How do you know?" Osnat asked.

"I just do," Ilan said. He pulled a potato out of the fire, broke it in half, and presented it to Osnat. "Some people are good at sports, and some people know about potatoes."

Osnat scooted closer to the flames. Maybe it really was handy having an internal potato timer. She thought about reaching over and touching Ilan. "So," she said finally, "you want to make out?"

Ilan snorted. "Are you kidding?" he said. "I hardly know you."

. . .

At the airport, security was tight and a woman border guard asked Jeannie the same questions over and over: "Are you sure you didn't go into the territories? Who were you staying with again?" The inspector's hair was pulled back into a tight slick ponytail. She checked Jeannie's passport and then Osnat's ID. When she opened up Jeannie's suitcase, Osnat imagined her forcing Jeannie to stay. They could be roommates, and Osnat could get Jeannie a job at her company. "Okay," the inspector told Jeannie. "You can go."

On the bus back to Tel Aviv, Osnat watched the gulls circling over the giant landfill that bordered the airport. Maybe one of them would get sucked into Jeannie's plane's engine, and the pilot would be forced to make an emergency landing. It had happened to Osnat's father once, and he had missed a meeting in Washington. When Osnat felt the bus come to a stop, at first she hoped it was that her wish had come true, and someone at the airport had radioed the driver to turn around, but when she sat up so she could see what was going on, she realized that up ahead two cars had gotten into an accident and now one of them was burning on the side of the road. Even though the police were already there and waved the drivers through, everyone was still slowing down for a better look.

Osnat turned to the woman who was sitting next to her. "Couldn't it explode?" she asked.

"It already did," the woman said. "Look at it."

And Osnat did look. The fire burned so brightly that looking at the flames hurt her eyes, and she could feel the heat when the bus finally made its way past the car's body. If there had been anyone inside it, you couldn't tell anymore.

"God," Osnat said. "I have to take a driving test at two."

"Maybe it's a sign," the woman said. "Drive extra carefully."

"I already failed it once," Osnat told her.

"That's nothing," the woman said. "I failed it four times. Why do you think I'm sitting here next to you?" The woman chuckled. "But that's okay," she said. "Despite everything, it's still safer riding a bus."

Earlier, before Jeannie had gotten on the escalators that would take her to her plane's boarding area, she had hugged Osnat and said, "It's not too late, you know. I bet it isn't a full flight."

"Sorry," Osnat had said. "I left my passport at home."

"Have it your way," Jeannie said. "But I think you're crazy. There are well-endowed men in Chicago too."

"Okay," Osnat said. She could feel herself getting all teary again. "If I fail my driver's test, I might just take you up on it."

"Then I hope you fail," Jeannie said. "But you won't."

Now Osnat sat in her driving instructor's car, with its passenger-side brakes, waiting for him to finish talking to the tester, who was standing with his back to her. "You're crazy," she could hear Jackie yelling. "No way is that dog getting in my car." Osnat hoped he was right—the dog was a large German shepherd who seemed to wink at Osnat seconds before it started dragging itself back and forth by its front legs and rubbing its butt on the sidewalk. "You see that," Jackie yelled. "It's a butt scootcher. Not on my upholstery. I make my living in that car."

"Fine," the tester said. "Have it your way." He got into the car and slammed the door behind him. "Osnat Greenberg," he said, "I'm Noam Halevi, your tester." He paused, and Osnat could feel him sizing her up. "Hey, didn't you used to have long hair?"

Osnat nodded. She gripped the steering wheel tighter. There was something familiar about him—she recognized his aftershave, the way he smelled—but she wasn't sure from where.

"I know you," the tester continued. "You're from Chicago. I used to work in a restaurant there, Ali Baba's."

Osnat couldn't help it: first she snorted, and then she started laughing. There he was, in the flesh, her first Israeli lay. There was nowhere to hide in this country. If it wasn't fortune-tellers accosting you in the bathroom, it was one-night stands accosting you in your car. She was going to have to learn to be more careful about who she slept with. She took a deep breath and choked down something that was between a hiccup and a sob.

"So," she said finally. "You came back."

"Of course I did," Noam said. "I had to. It was too big over there. I couldn't stay." He shrugged. "Everyone makes mistakes," he said, "but that's no reason to suffer."

"So this is your happy ending?" Osnat said.

"Sure," Noam said. "Why not? I deserve it." He smiled. "Well," he said. "I see you've got your seat belt on. You ready to go?"

Osnat considered his question. "Yes," she said finally. "I am." She turned the key in the ignition.

"Great," Noam said. "Let's do it."

Selling the Apartment

Your parents' friends, when they hit sixty, will begin moving south in couples: One to North Carolina. Another to Florida. A third to Texas. At Rosh Hashanah you'll be down to ten. Hanukkah, eight. Purim, four. Finally, one Passover, it will be just you and your parents. You will sit across from them in the dining room, eating gefilte fish by candlelight, when the phone rings—it will be your mother's sister from Israel, calling to wish her a happy holiday, shouting over the din of crying babies and someone plinking the Four Questions on the piano—and your mother will look so sad you will fantasize about running away—spending holidays by yourself eating turkey and mashed potatoes at the Big Boy—running away (like a teenager!) even though you're twenty-six and haven't finished paying off your student loans. Outside, it will be March and snowing and you will think, *God, please, anywhere but here, anywhere but here,* the next twenty years stretching in front of you flat and gray and silent, but how can you leave them—your parents—alone without friends? And there you'll be, watching your mother swallowing hard and trying to sound cheerful, and that's when it'll come to you. You have a perfectly good family, just not in the United States.

When you talk to the Israeli *shaliach,* you will find there is a category for people like you: *Returning Minor.* There are benefits as well: tax breaks, a free flight, graduate school, Hebrew lessons. Your parents, of course, will be supportive. They will notify the tenants living in your apartment that it's time to vacate. When your parents left Israel, they couldn't bear to sell the apartment, to admit they were leaving for good. Back then it was still wrong to leave—a kind of betrayal—and besides, they couldn't take money out of the country. Now they will tell you that they kept the apartment just in case, for this very reason, so you would have a place to go. In this respect, your parents are like all the other Israelis you meet in the States, forever going back just as soon as . . . and right after . . .

So you will go back and sleep in the same room you slept in as a child. The view from your windows will be exactly the one you remember: a smokestack, a small airport, a traffic light. Behind them: the Mediterranean, a flat blue line, thick or thin depending on the time of day. The part you won't remember is the way the heat keeps you sweating, how bright and relentless the sun is, the way it bleaches colors and washes them out.

Of course, it won't work out. You'll spend holidays with your extended family—Imagine! Eight first cousins! Forty-three second cousins!—but other days, they will be too married and pregnant and busy trying to keep up with inflation to see you. You will spend most of your time alone, or with other English speakers at work, writing technical manuals; at restaurants, complaining about the service; in cabs, trying to convince the drivers to turn on the meter—just turn it on!—while they speed along, charging you four times the going rate. In your apartment, the roof will leak every time it rains and the man who will come to fix it will take one look at you and tell you that what you need is a European man, one with manners, and not the typical Israeli who—you'll soon discover—thinks what American women want is sex without commitment (90 percent of Americans end up leaving anyway) and finds the fact that you already own an apartment as exotic as any of your American boyfriends ever found the dark hairs on your arms. You will want to make a snappy comeback, but your Hebrew will be too weak. Instead you will smile, baring your teeth like a dog, even though you already know Israelis don't smile at strangers.

There is more, all of it trivial, and you will be ashamed that the things that wear you down aren't the ones you expect: not the heat, nor the terror, nor the flying cockroaches. Instead, it will be the way people brush against you in the supermarket as if you're invisible, the way it's so easy to forget you're something more than a body and an accent, that you at one time had friends who wanted to be with you not just because there wasn't anyone else around. You'll give it two years and switch jobs four times, and when the third year rolls around you will start to fear that this new person whose body you've been walking around in—teeth clenched, heart pounding, shoulders hunched—is who you've really been all along, that you'll forget ever having felt any other way. And you will give up. Of course, your parents, tired of your 7 a.m. phone calls—who else can afford the long distance or put up with your whining—will be supportive and tell you to put the apartment up for sale—by then the laws will have changed, and it will be possible to take the money out—and come back. Come back.

When things don't work out, your parents will fly in to sign the papers. It's their apartment, after all. Before they come, you will find a real estate agent, a tanned man who dresses in linen. He will place an advertisement in the newspaper: In Ramat Aviv: 6th floor, 3 rooms, balcony, 92 m^2, spectacular view.

You'll want to show the ad to someone, so you'll knock on the door of the neighbor who still remembers you from when you were nine, and who still remembers your father with hair and your mother without glasses. From inside, you'll hear a shuffling and things falling on the floor. When he finally opens up, he'll be struggling with his shirt buttons. His stomach, unleashed, will seem white and fleshy, enormous. Behind him, you'll catch a glimpse of his wife wrestling with a lacy black nightgown, blue cream on her face. You'll check your watch: 4 p.m. You'll secretly suspect they are nudists, but still, you will show him the paper, and the neighbor will look at the ad and say, "You miss them, huh, your parents?"

The apartment is the same age you are. Your parents moved in the year you were born. You'll worry about what they'll think when they see it—the paint swollen and peeling where the walls got wet, the rust on the refrigerator door (the salt in the air eats through everything), the hairline crack in the bathroom sink. You'll order a cleaning service and—when the man promises to take twenty years off the floor tiles—you'll agree to pay him an extra three hundred dollars. After he leaves, two workers—a Nigerian and a Russian—will arrive. You'll trade jokes with the Nigerian (in English, of course!) and help him move furniture while the Russian scrubs the bathtub. They'll both work wearing nothing but shorts. Later, you will notice that every time the Russian man squats, his penis hangs out of his right leg opening. When he urinates, he'll leave the door open and stare right at you. You'll think about asking the Nigerian to do something, but how can you? The floor, when the Nigerian is done buffing it, will still look its age. Everything will still seem dirty, even though you know that it isn't. You'll spend the night cleaning the bathroom again. When you turn off the lights, you'll think you can see the places where the Russian's penis touched the porcelain shining yellow like glow-in-the-dark stars.

At the airport, you'll notice that your parents are white and fleshy too, and that they've already begun to shrink. Their ears, the tips of their noses, will seem too large for their faces. There will be three curly white hairs on your mother's chin. When she hugs you, she will feel less substantial than you remembered. You haven't been touched in months, and the hug will make your hands tremble. Although you'll feel tired and haggard, your parents will say you look wonderful, very tanned. When they see the apartment, though, they will suck in air through their teeth. You'll know how it must look to them—how it looked to you when you first returned—small, dirty, old. "My God," your mother will say, but this won't be when she starts crying. That will be later, over the phone, when she makes plans to meet your aunt. Your father will look at you grimly, then nod, as if he's just verified something. You will let them sleep in your bed—their bed—in your room, and you will sleep on the floor in the other room. You'll realize that you can look into the kitchen window of the penthouse apartment that sprawls above you from where you are lying (your building is shaped like an *X*). You will watch the upstairs neighbor eat microwave popcorn from a bag and read the newspaper. You'll have ridden in the elevator with him a few times, but you won't know his name, only that he has lost a leg in a motorcycle accident. To avoid thinking about what might be scurrying across the floor, you'll concentrate on willing him to stand up and look out the window and down at you. He won't.

In the morning you'll discover that your parents have gone on strike. They will sit on the couch in the living room, their arms crossed over their chests, and wait for you to go to the mini-market next door for fresh rolls and chocolate milk in a baggie. When you return, they will move to the kitchen table, where they will sit listlessly, propping their heads up on their arms, waiting for you to make coffee and set out silverware. Your father won't close his mouth when he chews and will make a thick rumbling noise—*mnnnnnh*—when he drinks. He'll pant slightly after swallowing. His Adam's apple, once prominent, will be hidden in the folds of his neck. It'll be the first time you notice it's gone missing. You'll look down at your plate: what other parts of him are lost?

When you're done eating, they'll take turns in the bathroom while you wash the dishes and make their bed. When you shake them out, their sheets will smell sour. You will open the windows to air the room out. Across the way, in the apartment in the next building, you will see a woman feeding a parakeet. When the traffic light below you turns red, you'll believe you can make out a distant chirping.

At 10 a.m., the real estate agent will stop by with the buyers he's found: a man, a woman, a teenage daughter with a slicked-back ponytail. The woman's hair will be hennaed red, and next to your mother, she will seem firm, fat, and vigorous, ready to knock down the wall between the kitchen and the living room all by herself. She will tell your mother they plan to put in central air, replace the Formica, redo the bathroom in muted maroons. After a while, her words will blur and all you'll hear will be the ugly parts of Hebrew—the guttural *ch* sounds that remind you of phlegm, the *r* that you'll never be able to pronounce properly. When the real estate agent tells her the leaky walls can easily be fixed, both your parents will look down at the floor, silent and guilty, and you'll realize that this is your chance to halt the sale. You'll stare at the husband—a short man with a solid gut and hairy ears and nostrils—and imagine him on top of his wife, balancing belly to belly, legs and arms in the air, a naked, hairy, human propeller. In this apartment? Where you grew up? Impossible.

After they leave—the daughter smiling thinly at you, lips clenched around her braces—the real estate agent will wipe his palms on his pants. The wet marks will dry before he's through shaking your parents' hands. You'll have an urge to lock the door behind him.

"That's that," your father will say once the real estate agent is gone. "Good riddance." He will pull out a camera and take pictures of all the wet spots on the walls, protecting himself against some future lawsuit. "Here's hoping for a drought."

You mother will say nothing and look at her hands. They'll be covered with liver spots and crisscrossed by veins. She'll sniff them cautiously. "I can smell his cologne."

The plan will be for your parents to drop you off at work—a tall building in Ramat Gan, next to the Diamond Exchange—and then drive up to Netanya to see your mother's sister. Instead, ten minutes after you arrive at your desk, your father will call you from the lobby downstairs: "I can't drive in this traffic. Take us home."

You'll explain the situation to your boss, a South African who lives in the West Bank. The bus he rides into work has steel mesh in its windows and dents from thrown stones. He is Orthodox and not frightened easily. When you gave him your notice, he said, "Yes, it's hard to live here without conviction." But you, you come from a family of atheists and leftists. In principle, you're against oppression and for a two-state solution. In reality, you have talked to exactly one Arab in your life: the seventeen-year-old boy who delivers your dry cleaning, and whom you tip generously as if that changes anything. What do you know about conviction, other than that you've got none?

About your parents, down in the lobby, your boss will say, "Do whatever you need to do." He's already managing without you. On his desk you'll see organizational charts on which your name has been crossed out. Downstairs, your father will have parked in the bus bay in front of your building. The incoming buses will be honking at your little Peugeot rental, the drivers yelling, "Move your car, *koos ochtok*!"

"Hurry up," your father will say, wringing his hands. "Get us out of here."

You will drive them up to Netanya, to your aunt's small house, and drop them off without going inside. Instead of returning to work, you'll decide to go visit the dogs that guard the airport. The airport, even though it's noisy, is the only reason you can see the Mediterranean from your apartment. You'll weave your way through rusted nails and broken bricks—construction waste from down the street—to the fence that blocks off the runway. Every few hundred yards there is a guard tower, and, in the nearest one, you'll be able to make out a soldier reading a book. When he hears your feet crunching in the sand, he'll look up at you and wave. The dogs are on the other side of the fence, chained to railings that are twenty yards long. They can run back and forth, their steel chains clanging behind them, but the railings are spaced so that neighboring dogs can never quite reach each other. When it's hot—and it's always hot when you visit—most of the dogs will be sleeping in the shade of their doghouses. Only the one farthest left, a Doberman pinscher who is missing an ear, will bother to bark at you. You used to imagine bringing them chewy toys and jerky treats, but when you finally did, the guard reached for his megaphone and yelled at you to stop: "Can't you see they're working?" The dogs depress you—their incessant panting, their mangy fur, their loneliness. Each time you visit them, you'll promise yourself it's the last. This time, it really will be.

All the first cousins—Eight! Not counting the children!—will gather at your aunt's for dinner. The women will each bring a casserole. You'll watch them slide easily in and out of the kind of small talk you never managed to master: reserve duty, day care, politics. You'll catch yourself mimicking their facial expressions: shoulder shrugs, raised eyebrows, pursed lips, open palms facing up. All of them—you too—have the same wide mouth, the same nose, the same dimple in the left cheek. How can you leave these people who look like you?

Back at the apartment, you'll be brushing your teeth when you hear someone announce: "Citizens, step away from your windows!" The voice will be staticky, the wording oddly formal. Your parents will obey and retreat to the hallway, but not you—you'll go stand on the balcony and lean over the railing, and try to make out the police blockade and the small robot that blows up suspicious objects. Your skin will prickle, waiting for the blast. This will be the first time they've found something in your neighborhood. The silence around you will buzz with energy—all the traffic below will be stopped—and you'll imagine all your neighbors standing on their balconies, in the dark, waiting, just like you, on the balls of their feet, ready to leap back if necessary. Nothing. Nothing. Then, just as you begin to relax, a small explosion, like a car backfiring.

You'll sense you mother standing beside you. "Well," she'll say, "that's one thing you won't miss."

The breeze off the Mediterranean will be cool and salty. In the distance, you'll see the blinking lights of a small plane getting ready to land. You will realize these are the moments you like best—the ones when you're near danger but not in it. You'll remember the time one of your Israeli coworkers gave you and a couple others a ride home. He asked you about the move, whether it was difficult learning to live with the terror, and you said you didn't know enough people to worry about who might be injured, who might be dead. Later, after he dropped the others off, the coworker told you that the man in the backseat had lost both his parents, the woman next to him a boyfriend in Lebanon. Now, watching the police clear the barricades and pack up their gear, you'll note how lucky you are, leaving unscathed: lucky enough to avoid busy markets and crowded intersections, always arriving a day too early, or else a day too late.

Instead of sleeping, you will listen to your father pacing up and down the hallway as if he's never heard of jet lag. He'll keep stepping on a loose tile in rhythmic intervals: tap tap tap clack, tap tap tap clack. You'll consider leaving the buyers' teenage daughter a gift under the tile—something she could use, like a purple marker or glitter makeup—but worry she'd lose them, or worse, throw them out. A better plan: carving your name in the door frame or the windowsill, something that can't be replaced the way this dour teenager with braces will be replacing you. The only thing that keeps you from doing it right then will be the sound of your father still pacing outside your room: tap tap tap clack, tap tap tap clack.

In the morning, after you're done feeding your parents and airing their room—the smell, if anything, is worse, not better—you'll start scratching the letters of your name into the frame of the west window with a screwdriver, in a place the teenage daughter will surely see when she watches the planes taking off. Before you have time to finish, the doorbell will ring. Your parents won't move—it's part of their strike—and when the doorbell rings again, you will tuck the screwdriver into the pocket of your shorts and let in the real estate agent and the mother, who—if anything—will seem to take up even more space than she did yesterday. You and your parents will trail the woman as she walks in and out of each room, looking closely at the furniture you've bought with your Returning Minor discount.

"This wardrobe isn't real wood," she'll say. "These burners don't ignite automatically."

She'll sit in front of the piano—the piano that waited patiently for your return, the one the technician had taken four hours to get back in tune—and tap out "Doe, a deer." You'll worry that she'll burst out singing, but she won't. Instead, she'll spin around on the rusty piano stool—again, the salt air—and say, "I'll give you a hundred shekels for the wardrobe. I don't want anything else."

When she leaves, the real estate agent will reveal that she is planning to install all new windows and replace all the doors. Your parents will nod and accept her offer, which is substantially less than the real estate agent's initial estimate, but still more than the apartment is worth.

"Don't forget," the real estate agent will say, "I get a percentage."

While they set up a time for the closing, you'll excuse yourself to pee. Washing your hands, you'll glance in the mirror and remember that you're actually closer to the mother's age than to the daughter's, that you already have gray hair and wrinkles and varicose veins of your own. Still, you'll think, there must be some way to leave a mark, some sort of signal that even this woman, with all her renovations, won't be able to erase until long after you've gone.

After the sun sets and the air cools a little, you will walk with your father to the Ramat Aviv mall. You will have to pause twice while your father wipes his forehead with a handkerchief and pretends he doesn't need to catch his breath. Inside, the stores' names are in English: Golf, Aldo's, McDonald's. Your father will sample the kosher Big Mac and say it's too salty. The French fries, though, still taste the same.

"This is hard on your mother," he'll tell you, as if you haven't figured this out. "It's like leaving Israel, all over again."

"What about you?"

"You know me." Your father will open another packet of ketchup. "It's your mother I worry about."

But he's wrong. You don't know him. You never paid attention. All you have are pictures of him in his army uniform, his hair cropped close to his head, or squinting into the sun, his arm casually draped around your mother's shoulders. Once you moved to the States, he started wearing shoes with socks instead of sandals and shaved off his sideburns. You'll know there has to be more, but what is it?

When it's time to head back home, even though it's only ten minutes by foot, your father will hail a cab. "I'm sixty-four," he'll remind you. "I'm tired of walking." When the driver refuses to turn on the meter, your father will shrug. "Look at that," he'll say in English. "He knows I'm American. It must be the clothes."

Back in the apartment, the two of you will find your mother making a list. "These are the things I want," she'll tell you, handing you the piece of paper. The list will include a vinyl tablecloth, a horsehair broom head, and rags with which to wash the floor.

"You can't be serious," your father will say.

"But I am." Your mother will sigh. "I just want *something*."

When you're through packing up your desk at work—a hot pink plastic Slinky; a picture of your dog, now long dead; three ballpoint pens with the company logo—you'll go home to discover the men who are supposed to cart away the piano (an Ecuadorian and a Thai) smoking in the lobby, listening impassively to your neighbor the nudist declaim the ills of foreign labor: "Look at this mirror, the way it hangs crooked! Look at the grout between the tiles, only two years old and flaking already!" When he sees you, he'll say, "These people all live together in camps, you know. Yell at one and you've yelled at them all." Then he'll ask, "Where are your parents? I keep knocking and knocking, and nobody opens."

Upstairs, your parents will be sitting at the kitchen table, arranging yesterday's crumbs into small piles. Your mother will accuse you: "There's no milk. Your father is starving." And you'll accuse her right back: "Why didn't you open the door?" Even though you're a family that never yells, you will feel a shout forming deep in your lungs and rising to the back of your throat. The only thing that will stop it is the Ecuadorian mover, who right then will announce in broken English that the piano doesn't fit in the elevator. You'll spend the next half hour on the phone reminding the man in charge that you did, in fact, tell him the elevator was too small, yelling at him instead of at your parents, who are now tracing the patterns on the tablecloth as if they've gone deaf. After a while, the owner will instruct the Ecuadorian and the Thai men to leave, and they will, not bothering to close the door behind them. After they go, you'll run downstairs and buy milk, run back upstairs, and slam it down on the kitchen table.

"What's the matter with you?" you'll ask. "Why are you doing this to me?"

For a while, your parents won't say anything. Then your mother will say, "To you? To *you*?" And you'll know you've done something wrong—but what? What? What could you have done that's bad enough for *this*?

Later, the three of you will go out to dinner in Jaffa with a rich old friend of your father's who likes to golf in Caesarea and go skiing in Switzerland. The friend will spend the evening grilling your father about money: "What are you getting for the apartment? How about that piano?" When your father finishes accounting for all of it, the friend will proclaim: "You've been robbed!" To you he'll say, "Why didn't you call me, if you were so lonely?"

Outside the restaurant, the air will smell like rust and urine and, while your father and his friend say their good-byes, you will watch a large rat who's missing a tail gnaw on what looks like a black piece of rubber.

"What is that?" you'll ask your mother.

She'll peer in the direction you're pointing, and even though she'll smile, you'll realize she can't see it. "I don't know," she'll say, "but wasn't the fish delicious?"

The three of you will climb slowly up the stairs that lead from the harbor to the Old City. There will be a full moon, and the stone buildings around you will shimmer. Below you, you will see waves crashing white into the wall.

"Maybe we shouldn't sell," your mother will say. "We could find new tenants."

Your father will be the one who notices she's shivering, who pulls her close and wraps his arms around her: "The roof leaks. The paint is peeling."

"So let's sell it and buy a different place," your mother will say. "Maybe over in Kfar Saba. A nice house or something."

"We're not coming back. You know that."

"No," your mother will agree. "We're not. But what if we change our minds? We have family here."

"We have family there too."

"Who?" your mother will ask. "We have no one."

"We have a daughter," your father will remind her, winking, and your mother, startled, will look up at you, her *daughter,* nearing thirty, older already than she was when she had you, and you'll find yourself thinking your father's friend was right: she's been robbed. She's been robbed.

While your parents sign the papers in the presence of the real estate agent and a lawyer, you will pass the time riding the elevator up and down, up and down. Other neighbors—the nudist, the family from number 9—will hop on and hop off, but you will stay in there and wait for the woman, the husband, and the dour teenage daughter to leave. Tomorrow, you will hold a moving sale. In two days, the packers will come. In three days, you'll follow. Seventy-two more hours, you'll think. You can get through this.

It's only when you're holding the elevator for the neighbor from the penthouse that a solution will come to you. You will ride up with him to seven, trying to work up the courage to ask, and then ride down to six and walk up the stairs. By then, he will already have gone inside, and you'll have to ring the bell.

"What is it?" he'll ask you. When you start stuttering, he'll say, "You can tell me in English."

"No," you'll say. "It's not that."

The apartment, behind him, will be dark, the furniture modern, with black metal frames, the shades closed against the afternoon sun. The neighbor will lean on one crutch, the left leg of his jeans pinned up neatly below the knee. He'll patiently listen to you tell him about the apartment, about leaving, about the teenage daughter and her thin-lipped smile. You'll follow him into the kitchen and wait while he looks for a screwdriver and a hammer. There will be a half-empty bag of popcorn on the breakfast table.

"There you go," he'll say when he gives you the tools. His hands, you will notice, are large, with dark thin hairs on the knuckles. "Let me know when you're done."

You'll clear a space on the counter underneath the window and climb up. From there, you'll be able to see down into your parents' old bedroom. Your sleeping bag, the pile of laundry in the corner—you need to do laundry—will look like shed skin left behind by some animal. The exterior of the building is a dusty beige stucco. To pound on it properly, you will need to stick your head, and your shoulders and arms, out the window. At first, the height will make you dizzy, but then you'll learn to avoid looking down at the parking lot. The bits of concrete you hammer loose will fall on the cars parked below, but will be too small to do any damage. Soon, you'll be sweating from the effort, and the neighbor, who will have showered by now and changed into sweats, will offer you a glass of water. Although in your mind you imagined him to be about your age, now you'll see that he's actually much older. He is losing hair on the crown of his head. There are laugh lines carved around his mouth and eyes. You'll watch him watching you drink, but you won't know what to say to him. It'll be too late anyhow—your flight already booked, your books sorted into piles, your parents in the living room shaking hands with strangers—you'll be leaving, and he'll be staying. So what if he's missing a leg?

"Can I see it?" he'll ask you once you've finished, and together you will take the elevator down to six and find your parents slumped on the sofa in their standard positions, their copy of the contract on the coffee table, pinned down by empty cups and saucers. In your parents' old room, you and the neighbor will take turns standing by the window, admiring your handiwork: your initials, large and loopy, the date, the apartment number, all carved into the building's façade, just above eye level and well out of reach.

"If she turns out to be nice," the upstairs neighbor will say about the teenage daughter, "I'll tell her to look for it." When you shake hands good-bye, he'll say, "I'm sorry things didn't work out better," and you'll say, "I am too."

That night, while you listen to your father pacing, you'll wait for the lights to go on in the penthouse kitchen, for the upstairs neighbor to come to the window and wave. He won't, of course. This is your story, not his.

All the things you can't sell, your family—Eight first cousins! Forty-three second cousins!—will pick through, checking the nonstick cookware for scratches, the sofa for broken springs. In the early afternoon, you'll drive down to Jaffa and pay the State of Israel back for the Returning Minor discounts and tax breaks it gave you—you didn't stay long enough for the loans to be forgiven. Back in the apartment, the bed will be gone. In its place you'll find your parents sitting on folding chairs the nudist neighbor has lent them, your father reading the newspaper, your mother folding fifty-shekel bills into complicated paper airplanes. The sour smell will seem sharper, like window cleaning fluid and sweat, but when you look around, all you'll see are discarded sheets, pillows, your parents' neatly packed suitcases.

"Where will we sleep?" your father will ask you, looking lost.

Emptied of furniture, the apartment, if anything, will seem smaller. You'll call up the Hilton and reserve a room for the night. Breakfast won't be included, but there will be cable TV. You will leave your parents in front of CNN, where the headlines will be about the peace process. The Israel you glimpse in this newscast—a yellow, dusty, third-world country where dirty children throw stones—will be nothing like the Israel you know.

After that there will be nothing left to do but haul the laundry off to the Laundromat, then sort it into the things you'll take with you and the things that you'll ship. The only other people there will be the American exchange students from Tel Aviv University, chubby and tan, their toenails painted a metallic blue. While you fold, you'll listen to one of them complain about her boyfriend: "He was like, What do you think this is? America?"

Only when you get home and stack everything into piles will you realize all but two of the towels are missing. The wardrobe will be empty, the bathroom cabinets too. You'll stand in the middle of your bedroom, chewing the loose nail on your index finger, and wonder where they've disappeared.

For dinner, the three of you will go to a dairy restaurant where they make smoothies and pancakes larger than your head. For once, your parents will seem cheerful, admiring the photographs of cows in the middle of the desert that are hanging on the walls.

"Too bad we don't have more time," your mother will say. "We could have gone down to the Dead Sea."

You'll feel like throttling her, but she's your mother, and you won't. Still, you'll resent her for perking up as if all she'd needed was some time away from the apartment, some time away from you.

Later, you'll stop by their suite to use the bathroom, and that's when you'll notice that the smell has followed them here, and that now it's so strong you think you can taste it. You'll pull back the shower curtain, then check under the sink. And that's where you'll find them, the missing towels, all five of them, and you'll realize it's much worse than what you've imagined—the towels, balled up and wrinkled, are damp with what can only be urine.

You'll stay in the bathroom so long your father will knock on the door and ask if you're all right. You won't know what to do, so you'll lie: "Must be something I ate." You'll wash your face and your hands, but the smell, you'll imagine it clinging to your hair and your clothes like a crying baby you can never set down.

When you're finally ready to come out, you'll flush the toilet and blow your nose. Your parents will be sitting up in bed, watching the news, and in the blue light of the television they will seem fragile and younger than you've ever known them: your children. The air in the hotel room will feel stuffy and close, but there it will be, the rest of your life: you will ship off your belongings and go back to the States, and in years to come—and there will be many—when friends ask you what went wrong, why you left, what happened exactly, over there in Israel, you'll have nothing to say. From where you'll be standing—on the other side of the fence, the dog chain pulling you back, your parents almost within reach—the simple truth will be this: you just won't remember.

Ascent

Sometime during the two years Osnat had been gone, her mother had replaced her with another, more easily accessible daughter named Harriet. It was a fact her mother had managed to hide during their transatlantic phone conversations, but now that Osnat was back from Israel, it was hard to miss. Harriet was the bookkeeper at Fantasy Bridal, where Osnat's mother was the general manager, and Osnat's parents were forever wining and dining her, inviting her for walks and to museums and to the movies. A couple of times, Osnat's mother and Harriet had even gone on weekend trips together, once to Cleveland, which was still somehow okay, and once to Niagara Falls, which wasn't. Osnat wasn't an idiot: she'd read enough about cheating in women's magazines to know what it was she was looking at. Still, she sat there and admired photo after photo of her mother and Harriet, their arms wrapped around each other, smiling in front of the Horseshoe Falls, the floral clock, the *Maid of the Mist,* or clad in bathing suits, soaking in a heart-shaped hot tub in a pink hotel room. Osnat's mother looked like Osnat's mother, but Harriet could have been anyone: small, blond, blue-eyed, completely unremarkable. In most of the pictures, she was wearing shorts and a tank top, and the muscles in her arms and legs made her look strong, like someone to be reckoned with. It was one of the things Osnat's mother liked about Harriet: "She looks like she could fight off any attackers."

"What attackers?"

"You know," Osnat's mother said. "Attackers." She flipped to a photo of Harriet posing next to one of the barrels that had gone over the falls. "She takes great pictures."

Osnat shrugged.

"Now don't get jealous," her mother said. "She's worked hard for it. I've seen her school pictures: frizzy black hair and big nose, a girl straight out of some shtetl. Even when she started at Fantasy Bridal she was nothing like the sleek professional she is now. You just can't tell where people come from anymore."

"I'm not jealous," Osnat said. "I was just thinking that maybe *we* could go on a trip sometime. I could even take a couple of days off work."

"If you're going to take a couple days off work," her mother said, "then maybe you could use them to unpack."

"I am unpacked," Osnat said.

"Well," Osnat's mother said, "I'm still waiting for my invitation to the housewarming." This was apparently the end of Osnat's visit, because her mother opened the freezer and pulled out four Tupperware containers filled with homemade chicken soup. "I'm sorry there isn't more," she said, "but Harriet has a cold."

"That's okay," Osnat said, because that was what she was supposed to say. "I'm nowhere near running out."

Osnat's mother looked surprised. "How can that be? You should've eaten the last bowl on Thursday. How are you going to get better if you don't eat any soup?"

Osnat stood up. "I'm going to go now," she said. "I don't need to get better. I'm fine the way I am."

"Okay," her mother said, but she sounded skeptical. "Then why aren't you unpacked?"

Not that unpacking mattered. If you ignored the boxes in Osnat's living room, it was easy to imagine that she had never left Ann Arbor in the first place. Here it was, her life, as ordinary as the next person's. The apartment she was renting was down the street from her old elementary school, only three blocks away from her parents' house. She still saw the same dentist she had seen as a child. She had a job writing press releases for one of the software companies near the same mall where she'd shopped for her prom dress. And every day, just about, she ran into people she'd known and hadn't liked in high school. Some of them had new haircuts, and some of them had babies, but the main difference was that everyone had gained weight. Sometimes, entire days went by when Osnat didn't hear any Hebrew, and that was just fine with her—because even this part hadn't changed, the part where she heard Hebrew on the street or in a restaurant and froze, unable to do anything more than stare meaningfully at the speakers in the hope that one of them would somehow recognize the Israeli part of her, no matter how small and shriveled it had become.

Of course, the only person who did recognize Osnat was Harriet, and she recognized her *everywhere*: in the dairy section of Kroger, in line at the post office, filling up at the gas station on Carpenter.

"Are you following me?" Harriet would ask when they ran into each other, and Osnat would say, "Are you following *me?*" and then they'd both pretend to laugh, or maybe they really did laugh.

"No, really," Harriet would say, wiping tears from her eyes, "it's like we're connected. Sisters even."

Just the thought made Osnat cringe. *No*, she wanted to say, *we're not. We're really not.* Although later, when her parents would call asking her to run this or that errand, her disgust didn't stop her from thinking, *Why me? If we're sisters, why not Harriet?*

"Because," her father said, "some jobs are just part of being a family." He was going to a conference in San Francisco and wanted Osnat to babysit her mother, only he phrased it as "keeping your mother company." He sighed. "Really," he said, "what are you, nine years old? I'm asking you for a favor here, so I don't have to worry about her remembering to take her medication or turning off her curling iron. Is that so much to ask?"

"No," Osnat said dutifully. "Of course it isn't." She dutifully packed an overnight bag and dutifully drove over to her mother's house, only to find her mother and Harriet sitting together at the kitchen table next to an empty box of pizza, laughing uproariously at some joke. "Did you save me a slice?" Osnat asked, even though it was clear they hadn't, but instead of apologizing, her mother whipped out a plate of cookies. "Look!" she said. "Harriet made *rugelach*! From scratch!"

Osnat pulled up a chair and did her best to ignore the way her mother was patting Harriet's hand. Something about the gesture reminded Osnat of the creepy old women in nursing homes who sat in the lobby and couldn't keep their hands off the visitors, women with cold, dry fingers that latched on to you and left chilly imprints on your skin. She shuddered and glanced at Harriet, who seemed unmoved, or perhaps *too* moved: instead of pulling away, as Osnat expected her to do, she patted Osnat's mother right back.

"Guess what?" Harriet said. "Your mom and I have a bet going. I say you'd never go to speed-dating at the JCC, and she says that you will."

"Speed-dating?" Osnat asked.

"You know," Osnat's mother said. "You go on ten ten-minute dates, and then you rank the men and decide which one you actually want to go out with."

"I can tell she's not going to bite," Harriet said. "Pay up."

"I'm right here," Osnat pointed out. Then, when her mother reached for a third cookie, she said, "Mom."

Much to Osnat's horror, her mother actually giggled. "What your father doesn't know won't hurt him."

"Unless you go blind."

For a moment no one said anything, but then Osnat's mom resumed chewing, and Harriet changed the subject. "Come on, Osnat. Maybe it'll be fun," she said. "Your mom's always saying that since you came back all you do is sit in your apartment and avoid unpacking."

Osnat could feel herself blushing. "She does?"

"You should go," Osnat's mother chimed in. "You should. You should really go. You'll meet some men, and it'll give you a chance to get to know Harriet. She's very interested in Israel."

"I am," Harriet agreed.

"She's going to move there," Osnat's mother added.

"When?" Osnat asked.

"Oh, I don't know—" Harriet started to say, but Osnat's mother interrupted her: "As soon as she finds an Israeli husband."

When Israeli buses started blowing up every week shortly after she'd returned to the States, Osnat was sure that her mother would finally admit that Osnat's return was a relief. But even when the peace talks derailed completely, the economy tanked, and things got really bad, Osnat's mother had been noncommittal at best, spouting platitudes about not letting fear run your life, and about how bad situations always seemed worse from a distance. It was unfair that Osnat's mother could feel that way and be considered not only motherly but brave and selfless. Other mothers cried bitterly when their children went away to college or took jobs in California. Not Osnat's mom. She could see the larger picture. She wanted—*wanted*—Osnat in Israel even if it meant they wouldn't be together. And now that Osnat was back, her mother turned her attention to Harriet, prepping her to go in Osnat's stead—someone, apparently, had to go and succeed where Osnat had clearly failed. How else to explain the things that were coming out of Osnat's mother's mouth?

"The Israelis who come to Michigan," she was lecturing a nodding, smiling Harriet, "come because of the university, so they're preselected for motivation and intelligence, like Osnat's father. Ann Arbor isn't like New York or L.A., where Israelis move furniture or drive cabs."

"Or sell off-brand electronics at deep discounts," Harriet added, as if it mattered.

"But you're the Israeli one," Osnat told her mother. "Not Dad."

"So what?" her mother said. "He's still very smart."

Later, when Osnat's father called to check in from California, he also testified to the inherent genius of Harriet's plan. "Everything's easier with a spouse," he told Osnat, who was listening in on the extension. "There are scientific studies that show it."

"Especially if you're the man," Osnat's mother said. "Marriage is especially good for the man."

"Which I just happen to be," Osnat's father pointed out.

"Yes," Osnat's mother agreed. "You certainly are."

After that, it was time for the entertainment portion of the evening: back-to-back episodes of the show where neighbors redecorated each other's houses and pretended to be pleased with the results. Or maybe they really were pleased.

"I don't know," Osnat's mother said. "I give that shoddy paint job a week before it starts peeling. Everything looks better on camera."

Osnat imagined the show about her and her mother in which

editors cut out all of their awkward silences, or, at least, cut them down. They would end up with two minutes of usable footage: empty pizza box, her mother crocheting, Osnat throwing away the rest of Harriet's cookies. Then there would be shots of Osnat lying awake on her old bed, listening to her mother toss and turn in the next room, her every move broadcast down the hall by the plastic protective covering under the sheets. Osnat felt embarrassed just thinking about it, downright mortified when commercials came on for adult undergarments. Her mother looked nothing like the silver-haired, grandmotherly women who discussed incontinence over coffee on TV. If they looked soft and powdered, then Osnat's mother looked hard: black hair dye, blue eye shadow, mascara, grooves carved into her leathery skin. No matter how much lotion Osnat rubbed into her face very night, she could already see the same lines forming in the corners of her own eyes, across her own forehead. She hated imagining the future in which furniture would have to be protected from her, from her body. She knew she was a terrible daughter for thinking it, but she thought it anyway. She wasn't anything like Harriet, who would probably change you whenever you needed it and not look horrified at all.

Osnat's mother yawned and turned off the TV. "Listen," she said, "I think you should go on this speed-dating. It would be good for you. I think you should go. You should go. You should definitely go. Just go. Why don't you go? You should go. Go."

"But I don't want to go," Osnat said.

"Do it for Harriet then. She did bring you those *rugelach.*"

"She brought *you* those *rugelach.*"

"You know," her mother said, "it isn't healthy to be so negative. Just because you're self-absorbed doesn't mean everyone else is too."

"I'm not self-absorbed," Osnat protested.

"Well then," her mother said, as if proving her point. "Harriet's making an overture. Now you make one too. After all, what are cookies if not overtures in disguise?"

There was just no arguing with that kind of logic. Osnat had to open three boxes before she found the one with her going-out clothes, and then it turned out that all her skirts were too short, her pants too tight: it was starting already. She switched back into her jeans.

The speed-dating took place in one of the bars downtown. It was loud, crowded, smoky with desperation. Everywhere Osnat looked, she saw short, pudgy Jewish men chatting up women with lots of cleavage. Standing next to them, Harriet seemed to glow, her blond hair almost fluorescent. "Boy," Osnat heard one man tell her, "are you *sure* you're Jewish?" and Harriet said, "I just like to blend in."

"Blend in where?" another man asked. "Utah?"

Everyone laughed heartily, so Osnat laughed heartily too. As far as she could tell—and Osnat could always tell—there wasn't one Israeli in the entire place, unless you counted Osnat herself, which you really couldn't. "Not only that," she told Harriet, "but that guy"—she indicated a man in a suit who was ordering a drink up at the bar—"isn't even Jewish."

"Wow," Harriet said, impressed. "That's a useful skill."

She sounded so sincere that Osnat could feel herself blushing, as if her ability to spot Israelis was something to be proud of rather than a sign of desperation. But before she could say anything else, the emcee announced that it was time for the women to take their seats. He was wearing a T-shirt featuring a Hasidic Jew wielding a whip and being chased by a giant rolling slab of ham. The caption read, "The Adventures of Indiana Jew." Every time he completed a sentence, everyone was supposed to cheer.

"So what do we do?" Harriet asked. "Do we leave?"

Osnat shrugged. "You're the expert."

"Me?" Harriet said. "This is my first time."

"Fine," Osnat said, trying to hide her disbelief. "Let's leave." And the truth was, she was glad to go. She wasn't even unpacked, and now she was supposed to start dating?

"What do you think?" Harriet asked once they were outside. "Pancakes? I'll drive." Then, inside her car, she waited patiently for Osnat to fasten her seat belt before she started the engine and drove to a small diner near I-94, where they were seated in a booth behind some high-school students who were swapping milk shakes. "Mmm . . ." one of them was saying, "milk shake," and another was saying, "Mmm . . . malt."

"Mmm . . . malt, indeed," Harriet said. She unwrapped her straw and busied herself folding the wrapper into a small square.

Osnat shrugged again. Something about Harriet was turning Osnat into an expert shrugger—she just couldn't think of anything to say. Plus, under the diner's bright lights, Harriet's eyes were such an intense blue that it was difficult to meet her gaze.

"Your mom is going to be pretty disappointed," Harriet continued. "She was really hoping we'd meet someone."

Osnat could feel herself cringing. *We?* she wanted to ask. *We?* Instead she said, "No double wedding for us."

"It's just as well," Harriet said. "The guests would have resented buying two gifts."

"On the downside," Osnat pointed out, "this delays your departure." When Harriet looked confused, she said, "To Israel. You know, with your Israeli husband." Then she added, "Are you wearing contacts?"

"I am," Harriet said. "Are they too much?"

This time, Osnat caught herself midshrug. "Maybe."

"It's hard to find blue contacts that look natural," Harriet said. “Nose jobs, hair color, no problem, but eyes are a different story.”

“Huh,” Osnat said. She craned her neck to see if she could catch a glimpse of their waitress. What was taking her so long with their food? “What’s wrong with brown eyes?”

“When you read about people who survived the Holocaust,” Harriet explained, “it’s often the blond, blue-eyed ones. And the ones with good footwear.”

“Are you serious?” Osnat said.

Harriet sniffed at the syrup dispenser that the waitress brought her and pushed it aside. “It can’t hurt to be prepared. That’s the thing about living here—everyone is so nice and helpful and then they paint swastikas on your synagogue in the middle of the night.”

“That’s so . . .”—Osnat searched for the right word—“paranoid.”

“No,” Harriet said. “It’s just how it is. I thought that you, of all people, would understand.”

“Me of all people?”

“Well,” Harriet said lightly, “you’re just so suspicious of everyone.” She reached across the table for Osnat’s hand, but Osnat pulled away. “See what I mean?”

“God,” Osnat said. “What is it with you and the handholding?”

“What is it with you and the sulking?”

Osnat stood up. “You’re not my mother,” she said. “Take me back to my car.”

Harriet took another bite of pancake. “Sit down,” she said calmly. “I’m not done eating, and it’s a long walk back to Main Street.” Then, when Osnat sat back down, she said, “And if you’re not a sulker, don’t sulk.”

And this, Osnat couldn’t help but think while Harriet took interminably long to eat her pancakes and even longer to drink her malt, was the person who had usurped Osnat's place by her mother's side: a blond-haired, blue-eyed fake with a nose job. Didn't Harriet have her own parents? Couldn't she get her own boyfriend? And how could she sit there chewing calmly while Osnat fumed across the table from her? It was almost enough to make Osnat call a cab.

Back at her parents' house, her mother was waiting up. "What do you mean, you didn't stay for the dating?" she asked. "And what do you mean, you don't love Harriet? How can anyone not love Harriet?"

"It's not that I don't love her," Osnat said. "I just don't really *know* her. Come on, Mom, we're practically strangers."

"You two have *me* in common," Osnat's mother said. "You could have talked about *me*. You could have even complained about me, and Harriet could have offered you some perspective."

"Why would I complain about you?"

Osnat's mother thought this over. "I can be moody. And sometimes I nag."

Osnat brought her hand to her mouth in a gesture of surprise. Then she said, "But doesn't Harriet have a mother of her own?"

"Of course she does," Osnat's mother said. "But her mother's down in Arizona—she moved there after the divorce—and you know what they say about love and real estate."

"What's that?"

"They're all about location. Location. Location. Location."

The next day was Saturday, and Osnat awoke to the smell of something scorching. Her father had been right, she thought. Her mother *was* dangerous. She rushed downstairs and found her mother in the kitchen, charring an eggplant over one of the burners.

"I thought I'd make some baba ghanoush," she announced.

"Harriet's coming over to help me, and then she's going to drive me to the shop. You're welcome to join us, you know."

"God, Mom," Osnat said. "You really scared me." Now that her heart wasn't pounding, what she mainly felt was embarrassment. She opened the refrigerator and pretended to look for something to eat. "Actually," she said, "I think I'll go home."

"Going to work on all that unpacking?" her mother asked.

"Look at that!" Osnat closed the refrigerator. "I don't need breakfast after all!"

Her mother rotated the eggplant. "I might even bake a cheesecake."

"Mom." Osnat put her hands on her hips. "Are you trying to die young?"

Her mother laughed. "I already missed the boat on that one," she said. "Anyway, your father gets to have fancy lobster dinners every night at his conference, so why can't I have some fun too? Do you think you could pick up some graham crackers for me, or should I ask Harriet?"

"I'll tell her not to," Osnat warned.

"It's none of her business."

"It will be if she has to start giving you insulin shots."

"No," Osnat's mother said. "That's why I have you."

"Mom," Osnat said. "I'm not your maid."

Her mother slammed the eggplant onto the counter, and it exploded spectacularly, spraying bits of flesh on the floor and on the cabinets. "No," she said. "A maid would never dare talk back like that." Then she disappeared upstairs, not even bothering to turn off the burner, and after a few seconds Osnat heard her bedroom door slam.

When Harriet showed up a little while later, Osnat was still trying to wipe all the bits of eggplant off the floor. "What happened here?" Harriet asked, reaching for a paper towel.

"You don't have to do that," Osnat told her. "Mom's in her room. I think she's watching TV."

"Okay," Harriet said, and started mopping the counter anyway.

"My God," Osnat said. "Is there anything you don't do?" She took a deep breath. "I'm sorry."

Harriet waved her right hand dismissively. "Eggplant brings out the worst in people."

She rinsed her paper towel in the sink and spread it out to dry, and, as if on cue, Osnat's mother came down the stairs. "Harriet," she said. "Is there anything you don't do?"

"Funny," Harriet said. "Osnat was just asking me the same thing."

Osnat's mother shrugged. "I guess it's that mystical mother-daughter connection everyone talks about." She was wearing her work clothes, her face was carefully made up, and she was holding her purse. "Okay," she said. "I'm ready. Osnat, remember to lock up when you're done."

Alone in her parents' house, the floor and cabinets finally clean, Osnat wasn't sure what to do next. She went upstairs into her parents' room, which seemed large and empty without her parents. The bed was made—her mother always made the bed as soon as she got up—the quilt lined up precisely so that its stripes were parallel to the headboard. On either side, the nightstands were loaded with photographs—Osnat's Israeli cousins in their wedding dresses, Osnat's Israeli cousins holding their brand-new babies, Osnat's Israeli cousins' Israeli children gnawing on watermelon rind or playing on the beach in wet bathing suits. Of course there was a picture of Osnat, but it was an old one. She was seventeen and wearing a pouffy black prom dress. Her bangs were huge, feathered, stiff with mousse. She was smiling politely, her mouth red with lipstick. She looked nothing like herself, nothing like who she'd been back then, which, as far as Osnat could remember, was a plain and too serious girl, the kind of girl who sat in the back of her high-school classroom and doodled on the margins of her notebook, then wept the night before she had a paper due while her mother said, "You knew about this assignment for weeks. What were you waiting for?" She was also the kind of girl who would spend the seven minutes between classes making out with the smart, nerdy boys who were too shy to make out with the girls they actually liked and who would place their pale hands on Osnat's dark skin, fingers spread like starfish, and make jokes about crosswalks. "Slut," the smart girls hissed whenever Osnat walked by them. "You snotty, snotty slut." Still, making out with the smart boys had made Osnat feel good, and made Osnat's friends, other girls who were too shy or too fat or too ugly or too foreign to make their own way up their high school's social ladder, admire her and ask her for advice: "He borrowed a pencil. Does he like me?" or "Are you supposed to kiss with your eyes closed or what?" or "Is it really like they showed us with the banana in Health and Wellness?" Osnat hadn't known the answer to this last one at the time—there was a limit to what could be accomplished in seven minutes in a public space unless you were willing to be tardy to your next class—but she still always answered, "Yes, exactly," with such an air of authority that no one questioned her.

For college, Osnat had gone away to a large university where she figured no one would know her and she could start fresh and be one of the smart girls herself this time, but it turned out that large universities weren't all that different from large high schools, except that there was more drinking, and not just on the weekends: sometimes, on her way to the cafeteria for breakfast, Osnat would walk by drunk people passed out on the steam vents for the tunnels that ran underneath the campus, which surely was the only reason they didn't freeze to death in winter. "That's Americans for you," Osnat's mother told her on the phone. "Nothing in moderation. Why not join a Jewish student organization like Hillel, where the others will be more like you?" But Osnat didn't want to join Hillel and spend her Friday nights with the Jews on campus who peppered their conversations with words like *schlep* and *putz* and who were always planning fund-raisers for Israel or trips to Israel or fund-raisers for trips to Israel and getting upset whenever some professor used *Jew* as a verb. Not only were they nothing like Osnat, but like her fat and ugly high-school friends, they looked to her as some kind of expert: "Say something in Hebrew," they'd say, or "Where are the best places to party in Tel Aviv?" or "Shouldn't you be in the army?" Osnat could say just about anything in Hebrew, but she didn't know where people partied in Tel Aviv, and she certainly didn't know if she should have gone into the army, where no doubt she'd be doing something that mattered instead of her Calculus I homework. Unlike with the sex stuff, though, she felt uncomfortable lying to the Hillel crowd, convinced that sooner or later they'd find her out. "Are you a dual citizen?" they asked. "Are you going back? *When* are you going back?" Then she'd come home for vacations and her mother would show her pictures of her Israeli cousins, tanned and tired in rumpled khaki uniforms, and say, "The army in peacetime is a great experience." It had been peacetime then, for a while, and Osnat knew that just like those students in Hillel, only less honestly, what her mother was really asking was, "Are you going back? *When* are you going back?" too.

Of course, Osnat didn't know when she was going back to Israel, and so she stopped going to Hillel meetings as well. Instead, she found herself a boyfriend named Chris and spent her nights with him (it *was* just like with the banana, it turned out, but not as pointy) and imagined a future for the two of them that maybe involved Israel, but only for brief vacations when they'd go snorkeling in the Red Sea. But then this Chris (Osnat's second, if you counted the Chris in high school) went abroad and never called, and the third Chris was just a one-night stand, and the fourth didn't want Jewish kids, and the fifth was engaged to someone else, and the sixth was just mind-numbingly boring, and then Osnat was twenty-five and in love with the seventh Chris, who loved her back and even proposed, but she was unable to marry him despite this, because the Israeli part of her, the part she'd thought was dead and buried long ago, suddenly came back to a vigorous, vengeful life, and Osnat, it turned out, *still* had no idea where she belonged, only that it wasn't with a Catholic Chris in Kenosha, Wisconsin. Her mother hadn't said good riddance, but she might as well have, the way she bided her time and waited for Osnat to arrive on her own at the conclusion that apparently had always been foregone: with her life in the States so Christian and empty, it was time for Osnat to give life in Israel a try.

Really it was no wonder that her mother preferred the Prom-going Osnat to all her other incarnations. Osnat put down her prom picture and lay back on her mother's side of the bed, the plastic sheet squeaking beneath her. Maybe Harriet's plan to find an Israeli husband wasn't so stupid after all. Osnat's mother certainly didn't seem to think so, and, as proof, had not one but two pictures of Harriet on her nightstand, both taken recently in the backyard, one in front of the hostas, the second in front of the peonies, which, still closed, looked like clenched, angry fists. Osnat rolled onto her side and opened her mother's nightstand drawer, examining the contents: a manicure set and Plum Red nail polish, a turquoise pendant on a tarnished silver chain, a small tube of Astroglide (which Osnat immediately pretended she hadn't seen), and one of those pill-a-day dispensers, which, it turned out, still contained that day's pills, numerous and colorful like jewels.

Of course, it figured that Osnat's mother hadn't taken her morning medication, because Osnat had apparently still not seen enough of Harriet over the past few days. She drove over to Fantasy Bridal, the pill dispenser in the passenger seat next to her, and worked on visualizing herself darting in, saying hello, handing her mother the pills, and darting back out. There was no reason the whole thing would take more than sixty seconds, unless her mother was with a client, which, of course, she was.

"Beam me up," she was saying to a woman who looked as if she were barely out of high school, "or May the force be with you?"

The woman wrung her hands. "Beam me up?" she said. "I think?"

"You're looking at a *Star Trek* wedding," Osnat's mother said. "Original or *Next Generation?*" When the woman didn't respond, she rephrased the question: "Captain Kirk or Captain Picard?" The woman shook her head. "Young and smarmy, or old, bald, and handsome?"

Harriet was sitting by the cash register, printing out some kind of report. She smiled at Osnat and gestured at a nearby chair. "Have a seat."

"That woman must really be in love," Osnat whispered.

"They're all like that," Harriet said. "It's one of the nice things about this job."

For a moment, they both watched Osnat's mother explain the various Starfleet uniform options. She looked competent and soothing, as if it actually did matter whether the groomsmen wore red or blue.

"You know," Osnat said—just to make conversation, of

course—"you could move to Israel and meet your Israeli husband there."

"Maybe," Harriet agreed, "but it would be harder. I've done a lot of reading, and apparently most Americans don't make it in Israel, at least not for very long. I'm guessing that doesn't make them very attractive as spouses."

"Hey," Osnat's mother said. She had finished up with the client and was now filing away the pamphlet about including aliens in your space-themed ceremony. "That's my husband you're talking about."

"That's different," Harriet said. "I mean, wasn't part of his allure that he was American and could take you away from it all?"

"No," Osnat's mother said, "he was just the person I fell in love with. The moving to America came later. You're very wise, Harriet, to consider your options so carefully. In retrospect, I would have done things differently, held off, I guess."

Osnat couldn't believe it, couldn't believe how calm her mother looked saying it. Her father was off in San Francisco, sitting through session after session of mathematicians talking about God knows what, his suit probably smudged from all the powdered doughnuts he was eating, confident that all was well with his wife and daughter back home. And here was his wife badmouthing their marriage behind his back. It was up to Osnat to defend him. "Well," she said, trying to keep her voice light, "if you'd held off, you wouldn't have had me."

"No," her mother agreed. "I'd probably have had some other kid." She patted Osnat's back in what she no doubt meant as consolation. "Now don't get mad," she said. "I'm just being honest. If I hadn't married your father, I would have married someone else. You can glare all you want, but why not learn from my experience?"

Osnat imagined standing up and walking out. She would drive

home, then lie in bed and stare at the ceiling. It was something she was good at. Then, after work, her mother would come over and apologize. Except that her mother never apologized. "So why did you agree to move, if you're so unhappy here?"

Her mother rolled her eyes, impatient. "Pay attention," she said. "A, I didn't know. B, I didn't want to raise you by myself. If ever a girl needed two parents, it was you, Osnat."

"Then we could have all stayed in Tel Aviv."

"No," Osnat's mother said. "Your father couldn't stay. That part wasn't negotiable. He was leaving, and I could go with him or stay behind."

Osnat felt her chest constrict. "So he gave you an ultimatum?"

"Who's talking about an ultimatum?" Osnat's mother said. "There was no ultimatum. He was leaving, and I could come with him, or I could stay in Israel."

"Mom," Osnat said, "that's an ultimatum."

"No," Osnat's mother said, "it's not."

Harriet cleared her throat. "Actually," she said, looking uncomfortable, "I'm afraid it is."

Once, an Israeli cabdriver who was bringing Osnat home from the airport told her that people didn't move *to* a place, they moved *away.* The driver had smiled. "So," he'd asked, "what are *you* leaving?" At the time, Osnat had been insulted, but now, at long last, she finally knew the answer. She was moving away from *this.* She was leaving *this.* She handed her mother the pill dispenser. "Here," she said. "You forgot to take these." Then she left, she walked out, she exited, she was out of there, she was gone before either her mother or Harriet had a chance to say good-bye.

It would have been easy for Osnat to run away: she was already packed. She could have maxed out her credit cards on airfare and designer luggage, and then, with bill collectors after her, she'd have no choice but to stay away. She tried imagining where she would go, but even as she pictured herself in a little walk-up in Paris or working on a cattle ranch in Australia, she knew she wouldn't do it, that if she were to go anywhere, it would be back to Tel Aviv, where at least she mattered a little—in a country that small, everybody did. Suddenly Osnat felt so wistful she could hardly breathe. "Call your cousins," her mother had advised her countless times back when she was still in Israel. "You don't have to be so alone. Call them. They'd love to see you. Call them. Why won't you call them?" But Osnat hadn't. She had bought into the hype about the way that Israelis welcomed their brothers and sisters from the Diaspora with open arms, that Israel was a smaller, refreshingly blunt version of America, that living in Israel was like riding a bike—she'd done it as a child, hadn't she? And when it turned out that she'd been wrong, that things were more complicated than she expected, did she stiffen her lip and roll up her sleeves, call her cousins, and start hacking away at the heavy labor of assimilation? Nope. She'd hopped on the first flight back to the States.

The more Osnat thought about it, the more she was convinced that Harriet had the right idea with her Israeli Husband Plan. An Israeli husband would help with the transition, would know how banks worked, which brand of cottage cheese tasted freshest, when it was appropriate to smile. And if things didn't go smoothly right away, an Israeli husband would make it that much harder to leave, especially if you loved him. Or else he would return to the States with you, cementing the two of you as wildly romantic, a couple not to be divided by anything as mundane as the INS. Really, it was the perfect plan. Maybe Osnat's big mistake had been thinking that she was above it.

The day was sunny and unseasonably warm. Outside Osnat's apartment building, a man was crouching in the middle of the street, drawing chalk arrows pointing south. When Osnat pulled up, he stopped and moved out of the way so she could park. He was sweating through his T-shirt.

"What are you doing?" Osnat asked him.

"There's a race tomorrow," he said. "A 5K run."

"Huh," Osnat said. She went inside. The boxes were still there, stacked neatly, ready to go. She touched one of them, and the cardboard felt clammy, as if the box were alive and sweating too while it awaited her decision. Osnat took a deep breath, and then another one. Charted out on a graph, her life would be a thick vertical line traced over and over between two points: how dare she expect her mother to want her to stay when clearly, no matter how hard she tried, all she could do was go, go, go, as if no one place was good enough, as if the problem were place, and not her, not Osnat. Maybe it was her destiny to think she was moving forward when, really, she was moving nowhere.

Osnat sat down, then stood up, then sat down again. She tried to imagine Harriet in the same situation, but, of course, Harriet would never be in this situation—she'd probably find something useful to do. Osnat walked into the kitchen and poured herself a glass of water, and then suddenly she found herself pouring one for the man with the chalk. By the time she got outside, he'd already moved on, but she followed the arrows for a couple of blocks until she found him.

"Here," she said. "You look like you could use some water."

The man smiled. He looked maybe fifty years old, his arms and legs lean and sinewy. "I appreciate it," he said. Osnat watched the way his Adam's apple bobbed up and down as he drank. When he was done, he handed the glass back to Osnat. "Thank you." He wiped away the trickle of sweat running along his neck.

"Good luck tomorrow," Osnat said. She was feeling calmer

now. She walked back to her apartment and rinsed the glass and put it in the drying rack.

For some reason, Osnat had expected that Harriet's betrayal, her decision to side with Osnat, would be the end of her romance with Osnat's mother. Instead, when she followed the chalk arrows back to her mother's house that evening, Harriet's car was in the driveway, and Osnat could hear laughter drifting out of the kitchen window.

"There you are," Harriet said as if nothing had happened. "We've been waiting for you."

"I made some cheesecake after all," Osnat's mother added.

They spent the evening watching TV, or, more accurately, Osnat watched her mother and Harriet watching TV. Occasionally, Osnat's mother would doze off, her head rolling forward slowly until her chin touched her chest. Sometimes her mouth opened, its corners turned down as if she were disappointed.

"So sweet," Harriet whispered, catching Osnat's eye.

It wasn't a word Osnat would have used to describe her mother, and, as if agreeing, her mother let out a loud, throaty snore.

"Mom," Osnat said, a little irritated. "Mom. Go to bed." She suddenly had an awful thought that her mother would fall into a sleep so deep she'd accidentally wet the sofa. "Go brush your teeth."

"I'm not bothering anyone," her mother said. Still, she shifted so that she sat up straighter. She blinked at the TV. "This show is boring. What time is it? I promised your father we'd call."

On the phone, her mother was suddenly perky and cheerful. "Let me guess," she was saying. "You had a Whopper and fries for lunch." She laughed and gave Osnat and Harriet a thumbs-up. "I always know." Then, as if she and Osnat and Harriet had all been sworn to some secret pact, she proceeded to tell Osnat's father about the wonderful day she'd had with some other imaginary daughter, a day that involved perfect weather, pleasant conversation, and a wacky eggplant explosion. "Yes," she said, sounding so sincere that Osnat almost believed her, "it's so nice to spend this much time together."

"On that note . . ." Harriet said after Osnat's mother had hung up. She stood up and hugged Osnat's mother and then hugged Osnat. "Have a good night."

"I'll walk you out," Osnat offered.

She held the door open while Harriet fished her keys out of her purse. Then, once they were outside, she said, "You can't keep encouraging her to eat all those sweets. She's prediabetic."

Harriet looked startled. "I didn't know."

"She won't listen to me," Osnat said, "but she really likes you." She swallowed and, for a moment, she thought she finally knew exactly what it was she was supposed to do. She would go to Israel with Harriet and Harriet's husband, and they would all three live as neighbors and wait patiently for Osnat's parents to retire and come join them, and then they would all spend the rest of their days expounding on exactly how thankful they were for the better weather and the socialized medicine and the hundreds of relatives milling around. Everyone would be happier that way, wouldn't they? Osnat swallowed again. Who was she kidding? "Is she very disappointed in me?" she asked Harriet. "Disappointed that I came back?"

"Are you?" Harriet asked.

"I don't know," Osnat said.

Harriet reached out and put her right hand on Osnat's left shoulder. "Well," she said, "you're the one with the sense for Israelis. Where do you think you belong?"

Osnat concentrated on not shrugging Harriet off. "I don't

know," she said again. "Maybe I didn't give it enough of a chance the first time around. Maybe I should give it another try."

"You think so?" Harriet asked, sounding dubious.

"You don't?"

"Uh-uh," Harriet said. "This one's all you, I'm afraid."

"Except that it's not," Osnat said. "Look at my mom. Look at how excited she is about your plan."

"My plan?"

"You know," Osnat said. Harriet's hand on her shoulder felt foreign and heavy. She shifted her weight from one foot to the other, but Harriet didn't seem to notice. "Finding an Israeli husband and going to Israel."

Harriet laughed. "That's not my plan."

"What do you mean?"

"If it happens, it happens," Harriet said. "But it certainly isn't a *plan*."

Osnat couldn't help it. She moved out of Harriet's reach. "But my mom—"

Harriet lowered her voice. "Look," she said, "I love your parents, your mom especially. They've been so warm and kind to me, treating me just like a daughter—"

"But *I'm* the one who's their daughter," Osnat interrupted. She knew she sounded petulant, but she couldn't help it.

"Exactly," Harriet said. "Which is why it doesn't matter if your mom is out there making plans for me—I'm just a hobby. But you're her daughter, and she's your mom, and you need to talk to her."

Osnat could feel the tears coming. "But I already know what she's going to say." She didn't know what was more upsetting—that she was humiliating herself in front of Harriet, or that Harriet wasn't planning to go to Israel after all, and that once again Osnat would be left alone, duty-bound to her parents and to a country where she might never feel at home. Something like despair was bubbling up inside her. She took another deep breath but it was no use. "Maybe we could go together," she heard herself telling Harriet, "you and me. We could be roommates. We could help each other out. I'll show you all the good places to eat." Osnat knew she needed to shut up, but she kept right on begging: "My mom's right, you know—Israeli men really are very good-looking, even if they are on the short side. But you're not that tall, so it won't be a problem. And they give you gifts. And they open doors."

"Osnat," Harriet said. "Stop. Please."

Her expression was so earnest and friendly—so sincere—that Osnat finally understood what her parents saw in her, why they'd adopted her as their own. She wanted to kick herself for not being nicer to Harriet, for being so sarcastic and rude when all Harriet had been was kind, offering rides, baking cookies. If Osnat had tried to be nice, if she'd given Harriet a chance, who was to say that Harriet wouldn't have at least considered moving to Israel with her now? But no. Osnat had blown even this one small thing.

Harriet took a step toward Osnat but kept her arms stiffly at her sides. "Osnat," she said, "are you *sure* your mother wants you to go back?"

Osnat nodded. Of course she was sure.

"But have you *asked* her?" Harriet said. "You need to ask her. This isn't an ultimatum, so don't turn it into one. You're her daughter. She can't divorce you."

"But—"

"Ask her," Harriet said firmly. She reached out again for Osnat's shoulder, and this time Osnat didn't flinch. She would work hard, and she would change. She had to.

"Okay," she told Harriet. "I'll ask her. I will."

. . .

Osnat expected that when she got back inside her mother would already be in her nightgown, but she wasn't. She was sitting in front of the TV, but instead of watching anything, she was fuming. "Even if I'm a little incontinent, I can hear just fine," she said. She waggled a finger at Osnat. "This behavior has got to stop. Right now. Right this minute, even."

Osnat could feel the skin on the back of her neck prickling. "Then start taking care of yourself," she said. "Do you think this whole diabetes thing is a joke?"

"I'm not talking about that," her mother said. "I'm talking about Israel. So it didn't work out. So you weren't happy there. Get over it and move on."

"But—"

"No buts. You tried. It didn't work out. Move on. For God's sake, Osnat, don't tell me that you're thinking about moving again. It's like you're stuck in an instant replay of your own life."

"It's not that simple," Osnat objected.

"Of course it isn't." Her mother sounded exasperated. "Don't you think *I* know that? But Israel's *my* home, not Harriet's, not your father's, and not even yours. If you truly want to live there, fine, but stop acting as if this is about me, for God's sake, and stop expecting a homecoming. Home isn't just about place, you know. It's beyond me why you keep thinking it is."

Osnat sat down. She felt her mind emptying out, going blank. Even though there was no use arguing with her mother, she felt like she had to try. "But you miss it so much," she said. "All you ever do is miss Israel."

Osnat's mother laughed. "That's not all I do," she said. "I have a job. I have friends. Sometimes I eat. Sometimes I go on vacation."

Instead of looking directly at her mother, Osnat watched her reflection on the blank screen of the TV. Both she and her mother looked very small and distant, as if their lives, with all their tiny, frantic gestures, were taking place in a faraway, washed-out room.

"Okay," her mother conceded. "Of course I miss it. Can you blame me? Of course I do. But at the same time, and here's the thing you need to ask yourself, so what if I miss Israel? So what?"

Osnat watched her chest rise and fall on the television screen. Next to her, she could hear her mother breathing too, as if, really, this was all you had to do to keep going: breathe in and breathe out, and breathe in again. It made Osnat feel light-headed. "I'm so tired," she said. "I'm *so* tired. I just want to go home."

"Look around," her mother said. "You are home."

Osnat closed her eyes and leaned back into the couch, feeling the cushions give a little against her. If she tried, she could make out sounds from the rest of the house: the clock in the dining room, the refrigerator in the kitchen, the crickets outside, and beyond them, barely audible, the traffic on US-23.

"Mom," she said again. "Mom. It's not that simple."

"Yes," her mother whispered, reaching over to squeeze her hand, and Osnat could feel the blood pulsing through her fingers. "Yes, Osnat, it is that simple. It really is."

The next morning, Osnat woke up to the sound of applause. "Good job!" someone on the street was yelling. "You can do it!" For a moment, she felt disoriented—were they applauding her? But then, when she listened some more, she could make out the slap of sneakers on pavement. She sat up and looked out the window, and, sure enough, there were runners making their way down the road, and, on the lawn across the street, there was an elderly couple sitting in lawn chairs and cheering them on. "All right!" the man was yelling. "Just a little farther!"

Osnat got dressed. She could hear her mother in the shower, singing. Outside the sun was making the asphalt sparkle, making the grass in people's yards shine as if it had been lacquered.

"Good morning," called the woman from across the street. "Great day for a race."

Osnat waited for a break in the runners, and then she crossed over. "You rooting for someone special?"

"Well," the man said, "I just saw my optometrist go by."

"And the guy from the bank," the woman reminded him.

Another group of runners approached them, and the couple paused to cheer. "Looking good!" the man shouted. "Almost there!"

Osnat sat down on the curb to watch. The runners weren't what she had expected. They were ordinary-looking, not particularly athletic, and some were downright fat. Some of them wore sweatbands, and some wore funny hats. Some shuffled, and some seemed to bound. As far as Osnat could tell, there just wasn't any connection between what people looked like and how they ran. It was nice, the way you didn't know exactly what to expect.

"Just wait until the stragglers start coming by," the woman told Osnat. "That's where we really make a difference."

"How?"

"Watch this," the woman said. She stepped out into the road and high-fived a red-faced man who was lumbering toward them, and just like that, he straightened up and started running faster. "See?" she said. "It doesn't take much."

After a while, the stream of runners rushing by lulled Osnat into a kind of stupor. She closed her eyes. The sun was warm on her skin, the wind gentle. She felt like the Wicked Witch of the West, disintegrating in a puddle of light this time, but still soaking back into the ground, where she belonged. All around her, the air hummed, its molecules vibrating, and underneath it she could hear the runners' breathing and the applause from a faraway finish line.

"Here they come," she heard the woman tell her, as if from a great distance. "Get ready."

Osnat breathed in and out, then in again. She opened her eyes and opened her mouth, and waited for the cheering to begin.

Acknowledgments

Thanks to Dorian Karchmar and Lexy Bloom for believing in this book, for their smart suggestions, and for their patience and pep talks. This book wouldn't be what it is without them. Thanks also to Dixon Gaines and the folks at Pantheon and to Georgia Cool and Adam Schear at William Morris.

Special thanks to Susan Finch, Bridget Hardy, and Steve Fife-Adams for their careful reading and unflagging encouragement, and for their friendship.

Thanks to Hannah Tinti and Maribeth Batcha, who continue to offer guidance and support with a generosity I can only hope one day to deserve.

Thanks to my teachers: Alyce Miller, Dana Johnson, Tony Ardizzone, John Schilb, Melanie Rae Thon, Michael Martone, Avram Heffner, Suzanne Paola, and Diane Vreuls. Special thanks to Linda Miller and Alyson Hagy, who took me on as an uptight, melodramatic teenager and never made me feel my writing was ridiculous, even when it was.

Thanks to my friends and fellow writers: Paul Maliszewski, Adam Rovner, Laurie Filipelli, David Ramm, Julie Story, Nathalie Arnold, Seamus Boshell, Loyal Miles, Marlaine Browning, Sarah L. Thomson, Sara Jane Stoner, Gudis Schneider, Zoe Clarkwest, and Jean Angel.

Above all, thanks to my family: my parents, Mort and Raya; my brother, Alon, and his wife, Heidi; and, of course, Bill and Ziv.

A NOTE ABOUT THE AUTHOR

Danit Brown holds an MFA in fiction from Indiana University. Her stories have appeared in numerous literary journals, including *Story, Glimmer Train, StoryQuarterly,* and *One Story.* She lives in Michigan with her family.

A NOTE ON THE TYPE

This book was set in a version of the well-known Monotype face Bembo. This letter was cut for the celebrated Venetian printer Aldus Manutius by Francesco Griffo, and first used in Pietro Cardinal Bembo's De Aetna of 1495.

The companion italic is an adaptation of the chancery script type designed by the calligrapher and printer Lodovico degli Arrighi.

Composed by TexTech, Brattleboro, Vermont
Printed and bound by R. R. Donnelley,
Harrisonburg, Virginia
Designed by Wesley Gott